Lady in Lace

Regency Timeslip

Regencies by Joanna Maitland

Unsuitable Matches Series
A Penniless Prospect
Marrying the Major
Rake's Reward

Star Crossed Lovers Series
My Lady Angel
Bride of the Solway
Star Crossed at Twilight*

The Aikenhead Honours Series
His Cavalry Lady
His Reluctant Mistress
His Forbidden Liaison
His Silken Seduction*

Individual Stories
A Poor Relation
The Earl's Mistletoe Bride
A Regency Invitation
[with Nicola Cornick & Elizabeth Rolls]

Regency Timeslip
Lady in Lace*

*published by Joanna Maitland Independent

LADY IN LACE

~Regency Timeslip~

JOANNA MAITLAND

Published in the United Kingdom
by Joanna Maitland Independent
https://libertabooks.com

LADY IN LACE
Regency Timeslip

ISBN-13 : 978-0-9957046-5-7
ISBN-10 : 0995704651

Requests to publish work from this book should be made to:
info@LibertaBooks.com

Cover Design: jdsmith-design.com
Cover Images: Shutterstock.com
Interior Formatting: Joanna Maitland

Dedication

To the members of the Marcher Chapter
of the Romantic Novelists' Association
with huge thanks
for their support and encouragement

Table of Contents

Chapter One

EMMA WAS ALONE IN THE PASSAGE. She hadn't been down here since her first day. She remembered being shown round then, peering into all these museum store rooms. Today it felt different. Was it because it was so late? But surely it hadn't been this gloomy down here before? Or this cold?

A strange shiver danced down her spine. That mahogany door. She hadn't noticed it before. It seemed totally out of place in a museum. But it was real. Solid.

She paused in the act of reaching for the intricate brass handle. She could just about make out her own frozen shape, dimly reflected in the door's fielded panels. There was something ghostly about her fuzzy outline, as if it were half real, half melting.

Nonsense. It was just a door. If she wanted to know where it led, she would have to open it.

Her extended arm seemed reluctant to make that last effort, her fingers unwilling to grasp the cold metal. That strange shiver came again, this time tingling down her arm and into her outstretched fingers. For a single mad moment, she thought she saw... She could have sworn she saw jagged streaks of blue lightning joining her hand to the brass.

Too much wine last night, she told herself sternly, trying to dismiss the weird feelings. *Or those mussels. You should never*

1

trust mussels.

She forced her rigid body to move. Only a wimp would be frightened off by a dim reflection and a slightly queasy stomach. And she'd promised herself she wouldn't be a coward any more. Hadn't she?

She grasped the handle at last. It was strangely cold, almost icy. She shuddered again, but refused to let go. She began to turn it, to pull the door open.

Immediately, too soon, the door began to swing towards her, as if it had a mind of its own. Under her fingers, the metal began to heat.

Emma gasped in shock and snatched her hand away. In less than a second, the brass had become too hot to touch. It was impossible. Cold... hot... blue lightning? Was she in the middle of some strange dream? Would she wake up soon?

The door had swung open on silent hinges. Expectantly. Waiting for her to step inside. Into the louring darkness beyond.

I am not afraid of you, whatever you are. She had taught herself to conquer her fears. She would not stand here on the threshold, petrified, like some kind of statue.

"Damn those mussels," she spat. Her wild words seemed to echo for a second. Then they were swallowed up by the dark silence in front of her. But they had broken the spell. She could move at last. And it would be forward. She was her own woman now. She would not run ever again.

She took two firm steps through the doorway. Into the gloom.

Why was it so dark? A room, even a corridor, should have windows somewhere. Even here in the museum. What was this place?

She stood still, trying to make sense of her surroundings. Behind her was the open door and the dim light of the hallway. In front, nothing. Or so it seemed. Yet she sensed that there was a great space in front of her, as if this darkness went on and on.

For the moment, her eyes were worse than useless. She reached her arms out sideways, feeling for walls. If this were merely a dark corridor, there should be walls.

Her right hand met something soft. Yielding. At her touch, it swung away.

She cried out, "Who's there?"

The softness swung back against her hand. Pile. Velvet? But not alive at all. She understood that instinctively, even in the dark, for there was no smell of life. It was some kind of velvet wrap, suspended here, swaying at her touch.

Not a corridor, then. A storage cupboard? But why so enormous?

She was beginning to overcome her childish fancies at last. Her mysterious door led to a huge cupboard, big enough to walk into. She put both hands on the velvet and groped her way towards a hanger and a rail, then on to more hangers and more suspended garments: furs, heavy wool, then fine silk and gauze. It was an enormous clothes store.

But whose clothes? This was no way to store museum exhibits.

She was finally beginning to see through the gloom, helped by the faint light from the hall at her back. The racks of hanging garments stretched into the distance and disappeared. As if the rail went on for ever.

She forced herself to straighten her shoulders. She would not be intimidated by a mere cupboard. She lifted her chin and took a deep breath, ready to challenge anything. Anyone.

She could smell the sea.

Impossible. Her mind was playing tricks. It had to be that. Didn't it?

She could smell the sea. As strongly as if she were standing on a beach, with banks of drying kelp and crashing breakers.

Her shoes began to sink into soft sand. Her toes curled automatically, trying for grip. She grabbed for the coat rail, desperate to keep her balance.

The coat rail was gone.

Her flailing arms met wool, warm wool, and warm flesh beneath.

"Take care, or you will fall." It was a man's voice, strong and reassuring. It seemed familiar. As did his touch.

Her body knew him. This time, she was not afraid.

3

She had come home at last.

She had been holding her breath, desperately trying to fathom what was happening to her. Now, relaxing, she breathed in the comforting scents of sand and sea and warm, living man. He smelt of fresh winds and freedom. His touch, where he held her up, was merely a polite support. Yet it was more, too. A caress, a knowing caress, of two bodies that had lain together, naked skin against naked skin.

So familiar. So loved. And yet she did not know him.

She tried to speak, but her throat would not open. She reached for him with her free hand, clutching for his arm where he held her up, and beyond, to the body she longed to find. It was eluding her.

"Oh, where are you, my love?" she managed at last, in a voice that sounded nothing like her own. Had she really said those words? To a man she didn't know?

His reply was wordless, a soft laugh deep in his chest. Then the contact was broken. The warmth of him was gone.

She was alone.

The ground beneath her feet was solid again.

He was gone. And so was the smell of the sea.

Tears of frustration welled up in her straining eyes. Her lover, her life, the man she was destined for – he had been here, holding her. Then, so swiftly, he was gone.

She peered into the darkness, narrowing her eyes. Surely there was movement, somewhere in the distance? A shadow, a shape. Yes, someone was there. He was still with her.

"Don't go, my love. Please don't leave me." She spoke without hesitation this time. Her heart was pounding like a racing engine. It was vital not to lose him. He had to understand that she was his. Always.

That deep laugh again, but no words. She saw the dim shape of a tall man in some kind of tail coat. For a split second, she caught the gleam of something gold before he turned away. And a flash of white teeth as he smiled back at her.

No need for words. His smile said it all. *Wait for me, love. We will meet again.*

She started towards him, arms outstretched to embrace his

beloved form. Her questing hands met another rack of clothes, soft, and full, and yielding. But lifeless.

He had been here, touching her, reaching for her. She could have been safe in his arms. Should have been. But now he was gone. And her heart was empty.

She clung to the rail, racked by sudden shuddering sobs. Nothing she had suffered could begin to approach this searing emotion, this harrowing sense of loss. As if her heart had been torn from her living body and trampled in the dirt.

Under her hand, something scratched her skin.

Beckoning.

It was ridiculous to think that racks of clothes could call to her, but she was prepared to believe almost anything now. She stroked a hand blindly across the hanger. This was a flimsy gown made of something she could not identify. Fairy gauze? Nothing could surprise her any more.

She made to lift the hanger from the rail. It stuck. She leaned closer, determined not to be beaten. It had summoned her, so she would have it.

It smelled of the sea.

For a second only, and the scent was gone. Then the gown came sweetly into her hands, as if it had leapt from the rail of its own volition. As if it were alive.

She brought it to her face, to touch, to caress, to breathe in its elusive scent. Her love came with the sea, and this gown was the link.

The gown's own scent was almost too faint to discern.

It was not the sea after all. It was lavender.

~ ~ ~

"What have you got there, Emma?"

She was standing in the passageway, gazing down at the golden lace and gauze draped over her arms. But she had been somewhere else entirely.

"Emma?" It was Richard, another of the museum curators, one who had begun to feel like a friend in spite of the difference in their ages. "Are you OK?"

She looked at the golden gown, then at Richard, and then swung round to the wall behind her. Yes, there was a door. No, it wasn't made of mahogany. It was a standard museum door, one she had definitely seen before. It led to the racks where they stored the costume collection in specially controlled conditions. "I...I...I'm fine. It was just this gown. It—"

His frown evaporated. "Oh, yes. That one. Your predecessor showed it to me once. Shame it's in such a state. It must have been stunning when it was new. What date do you reckon it is?"

Emma stared at him and then glanced down at the dress. "Er, middle to late Regency, I think. Somewhere between 1815 and 1820." She looked again, really looking this time. Just minutes ago, in the gloom, it had been floating on that hanger like woven gossamer in a summer breeze. But the gown in her arms was little more than shreds of golden overskirts, suspended from a fragile lace bodice and a silken petticoat. One puff sleeve was almost intact; the other was a wreck.

"I'd have thought it was beyond restoration," Richard said with a knowledgeable nod, "but you're the expert. It would be great if you could put it on display. Regency exhibits always pull in the punters. It's all those Jane Austen fans, I suppose."

"And memories of Colin Firth in a wet shirt," Emma quipped with a smile, glad to be brought back to earth again.

Richard raised his eyebrows. Well, he was a man and well past forty. He probably wouldn't understand how that iconic TV adaptation could feed fantasies, more than twenty years on.

A fantasy? Was that what she'd had? It had seemed so real. You didn't smell lavender in fantasies, did you? Or the sea? Or—?

She banished the image of white teeth and glinting gold to the back of her mind. She was a serious woman, with an important new job here. And a whole new life.

"I'm going to have a look at it under the lights in the research room," she announced in her best reliable-colleague voice. "Need the magnifiers to see exactly how bad the damage is. We might be able to do something. You never know." She turned and started along the corridor. Then she remembered how late it was. "There's time before we have to lock up, isn't there?" she called over her shoulder. Richard, as the longest-serving curator, was responsible for locking up the museum at the end of the day. He replied with a cheery wave.

~ ~ ~

She was still examining the gown when closing time actually came. She wanted to weep over it. Under the magnifiers, she had discovered, with a shock, that at least some of the rents were not caused by age or vermin. Some of the gold lace had been cut. Someone – someone out of their mind, surely? – had taken a knife or scissors to this fairytale ballgown and deliberately shredded the overskirt. Someone had wanted to be sure this gown could never be worn again.

Someone hateful.

She leaned back in her chair and began to muse on the owner of the gown. The museum had no information about who she might have been. It would have been someone rich, perhaps aristocratic. Young, but not too young. Really young girls wore white ballgowns in those days. This one probably belonged to a married lady. A rich, young, married lady. Was it her husband who had destroyed the gown? Had he found her in some compromising—?

"Emma?" It was Richard, doing his final rounds to check everything was locked away. "Oh. I didn't realise you still had that gown out." He muttered a curse. "I've locked all the stores." He glanced across at the clock on the church opposite the museum. He was due to meet his wife and baby daughter immediately after work, Emma knew. He wouldn't want to keep them waiting in the cold. It was spring, but the wind was bitter.

Emma leapt to her feet, conscience-stricken. It would take a good ten minutes to open up the stores again. "I'm sorry, Richard. I lost track. Look, it's about time I took a turn at locking up, anyway. Has everyone else gone?" When he nodded, she said decisively, "Fine, well, leave me the keys and I'll finish doing the security checks after I've put this away. I know how to set the alarms. You can rely on me."

He chuckled. "You do realise you'll have to be first in tomorrow if you have the keys? I thought you weren't a morning person?"

She smiled at him. "It's amazing what caffeine can do, you know."

He looked relieved as he tossed her the huge bunch of keys. "See you tomorrow then. Early. *Very* early." He was still smiling as he left.

Emma laid the keys on the big round table and sat down again to gaze at the gown. Silence settled. Richard had switched off most of the lights. It was like being on an island of light surrounded by darkness.

She could smell the sea.

Rubbish. She was nowhere near the sea. It must be simply that idiotic idea of being on an island. Islands were surrounded by sea, not darkness. So she had *fancied* she smelt it. Was she going down with something, maybe?

She touched the back of her hand to her forehead. It felt normal. Well, it would, wouldn't it? You could never feel your own fever.

Get back to work, Emma Stanley, she told herself. *You are supposed to be a sensible, dependable, professional woman. Put the gown away, lock up the building, and go home. You can always check your temperature once you're there.*

It didn't matter if she had a temperature like a furnace tomorrow morning. She was in charge of the keys now. No matter what, she would have to be here early enough to open up.

~ ~ ~

The clock of St Mary's struck the half hour.

Shocked back to reality, Emma gasped aloud. How long had she been sitting here in the research room, marvelling at the shredded beauty of the golden gown?

She shook her head in disbelief at her own strange behaviour. She had won the job of regional costume curator because of her innovative but level-headed approach to planning the future of the collection. Her ideas and passion had persuaded the panel to overlook her patchy employment record.

Yet here she was, barely a few weeks into her new job, and without a single level-headed thought in her mind.

She was seeing things, and feeling things, and, most

8

outrageous of all, smelling things that could not possibly be real.

She lurched to her feet, toppling her chair in her haste. She had to put the gown away safely in the storeroom. But first, she would put a little distance between them. To catch her breath. She would go and change into her travelling clothes. A splash of cold water on her face and neck might help, too. Anything to bring her back to reality.

A few minutes later, Emma was smoothing her navy pencil skirt onto its hanger. That suit had been a good buy, in spite of the high cost. Creases fell out of the material when it was hung up and the cut flattered her figure, even though the suit was now a little loose. She had lost a lot of weight during the long months of her hellish divorce, but she had resolved to fix that. From now on, she would eat regularly, and properly. She had a new career and a bold new life, and she was going to make a success of both. There was no one trying to control her any more and she would never, *never* let it happen again.

She took a step back and gazed at her reflection in the long mirror. Much too thin, but otherwise not bad. Her dark red hair, definitely her best feature, was piled on top of her head in loose curls, in vague imitation of the Regency styles she had always admired. Her new gold underwear looked classy and flattering.

A strange coincidence that she had chosen to wear gold today, the same colour as that amazing Regency gown. Almost as if she had been meant to try it on…

Barely a minute later, Emma found herself back in the research room with the damaged gown in her hands. It would do no harm to try it on, just for a moment or two, just to see how it looked. And then she would return it reverently to the store room and never be tempted again.

The bell of St Mary's began to toll. It was almost seven. Where on earth had the time gone?

All the same, it was not too late just to… With infinite care, Emma started to push an arm into the undamaged sleeve.

Blue lightning shot along her arm. It should have burned, but instead it was freezing cold. A moment later, Emma felt a whoosh of icy air howling through the room, like the bitterest

Arctic gale. The noise was even worse than the cold. It sounded as if some hideous giant was sucking the life out of everything, swallowing it down into consuming darkness. Emma cried out in terror. At least, she tried to. But her voice was sucked into the void along with everything else.

She was in the dark. She was falling.

And she was alone.

Chapter Two

IT WAS MUCH TOO DARK TO SEE where she was. But it smelt small, enclosed… and wrong. What was so different?

Emma took a deep breath and tried to conquer her fears. She had no idea where she was but, as with that mysterious cupboard filled with racks of clothes and disappearing sandy beaches, it was somewhere other-worldly.

Candles. That was what she could smell. Burning candles. Had there been a power cut, maybe?

As her eyes began to adjust to the pervasive gloom, she took a tiny step forward. Something hushed against her ankles. A long, full skirt.

But I wasn't wearing a skirt. Just underwear. How can I have—?

Automatically she touched her hands to it. And realised at once what she was wearing. She could feel the undulating textures of lace. She was dressed in that golden gown and somehow, impossibly, it was whole again.

She was having a nightmare. This wasn't possible.

She swallowed hard. What on earth was she going to do?

Her eyes were finally adjusting to the gloom. She made out a curtained window and a wooden door, ever so slightly ajar. A glimmer of light flickering through the crack suggested there was someone in the room beyond.

Emma gulped. Her heart began to race. Now what?

She heard a rumble of voices from beyond the door. Male voices. Or one male voice, at least. Did she dare?

It was a dream. Only a dream. Whatever might appear to happen in a dream, you were always fine again when you woke up. So it wouldn't matter if she went in there. Nothing could actually happen to her.

She wasn't brave enough to throw the door wide open, though. Instead, she eased it open a fraction more. Enough to hear what was going on. And, if she put her eye to the crack, enough to see.

She had to choke back her gasp of astonishment. She closed her eyes, trying to stop her dream in its ridiculous tracks. But when she opened them again, it was all still there. And still real.

She was staring into an enormous, and opulent, bedchamber. It was brightly lit. And very warm. There were candlesticks on the mantelpiece and silver candelabra on spindle-legged tables around the room. A huge log fire was crackling merrily in the grate. Heavy green velvet curtains, matching the ones around the raised tester bed, were drawn across one wall, presumably concealing floor-to-ceiling windows.

All of that was obvious from the first quick peek. Emma's sensible self was saying that her dream had taken her back into history, by a couple of centuries or so. Her sensible self was wittering on about period furniture and priceless Georgian silverware.

She was not listening to a word from her sensible self. Her gaze was riveted on the tableau in front of that blazing fire, where a youngish female servant stood, holding a water can of polished copper and staring longingly at the back of a man, naked from the waist up, sitting in a bath.

He'll be naked from the waist down, too. Emma's thought came unbidden, and certainly not from her sensible self.

The man was soaping his hair, massaging his scalp energetically, the muscles in his shoulders and arms working. From the back view, he had a very fine body – lean, lithe and strong. Young, probably. And he seemed to have a fine head of hair, though it was difficult to be sure of the colour, or the length, under all that lather.

"Pour the water over my hair. Slowly. I need to get rid of this soap." Crisp instructions, delivered in a rich baritone. This man was used to giving orders.

The maid raised the can a little higher – she seemed to have good muscles, too – and began to pour. A little, then a pause, then a little more as the man stroked away the soap. It took a while, but eventually the can was empty and the man's hair was clean. He ran his fingers through it, pressing out the excess water and combing through the tangles.

The servant's task seemed to be over. She put the can on the floor beside the bath and moved away. But as soon as the man could no longer see her, she wiped her damp hands down her skirts and began to unbutton her bodice. In a trice, the buttons were all undone, and she was exposed to the waist.

What kind of place was it? And why was a female servant attending a man in his bath, anyway? Had this absurd dream transported her into a brothel?

Emma was shocked. But not shocked enough to stop looking. This fascinating dream was turning into something like a scene from a film, and a raunchy, X-rated one, at that. What's more, it was getting to her. Heat was beginning to flare in her gut. She had to see what would happen next. And she had to see the man. All of him.

I don't care if it is a brothel. It's my *dream. So I'm entitled to see.*

The man glanced sideways, as if looking for the missing servant, shrugged, and rose to his feet in a single athletic movement. "Fetch my towel, woman," he snapped, holding out his hands to the warmth of the fire. When the servant failed to obey – she did not move an inch towards him, but she did plaster an inviting smile on her face – he stepped out of the water and turned to look for her. He was frowning. "I said—"

A look of total astonishment replaced his angry frown. A split second later, an even blacker frown took its place. There was something more in his eyes, too. It should have been anger, but Emma was almost certain it was not. Frustration? Resignation? But why?

The man and the servant stared at each other for a long, long moment. The maid had thrown her shoulders back so that her ample breasts gleamed in the firelight. She intended to entice, clearly, but the man made no move towards her. Nor did he do anything to hide his nakedness. He let the girl feast her eyes on his body, which was as beautiful as any classical statue, to Emma's mind, and waited for the servant to get the message. His body was not reacting at all to the merchandise on offer. The maid's smile, so eager at first, faltered. Her mouth fell open. Then she started to babble incoherently.

"Enough. Cover yourself, woman."

"Sir, I only wanted to—"

"You don't have to tell me. I've heard it too often before. You wanted to find out what it was like to be bedded by the 'Greatest Lover in London'." He smiled sourly and gestured towards his drooping genitals. "As you can see, the so-called 'Greatest Lover in London' has no interest in women who throw themselves at him."

Head bent, the maid had begun to fumble with her fastenings, dragging the halves of her bodice together over her nakedness. She was scarlet to the roots of her hair, Emma saw, and her fingers were trembling. But she was not totally cowed. She muttered something under her breath.

"You spoke?" he said very softly.

Emma had never heard anything quite so haughty. Or so menacing.

Evidently, his tone caught the servant on the raw. "Aye, I did." She jerked her head up and stared him full in the face. Her embarrassment had faded. She looked to be livid with anger. "Think I'm not good enough for your bed, don't yer? 'Cos I'm only a servant. If I'd been one of yer high-and-mighty lady friends, you'd have thrown up my skirts quick enough. You're a—!"

He stopped her with a contemptuous gesture. "I wouldn't touch a *duchess* if she threw herself at me as you have. Whatever *I* may be, *you* are no better than a harlot. Now, get out of here, before I toss you out." He took a single step towards her.

She gasped and fled.

The man gave a snort of mirthless laughter and padded across the carpet after her. In a second, he was lost to Emma's view.

He couldn't walk out of the room, surely? Not stark naked. Emma eased her door open a fraction more. She had to crane her neck to see the other door. The panicking maid had left it open and Emma could make out a gloomy corridor beyond.

The man shut the outer door quietly, pressing the flat of his free hand on the panel of the door, as if to ensure it was well and truly closed. He shook his head. At the folly of women? Then, with a sigh, he turned the key in the lock.

Emma started to shrink back into her hiding place but he spun round with sudden decision and started for her dressing room. Had he suddenly remembered there was another door to be locked against predatory females?

After barely a couple of steps, he stopped dead. This time, the expression of astonishment came and stayed. "Emma," he breathed. Then, with joy in his face and in his voice, "Emma. Emma, my darling, you've come back to me."

It was impossible. How could he know her name? And what was she to do now?

He took another step towards her door and stopped again, looking down at his unruly body. He now had a splendid erection. "It's no use pretending that I'm not pleased to see you, is it, love?" he said with a disarming smile. "But to spare your blushes, I'll cover the evidence of my, er, preferences." He strode over to the fireplace, grabbed the towel from the warming rack and wrapped it tightly round his lower body. It didn't help his modesty. Not one bit. It merely made his erection even more blatant.

Wherever Emma was in this absurd dream, she was behaving like a gormless idiot. It was time to take charge. She pulled the dressing-room door open and stepped into the bedroom. "In terms of concealment, that towel is definitely *not* working."

Not a single wobble in her voice, she was proud to note. She was being braver in her dream than she had been in real life.

He looked down at himself again and grinned, a little

15

ruefully. "It's your fault, you know, love. You're the one who bewitched me. You know I can't get enough of you. But now that you've come back to me…"

There was such longing in his voice that Emma began to respond. She had no idea who this man was, but she understood yearning. She had learnt to understand it when she stood on her phantom beach, reaching for a lover who was leaving her. But this was a different man, wasn't it? Her body had not recognised this one. "I…" The words would not come.

He wasn't interested in talking. He crossed the space between them in a couple of quick strides and drew her into his arms, nuzzling her hair and muttering her name, over and over. "Emma, darling Emma. Don't leave me again. I'm lost without you. You're the only woman that I—" He tried to shake his head but he was hugging her so close he couldn't move. He groaned instead. In frustration?

He took a step back from her, but left his hands resting lightly on her shoulders as he examined her from head to toe. "Beautiful. And so very desirable. You are the only woman I want to take to my bed, Emma. You must know that."

Emma managed to make a strangled noise in her throat.

"Don't you believe me? It's the truth. I may have had the reputation as the greatest rake in England, but I've turned down every single offer since you left me. Lately, there have been more and more of them." He made a face. When Emma said nothing – she was quite unable to say a word – he went on, "Before, the ladies wanted to discover whether the experience was everything their friends had described – I do not doubt that my prowess was *much* exaggerated by those damsels – but now they're vying to be the one who lures me out of what they're calling my 'monkish habits'. Not a chance. It could only be you. The moment I saw you again, I wanted you."

Emma bit her lip.

"I want you now, Emma. And I know you want me, too. Will you take off that beautiful gown, or shall I?"

He reached for her and, without a second's hesitation, she melted into his arms. This was meant. Even though it was only a dream.

His kiss was like nothing she had ever experienced before, awake or dreaming. At the first touch of his lips, the warmth in her belly exploded into searing flames. Her body had recognised its soulmate again. How had she failed to see that from the first?

He wanted her. Urgently. But her urgency was as great as his. She returned his kisses with equal passion, their tongues dancing together as each demanded and then willingly gave. Without breaking that fervent kiss for even a second, he propelled her across the floor and lifted her on to the great bed. He pushed up her skirts, groaning her name into her mouth.

It was what she wanted. With this unnamed, but beloved man. Here. Now! She dragged off his skimpy towel and opened herself to him.

His body still had drops of water on his chest and in his hair. They fell onto her bare shoulders, sizzling like water on a hotplate, as the lovers came together in a frenzy of mutual need and desire.

And then it was over. Complete. Perfect.

He rolled off her with a great sigh of content and closed his eyes. "My darling. Oh, my darling Emma," he breathed, carrying her hand to his lips to kiss each fingertip in turn. For a moment, his sharp teeth nibbled at her little finger. Soon he drifted into sleep and their joined hands slid back to the coverlet.

Emma relaxed back onto the pillows and smiled up into the canopy. Later, she decided, they would make love again and next time, it would be a more leisurely affair. They had both needed that first, urgent, joining and it had been glorious, but she wanted more time to enjoy their lovemaking. Perhaps she might even find out his name? He knew her, clearly, but she had not the foggiest idea who he was.

Her damp hair was tickling her temple. She lifted her hand to push it away and saw, to her horror, that she was wearing a wedding ring. She couldn't be. She had taken her ring off for good, months before her divorce.

But this was a dream – and in her dream she seemed to be married. Who was she? Who was her husband? Was it this

17

man? Could she be married to this man, the greatest stud in London? Or was she an adulterous wife, another of this man's many conquests?

What do I do now? I can't very well ask him, can I? "By the way, sir, are we married? Or am I just your mistress?"

She had to get away. She couldn't possibly think clearly while he was lying there next to her, naked and so very desirable.

But he was holding her hand. If she pulled away, he might wake up. She swore silently. There must be something she could do? A practised courtesan would know ways of extracting herself from such a situation. But Emma was no courtesan, and not so very practised, either.

Desperation gave her an idea. She leaned across and put her lips close to his ear, gently huffing aside his damp hair. "Forgive me, dearest," she breathed, trying to sound as sexy as she could, "but I need to clean myself."

He seemed to hear though he did not wake up. However, his grip relaxed a little and slowly, carefully, she pulled her fingers free. "Thank you, my darling," she said softly, automatically leaning across and kissing him, full on the mouth.

It was a mad thing to do. He'd wake up. He was bound to.

But he didn't. He moaned a little in his throat – a purr of pleasure, Emma fancied – and then he turned onto his side, still asleep.

She had to go. Immediately. But how was she to escape?

First things first. She would go back to the dressing room where this incredible dream had begun. Once there, she would think of something. She had to.

Seconds later, she was back in the dressing room and the door was shut and locked behind her. The outer door was locked too. She had seen to that. She'd even removed the key, to be doubly safe. So, now what?

There was a long pier glass in the dressing room, for the use of the master, Emma supposed. It showed her a Regency woman in a crumpled golden gown, with her hair falling down onto her shoulders and a mouth swollen from a hundred passionate kisses. She looked exactly what she was – a woman who had been thoroughly bedded. And who had definitely enjoyed the experience, too.

Emma started to pin up her hair again but, with her arms raised, the edging of her tight bodice was cutting into her flesh. It hurt. "Damn this dress," she spat. "None of this would have happened without it. I can't even redo my hair without taking it off. And I certainly can't leave here looking as if I'd been dragged through a hedge backwards."

Determined, she began to undo the fastenings so that she could peel off the golden gown...

Chapter Three

THE BELL OF ST MARY'S FINISHED tolling the hour.

Followed by a silence that echoed eerily in the dark, empty museum.

St Mary's stood across the road, solid sandstone as ever, obscuring much of the view from the research room window. The hands on its clock read seven.

Emma's head was pounding. Her whole body began to shake. She grabbed the edge of the table to stop herself from falling. Seven o'clock? It couldn't be. It had been striking seven when she started to put the gown on and she had been gone for hours.

Hadn't she?

She closed her eyes for a long moment. Mistake. The room started to swim. In desperation, she clutched the table even harder.

Was she going totally mad?

She took a long deep breath. Then another. She forced herself to open her eyes and look around. The research room was the same as ever. The damaged lace gown was draped across the huge round table. The spotlights in the magnifiers were shining down onto it, making the shreds of gold lace sparkle, even after two centuries. Underneath, the delicate silken petticoat gleamed enticingly.

Emma dragged a chair out from under the table and collapsed on to it. Her whole body was shuddering so much she didn't dare to let go of her support.

Had she had some kind of seizure? Thinking she'd been transported to another place and another time? Like a daydream?

It was no daydream. A nightmare, perhaps? If so, it was a waking nightmare. But then again, that was impossible, too. Even nightmares took time and – she checked the clock which now showed a minute or so after seven – no time had passed. She had been here when the bell began to strike seven. She had started to try on the shredded golden gown. Then she had been somewhere else, in another time and another place altogether, wearing the undamaged gown as if it had been made for her.

And…and…

Shocked, she realised that her body was feeling heavy and sated. Satisfied. She recognised that feeling, from long ago in the early, naively happy, days of her marriage, when sex had been joyful and fulfilling. In her daydream – and it *must* have been a daydream, surely? – the greatest stud in Regency London had made love to her. Here in the real world, her body had responded. It was perfectly possible to have an orgasm in a dream, she knew. The orgasm would be real, even though the dream lover wasn't.

She forced herself to hold up her left hand. It was shaking. There was no wedding ring but there was a tiny bruise on the side of her little finger, as if someone's teeth had—

"I'm going mad," she said aloud, transfixed by the mark on her hand. It wasn't possible. Such things couldn't happen.

She screwed her eyes shut and dropped her head into her hands with a groan.

I'm a sensible, professional woman. I can sort this out. I just have to think it through. There has to be a rational explanation for what I'm feeling.

Doesn't there?

She swallowed hard. Her heart was pounding almost fit to burst. Frighteningly. Was she going to have a heart attack? She concentrated on breathing. Long and slow, long and slow.

Eventually, her heart rate dropped and her terror began to subside. She'd had a shock but she was OK. Even if she couldn't work out quite what had happened to her.

She made herself raise her head and open her eyes. The ripped gold lace was still there, lying across the table like a threat.

Enough of this.

Emma forced herself to her feet. If this golden wreck of a gown had some kind of mystical power, she would find out what it was. Right now. She had fancied that putting her arm into that puff sleeve had carried her off into Regency England, had she? Well, she would do it again. Right here. Right now.

She picked up the damaged gown and—

She almost screamed. Underneath the gold lace gown lay a key. It looked like the key she had removed after locking the dressing room door.

Not only had she been transported back to her own time but she had brought back more than the magic gown. What did it mean? If she had brought back a key from her Regency dream, then the dream had to have been real, didn't it?

She steeled herself to reach down and pick up the key. It felt solid. Like a real key. It hadn't been in the research room before, so she must have brought it back with her. There was no other explanation, was there?

Another thought struck her, even though her head was spinning. She had locked *both* the doors into the dressing room. From the inside. Her lover would try to get in, but wouldn't be able to. How would he explain that?

The key seemed to warm in her hand. As if it had something to tell her.

She carried it to her lips and, in that same moment, she understood. She had been fated to remove that key. Her lover would assume she had left via the outer door, locking it behind her and taking away the key. It made everything plausible. Just.

She heaved a sigh of relief. But she was not really convinced. Her lover would wonder why no one had seen her making her escape. Locked room mysteries were always a problem. It would be better if she could go back, unlock the door again, and leave the key on the inside where it belonged.

She had the gown. She could do it. *Now*.

Grasping the key in one hand, she carefully began to slide the other into the undamaged sleeve. She held her breath, waiting for the blue lightning, the icy wind, the shock.

Nothing.

She slid her hand a little further, gently pulling the gown up her arm.

Nothing. Nothing at all.

Whatever she thought had happened last time, it clearly wasn't going to happen again. The tattered gold lace gown was nothing more than a rather sad museum artefact. In spite of that mysterious time travelling key.

With a sigh of disappointment tinged with relief, Emma dropped the key onto the table. She'd think about that later. What mattered now was the magic gown. She peeled it off her arm and draped it across the table. "You have a story to tell, haven't you?" she said, glaring down at it. She felt a little more in control at last. "But you've decided not to say another word today. Why is that, I wonder?"

Very gently, she stroked her fingers across the scraps of torn lace. So costly, so delicate, so beautiful. It had been even more beautiful when it was whole and she was wearing it. A sob rose in her throat for the loss of something so precious.

And for the man whose hands had caressed the body that wore it and taken Emma to a place of ecstasy.

~ ~ ~

A night's sleep should have cleared Emma's head. But she hardly slept at all. She kept dreaming about her lover – the man on the beach and the man in the bedroom were one and the same, according to her calculating subconscious – but she would always wake up at the awful moment when she was saying something supremely foolish, like asking him his name.

At five in the morning, she gave up and went to the kitchen to make a cup of tea. Decent sleep was impossible, so she would do some research. She went to the desk in the corner of her tiny living room and began to trawl the internet for "the Greatest Lover in London" in the Regency period. Predictably,

23

she found nothing very useful. Her search parameters were too vague. She needed a *name*.

She sighed out a long breath and tried to relax the tension in her shoulders. Time to take stock. She'd had an out-of-body experience, and *what* an experience, with a dream lover in the Regency period. What's more, he had recognised her, named her, so he had met her before. Somewhere. And he loved her. Or he *said* he did. He was a stud, reputed to be the best lover in London, so he might say that to all his mistresses. On the other hand, Emma had seen, with her own eyes, how coldly he had rejected that buxom serving maid. The girl had been attractive enough, and very willing, but he had shown not a flicker of interest. The instant he set eyes on Emma though... Phew. That had been a reaction and a half.

Had her out-of-body experience actually happened? That was the jackpot question and she had no idea how to answer it, though her body was screaming that it had been real. She could see that she had two obvious courses of action. She could be sensible and professional, putting the whole episode behind her and trying to forget it as a moment's mental aberration. Or she could try to recreate it in order to find out more about her Regency doppelgänger, and about the unnamed man who made her hormones do cartwheels the moment his lips touched her skin.

"I should be focusing on my new life and my new job," she said to her computer screen. "Any sensible woman would do that. But I'm not going to be sensible, am I?" She shook her head at her dim reflection. "I'm going to do it all over again, exactly the same as last night, just in case it works. Just in case I can get back there, and find out more, and see him..." Even alone, she didn't dare to say the rest of the words out loud but, in the secret recesses of her mind, she added, "...and make love again."

~ ~ ~

Richard laughed when he arrived and found her hard at work on cataloguing the costume collection. "You must have been here for hours. You didn't have to arrive *that* early to open up. I'm usually the first in and Melanie never gets me here before half past eight." Melanie was his second wife, nearly twenty

24

years younger than Richard, and he doted on her. Three days a week, she took their daughter to nursery on her way to her part-time job. She dropped Richard off at the museum, too, since they couldn't afford a second car. Being a museum curator didn't pay enough for that, especially since he was supporting the teenage children of his first marriage.

Emma felt herself beginning to blush. She had never been very good at lying. "Oh, I didn't sleep very well last night." That, at least, was the truth. "So I gave up trying and decided to come in to work. There's plenty to be done." She gestured to the box of index cards and the computer screen. "There's weeks of work here, so even a few extra hours is a help."

"It's not the kind of work you should be doing, though. Maybe we could get one of the volunteers to do it?"

"Good idea. I'll have a chat during the coffee break, next time any of them come in. It's pretty boring stuff, though. They might not want to do it."

"You could make it worth their while. Trade a couple of weeks of data entry for a day or two getting really hands-on with the costume collection. Most of them would jump at the chance, I'd say."

Emma smiled up at him. "That's a very clever wheeze. Have you got Machiavelli somewhere in your family tree, by any chance?"

He laughed back at her. "Maybe. You never know." He turned for the door, just as Emma tried to stifle a yawn. "Ha. Caught you. It's not my place to tell you what to do – you're your own boss – but it might be a good plan to knock off early. Catch up on your lost sleep? It's my turn to lock up."

No, that was *not* the plan at all.

"Um… Actually, I thought I might take a couple of hours off at lunchtime for a rest. I'd really like to do some more of this computer stuff and I concentrate best when it's quiet. So I was planning to stay late again. No point in two of us hanging around, is there? I'm happy to do the security stuff. Why don't you go home early, read little Chloë her bedtime story for once?"

Richard's neck turned slightly pink above his collar. Little Chloë was her daddy's darling – his older children were both boys – and everyone at the museum knew it. "You really are a sucker for punishment, aren't you?" he said lightly.

"Not really. If I do a couple of hours every evening, once it's quiet, I should be able to make real inroads into the backlog. Just for a week or two, until we can find a willing volunteer to take it on. It'll make it easier to sell the cataloguing, too, if the volunteers know the curator has been doing her bit. Don't you think?"

Richard nodded. "OK. But if you're going to make a habit of working late, we'd better get a spare set of keys made for the staff entrance so you're not doing late nights *and* early mornings as well." He grinned suddenly. It made him look much younger. "I'm certainly not going to argue if you're determined to send me off home early today. Melanie *will* be surprised."

"And so will Chloë. She's the one who really matters when it comes to bedtime stories, isn't she?"

"You're a star, Emma. And I owe you. Thanks a lot."

Emma watched his retreating back. He definitely had an extra spring in his step. Such a little thing, but it meant so much to him.

And to her, too.

It meant a chance – several chances, since she'd bought herself at least a week – to get the golden gown to work its magic again. A few more hours and she would know. Perhaps.

She yawned again. She couldn't help it. Richard was right that the data entry was mind-numbingly boring. She would go to the staff room for a caffeine top-up. Then she would go for a quick walk around the block in the fresh air. Between them, they should wake her up enough to do the rest of her day's work.

~ ~ ~

By half past six, Emma's nerves were jangling. The rest of the staff had left ages before and she was alone again in the research room with the golden lace gown laid out on the big table under the spotlights. The external doors of the museum were all locked. She didn't dare take the risk that a member of staff might find her sitting here in nothing but her underwear. It was the same golden underwear as yesterday. Because

26

everything, absolutely everything, had to be the same. It wasn't just a question of putting on the dress. She'd discovered that after she "returned" last night. Unless she'd failed because she'd been holding that key? There was more to it than the key, she was almost sure, but she had no way of knowing what the vital elements were. So she would recreate every single one.

St Mary's chimed three-quarters.

Soon. Very soon.

At a couple of minutes to seven, Emma was standing by the table, holding the glorious tattered gown in her arms, waiting. She could scarcely bear to breathe as she watched the church clock move slowly towards the hour. It didn't actually tick but she felt as if she could hear it. Perhaps it was the beat of her own hesitant heart?

St Mary's began to strike the hour.

Now.

Emma pushed her arm, ever so carefully, through the puffed sleeve of the golden gown.

And there it was again. Blue lightning, piercing cold, sucking wind.

But this time she was not afraid. She knew where she was going. And it was what she wanted.

She was going to meet her soulmate. All over again.

Chapter Four

"LADY EMMA?" THE FAIR-HAIRED MAID bobbed a curtsey, but waited by the door.

Lady? Shocked and breathless, Emma looked around for her aristocratic namesake. She was in a totally new place this time, a salon of some kind, furnished with sofas, chairs and screens. It was lit by candles, so it was late. And there was no one else in the room, apart from a soberly dressed older woman kneeling at Emma's feet, needle in hand.

The woman snipped her thread and smoothed the hem of Emma's delicate golden gown with the confidence of years of experience. A lady's maid, obviously. She rose to her feet, smiling shyly. "That will see your ladyship through the rest of the evening. But your own abigail should look at it. It would be a shame if such a beautiful gown were really damaged."

"Um, yes. Er, thank you," Emma mumbled automatically. *Ladyship?* Plain Emma Stanley was *Lady* Emma? She swallowed and managed to stammer, "I–I will."

The questions came crowding in. Where was she? In the same house as before? And where was he?

Oh, please, please, *let him be here.*

The younger maid by the door curtseyed again. "Lady Mumford asked me to find your ladyship. May I bring you to her?"

28

Lady Mumford? Who was Lady Mumford? And who on earth was Lady Emma? Was that who she'd been last time? An aristocrat? With him?

In the tumbling recesses of her mind, Emma the historian knew one thing for sure: if she was "Lady Emma", she had her title by birth and not by marriage. She had to be the daughter of an earl, at least. A subversive little voice was whispering in her head that this dream was right up there in the Harrods class. Maybe, this time, if she closed her eyes and opened them again, she would wake up?

But did she want to?

She swallowed hard, lifted her chin and straightened her spine.

She was here. She was going to stay until she found out who she was and whether he was here, too. She had to know.

~ ~ ~

As Emma followed the fair-haired maid along seemingly endless corridors, her mind was working nineteen to the dozen. OK, she was Lady Emma. But Lady Emma what? Lady Emma Earlsdaughter, she supposed. Or even Lady Emma Dukesdaughter? Wow, wouldn't that be a turn-up for a divorced woman of no social standing?

How was she to find out the truth about herself? Her history degree was no real help. But she also had Georgette Heyer, whose Regency and Georgian romances had sparked Emma's interest in history and costume in the first place. As a teenager, Emma had read some of them so often she almost knew them by heart. And they provided the fine detail that history lectures had not.

The problem was that no one would ever call her by her full name. To servants she was "your ladyship"; to members of her own class, she would be "Lady Emma"; to her intimates, she would be simply "Emma."

Intimates? Not a good word to choose. So far I only have one of those. Very, very intimate, too.

She went back to the problem of her name and family. Perhaps she might refer to her father and mother, quite obliquely, and then someone else might mention them by name?

It probably wouldn't help. The daughter of an earl took the family name. The father's title was usually totally different. He might be the Earl of Gladstone but his daughter would be a mere Lady Emma Bagg. And what if her unnamed father was already dead? It would sound very odd to have a daughter of the house speaking as if a dead earl were still alive. No, she had to find a better way.

Of course. If someone sent her a letter, it would have her full name on it. Easy.

She floated along the corridor for a few yards. Then she came down to earth with a bump. What pretext would she use to get someone to write to her? She didn't know anyone, except him, and writing letters to her was the last thing he intended to do.

Then another nasty thought struck her. What had happened to her shrewd business brain? Lady Emma was a married woman. She brought her courtesy title from her family, but her surname would be her husband's. Whoever he was, she must outrank him, or she would have been addressed by his title, not hers. Had Lady Emma Earlsdaughter married a mere Mister Brown? If so, he must have wealth and power. Daughters of earls were not permitted to marry where they pleased.

If her husband had wealth and power, he might well have strong ideas about honour. That type of man would not take kindly to being betrayed by his wife. He certainly wouldn't be happy to find himself playing second fiddle to the greatest rake in London.

She was getting in deeper than she could possibly deal with and—

Uh-oh. Too late. The maid was holding a door open for Emma to pass through.

Emma was in over her head now and, heaven help her, she was just going to have to muddle through as best she could.

She straightened her shoulders, lifted her chin and walked into the room, remembering to take small dainty steps and to plant an aristocratic half-smile on her lips. She was an earl's daughter, at the very least. She had to behave like one, even though she wasn't really sure how an earl's daughter should behave. When in doubt, she would say nothing, but smile knowingly.

"Ah, Lady Emma. How delightful." A middle-aged lady with an overflowing bosom was making for Emma with both hands outstretched. She was smiling broadly but the look in her eyes was more calculating than friendly.

Emma was instantly on her guard and schooled her features into a slightly wider smile.

The older lady took Emma's right hand in both of her own and shook it warmly. "Such a long time since we last saw you, my dear. When I heard that you were attending this soirée after all, I just *had* to see you and tell you how much we had missed you here in London. When did you arrive? I collect it was in the last few days? I saw no mention of your name in any of the newspapers."

Adrenaline kick-started Emma's brain. Her response came instantly. "I arrived only very recently and have barely had time to set things to rights. But it is most kind of you, ma'am, to trouble yourself so over me. I declare I do not deserve such a courtesy." Goodness, not only glib, but haughty and highfalutin' as well. Where had all those tongue-twisting phrases appeared from? And that cut-glass accent? Her subconscious was working miracles, it seemed. It had even known, somehow, that she should address the older lady as "ma'am" and so avoid having to use a name. This might be the Lady Mumford who had summoned Emma, but if she were not, it would be a terrible *faux pas* to call her by the wrong name.

Emma decided to do a bit of a bulldozer act, to keep the initiative in her own hands. "It is delightful to see you again, ma'am. Tell me, how do you go on?"

The lady rambled on for some minutes, about the parties and balls she had attended – all of them "such a dreadful squeeze" – and the problems of servants in London where there were far too many distractions, often involving drink and gambling. "One sends one's footman out to deliver a note and it may be hours, *hours*, before he returns to his duties. With some sort of lame excuse about losing his way, or having to wait to deliver the note. I said to Mumford only yesterday—"

31

Yes. One up to me. She is *Lady Mumford.*

"—only yesterday that I was almost *certain* I could smell alcohol on the footman's breath."

"Indeed? How trying that must have been, Lady Mumford. Did you dismiss him?"

"Ah, now, I know what a stickler you are, Lady Emma, and I am sure you would have done so, on the spot. However, Mumford is, er, very particular about his footmen and I did not feel..." Her voice trailed off and she looked at her feet. She was actually blushing, too. Emma began to suspect that Mumford's interest in footmen – handsome well-muscled footmen, perhaps? – was very particular indeed.

"I quite understand," Emma said hastily.

And I'm a high stickler, am I? Interesting.

"It might have been a single lapse," she went on smoothly. "And it is so *very* difficult to recruit new staff in London at the height of the season, is it not? I collect you gave him a stern set-down?"

"I, er, yes, of course. He can be in no doubt that he risks his place if he transgresses again." Lady Mumford's smile was tinged with uncertainty.

Time to change the subject, Emma decided. It would not do to press too hard. Lady Mumford might be desperate enough to start asking awkward questions about Emma. "Is your husband with you this evening, ma'am?" That was safe enough. There were no men in the room, only a handful of ladies standing by a piano with their heads close together. No doubt exchanging scandal.

What if it was scandal about Emma? She wouldn't know whether it was true or not.

"He did say he might look in but I have not seen him. If he is here, he will be in the card room, I imagine." Lady Mumford's smile faltered. "They do play very high here," she added. "Not that it would be anything to you."

So I'm rich, as well. Is that my money, or my husband's?

"I find I have lost the taste for high play," Emma said solemnly. Let her ladyship make what she could of that. Emma did not know how to play, so she would stay well away from the tables. Unless her wily subconscious could dredge up

Regency gambling skills as easily as that cut-glass accent?

Lady Mumford was suddenly looking decidedly glum. Because of Emma's comment about high play? Were the Mumfords in debt, perhaps?

In an attempt to humour the woman, Emma said kindly, "Shall we join the other ladies?" She gestured towards the piano. "They look to be having a *most* interesting discussion, do they not?"

"Scandal, Lady Emma. Scandal. They cannot get enough of the *on dits*. Indiscretions. Crim Cons." She shook her head. "I dare swear that young women today are not above boasting about the number and quality of their own lovers."

Emma threw Lady Mumford a conspiratorial smile and started across the room. Lady Mumford had no choice but to follow.

"And *now* he has—" The lady in maroon silk stopped in mid-sentence. "Oh. Lady Emma. How delightful that you could join us."

Emma nodded graciously. She prayed that someone would give her a name.

"I think you know everyone, do you not?"

Emma nodded again, rather vaguely. What else could she do? She was clearly going to get no help with her hunt for names.

The lady in maroon seemed to have decided it was safe to continue her gossipy tale. "I was just telling our friends here, Lady Emma, the latest *on dit* about Captain Will. Will Allmay, you know?" Emma must have looked blank. The maroon lady hurried to explain. "Oh, yes. You have been out of town for so long, haven't you? When Captain Will was first on the town after his return from the wars, he had the reputation for being the most fearful rake. No lady was safe from him."

"No lady *wanted* to be safe from him," put in a saucy young matron in pale blue. Two others laughed. The maroon lady blushed rosily.

Emma, the woman who had once believed fervently in faithful monogamy, found herself shocked. Another one. Was the whole of London full of rakes and adulterous wives? However all information could be useful, so she listened carefully and stored it all away. A *Captain*? A naval captain would be older and richer than an army man. On the other hand, an army captain might be young enough, and fit enough, to be the inexhaustible lover the ladies were describing. Army, then. Probably. And fairly recently sold out.

The ladies seemed to be expecting a reaction from Emma. She swallowed. "I hope he has not been indiscreet," she ventured. "A gentleman, after all..."

The pale blue lady took up the story again. "Whatever else they say about Will Allmay, no one has ever accused him of being indiscreet. His liaisons do not last more than a week or two, to be sure, but he always remains on the best of terms with his, er, lady friends. And he never, ever gossips. The ladies, on the other hand... Well, some do like to recount their exploits to a few select friends. He does seem to have rather, er, inventive ideas. And the stories are exaggerated, too, I do not doubt."

The maroon lady drew in a deep breath. Her bosom was almost bursting out of her low-cut bodice. "Exaggerated? Yes, indeed. I cannot for a moment believe that he is quite as much of an expert in...in intimate matters as some of his conquests have suggested."

She wishes she'd been one of his conquests, Emma realised. *Poor Captain Allmay. All these ladies are after him, in one way or another.*

The pale blue lady bent forward and said, in a conspiratorial whisper, "Have you heard what they call him *now*? His friends in the clubs, I mean?"

All the heads shook as one. Two of the ladies leaned in more closely.

"Will May All!" The pale blue lady giggled. "They are envious of his, er, prowess, I suppose." She was blushing a little. "We ladies, naturally, would know nothing of such things."

"No, indeed," agreed the maroon lady, nodding vigorously.

Emma noticed that the other ladies said nothing. Some looked more than a little knowing. Had the notorious Captain bedded them all?

The pale blue lady suddenly straightened and blushed

scarlet. She was looking past Emma's shoulder. With an expression of horror in her eyes.

Emma felt a tiny touch on her arm, between her long evening glove and the puff sleeve of her dress. Her insides went up in flames. Instantly. For a split second, she fancied she could smell the sea. She did not need to turn to know who was there. She could only pray she was not blushing.

"Why, Lady Emma," said that well-remembered voice. "How delightful to see you in Town again at last. I hope I find you well?"

She turned. He was wearing immaculate black evening dress, its stark simplicity leavened only by a curious gold pin in the folds of his snowy cravat. He looked magnificent. Emma swallowed hard. She dipped her head and dropped a small curtsey but she did not offer her hand. She did not dare risk another touch, even through her kid glove.

The maroon lady gushed forward and seized his hand before he could finish bowing to Emma. "Good evening, sir. How kind of you to join us. We were only this moment speaking of— That is, we were saying...um...that Lady Emma is blooming and we are so pleased that she is returned to London society. No doubt you would agree, Captain? Oh." She clapped a gloved hand to her mouth. "I beg your pardon. I was forgetting. It is *Sir* William now, is it not?"

Sir William? Captain? Emma's heart sank to her flimsy evening slippers.

She should have known. With her luck as a picker of men, it was bound to be him. And none of his liaisons lasted more than a week or two?

A bubble of hysterical laughter gathered in her throat. She managed to swallow it, but only just. She kept her gaze fixed on the hem of her gown.

Will May All? He certainly believes he May All with me.

But I swore I would not allow another philandering bastard to control me. Never again.

Chapter Five

I<small>T TOOK</small> E<small>MMA LONG</small>, <small>HEART-THUMPING</small> minutes to extricate herself from the gossiping women. She had learned exactly what he was now: a naval captain, recently created a Knight Companion of the Bath for outstanding military service. For her own survival, she had to get away from him.

Because she knew the *kind* of man he was.

Also what he was not, she realised with sudden insight. He had greeted her as an acquaintance, when he arrived in the music room. So – *not* her husband.

Better?

No, worse. For it made conventional Emma Stanley into an adulteress.

With a final, and pretty lame, excuse, she made for the door and the succession of corridors leading back to the ladies' retiring room where she had first made her entrance. It seemed safest to assume that returning to her modern life, like making the transition from modern to Regency times, required her to go back to where she first came in. She had done that the previous time, via the dressing room.

If absolutely everything had to be the same this time, though, including the ministering lady's maid, she could be in deep trouble. Would she have to rip her hem again, deliberately?

I'll be Lady Emma the Accident Prone instead of Lady Emma the Stickler.

She found herself laughing out loud, but it was nothing to do with mirth: she was on the verge of hysteria. She was truly frightened. Frightened of where she was, frightened that it might not be a dream after all, frightened that she might never wake up. What if she were trapped here in this alien world? What if—?

What-ifs get you nowhere, Emma Stanley. Go back to the retiring room, go behind the screen and start taking the gown off. That should do it. And if it doesn't, you can cross that bridge when you come to it.

She turned more corners. This was the way the maid had brought her, wasn't it?

No. She hadn't been down this corridor before. She was lost.

Emma swallowed hard, trying to keep herself from shaking. She mustn't lose her head. She had to think.

There had to be someone around, a servant, or another guest, who could direct her to the ladies' retiring room. She just had to find someone. Anyone at all would do.

She looked around and behind her. The corridor was totally empty. Fine. She would find another corridor, other rooms, other places. There must be people in this great barn of a house.

She hurried on. Round another corner and another. It seemed to be a maze. But finally she thought she recognised a huge oriental vase on a carved wooden stand. Yes. She had seen that before. There couldn't be two as ugly as that, surely? It had been quite near the entrance to the retiring room. Round this next corner, perhaps?

At that moment, the door opposite the oriental monstrosity opened. She heard the murmur of voices from the gloom beyond. Then a single word, quiet but incisive. "Emma."

His voice.

An arm snaked out and grabbed her hand before she could make a dash for safety. "Emma, is something wrong? Why did you run from me? Why do you keep disappearing?"

There was no answer to that. Not one that he would

37

believe, anyway. Desperate, she tugged her hand out of his grasp. Touching him was sheer torture.

He allowed her to put a little distance between them. A sad smile quirked one corner of his mouth. "Anyone would think you were afraid of me," he said, in a voice that stroked her skin as gently as the caress of a flower petal.

Emma's muscles were starting to melt. Any moment, she would collapse in a heap at his feet.

His gaze was fixed on her face. "But that is not possible." His voice dropped even further until it was barely a rumble, deep in his chest. "Not after how we have been to each other. *With* each other."

Emma forced herself back against the corridor wall. For support. "Do not say such things," she hissed at last. "Would you ruin me, sir?" She glanced to right and left, as if expecting one of the gossipy matrons to materialise and denounce her.

He shook his head sadly. "I would do nothing to upset you in any way, Emma. You know that. You know how much I want you, how I...we..." He let his voice tail off. In that moment, something changed.

He looked up and down the corridor. It was totally empty. Then he made sure that the door opposite the oriental vase was firmly closed. As he turned back to Emma, he dropped his hands to his sides, palms open and pleading.

"Emma, my darling, you must help me. Please. I do not understand how you can make love to me at one moment, and flee the next. Is it something I have done? *Tell* me, my dear. I can't go on like this. This diabolical hide-and-seek of yours is like to drive me stark mad."

He *seemed* to be telling the truth. There was a stricken look in his eyes. Mixed with something that could have been longing. But what on earth could she say to him?

"I...I... Forgive me, but I cannot explain things now." She glanced down the corridor. Someone might appear at any moment. "Not here. I—"

"Then let me take you somewhere else. Where we can be alone. And safe." He reached out to take her arm.

She wriggled away from his questing hand. "No! Nowhere is safe here."

He was frowning now. And he was clearly going to argue.

"I will meet you," she said in desperation. "Early tomorrow. In the park."

"Which park?" he bit out. "Or would you have me tour them all?"

Which park? How should I know which park would be safe for a lovers' tryst? "Er… You choose. You are more practised than I in the art of dalliance, are you not?"

That definitely hit home. She saw his eyes darken. He clearly did not like to be reminded of his reputation as a rake.

"Not Hyde Park. Too many ex-soldiers out exercising their horses first thing. No. Green Park. By the milk maids. We can meet as if by chance."

Emma nodded. She found she could not speak.

"I shall wait for you there. Do not fail me. Have I your promise?"

What choice did she have? "Green Park," she whispered. "Tomorrow. As early as I can." Then it was all too much. She fled round the corner. There, as she had hoped, was the door to the ladies' retiring room, her refuge from Will and, she fervently hoped, her passage to the modern world.

The retiring room was empty. She closed the door firmly at her back. There was no key, but she would not have dared to lock it anyway, now that she knew the dangers of locking rooms from the inside. She scurried behind the screen before anyone else should come into the room.

Please let it work, even without the ministering abigail. Please.

Emma took a deep breath and started to remove the golden gown.

~ ~ ~

The chiming of the church clock was balm to Emma's shredded nerves. She grabbed a chair and collapsed onto it, dropping her head into her hands with a groan.

It's over. I'm back. I'm safe.

She laid a hand on the tattered golden gown, safely spread across the research room table. It had not changed, or moved, not even a fraction.

It's over. Thank goodness.

But it wasn't over. She had made a promise to her lover. If she did not arrive at their rendezvous, what would Will do? He had said she was driving him mad. And he had certainly looked as if her disappearing acts were getting to him. He wouldn't do away with himself, would he?

No, of course not. He's a rake. He may be temporarily infatuated with Lady Emma – me! – but he'll recover once he realises she's not coming back to him. He'll give up and find another lover. It's what rakes do.

What rakes did. She corrected herself automatically. It was *not* real. None of it. She had been in some kind of trance, but she was still here, still in the museum, still plain Emma Stanley. Will Allmay must be a figment of her sex-starved imagination.

She took a deep breath and tried to force her thoughts into some kind of order. If…? No, she couldn't possibly go back to Will. For a start, no Regency lady could appear in Green Park dressed in nothing but a lace evening gown. Especially at seven in the morning. And how would she get there, anyway? On foot? In those flimsy evening slippers? They'd be in shreds before she'd walked a hundred yards.

But what would he do when she didn't appear?

Her stomach clenched. She felt a little sick and had to swallow hard to control it.

No point in agonising over that. Her window of opportunity had closed. The earliest she could go back to Will, if she were mad enough to do it again, was the following evening, when the church clock began to strike seven. And—

And she couldn't do it the next day, in any case. They were expecting her at the Lamb House to work on the collection there. It was miles away. By the time she'd finished there and driven back, Richard would have locked up the museum and she wouldn't be able to get in.

The subversive voice in the back of her mind would not be silenced. It was suggesting that even a two day wait in the real world might not prevent her from keeping her promise to Will. After all, she had made the transition twice now, to different times and different places. From Will's reaction in the corridor by the oriental monstrosity, more than a day had passed in

40

Regency London between her first and second visits. If Regency time could expand, perhaps it could contract, too?

Emma shook her woozy head, trying to clear it. It didn't work. Was Will a ghost? But how could a modern woman make love to a ghost? And hadn't she vowed to have nothing more to do with philandering men?

One thing she was sure of. She needed to see Will again. He was her lover. The lover with whom she had committed adultery, breaking her marriage vows to a husband whose name she didn't even know.

~ ~ ~

Emma went to the museum early to open up. As soon as Richard arrived to take charge of the keys, she set off for the Lamb House. She really enjoyed the drive. It was early spring and, although it was cold, the sun was shining out of a cloudless sky, so blue it could have been the Alps rather than England. Some of the trees already had little puffs of acid green clouding their branches, like fuzz on a baby's head, and soon they would burst into fresh leaves. She had promised herself that this year, by the spring, she would be happily settled into her new life.

Will Allmay – Captain Sir William Allmay, KCB, RN, according to the clues she had put together – had put the kibosh on that. She would never be able to settle to anything until she sorted out what was really going on with her strange visions, or dreams, or whatever they were. She had found a man she truly loved, but was he real? A quick internet search for a Regency Sir William Allmay had produced nothing at all, even with variant spellings. Maybe she'd misheard the name?

She racked her brains. As far as she could remember, the gossips had called him all sorts of things, including "Captain Will", "rake" and "Will May All". To his face, the women had said only "Captain" or "Sir William". Neither helped narrow down Emma's search.

Will Allmay might never have existed at all.

And even if he were real, somehow, did he love her in return? After all, he was renowned for how quickly he moved from one lover to the next.

Worrying won't help me. I can't do anything until tomorrow evening at the earliest, so better to enjoy the sunshine and the treasures of the Lamb House.

That prospect made her smile. She had visited the Lamb House as a tourist, ages before, but now that she was the costume curator, she would be able to go behind the scenes and explore all the nooks and crannies of that little jewel of a house. Plus the wonders of its costume collection.

And she was being paid to do this? She felt blessed.

Following the directions she'd been given, she drove round to the back of the Hall and parked alongside a couple of other cars by the kitchen door. The Lamb House wasn't yet open to the public. The staff, mostly volunteers, would be finishing the preseason clean and restoring all the treasures to their places, ready for the visitors who would soon be trooping through the massive front door. Emma had noticed on her previous visit that the medieval stone lamb above the lintel was totally out of keeping with the architecture of the house, but the guide had explained that it was a talisman for the then owners, the Lambester family, and had been recovered undamaged after the fire that destroyed the medieval manor house. It was not recognisably a lamb – its lumpy body and four legs could have been anything – but Emma accepted it had been a lamb. Once.

The Lamb House's costume collection wasn't on display, apart from a handful of items, but it could be viewed by appointment during the season. And Emma Stanley, costume curator, would be conducting those viewings, so she had to learn all about the collection, in double quick time.

She beamed at the thought as she made for the kitchen door.

~ ~ ~

Three hours later, she hadn't stopped beaming inside. But her back ached from lifting and replacing the long costume boxes, stacked on rudimentary racks about eight feet high. The Lamb House, as visitors saw it, was an delightful Regency gem but, behind the scenes, it was pretty basic. The back stairs were gloomy and forbidding in their austerity; the costume stores were little different except that they had long windows, shrouded by blinds to keep out the destructive sunlight.

Emma stretched her back and flexed her shoulders. She needed caffeine, she decided. After working so long, she reckoned she deserved it. No problem about finding it, either, since the house manager had shown her where the volunteers congregated to make coffee.

She rattled down the servants' staircase and through the kitchen to the snug that had once been the housekeeper's room. It was empty. She made a cup of coffee and sank into an old leather armchair with a sigh of contentment. She had spent a blissful morning unpacking treasures, not all from the Regency period. She particularly admired the velvet waistcoats from the Georgian period when gentlemen were happy to parade around like peacocks. The workmanship was exquisite: not just fine embroidery, but silver and gold thread decoration as well. No doubt the poor seamstresses were paid a pittance for their weeks of work, but it was probably that or starvation. And better than the brothel.

The Regency period was no better, she knew. Years and years of war took their toll until Napoleon was finally defeated at Waterloo in 1815. When everything should have been back to normal, with returning soldiers to till the fields and sailors to man the trading ships, Britain had been hit by the Year Without a Summer. Instead of peaceful harvests, there was famine. People begged for food. And some starved.

What year was it when I was with Will? Before or after Waterloo?

Emma thought hard. The ladies' gowns were no help. Even for an expert like Emma, it was difficult to place a style in a single year, because not everyone could afford to follow the latest fashions. She had reckoned that her gold lace gown dated from the later part of the Regency, but it could have been pre-Waterloo. Just.

Had Will said anything helpful?

Actually, no. Everything he had said was related to *her*, or rather to Lady Emma. He had spoken about how he desired her. Even in the music room, surrounded by lustful, leering ladies, he had been focused solely on her.

A vague memory stirred.

Yes, hadn't he mentioned ex-soldiers riding in the park?

That might mean the war was over. And the fact that Will himself had retired from the Navy might suggest the same. Then again, possibly not. Officers had retired throughout the war.

She'd have to find out. She was bound to put her foot in it otherwise. What if she said something about the Regent's daughter when the poor girl was already dead?

Princess Charlotte could be Emma's route to the answer. Or perhaps the Regent's wife would be better? Caroline had lived for some years after her daughter's death. She had even become George IV's queen, though he had stopped her from being crowned. If Emma could get someone to tell her the latest gossip about the royal family, it might be possible to work out which year she was in.

So, next time she was with Will, she would—

"Emma. There you are." It was the house manager, Geraldine. "Glad to see you're taking a break. If you're not going back to work right away, would you like to do that house tour now?" Geraldine had promised to take Emma round all the rooms that were not open to the public. Some were in the process of restoration. Some were so far gone that public access would never be possible.

Emma grinned and got up at once. "That would be great, Geraldine."

They spent an hour exploring rooms and peering into cupboards. In one imposing bedroom, the floorboards shifted unnervingly under their feet. "Couldn't let the public in here without very expensive repairs to the floor," Geraldine said with a grimace. "And the budget won't run to anything like that, not for years. Come and look at the master bedroom instead. We've got all the original furniture. Even the bed. And the restoration should be finished before we open."

Geraldine led the way along the corridor and threw a door wide. The red velvet curtains had been drawn back and the sun was straining to penetrate the blinds on the floor-to-ceiling windows. In the half-light, candelabra and ornaments gleamed on tables and chests. The huge fireplace was empty and cold; there was no fire screen. The canopy and curtains had been replaced on the tester bed, but the bed itself was not made up.

That same bed? That same fireplace? And candelabra, too? Emma's brain refused to believe what her eyes were seeing. She was so shocked that she blurted out the first words that came into her head. "But shouldn't the curtains be green?"

Chapter Six

EMMA FIXED HER GAZE ON HER RACKS of costume boxes and forced herself to focus.

It had been the same bedroom. She was sure of it. She'd found Will naked in the bath, right here in the Lamb House. The windows, the bed, the fireplace, the dressing room; everything was exactly the same. And she'd felt that it was Will's room. There was a sort of presence that she'd recognised instantly.

That gold lace gown has history here. It must have. It took me to the Lamb House for our first kiss. So Will must have history here, too.

In the master bedroom, Emma had shivered as if he were touching her again. As if he were *there*, in the room, beside her. She was reminded of their very first encounter, in the museum store room, with sand beneath her toes. She had touched him but he had melted away. Would he desert her again if she went back into the master bedroom alone? Or would he stay?

That annoyingly sensible part of her brain reasserted itself yet again. Even if she had had sex with a ghost – and she had surely dreamed that, since it was impossible – it had happened in *his* time, not hers. To meet him again, she had to go to *his* time and she needed to wear the lace gown to do it. When she

46

wasn't wearing it, Will had been a shadowy apparition that faded at a touch. So nothing could possibly happen in the restored master bedroom of the Lamb House.

Emma had done her best to pass off her comment to Geraldine as a strange fancy from the books on Regency design she'd been studying, but the house manager had given her a very old-fashioned look and had become a little distant for the rest of their tour. No wonder. She probably thought Emma was soft in the head. And she might not be far wrong, either.

Emma resolved to make an effort to be extra professional around the house manager in future. With her brain in gear, so there would be no more betraying slips.

Especially not about Will Allmay and his relationship to the house.

Emma needed to get closer to Geraldine, who was the keeper of all the history of the Lamb House. Now that Emma was sure Will had been here, it was vital to find out everything she could about the place.

Was there a real Lady Emma? And was she ever here? I need *to know.*

~ ~ ~

The sun had gone down long before Emma left the Lamb House. Halfway back, it started to drizzle, just enough to make the wipers smear the windscreen. It made the roads greasy, too. For some reason, she was feeling cold, so she turned the car heater up to max. It would be nice to get back to her cosy flat. She would heat up a tin of soup, perhaps, or have tea and hot buttered toast. Familiar, comforting things might help her to come to terms with what she'd discovered at the mansion.

At *Will's* mansion, she corrected herself. Since she'd found him in the master bedroom, and she knew she had, then he was clearly the master. But his name wasn't "Lambester". So how had he come to be there? Was he a tenant, rather than the owner? The house records might contain some clues. The research would probably be fascinating, exactly the kind of work that Emma loved.

But I don't have time to do it. I'm not due back at the Lamb House for several days and Will is expecting me to meet him in Green Park— Correction: Will was *expecting me to meet him in the park. This morning. Hours and hours ago.*

If she waited another twenty-four hours before she put the lace dress on again, she might miss him altogether. Tonight, on the other hand...

She put her foot down. She was driving too fast for the conditions, she knew, but at this speed she'd get back to the museum before seven. If she was lucky, Richard would have stayed late and she'd be able to get in.

OK, it was a one in a thousand chance. He always left on time. But after the shock of seeing that bedroom today, Emma had to check.

By the time she reached the museum car park, it was raining hard and very dark. The car park was empty. She told herself that didn't matter. Since today was one of little Chloë's nursery days, Richard wouldn't have had the car. He *might* still be here.

St Mary's clock was showing ten minutes to seven as Emma ran across the car park with her driving coat slung over her head to keep the rain off. At the staff door, she pressed the bell and waited. After a minute, she pressed it again. Her coat slid down onto her shoulders and she caught it just before it slipped to the ground. With a struggle, she managed to push her arms into its wet, tangled sleeves. "Damn the thing," she said aloud, huddling back against the door to make the most of the little shelter it offered.

She was cursing the fact that the museum was locked up and she had no chance of getting in. The precious lace gown was in there, only feet from where she stood, but it might as well have been on the top of Everest. In desperation, she pressed the bell again, holding it down. No one inside could possibly fail to hear that strident jangle.

No one came.

Then St Mary's struck seven.

She swore again, louder and longer. It had been stupid even to try, stupid to drive so fast on wet roads, stupid to imagine that Richard might have stayed late for once.

She leaned back against the cruel door. She would not cry. She would *not.*

Time to go home to that hot buttered toast. She straightened her shoulders. Did she need to put her coat over her head again? Or could she make it back to the car without getting too wet?

At the edge of her field of vision, something moved. Something human-shaped.

Emma's breath caught. Who would be in a deserted museum car park at this time of night? It wasn't on the way to anywhere.

All she could make out was a dark shadow, half hidden in the hedge. Someone tall and quite broad. A man, then. Wearing a hood, pulled low.

Why shouldn't he wear a hood? It's raining hard.

The hooded figure didn't move out of the shadows. It just stood there, motionless. She knew it was staring at her, even though she couldn't see its face. Something about the set of the shoulders seemed familiar.

Emma's stomach clenched. She had to swallow hard to stop herself from throwing up. She recognised that sinister shape now. She glanced across at her car, measuring the distance. Then back at the shadow. If she ran, could she make it to her car before he caught her?

She slid her fingers into her soggy pocket for her car keys. She could use them as a weapon if she had to. And, with the keys ready in her hand, she had a chance of starting the car in time to get away. Provided she could reach it before he—

She launched herself out into the rain, sprinting towards her car. Five yards from it, she pinged the lock. Seconds later, she was wrenching the door open and throwing herself inside.

Lock the doors. Shit. Where's the switch to lock the doors?

Her desperate fingers found it at last. Followed by a lovely solid click. She let out the breath she'd been holding and started the engine. Feeling fractionally safer, she dared to glance out into the gloom to see where he was.

The bastard hadn't moved. Still hidden in the hedge. Still hooded. Still staring.

He'd got to her just by being there. Without having to do anything but stare.

She cursed him again as she gunned the engine and shot

out of the car park onto the main road. But in her mind, she could hear him laughing.

Julian had always laughed when he saw her fear.

~ ~ ~

She slammed the door of her flat and double-locked it. Then, before she'd even taken her coat off, she grabbed the landline and dialled her police liaison officer.

It went to Flo's voicemail.

Emma had run out of curses. So she left a fairly polite message, reporting what had happened. With luck, Flo would ring back later in the evening. But she might have moved on. After all, it was months since they had spoken. They had both assumed that Emma was safe here, in a new location, with a new job and a new place to live.

I should have known, Emma thought. *As far as Julian's concerned, nothing has changed. That devil thinks he owns me.*

She realised she was clutching the phone so hard that her fingers were going numb. She flung it down in disgust.

This time, she was going to sort him. Properly. She refused to be afraid again.

~ ~ ~

By the time Emma fell into a troubled sleep, Flo hadn't returned her call. Emma tossed and turned, pursued by shadowy figures in her dreams. So when the phone did ring, eventually, her brain was too groggy to produce more than a slurred "H'lo?"

Silence.

A little of the fog cleared. "Flo? Is that you?"

Silence. Followed by loud, heavy breathing.

It took another few moments for Emma to realise what was happening. It wasn't the first time. And knowing who must be on the other end of the phone line brought her fully awake at last. She'd been frightened in the car park, sure, but that had been the shock of seeing him again. She would *not* let him frighten her with his stupid tricks. Besides, Flo had provided a remedy, months and months ago.

But where on earth had Emma put it? Where?

She pulled out the drawer from the bedside table, emptied

50

all the contents onto the bed and began to rummage around with her free hand. Yes, there. She grabbed the silver metal and put it against the mouthpiece of the phone. Then she blew, hard and long, using every ounce of her lung power.

The whistle was ear-splittingly loud and piercing. Emma thought she heard a cry of pain.

Yes! You won't try that again, you bastard.

She cut the call and slotted the receiver back into its cradle. Then she patted it. "Thank you, Flo," she said and went to make a restorative cup of tea.

The kettle was beginning to sing when she remembered. She ran back to the phone and dialled 1471. No joy. Number withheld.

As usual, he was much too canny to leave evidence when he didn't have to.

She dug out the little notebook from the heap of stuff on the bed, found a clean page and made notes about the time of the call and exactly what had happened. Flo had always said that "contemporaneous notes make good evidence."

The phone rang again.

Emma jumped. Even Julian couldn't be that crass, could he?

Nonetheless, she grabbed her whistle again before she picked up the phone. She put it to her ear without saying a word.

"Emma? Is that you, Emma? It's Flo."

"Oh, Flo. Thank goodness. I thought it was Julian again. I—"

"Julian *again*?" Flo repeated. "On the phone? Why didn't you say so before?"

"Because it's only just happened. Heavy breathing. But I used the whistle trick, just the way you showed me." Emma was feeling quite proud of how she had reacted.

"Oh," said Flo slowly. She didn't sound all that impressed. "Then I'm afraid— Emma, how did he get your phone number?"

Emma felt the familiar tensing in her stomach. "I'm in the phone book," she said miserably. "Name, address, phone number. How could I have been so stupid?"

Flo was too professional to answer that. She said briskly, "So he knows where you live. Pity. But I'm more concerned about that meeting in the car park. Did he attack you?"

"No."

"What did he say? Were there threats? Can you remember his exact words?"

"He didn't say anything. Not a word."

"Oh." Even less impressed, clearly. "Did he touch you at all?"

Emma could see where this was going. Again. "He didn't come near me. He stood in the shadows, half in the hedge, actually, and stared at me from under that blasted hoodie thing. Until I bolted for the car and drove off."

"Emma, I have to ask this. Sorry, but are you quite *sure* it was him?"

Emma wanted to scream with frustration. But this was just Flo doing her job. Flo who had supported her through the worst of bad times. If Flo didn't ask the nasty questions, someone else would.

"I know you have to ask, Flo. But yes, I am absolutely sure it was him. I'd recognise that shape anywhere. I had years with him, remember. And after all he did to me, I am very familiar with that particular male body."

"Of course you are," Flo replied. Too quickly.

Emma knew what was coming next. So she supplied it before Flo could. "You're going to tell me that he didn't actually *do* anything, so he can't be arrested. Aren't you? You're going to say that seeing a shadowy figure in a car park isn't evidence that he meant me harm. And that there's no evidence that it really was who I said it was."

"I believe you, Emma. But a magistrate wouldn't know you the way I do."

"You mean that the magistrate would think I was a hysterical woman who was seeing things in the dark. It's OK, Flo, I know you're on my side. I just wish the law was, too."

Flo didn't answer. After a minute, she said, "The phone call. Did you check for the caller's number?"

"No go," Emma replied at once. "Number withheld. He won't be caught that way. He's too clever."

"So are we. Tomorrow, we'll install call screening and block anyone who calls with their number withheld. We'll block pay phones, too. If he wants to do his heavy-breathing bit again, he'll have to do it in a way we can trace."

Emma wasn't at all sure that Flo's solution was foolproof but she said warmly, "Thanks, Flo. And I'll keep my trusty whistle by the phone, too. Just in case."

Flo sighed. "Yes, he's devious. Unfortunately, being a devious bastard isn't an arrestable offence. We need more. Can you come in tomorrow to give me a written statement?"

Emma found herself wishing she'd never left that message on Flo's voicemail. Working with the police hadn't got her anywhere last time. Her oh-so-charming ex-husband had produced glib-tongued reasons for everything, even Emma's injuries, and the prosecuting authorities had said there was no realistic prospect of a conviction. This time round, Julian would probably be even better at spinning convincing lies. He'd had lots of practice over the years, with lots of gullible women, though Emma was the only one he'd actually married.

When Emma didn't reply, Flo said, "Look, Emma, I do know how hard this is for you. Last time, when you—"

Emma cut her off before she could start reciting things that Emma most definitely did not want to hear. "I don't want to talk about last time, Flo. Just tell me when and where you want me for the statement and I'll see if I can make it. You have to understand," she added, with a brittle laugh, "that I'm a full-time professional woman these days, with diary commitments that I can't break."

"Yes, indeedy, ma'am," Flo said in a false American accent, laughing back. After a little haggling, they agreed a time and Flo rang off.

Emma's shoulders slumped; a nasty little pain prickled above her left eye. So the whole horrible circus had started again. With Julian as ringmaster, cracking his whip over the heads of caged female charges to make them dance to his tune. He'd found out where Emma's new home was. He thought he could control her again, get her back into his cage. But Emma had decided, long ago, that she would not do Julian's dance. She was not going back in his fear-cage, either.

Chapter Seven

BY SIX-THIRTY THE FOLLOWING EVENING, Emma was alone in the deserted museum and back on an even keel, more or less. She'd stolen out in her lunch break to give Flo the formal statement. Emma could not face telling her colleagues that she had a stalker – correction: potential stalker – and that he was, in all probability, her ex-husband.

She'd given her statement, but nothing would come of it. Flo was hopeful. But Flo had been hopeful last time, right up to the point where the prosecutors had abandoned the case against Julian.

Emma had been frightened, a bit, by his heavy-breathing phone call. Shock, really. Flo had urged her to be careful, to take precautions, and she would – she'd taken self-defence classes the previous year and she always carried a rape alarm – but she would *not* allow Julian to control her life. If she saw him again, she'd take video evidence. What else were smartphones for? And her martial arts instructor had shown her that a well-aimed car key could do a lot of damage.

Her car was parked much closer to the museum entrance today; a long way away from that concealing hedge. She would make sure she always had her rape alarm in her pocket and her keys in her hand when she left the museum. For now, she had more important things to do here. With the lace gown.

In the back of her brain, a warning voice, which sounded rather like Flo's, was telling her that she should have left the museum earlier, at the same time as everyone else. Safety in numbers and all that. But the truth was that she hadn't been prepared to.

Emma wasn't prepared to give up on the mystery of Will and Lady Emma. It was intriguing. She had to find out the truth about them, didn't she?

Rubbish. She was kidding herself and she knew it. It was a lot more than the mystery of it. It was a once-in-a-lifetime love affair, and Emma was desperate to know if it was *her* love affair.

At the thought of that love affair, she couldn't help but picture Will rising from his bath. That searing image was enough to fill her stomach with tumbling butterflies and make her throat dry. He was built like a Greek god and he made love like— Well, he was a bit like a Greek god in that department, too. Assuming that Greek gods took their lovers to paradise and beyond. From the myths she had read, the lovemaking of Greek gods was more about the creation of demigod children than the giving of pleasure, but that might have been because the Greek poets took sexual pleasure for granted. They *were* usually men, after all.

It was totally idiotic train of thought, but its off-the-wall quality was reassuringly familiar. Emma laughed out loud.

"Good," she said, grinning at the empty research table. "I'm me again. Daft as a brush under the businesslike exterior. But back in control of my life." She glanced out at the church clock. She had just under fifteen minutes.

"Right. I'd better go and find the magic lace gown, hadn't I?"

~ ~ ~

This time, Emma was no longer shocked by the blue lightning or the sucking cold. She expected those. What mattered, and what she could not forecast, was where she would appear. Would she be in Will's dressing room again?

No such luck.

She'd arrived somewhere completely new: the marble-floored entrance hall of a grand house. Where was she? *When* was she? She nudged aside the edge of the velvet evening cloak that covered her from neck to toes. The cloak told her nothing. But underneath? Ah. The magic lace gown. A quick glance round showed that she was alone in the hall, so she pulled up her skirt to examine the hemline. *Yes.* The temporary repair was quite noticeable. If more than a few hours had passed, someone with sewing skills would have made a better job of mending the tear, she was sure.

She dropped the hem to the floor where it danced across the toes of her evening slippers. Another clue. She stuck out a foot. Yes, she was wearing the same slippers she had worn at the soirée. So, apart from a velvet evening cloak, she was dressed exactly as she had been when she last saw Will by the oriental vase. It looked as if hardly any time had passed since she left him.

She looked harder at her slippered foot. There was no sign of dirt or wear to be seen. So how had she got to this mansion? And whose house was it?

She hesitated. Should she find a bell and ring for a servant? How would she explain her arrival if she did?

A scuffling noise behind her. Then a voice. "Oh, your ladyship. So sorry, your ladyship. I didn't hear the carriage. Or the door. Oh, your ladyship, I—"

Emma turned to see an old servant who appeared to have shot out of the porter's chair near the door. He looked a little bleary eyed but he was also bright red with embarrassment. Did he expect to be fired for failing to open the door to her? Emma was pretty sure she had arrived without opening the front door at all.

Her understanding smile cut his apologies off in mid-sentence. His high colour began to fade a little.

"No matter," she said, wishing she knew what he was called. She smiled again to cover up her failings in the naming stakes. "I am here now. Can you tell me what time it is?"

The porter glanced past Emma to a small carriage clock on a shelf above the oil lamp. "It's just gone half past three, your ladyship. Shall I ring for Miss Bailey?"

Who on earth was Miss Bailey? The porter seemed to think it was normal to ring for her, so Emma agreed he should, in spite of the ungodly hour. Behind her back, she crossed her fingers. She was counting on being able to tell from Miss Bailey's dress and demeanour whether she was hostess or servant.

Emma smiled encouragingly at the porter. "So Miss Bailey is waiting up?" That was a fairly safe question, she hoped. Her fingers were still crossed.

The man nodded vigorously. "Her said she would wait downstairs for yer ladyship's return. Said I was to ring the moment yer ladyship stepped through the door." His accent was becoming more pronounced. He was clearly relaxing a bit.

"Tell me—" Emma began, but was cut off by the arrival of a stately woman dressed in a neat dark gown made high to the neck. Not evening wear. Did that make her a servant?

"Good evening, m'lady," she said, dipping a tiny curtsey. "How late you are. And you must be cold in that thin gown. Shall I make you a hot drink before you go up?"

A servant, certainly. Her own servant? Probably. And Emma was obviously expected to sleep here. Did that make this *her* house? Or was she merely a guest here?

Whatever she was, she had no chance of finding the way to her bedroom on her own. "Thank you," she said quickly, "but I'd prefer to go straight to bed." Then, trusting to luck, she added, "I am very tired. Lead the way, if you please, Bailey."

The servant gave her a questioning look. Was that because Emma had called her "Bailey"? Surely that was the usual mode of address in the Regency? Or was it because the maid had been invited to precede her mistress? No way of knowing. Aristocrats were allowed to have their foibles – they were the bosses, after all – so even if Emma had got something wrong, Miss Bailey was unlikely to say so.

Miss Bailey started up the stairs and Emma followed, feigning tiredness by leaning heavily on the bannister rail. Halfway up the first flight, she stopped, shocked into momentary immobility. Her husband. Heavens, was this her husband's house? Was he here? Would he expect to share her bed? She had been thinking so much about seeing Will again that she had completely forgotten the anonymous husband.

Nothing to be done. It was a dream. What happened in dreams, even with an unknown husband, was not real. When she took off the lace gown, she would wake up, and then she would laugh at her fears.

She crossed her fingers yet again and continued to climb.

On the second floor, Bailey flung open a door for Emma to precede her into the bedroom. It proved to be empty, to Emma's great relief. Head held high, she crossed to the blazing fire, holding out her hands to warm them.

"I knew you were cold, m'lady," Bailey chided, taking the cloak from Emma's shoulders. "Are you sure you wouldn't like a hot drink?"

Definitely a lady's maid. An abigail, as they called them back then. And from the familiarity of her comments, the woman might have been with Emma for many years.

Go carefully with this one.

"Thank you, no. I should like to sleep for a little. I have to go out again soon. I promised to meet— Um, that is, I have decided to go for a walk in Green Park. As soon as it's light."

The abigail's eyebrows almost hit her hairline. She opened her mouth, presumably to remonstrate, and then closed it again. Firmly. But she was frowning as she reached for the fastenings of Emma's gown. "I will be ready to accompany you whenever you wish, m'lady," she said, fingers working rapidly.

"Oh no. Don't do tha—"

Too late. The gown was whisked over Emma's head. She waited for the inevitable.

Nothing happened.

Emma was standing in front of the fire in her underthings. Bailey had the gown in her hands and was examining the hem critically. She tutted quietly. "A very poor quality of repair, I must say. Done at the soirée, was it, m'lady?"

"Er, yes." Why was she still here?

An even more frightening thought crowded in on her. Would she be here for ever, now? In the power of her unknown husband?

He might come through that door at any moment, demanding his conjugal rights. He might be mean, or cruel, or even violent. And there would be nothing at all that she could do to fight him. For he would own her. Everything she had, including her body, would be his property.

She closed her eyes, desperate to will away the presence of this alien world. She longed to be back in her own time. Where she was safe. How could it all have gone so terribly wrong? She began to shiver in earnest. She had been a fool to do this again when she had not the slightest idea how the golden gown worked its magic. This was no game. The Regency world was suddenly all too real, and very threatening.

Bailey wrapped a heavy robe around Emma's shoulders and pushed her closer to the fire, scolding in an undervoice as she did so. Eventually, Emma's shivering stopped. The warmth, and the contact, was bringing her back to reality.

Regency reality.

She swallowed hard. She had better know the worst. Who was this man who owned her? Was he here, in this house, ready to pounce?

She had to know. But she couldn't blatantly ask who her husband was. Perhaps if the abigail could be made to start talking about him? A confidential servant was bound to know everything that went on, even in the bedroom. She'd been with Emma for ever, clearly, so she might open up about Emma's husband.

Staring down into the fire, Emma sighed dreamily and murmured, "My husband…?"

Bailey gave a snort. "Your husband, God rest his soul, would not have approved. He—"

Eureka! I'm a widow. A WIDOW.

No furious stranger was going to force himself into her bed. Or beat her for her adulterous liaison with Will.

No, that wasn't right. If she was a widow, she wasn't an adulteress after all.

The relief was overwhelming. Emma wanted to sing at the top of her voice and dance around the room. But Bailey was grumbling on about what Emma's late husband would have thought and said. In that moment, Emma realised she needed to curb her elation and pay attention. Important information could be gleaned from what Bailey had to say.

"—and as for meeting someone in Green Park when all right-thinking folk are abed— Sir John would not have approved, that's certain. It might have been his dying wish that you should marry again, m'lady, but he would not have held with your meeting a gentleman in the park at dawn."

"What makes you think that—?"

Bailey didn't allow Emma to finish. "Because I know you, missy. Always up to mischief, even when you was a nipper. And what else would you be going to the park for, at such an hour?"

Definitely an old retainer.

Time to push her luck. She'd done OK, so far. And it would be a good idea to change the subject, anyway. "By the way, the porter downstairs. He did not open the door for me." She let the comment hang, and waited.

Bailey did not disappoint. "Typical," she spat. "Filch is always asleep on the job. I suppose he jumped up from his chair the moment you were inside and was swearing black was white, as usual? Sir John always said he was too old for the job. Surely now you can see he was right?"

Filch? Did she really employ a night porter with a name like *Filch?* Shades of Dickens, several decades too early. Emma swallowed her smile and said calmly, "Old retainers are valuable, Bailey. Surely *you* know that more than anyone? No, Filch stays in his post as long as he is able and as long as he wishes to." At least she now knew that the servants were hers, even if the house was not. Progress, of a kind.

Bailey harrumphed. "You were about to tell me, m'lady, about the gentleman you are meeting in the park? I take it there *is* a gentleman?"

"Oh, very well." Emma needed to confide in someone in this alien world, and a faithful old retainer like Bailey was probably the best on offer. "You are right, as usual, Bailey. I am going to meet a gentleman. But it will be a perfectly respectable meeting. You will accompany me." At the abigail's half-smile, Emma added, "You will stay out of earshot, however. I wish to have a private conversation with the gentleman."

"As you wish, m'lady." Bailey did not sound happy at all.

At least there was one consolation. Emma might be stranded here in the Regency, but she wouldn't have to wear that skimpy lace evening gown to meet Will in the park. She would be able to wear something more appropriate, and a lot warmer, for their rendezvous. "Lay out a warm walking dress, if you please," she instructed. "And boots." She was determined that she was not going to freeze in the early spring wind. "I will lie down on my bed for a little rest. Wake me at six. I wish to be out of the house by half past."

Bailey glowered at her but said only, "As you wish, m'lady. At six."

Emma lay down on her bed and closed her eyes. But she didn't sleep. There were too many clues to piece together and she didn't have much time. She needed to have things straight in her mind, or at least a bit straighter, before she saw him again.

She had no idea yet what her name was, but she did know she was a widow. So all the matrons' chat about her being away from town had an obvious cause. She'd most probably been in mourning. And if she remembered rightly, mourning for a husband was two years, one year in black and one in grey. Lady Emma was wearing colours now, so her husband must have died more than two years ago.

Was this house hers? Possibly, but she'd have to find out for sure. It might be rented or it might belong to relatives. Having her own servants here proved nothing. And where had she been living during her mourning? Did she have a house in the country somewhere? She'd have to find out about that, too. She was going to have to do a lot of careful thinking before she allowed herself to ask any questions.

A devastating thought struck her: did she have children? She'd always wanted children but it had turned out to be a blessing that she and Julian hadn't had any. Bringing up children in a household with Julian as the father would have been dangerous for the poor things. But her Regency husband might have been a good man, for all she knew.

No way of telling. She'd have to wait and see. She would never dare even to hint.

61

The crunch question, apart from Will, was the gold lace gown. Would she ever get back to her own time? If so, how? It clearly wasn't just a matter of taking it off. Bailey had done that and nothing at all had happened. Perhaps because Emma wasn't in the place where she'd arrived?

Good grief. Am I going to have to start undressing in my own hallway while Filch watches from his porter's chair?

It would have been funny if it hadn't been quite so frightening. If the gown had lost its magic, Emma might be here in an alien time for ever.

No, there had to be a way. She'd just have to work it out.

She went back to the beginning. To leave the museum, she had to put the gown on at precisely seven in the evening, while the church clock was striking. She'd tried a different time and it hadn't worked. So time was crucial. But place? She couldn't be sure because she'd never tried to do it anywhere but the research room.

To leave the Regency, she'd twice gone back to the place where she'd arrived. The time of day had been different each time and it hadn't mattered. The place had been the same, though. The lack of a ministering abigail hadn't stopped her successful return from the ladies' retiring room, either, so people didn't seem to matter.

She pondered the conclusions she'd reached. Was it time that mattered in the twenty-first century and place in the nineteenth? Plus wearing the gown.

She needed a plan. Perhaps she could go down to the hall in the lace gown and send Filch off on some kind of errand? Then as soon as she was alone, she could start to take off the gown. It had only needed a sleeve before. If it worked, she'd be long gone before Filch got back.

And what would the poor old man do? Her household would imagine their Lady Emma had been abducted, or worse, wouldn't they? Filch might be thrown into the gutter to starve.

As a plan, it wasn't nearly good enough. But perhaps she could build on it. Later.

What about Will? She was to meet him in Green Park, by the milk maids. And say what? He had demanded an explanation for what he called her "diabolical hide-and-seek".

She wanted to tell him. She wanted to trust him. She did trust him. But there were limits to how far trust could be stretched, even for lovers. Especially when one of them was bound to have the mindset of an unreconstructed Regency male. If she told him the truth, that she was actually a visitor from two centuries in the future, he'd think she'd flipped. Even if he didn't say she was mad, he would certainly never believe her explanation. So she needed something much more plausible than the truth. But what?

It was almost six when the idea came to her.

Chapter Eight

EMMA WASN'T SURPRISED TO DISCOVER THAT the walking boots were an excellent fit. Presumably Lady Emma was rich enough to have all her footwear made to measure. The walking dress, in dark leaf green, was more flattering than she expected, with plenty of petticoats underneath to keep her warm.

Emma looked at herself in the pier glass. Not bad. She wouldn't be out of place, dressed as she was. Except for the early hour, of course. Would any aristocratic lady be seen in the park with a gentleman so early in the morning, except for nefarious purposes?

There was nothing to be done. She had promised; and promises had to be kept. She could only hope that no one would recognise her.

Fingers crossed again? Her inner voice was trying to sound a warning but she refused to listen. She was going to meet her lover, the man of her dreams – literally, she realised – and her heart was singing at the prospect of being in his arms again. Even if they couldn't find somewhere private for an embrace, she would settle for being able to touch his hand and to hear his beloved voice. In all her time in the modern world, she had never known longing like this.

She smiled at her reflection. It was the secretive, cream-pot smile of a woman about to meet the man who could ignite her passions with just a single glance.

At her back, Bailey harrumphed. She had probably understood that smile, too, and definitely disapproved. But she said only, "You'll need a spencer as well, m'lady, to keep the wind off. I know you prefer the cream one with this gown, but if I might suggest..."

Emma turned. Bailey had two spencers over her arm, one cream and one in a rusty brown colour. Emma raised an eyebrow.

"If you wear the cream spencer, you'll have to wear the matching hat. Or else your straw bonnet with the dark green ribbons. But if you was to wear this spencer—" she held up the brownish one "—you could wear the matching hat. The one with the veil," she added, with emphasis.

Bailey was not only an old retainer, she was clearly also a born conspirator, and fiercely loyal even when she didn't approve of her mistress's shenanigans.

Emma nodded gratefully and said, "That's an excellent notion, Bailey. That is precisely what I shall do." She wouldn't be the first Regency lady to wear clashing colours. She had seen plenty of fashion plates with much worse combinations than dark green and rust.

It was only when she reached the front hall, very much the aristocratic lady in rusty spencer and matching veiled hat, and with her abigail two paces behind, that she realised she didn't have a clue how to get to Green Park. Because she had no idea at all where she was starting from. Even if she knew the name of her street, and she didn't, not yet, she might not be able to find her way because she was only vaguely familiar with this part of London. Lady Emma, needless to say, would have known it like the back of her hand, but poor Emma Stanley didn't have the faintest.

She was chewing her lip when the front door opened and Filch slipped in.

The old porter, apparently fully recovered from his earlier embarrassment, straightened and bowed to her. The expression in his eyes was eloquent. Did everyone in this household know what she was doing?

Filch waved towards the door and said, "Your ladyship's

carriage is here. I gave the coachman Miss Bailey's instructions." He swung the door wide and waited for Emma and the abigail to pass through and down the steps to the waiting carriage.

Saved by the bell. No, saved by Bailey. She'd obviously decided that her lady shouldn't risk being seen walking through the streets at such an hour. First a veil, then a carriage.

A closed carriage was a lifesaver. No one would see her and no one was likely to recognise the carriage, since there was no crest on the door. Emma pushed her shoulders back and started for the steps. "Thank you, Filch," she said and was rewarded with a beaming smile. "And thank you, too, Bailey," she added in a low murmur. As soon as they were both seated, the abigail with her back to the horses, naturally, Emma asked about those mysterious instructions to the coachman.

Bailey allowed herself a knowing little nod. "Couldn't have you walking through the streets at this hour, m'lady, now could I? I told them you were unable to sleep after all the excitement of last night's soirée and arriving home so very late, and so you'd decided to go for an early drive to see if some fresh air would clear your head. When we arrive at Green Park, you'll just decide, on a sudden whim, that you'd like to go for a stroll. With your faithful abigail behind for propriety's sake, naturally. The carriage will return for you in, er... How long do you think this head-clearing walk might take?"

Emma had to grin. "I think an hour should be enough." Bailey nodded, satisfied. "But if it isn't," Emma added mischievously, "I can always send you back to tell them to wait a little longer."

~ ~ ~

The carriage reached Piccadilly and the park much too soon. Emma had intended to work out exactly what she was going to say to Will, but now, before she had concocted a single satisfactory sentence, Bailey was pulling the check string and telling the coachman that her ladyship had decided to take a walk in the fresh air. "Her ladyship wishes you to return here in an hour," Bailey instructed.

Emma heard only the sound of her blood drumming in her

ears. In a moment, she would have to walk into the park. And meet her nemesis. The word came into her mind unbidden. Nemesis? Downfall? Was that what Will was? Yet, in his bed, she'd felt he was her soulmate.

"Have you changed your mind, m'lady?" Bailey asked. Fellow-conspirator she might be, but there was a hopeful note in her voice.

That decided it for Emma. She had promised herself, long ago, that she was not going to be a coward any more. She stood up and shook out her skirts. "Certainly not," she said curtly. "A lady does not break her word."

Bailey said nothing. She simply twitched Emma's veil into place as the door swung open.

"I think," Emma said, loudly enough for the footman to hear, "that I should enjoy a glass of fresh milk this fine Spring morning. Come, Bailey, let us find the milkmaids." A plausible enough tale. Probably. "Er, do you know where they likely to be, at this time of the day, Bailey?"

"Well, I can't be sure, m'lady, not ever having been asked to find fresh milk at this hour of the morning, but I believe they're usually over that way." Bailey pointed along a path that led away from the road and towards several clumps of trees.

Would Will be waiting among those trees? Had he been watching for her arrival? Was he watching now? He must not be allowed to think that she lacked the courage to face him. She lifted her chin, squared her shoulders and began to march along the path.

Half a pace behind her, Bailey whispered, "You're supposed to be out for a morning stroll, m'lady. May I suggest it's best not to look too, er, purposeful?"

The abigail was quite right. Emma let her shoulders relax and reduced her pace to a gentle stroll. She even began to fiddle idly with her gloves. "These gloves are not right," she said. "The thumb is too long. I think they should go back to the glover. I hope I have not already paid for them?"

Bailey failed to smother a smile. "I'll see to it as soon as may be, m'lady."

"Good."

It wasn't good at all. She could see the milkmaids now.

And yes, there was a shadow by the trees. Emma was pretty sure she recognised the shape. Will was waiting, as he had promised. A few yards more and she saw him clearly. He was wearing morning dress, a beautifully tailored blue coat, pale pantaloons and shiny Hessian boots. The modern part of Emma's mind said he looked good enough to eat.

He gave a nicely judged start of surprise at the sight of the two women – it seemed he was a good actor, too – and came forward to greet them, raising his beaver hat. "Why, Lady Emma. Good morning. What a pleasant surprise. There are not many ladies who frequent the park at this hour, especially after such a late night."

Now it was Emma's turn. "Good morning, Sir William. I could say the same for you, could I not?"

His eyes smiled down at her. "I am always up betimes, ma'am. All those years at sea, I fear, have created a habit I cannot break, so when I am in London, I ride out early or take a brisk walk in the park. Today my favourite mare is lame so I am on foot. Were you going anywhere in particular? May I escort you?"

Neatly done, Will Allmay. But I suppose you've had lots of practice. All those lovers, and so many, many assignations. Emma waved a careless hand towards the milkmaids. "Oh, I have no particular destination in mind. I simply wanted some fresh air and a little exercise. London becomes so hot and dusty later in the day, even this early in the year. If you were planning to take a turn round the park, I should gladly accept your escort, though I am not, perhaps, as *brisk* a walker as you." She smiled archly up at him through her lashes. A moment later, she realised that her flirtatious move had probably been wasted. He could not have seen it through her veil.

So how had he recognised her?

"Bailey, you may fall behind for a space. I shall walk on Sir William's arm."

Emma made to lay the tips of her fingers on his sleeve, but he took her arm and tucked it into his, so that her forearm was held tight against his ribcage and only her gloved fingertips peeped out into the open air. She could feel the warmth of his body, burning through the layers of his clothes and hers. He was on fire. And so, heaven help her, was she, in the middle of a public park. Emma felt her face beginning to heat and was grateful once more for her veil. His moves were all deliberate. He must know exactly the response that his nearness was conjuring up.

"Fie, sir, 'tis unseemly to hold me so tight," she protested in a sharp undertone. She did not attempt to pull away, though. Any signs of struggle could bring Bailey up at the run. Or, worse, any gentleman who happened to be watching.

Will relaxed his grip, a little. "Unseemly it may be, Emma," he said with a distinct laugh in his voice, "but practical, nonetheless. Every time I let go of you, you disappear. So you will concede, I hope, that I have cause for my behaviour?"

That was taking the conversation in a direction that Emma wanted to avoid. So instead of replying, she said, "Tell me, sir, how is it that you recognised me from such a distance? I had thought that my veil would protect me from prying eyes."

"There is no veil that could prevent me from recognising you, my love." His voice had dropped to a throaty whisper that shivered along her bones. "Your shape, the way you move, the way you carry your head... Indeed, I swear I would recognise you even if I were blind."

Emma gulped. "Now that, sir, is a compliment too far," she said airily, trying to force a chuckle. He must know that his declaration of love, in such a public place, was making her very uneasy. "Such exaggeration. No lady of sense would ever believe a word you say."

"You may believe it, Emma. Every word. But I would not have you put out of countenance, so I will say no more here. May I procure a glass of fresh milk for you?"

She smiled her thanks, for he was granting her a moment without touching him, a moment to collect her wits. But all too soon he was back, offering a glass of milk. "I'm afraid you will have to raise your veil, my love."

Emma swore inwardly. Why hadn't she thought of that? Stupid, stupid.

Well, in for a penny, in for a pound. Rich aristocrats were

known to be fickle. She waved the milk away. "I have changed my mind," she said, trying to sound pettish. "It looks so foamy. What is more, it is warm from the cow. I had forgot that. It would not be refreshing. I suggest you drink it yourself."

He gave a snort of laughter. For a second, she thought he would challenge her, but then he tossed off the whole glass in a single swallow. "Excellent."

There was a speck of foam on his upper lip. Emma had a sudden urge to lean into him and lick it away. Slowly. Tenderly. She managed to stop herself from swaying towards him. But only just.

His eyes were sparkling down at her. He'd kept a straight face, but he knew. With exaggerated care, he set the empty glass on the grass, pulled out a snowy handkerchief and slowly wiped the milk from his mouth. "Yes, excellent. You have missed something…ah… quite special." His gaze was fixed on her mouth. Oh yes, he knew all right.

Emma tried to speak, but no words came out.

He offered his arm again. "Shall we walk on, ma'am?"

Emma glanced behind them as she took his arm. Bailey was following, as instructed, some ten paces away. She would have heard nothing. But what had she seen? Emma told herself it didn't matter. Bailey might rail at Emma in private but she would never betray her mistress's secrets.

Will wasn't pushing his luck with the handclasp, this time. From a distance, the pair probably looked a model of decorum, a gentleman and a lady taking a morning stroll and exchanging the latest gossip. The veil was a slight problem. Why would a lady wear a veil if her behaviour was beyond reproach?

It couldn't be helped. In any case, anyone who recognised Will Allmay would also recognise the reason for the veil. Any lady seen consorting with Will May All risked losing her reputation. So of course she would wear a veil.

"A penny for 'em, Emma."

"Er, what?"

"You were miles away, my love. Thinking on happier times, perhaps? And with me, I dare to hope."

"You, sir, have a great conceit of yourself." Yes, that was good. That was what an aristocratic lady of the *ton* would riposte.

"Is that what you think of me? Truly, Emma?" He sounded wounded. Was this more acting? More of the practised rake?

She sighed deeply. "You *know* what I think of you," she whispered. Let him work that one out for himself.

"Hmm. Perhaps I do. Then again, perhaps not. For I do not know why you continue to run from me. You promised to tell me the truth, Emma. Here. Today. Be warned. I shall hold you to your promise, even if it takes all day." His tone said he meant it.

"Yes, I did promise. And it is hard for me, too. You must understand, Will, that promises matter to me. And not just promises to you. I made a solemn promise, to Sir John, my husband. Almost on his deathbed. He was a good man. He was kind to me, even when he was dying." She scrabbled for her pocket and a handkerchief. Before she could find it, he was offering her his own. Not the one he had used to wipe away the milk, but another, clean and fresh. She took it and tried to smile her thanks. She had no memory of her husband, Sir John, but she was feeling intensely emotional as she spoke of his death.

"I did not have the honour of meeting your husband, but I know that he was held in high esteem by many men of my acquaintance, including senior admirals. He was a very fine man, I believe."

"Yes, he was. And he was proud of his name. That is, er, the crux of my problem. He did not ask me to remain a widow, indeed, he insisted I should not, but he did ask me to promise that I should never do anything during my widowhood to bring his name into disrepute. So you see, you must see, why my name must not be linked with yours."

"Lady Emma, the prey of the worst rake in London?' he said bitterly.

"Something of the sort," she muttered and instantly regretted her words. Her throwaway comment must have hurt him deeply.

There was a long, long silence. They walked on, both

71

staring straight ahead. At last, he said softly, "So what do you propose to do now, Emma, lady of promises? You have shared my bed, and more than once, even if no one else knows of it. Do you intend to continue our affair, in defiance of your vow to your husband? Or perhaps it is only the *appearance* of propriety that matters to you? For the spirit of your promise to Sir John was broken every single time you touched me."

Emma felt wretched. Yes, his words were hurtful, deliberately so, but she deserved it all. The "vow" to Sir John had seemed to be such a splendid solution, barely a few hours ago. But now she was tying herself in knots of untruths. How could Will ever think well of her when he believed she had broken a solemn promise made on her husband's deathbed? In desperation, she clutched at the first idea that came into her head. "Sir John had an ancient name, it is true, and he was an upright man, but there were plenty of black sheep in his family too. What he most detested was nasty tittle-tattle about members of his family, or about himself. He wished people to think the best of us. He knew perfectly well that it was not always true, that there were hidden secrets and that some of them were very dark. He went to considerable lengths to keep his family secrets secret. Appearances mattered to him, you see. Very much."

"He would have had you *appear* to be the virtuous widow even if you are not?"

She was losing him. She could hear it in his voice. Her shoulders slumped. "You put it very bluntly, Sir William," she said sadly, "but I suppose you have the right of it. Yes, he was a man who valued appearances, and convention, very highly. I did not think the worse of him for it. None of us can be perfect."

He laughed briefly, surprising her. And then he squeezed her fingers. "You are right, Emma. And your late husband was right too. Appearances do matter in the lives we lead. And you cannot afford to have your fair name linked with mine. That is true. But—" he stopped dead and turned to her "—I cannot give you up, Emma. You say that none of us is perfect. But *you* are. To me. You are the woman who makes me complete. Whatever restrictions you put on our being together, I will accept. I am a fool perhaps, but I cannot live without you."

And I am beginning to fear that I can't live without you, either, even though we don't belong in the same world.

The longing closed Emma's throat completely. She couldn't speak. She could only return the pressure of his fingers. They walked on together for a space.

"When shall I see you again, Emma?"

"I don't know, if I'm honest. I need to think and I cannot do so when you are with me. Give me a little time, Will. Please."

"Very well. Shall I see you at the Rutherford ball? Perhaps you will give me an answer then?"

"I will try to give you an answer the next time we meet. Will that content you?" She was not at all sure she would dare to risk another meeting with this man. Ever. And she felt hollow inside to be misleading him so.

"It will have to. And now I note that your abigail is hovering anxiously. She clearly believes that you have spent far too much time walking with a notorious rake." He grinned suddenly. It made him look much younger. And devastatingly attractive. "I shall return you to your chaperon. For she is almost certainly right."

Chapter Nine

EMMA'S HEAD WAS IN A WHIRL, but she had just enough presence of mind to take note of the route home through the Mayfair streets. She needed to know exactly where her house was so that she could find it again. Or give someone her address if they should ask. Besides, if she focused on making a map of London in her head, there should be no room left for thoughts of Will and the incredible feelings he had stirred up inside her. He had said she made him complete; even that she was—

No, don't go there, Emma. Don't turn yourself into a puddle of lust in a carriage in the middle of a public street.

As soon as she arrived back at the grand house, Emma fled to her bedroom. Bailey was dismissed. Emma desperately needed to be alone, to think, to decide what to do. Was she stuck here in the Regency? Was there any way of getting back to her own world?

Was it even her own world any more? Was she Modern woman? Or had she become Regency woman instead?

I don't know who I am. And it terrifies me. If I can't get back to my own time, back home, what shall I do?

In the Regency, she was a rich widow, bound by the conventions of high society. She was in love with the most notorious rake in London – that bit was true, at least – but she

74

and Will could never be together in any respectable way. Rakes didn't marry. Rakes amused themselves, got bored and moved on. And because Emma was the virtuous widow of upright Sir John Something-or-other, she could never be seen to dally with Will Allmay in any case. The most they could have would be a clandestine affair, always meeting in secret, always worried that someone would find out and spread the gossip that would be the downfall of Lady Emma the High Stickler.

Ruin. Do I want to risk that?

She wasn't sure that she did. Nor that she could cope with it if it happened. She'd always believed in faithful monogamy, even though that was not what she'd had in her married life. And yet she loved Will. She knew it in her bones. She'd love him in this world or in any other. She knew, too, that she could not expect the same devotion from him, no matter how vehement his protests. He was a Regency Casanova. He was bound to tire of her and move on.

That hurt.

But it helped her to focus. There was no happy ending for Regency Emma, just heartbreak, and probably exclusion from society once her reputation lay in tatters. She didn't fancy the life of a Regency outcast, no matter how rich she might be.

I can't have Will, so I need to get back to my own life. I need A Plan.

A Plan. That revolved around the gold lace gown. It had to.

On each previous occasion, starting to take off the golden gown had transported her back to the modern day. Except for this last time. This last time, the gown had been removed and nothing had happened.

But Bailey was there. Bailey was the one who had removed it.

Was that it? Could Emma only transition back to her own time when she was alone? She'd been alone in Will's dressing room, that first time, and alone behind the screen in the ladies' retiring room, too.

Decision made. She was alone now. She would fetch the gold lace gown, right this very minute, put it on and then start to take it off again.

Please let it work.

The gold lace gown was nowhere to be found.

For once, Emma failed to swallow her frustration. She swore out loud, using the worst oaths she knew. It wasn't enough. She picked up the silver-backed hairbrush from her dressing table and threw it at the wall. That wasn't enough, either. So she seized two little china figurines from the mantelpiece and dashed them into the hearth. They broke into dozens of pieces with a hideous noise.

Perhaps someone would hear and come running? Oh the joys of being rich and powerful. Servants round every corner, behind every door, ready to satisfy her every whim. Watching every single thing she did, too.

Privacy? Secrets? Not a chance.

She waited a beat. It seemed that this time no one had heard, for no one came.

And Emma was still trapped in an alien world. Tears welled up in her eyes but she wiped them away ruthlessly. She would find an answer. She would.

The lace gown was the key.

She marched across to her bedside and tugged the bell.

~ ~ ~

Bailey had taken away the lace gown to mend the tear at the hem, of course. She would not tolerate a visible and very temporary repair in a gown belonging to her illustrious mistress. In fact, the abigail even went so far as to suggest that the damage meant the gown would have to be discarded altogether.

"No," Emma said flatly. "It is my favourite. I absolutely refuse to part with it. I know I can rely on you, Bailey, to furbish it up like new. You are so very skilled with your needle." She was laying it on very thick, but Bailey controlled everything in Emma's wardrobe. It was in the woman's power to make the magic gown disappear altogether, or perhaps to alter it so much that the magic would stop working. Such a fearsome risk.

"If you will allow me to say so, m'lady, you wear that gown too often. People will start to gossip, thinking you can't afford to replace it."

"Let them think what they like. Let them say that I am too penny-pinching to spend my money on the latest fashions. *I* shall say that I am trying to show a good example. There are so many poor in London, especially now that the soldiers are returned from the wars." A new idea struck her: she remembered some of the beggars she'd seen in Piccadilly. She had found a fine new thread to weave into Her Plan. "I shall set up a charity for wounded soldiers, I think. I shall invite ladies of my acquaintance to donate the money they save by forgoing new gowns. And every time I appear in my gold lace gown, I shall use it to remind them of their duty to the poor and needy."

"If you say so, m'lady." Bailey's reply was definitely grudging.

"So I should like to have my lace gown back as soon as may be, Bailey. I shall be wearing it again very soon."

"If you say so, m'lady."

Emma smiled encouragingly. "Put it down to my fickle nature, Bailey. And I shan't need you for the rest of the day, so you'll be able to devote yourself to mending my lace, won't you?"

"But your ladyship is promised to the Rutherford ball this evening—"

Oh hell! Hadn't Will mentioned a Rutherford ball? But he hadn't said it was tonight. No, she couldn't possibly go. Emma wasn't anything like ready to see him again. Besides, she had to find out about the magic gown; she had to know whether she could transition back to her own time.

"I've changed my mind about going to the Rutherford ball. I am too tired after everything that has gone on. Pray send up a tray of tea. I fancy that will restore me. Oh, and send up today's newspaper also. I find I am sadly out of touch with life in London." Why hadn't she thought of that before? A newspaper would have a date on it. And lots of detail to help Emma avoid putting her foot in it with all those gossiping matrons.

"If you say so, m'lady."

"I will read the newspaper, but I shall leave it until later. I fear I have the beginnings of the headache."

She put a languid hand to her brow.

Bailey looked askance and said sharply, "Lack of sleep, m'lady. You should have gone to bed properly, as soon as you got back. And stayed there," she added, with dark emphasis.

Emma knew that ego-stroking was the only answer to the Bailey problem. "You are right, Bailey. And to please you, I will take myself off to my bed once I have drunk my tea. And since I shall not be going out this evening, you will have all the time in the world to mend my gown. There. Will that satisfy you?"

"If you say so, m'lady." Bailey left without another word. It seemed that more ego-stroking was going to be required.

Emma fell on the newspaper as soon as the maid had delivered the tea. Her guess hadn't been bad at all. Waterloo was indeed long over, for it was April, 1817. With a sigh of satisfaction, she poured herself a cup of tea and began to leaf through the paper. There was bound to be useful information here, and probably gossip as well.

One little paragraph seemed to leap out at her: "We are pleased to report that Lady E… G… has returned to London at last and has put off her blacks. Lady E… was welcomed warmly at the F… soirée last evening and was seen to be in excellent health and spirits."

Emma gulped. *It's me. Or rather, it's Lady Emma. It has to be.*

Lady Mumford had said that Emma's return had not yet been reported in the papers. Well, it had now. Someone had been quick off the mark after last night's party. In return for payment, no doubt.

But, much more important, Emma had another clue to her identity in the Regency. She might not know what her surname was, but she did know it began with G. Progress.

She settled down to learn all she could. She would study the paper for a while and then she would have a snooze for a few hours. Later, if she was hungry, she'd have a light meal sent up. Being a rich aristocrat definitely had some advantages. There was no point in getting stressed about what was to come, since she had hours and hours to wait.

~ ~ ~

Emma checked the clock for perhaps the hundredth time. As she looked away again, it began to strike twelve. It had a very sweet-sounding chime.

Confident that Bailey would not now appear again until morning, Emma quietly opened the clothes press and took out the precious gown. Her abigail had done a marvellous job on the damaged hem. Even though Emma knew the mend was there, it was almost impossible to detect it. Certainly no stern matron's eye would ever be able to find fault with the gown when Emma wore it. As she would.

If I stay here. Only if I stay. And I don't want to, do I?

She ran a hand over the delicate lace, wishing yet again that she knew precisely how the magic worked. Did she have to be alone? Did the time have to be the same as when she arrived? Or the place?

It was hopeless. She was marooned, with nothing at all by way of life raft.

The gown seemed to glow beneath her fingers. Was it trying to tell her something? To encourage her to try once more?

She took a deep breath, shrugged off her silken bed robe and began to put on the lace gown. She would have trouble doing up all the fastenings at the back, but that probably didn't matter. After all, when she'd been at the museum, she'd been transported into the Regency, just by putting one arm through a sleeve.

After a bit of a struggle, the gown was on and the tapes at the back of the neck were tied. Sort of. She'd even managed to do a makeshift bow with the underbust tapes, which were much more difficult to reach.

Thank goodness for modern bras. We modern women have so much practice reaching round to fastenings in the middle of our backs.

She was putting off the moment of decision and she knew it. She had to stop letting her mind wander down procrastination avenue. She needed to concentrate on finding out how to make the gown work its magic. It *did* work. So how?

She ran her fingers gently over the draped skirt, hoping for inspiration. And it came, after a fashion. What time had it been when she arrived in the front hall? Ah yes, she'd asked the porter and he'd said— What *had* he said? She couldn't remember.

An instant later, her mind cleared miraculously. Bless it, her lace was working again. He'd said it was half past three.

She glanced again at her clock. Almost half past twelve. So, three hours to wait. At half past three, or just before, she would steal down into the hall and start to remove the lace gown. Filch was bound to be asleep in his porter's chair so he was unlikely to hear her. And since no one else would know what she had done, no one would be blamed for her disappearance. Very neat.

And if it didn't work – *please, please let it work*, she prayed – she would be able to creep back upstairs again unseen. Probably.

Unfortunately, her plan wouldn't tell her whether it was time, or place, or both together that mattered. But what choice did she have? She had only this one night to try to get away. So she had to do everything as before.

Should she wear the dancing slippers and the velvet cloak too? She hadn't considered that. Probably best to take no unnecessary chances.

She found the slippers easily enough – they were in the bottom of the clothes press – but the cloak was missing. Something else that Bailey was working on?

Emma was going to have to summon Bailey again, even though it was the middle of the night, and demand that the cloak be produced. Bailey was bound to think that her mistress was losing her marbles. What's more, as a trusted retainer, the abigail would demand to know why Lady Emma wanted her evening cloak at one o'clock in the morning when she was not planning to go out.

Emma began to rack her brains for a convincing excuse. She didn't find one. Then she realised that Bailey mustn't find her wearing the lace gown, either. Ladies didn't dress without the help of a maid unless something clandestine was going on. And they certainly wouldn't choose a ballgown for a legitimate midnight outing.

Perhaps the silk bed robe would hide it? Emma picked up her discarded robe from the floor, noting guiltily that she had acquired slovenly aristocratic habits without even thinking about it. Was she still the woman who had been expected to pick up her husband's discarded clothing and who'd come to hate him for turning her into a menial? But that was in another life, another time. She refused to think about it.

She slid her arms into the long sleek sleeves and tied the belt, before checking her reflection to make sure none of the gold lace was visible. It was OK.

No, it wasn't. All the lace was covered, but the silk of the bed robe was so thin that the texture of the lace showed through. Nothing else for it. Both the bed robe and the lace gown would have to come off until the velvet cloak had been retrieved. What a pain.

The bed robe was the easy bit. The tapes at the back of the lace gown were much more difficult. When Emma had tied them, she hadn't been thinking about untying them again. In fact, she'd been sure she wouldn't have to.

Practice with modern bras, my foot. Bra hooks never tied themselves in impossible knots.

The Gordian knot was untied with a sword, Emma remembered. But she couldn't possibly manipulate scissors to cut a knot in the middle of her back. She'd just have to persevere until the blasted knots came undone.

It took her more than ten minutes but she managed it, eventually. At last she could slide out of the lace gown and return it to its home in the clothes press, just in case Bailey should look in there and notice it had been moved.

Careful now. Make sure you don't damage the gown as you take it off. Bailey would be sure to notice.

Had the gown been folded in the clothes press? Emma concentrated, trying hard to remember, as she began to ease her arm out of the puff sleeve. No doubt the abigail had her own precise ways of folding garments to prevent them from getting creased, but Emma hadn't been paying enough attention. She'd have to do her best to—

The clock was striking again.

But it wasn't her bedroom clock.

It was St Mary's. And the church clock showed seven.
She was back.

Chapter Ten

SHE WAS BACK IN THE RESEARCH room and the clock of St Mary's church was still striking seven. In the modern world, no time at all had passed.

It was just as before.

But in the Regency?

Questions tumbled into Emma's brain. If she was back in the modern world, where was *Lady* Emma now? It was clear that at least a few days had passed between Emma's first two visits. Perhaps longer, judging by Will's angry outburst at the soirée. So either there was no Regency Lady Emma during that period or there was someone else who took her place. Did a doppelgänger materialise like some kind of ectoplasm? If so, where did she go when Emma put on the golden gown and was transported back in time? The doppelgänger couldn't be taking Emma's place here in the modern world because no time was passing. So was her double translated to some kind of between-world? Or vaporised?

It was all more than Emma's poor frazzled brain could handle. She sank into her chair and dropped her head into her hands. She was back where she belonged, in a world she could cope with. She couldn't cope with the Regency world. Too many ridiculous rules about what a woman could do and who she could be seen with. Too many gimlet-eyed harridans searching for an excuse to ruin a besotted woman's reputation and consign her to outer darkness. The pampered, moneyed ladies of the *ton* trashed reputations for sport.

Emma gazed at the remnants of the lace gown, spread across the research room table. Yes, the gown was magic, but it was much too dangerous for her to dare to make the transition again. She would not do it.

But you know how to go both ways. There's no risk of getting stranded any more.

That mischievous voice inside her head would not be silenced. Because the blasted thing was right. Purely by chance, Emma had now discovered how to get back. If it hadn't been for that missing cloak, she'd have gone down to the hallway at half past three to begin her striptease. Instead, she'd done it at a different time and in a different place, but the magic had still worked.

So it wasn't a matter of matching the time or the place. There had never been any need for her to creep down into the hallway and make sure she didn't wake Filch. It was much, much simpler than that. She just had to be alone, wearing the gown, and to start to remove it.

A minute was all she would ever need to start undoing the fastenings of the gown. All she would ever need to get back. She had the knowledge, now, to avoid been marooned in an alien time. She could go back to the Regency whenever she wanted. She would be in control. Safe.

She could go back and meet Will again.

~ ~ ~

By the time Emma had put the lace gown back in the storeroom and locked up securely, she had a thumping headache for real.

Serves me right, she told herself as she stowed the bunch of keys in the key safe and spun the combination lock. She'd spent ages going back and forward through the arguments. Should she go back? No, she'd be mad to. But she longed to be with Will.

In the end, her sensible self asserted itself. It was Friday, so there was nothing she could do until she came back to work on Monday. She had the weekend to get her head together. If the weather was fine, she would go for long walks which always helped her to relax. For now, she should go home, have some food – when had she last eaten? – and then some sleep. If necessary, she could take some pills for her headache, even though she hated swallowing any kind of medication. She'd had enough of that when Julian was trying to convince the medics that she was mentally ill and should be sectioned. She shuddered at the memory. He had so nearly succeeded.

She went back to the staff room for her car coat. It was cold today, so she needed a warm outer layer. And her gloves. Had she remembered to bring them? She dug her hands into her coat pockets and—

Her fingers found a key. Will's dressing room key.

That key had been trying to tell her something. And she, like a fool, hadn't even attempted to listen. Modern-day Emma Stanley had returned from two hundred years in the past and had brought a key with her. Your actual one-hundred-percent genuine Regency artefact. Intact. Across time.

It meant something. But what? That she could steal priceless Regency items and bring them back to sell in the modern day? She would never do that. It would be like stealing. The dressing-room key was about more than that.

She examined it carefully. She'd seen loads of similar keys in stately homes. There were some in the museum, too.

Would it still fit the door in the Lamb House?

That thought sent a real shiver down her spine. She'd become so bewildered while brooding over returning to Will that she'd completely forgotten about the Lamb House. It contained the bedroom where she and Will had made love. And the dressing room was there too. She'd seen it with her own eyes. So she could take the key to the Lamb House and try it in the door. What would happen then? Maybe nothing. But then again, maybe something wonderful...

She was lying in her own bed, her headache blessedly gone, when the idea popped into her head. It was almost like walking through a dream. Another few moments and she would have been asleep. She'd have missed it.

It felt momentous. A challenge.

And this time, she decided, she was going out to meet it.

~ ~ ~

Next morning, Emma woke refreshed. She sensed that she had important decisions to make, even before she went out for her walk. On Monday, she was going to drive out to the Lamb House. She'd tell the museum that she had urgent work there. She no longer had to be at the museum early to open up – Richard was in charge of the staff entrance key now while Emma had the new spare – and she was her own boss, so there was no one to quibble about how she divided her hours between the two locations. But what was she going to take with her?

She sat down with a pot of tea and thought hard. She needed clever choices, in case her off-the-wall idea worked. If it didn't, there would be no harm done. But if it did? Goodness, she could learn such a lot. For a historian, it was doubly exciting.

You ARE going back then? The sensible voice in her head was beginning to sound a bit like the stern headmistress who had terrified Emma and all her classmates into obedience and submission. For a while. Emma chuckled to herself. Miss Brimstone, as they'd nicknamed the woman, was eminently sensible, yes, but often wrong.

Emma *was* going back, she realised. Safe in the knowledge that she could escape back to the modern day at a moment's notice, she was going to satisfy her professional curiosity and make the transition one last time.

Probably one last time.

It would all depend on what she found out once she got to the other side.

And on who was there to meet her.

~ ~ ~

Early on Monday morning, she drove to the local supermarket to buy what she needed. Nowadays, it was possible to buy almost anything at any time of year. And technology was everywhere, nowadays. No problems there.

She felt herself smiling her cream-pot smile as she packed up her shopping and paid.

"You're looking very pleased with yourself for this time in the morning, dearie," the grey-haired assistant said, with a conspiratorial look. "Going to meet someone special, are we?"

86

"I don't know yet," Emma replied, honestly enough. She felt a childish urge to share her glee with someone. This woman was almost old enough to be her mother. So why not? "But it *is* just possible that today could be a special day."

"Good on yer, then. Come back and tell me how it works out. I'm usually here, early mornings."

Emma's smile broadened. "You know what? I just might. If it works out."

She was still smiling to herself as she got into her car to drive to the Lamb House. She turned on the car radio and wasn't in the least surprised to find that Beethoven's *Eroica* was being played. Just right for a quasi-Regency museum curator. Putting Emma in a light-hearted mood for whatever was to come. She put her hand on the shift and glanced in the rear-view mirror, ready to put her car into gear.

Julian. Sitting in the car immediately behind hers. Staring at her, with the unblinking laser focus that had always scared her to death. This time, there was no chance that Emma was mistaken. There was no shadow, no hoodie to make recognition doubtful. It was definitely him. He was watching her, spying on her, and he didn't care who saw him doing it.

Emma hit the lock on her car door. Then she pulled out her mobile phone and dialled Flo. The policewoman picked up at once. "Flo, it's Emma. Julian's here, parked right behind me. He's following me again. Help me, please."

"Calm down, Emma. Are you in your car? Good. Tell me where you are and I'll come to meet you. I'll deal with him."

Emma took a deep breath and gave her location.

"Stay there. I'll come to you. What car is he driving? What's the registration?"

"It's silver. A Ford, I think, but I'm not sure. I can't see the registration. He's parked almost against my back bumper. I'd need to get out to see the number plate and I don't want—"

"Don't do that. Stay in your car. Keep your door locked. I'll be with you in a few minutes. If he makes a move before I get there, set off your rape alarm."

Emma dived into her pocket for her alarm but her hand was shaking so much she could barely grasp it. After a couple of tries, she managed to pull it out and held it against her throat, like a talisman. "You bastard," she swore aloud. "I'll get you for this. I will."

Her heart was thumping fit to burst. Julian just had to stare at her, with those piercing, pitiless eyes, for her to crumple into a helpless heap. She needed to fight back. Fight *him*. He was only a man. And he didn't even have the law on his side.

My engine's running. If I drive across the car park, I'll be able to see his number plate. Once Flo has the registration, she'll be able to track him.

There was a parking space immediately opposite hers, so she slipped her car into first gear and slid forward into it. Then she realised what a mistake she'd made. She couldn't move forward because the space in front of her was occupied, and to get out of her own space, she'd have to reverse. If Julian drove forward, he could pin her in this space with his car, get out and come round to—

She could risk another look in her rear-view mirror. She would get the car's make and registration, at least. And she did have her rape alarm. He wouldn't dare try anything once she set off that ear-splitting racket.

The silver car had gone. Julian must have seen her making that phone call and quietly backed out before he was caught. He was a nasty beast, sure enough, but he was definitely a clever one.

Flo arrived a few minutes later, blue lights flashing. She was alone, so she hadn't thought the situation dangerous enough to need backup. She climbed into the car with Emma and gently teased out all the details, making notes as Emma spoke.

"He's sharp enough to have guessed you were calling the police. But he's missed a trick, for once. He shouldn't have tried it on in a supermarket car park. There's CCTV here. The camera will have caught his car make and registration as he drove out. It couldn't have been more than 10 minutes ago."

Flo reached across to pat Emma's hand reassuringly. "Don't worry. With your testimony, plus the CCTV pictures, we'll be able to prove that he's stalking you again. Stay here. Keep your door locked. I'll go and talk to the supermarket manager and get the recordings."

Emma spent the next half hour telling herself that everything would be fine. But as the minutes passed, she worried more and more. What was taking Flo so long?

By the time Flo returned, Emma was clutching her rape alarm so hard that her fingers were white. It almost felt as if she had made a dent in the metal casing.

Flo's face told the story before she said a word. "I'm so sorry, Emma. CCTV malfunction last night. They're waiting for the technician to arrive to repair it. It was only broken at one of the exits, but Julian was lucky. Again. He must have driven out through the one where the camera wasn't working. I checked the footage from the second exit and there was no sign of a silver car driven by a lone male in the last hour."

"When it comes to evidence, Julian is always lucky," Emma said despondently. "And I suppose my testimony isn't good enough on its own?"

"Probably not. You know what happened before. We need third party verification. CCTV would have been great. We could explain to the magistrate how Julian could have got away without being seen, but it would be no more than plausible. We need something that would back up your statement. And at the moment, we don't have it."

"And my phone call to you doesn't count, I suppose?"

"No. Sorry. It helps to pinpoint the time, but it's not third-party evidence. Do you want to come to the station and—"

"Come on, Flo. There's no point in making another statement. It wouldn't do any good. Let's just leave it for now, shall we? But thank you for responding so quickly." She sighed deeply. "I don't know what I'd do without you."

"Only doing my job," Flo said, but she smiled warmly. She knew.

~ ~ ~

Back in her flat, with the door double-locked and bolted, Emma phoned the Lamb House to tell them her visit had had to be postponed. She didn't say why. Phoning the museum was slightly trickier. She took a deep breath and lied blatantly. She'd had a sudden attack of migraine, she said, trying to sound stricken, and so she was unable to drive. She hadn't had an attack like that for years, she added, but she was sure she'd be fine after a day in bed. She'd be back at the museum tomorrow, as planned.

Her hand was shaking as she replaced the receiver. She didn't have a migraine but her heart was racing and her skin was clammy. In spite of Flo's reassurances, Emma was afraid.

Her supermarket shopping bag sat at a drunken angle on the kitchen table. Staring at her. Accusingly.

"So much for my grand scheme," she spat at it. She upended the bag and her purchases tumbled out. She put the bread in the bread bin and the tins in the cupboard. She stuffed the cardboard box and its garish contents into the kitchen drawer. Then she pushed her last purchase to the back of the fridge. Let it rot there. She couldn't possibly face it now. She wouldn't be going back to talk to that chatty checkout lady either. There was no good news to report. Absolutely none at all.

Chapter Eleven

EMMA DIDN'T MAKE IT TO THE museum the following day, as she had promised. She slept badly, tossing and turning for hours, and when she did eventually fall into a troubled sleep, it was only to wake up with a real, honest-to-goodness migraine. It was so long since she'd had one of those that she didn't even possess any migraine pills any more. So she fell back on her old remedies. She drank some ginger ale and ate half a slice of dry toast in an attempt to settle her queasy stomach. Then she downed a couple of headache pills and went back to bed with the curtains firmly closed to keep out as much light as possible.

It was only when she woke up again, around eleven in the morning, that she realised she hadn't told the museum that she wouldn't be in today, either. They'd be sympathetic, she was sure, but they'd think she wasn't very professional after all.

She sat down with a mug of tea at the kitchen table and tried to work out what to do now. The nausea had gone but the migraine continued to hover, a little threateningly, behind her eyes. She would be unwise to drive anywhere today, even the short distance to the museum. She certainly couldn't go to the Lamb House. So she would stay at home, nurse her delicate head, and try to plan what to do next.

It was all about Will. She'd promised to give him an answer when they met again. And she was pretty sure that, as soon as she went back to the Regency, she'd see him, no matter where she was when she landed there. Every transition seemed to be about Will. And Lady Emma. Together.

So she'd better have her answer ready.

But what *exactly* was the question? What did he really want of her?

She thought hard, trying to remember precisely what he had said in the park. Not *will you marry me?* That was for sure. Rakes certainly did not marry their mistresses.

No, he wanted to continue their affair. Which had been going on, she supposed, for a while, on and off. During her mourning? Possibly. It might be useful to find out how they'd first met. If she was subtle enough, she might be able to get him to talk about it – what he'd thought when he first set eyes on her, why he'd been attracted to her in the first place, that sort of thing – and pick up clues about the when and where.

But what really mattered was whether it was going to continue. And that was to be Emma's decision. He'd even said he would abide by any restrictions she wanted to impose. That was quite a concession. Most rakes, she imagined, would want to brag about their conquests to their drinking mates. Will, it seemed, was different. Hadn't the ladies at the soirée commented on how discreet he was? So Emma could probably trust him with Lady Emma's reputation.

There was always chance, though. Someone might see them together. And her servants would know, too. Would it be possible to stop them from gossiping? Hmm. She'd have to consult Bailey about that.

So you've decided to go back AND to continue the affair, have you?

Emma told her inner voice to shut up. Or to concentrate on identifying the most sensible way to keep on meeting Will.

The Lamb House. The Lamb House and the golden lace. They were tied together somehow. That was where she'd first seen Will, in all his naked beauty.

She had to swallow hard at the thought of him and force herself to focus on reason instead of lust. The Lamb House was where they'd first made love, at least, the first that Modern Emma had experienced with him. Will had some kind of relationship with the house, hadn't he? So perhaps they could meet there?

Hmm. Difficult. How would Emma get there when she was living in Mayfair? If she travelled by carriage, she could be seen. And her servants would certainly guess what she was doing.

The best solution would be to materialise at the Lamb House from the modern-day museum. But she didn't seem to have any control at all over where she arrived. It had been the Lamb House once; but it had been a London soirée on the second occasion and her own London house on the third.

What if Emma took the lace gown to the Lamb House and put it on there?

It wouldn't work. She knew perfectly well that it had to be exactly seven in the evening. And she had to be in the research room, listening to St Mary's bells.

But what if she was wrong about that?

She had no answer to that one, so she filled the void by phoning the museum to apologise for taking a second sick day. This time, she spoke to Richard. He was very sympathetic. His wife, Melanie, had suffered from migraines when they were first married, he said, though they hadn't recurred since Chloë was born. The museum had nothing urgent on, so she should take the time to get well. Even if it took a third day.

Emma was smiling as she put the phone down. *No, I can't bear to wait another day before I see Will again. I need to BE with him.*

She hugged herself and did a little dance round the kitchen table, imagining herself in Will's arms. But her nagging inner voice soon put a stop to that. It reminded her she needed to know what she would actually *do* when she found him again.

She fetched a pad and pen from her desk and sat down to explore options.

~ ~ ~

Her options hadn't amounted to all that much, in the end. Taking the gown to the Lamb House could never be made to work, because the house closed to the public at five in the evening. There was no way Emma could be alone inside at seven. The house manager was responsible for the security of the property and she always made a point of locking up and setting the alarms by no later than six.

It had to be the museum and the lace gown. At precisely seven o'clock.

Once she was back in the Regency, she would have to find a way of getting to the Lamb House. She would enlist Bailey's aid, she decided. And she would take back Will's dressing room key, too. If she did make it back to the Lamb House, she'd find a way of dropping it there. Someone would be sure to find it and restore it to its place.

So she ensured it was safely stowed in her coat pocket when she set out for the museum, very early on Wednesday morning. She needed to get in early in order to catch up on some of the computer work she had *said* she was doing on Friday night. She couldn't afford for any of the museum staff to notice that almost no records had been added to the catalogue, in spite of all the extra hours the costume curator was supposedly putting in to deal with the backlog.

In any case, it would salve her conscience to do some routine work. She might even enjoy it.

Perhaps surprisingly, she did. By the time Richard arrived, about ten minutes later than normal, she had dealt with a large bundle of index cards and she was pretty sure that no one could now question how much she'd done. Or when exactly she'd done it. Her brain had been buzzing and she'd been able to do each entry amazingly fast.

Self-preservation? Probably.

But it didn't matter. As long as it worked.

"Goodness. You're in early again, Emma. Are you sure it's a good idea? Migraines can be horrendous, I know. Shouldn't you be taking it easy?"

Emma smiled up at him and shook her head. "I'm absolutely fine now, Richard. Honestly. But my conscience was getting at me. I've hardly been in the job two minutes and here I am, taking two days off sick with a migraine. So I thought I'd come in early and do a few more cards. If I keep at it, I may even speed up enough to get through the pile. Seems to take me ages to do each one." If her colleagues assumed she took a long time over each card, they wouldn't question her slow progress overall. Her little lie was justified.

In order to be with Will.

The mere thought of him made her insides start to melt, all over again. His naked image was so real in her mind that she felt she could almost reach out and touch him. And his reaction when he'd seen her— There was certainly no room for doubt about just how much he wanted her.

"Er– if you're really sure you're feeling OK..." Richard was hovering, almost hopping from foot to foot. Emma had been so absorbed in her own daydream that she had forgotten him.

This time she made a real effort to reassure him. She got up from her chair and put a friendly hand on his arm. "I'm absolutely fine, I promise you, Richard. It's a long time since I had anything like this, but in the past they always cleared up after a day, or two at most, and I would be right as rain."

"Until the next time?" His mouth quirked into a rueful smile. It seemed he did know about migraines.

"Yes, well, that was then. There's no reason to assume I'll have any more. At least, I'm hoping so. I had, er, some personal problems at the weekend and they obviously got to me a bit. But they're sorted now," she finished firmly. She really didn't want him to ask.

Unfortunately, he did. "Would it help to talk about it? I can be very discreet, you know."

She shook her head. "Thank you, but no. It's not something I'm prepared to talk about, even with someone as sympathetic and discreet as you. Sorry."

"Um. Yes, I see. But if you change your mind, the offer is always open."

"Thank you. You're a good friend, Richard. I do appreciate it." When he still didn't leave, Emma realised she must have missed an earlier signal. "But that wasn't what you originally wanted to say, was it?" She smiled invitingly.

"No, actually. We're in a bit of a fix, Melanie and I. We've got tickets for the Met opera on Saturday – the screening at the local cinema, you know? – and Melanie doesn't want to miss it. Unfortunately our usual babysitter has double-booked herself and so I was wondering if you might—?"

"Babysit for Chloë? Saturday night? Of course I will. I'd love to. What's the opera?"

"*Madam Butterfly*. It's Melanie's favourite."

"Have to say it's not mine," Emma said with a grimace. "Oh, the music is lovely, but the plot infuriates me – a grown man going through a sham marriage with an underage girl in order to have sex with her? And then declaring his eternal love for Butterfly, knowing all the time that he's going to abandon her? No, Pinkerton is a predatory bastard of the first order, I reckon. No amount of beautiful music can make up for that." She stopped herself before she said something even more revealing about betraying husbands. Richard might start to put two and two together, given what Emma had said about personal problems. "Don't tell Melanie I detest her favourite opera, though," she added quickly, with a conspiratorial grin. "I wouldn't want to spoil her special night out."

~ ~ ~

"I've forgotten the blasted key."

The words were out before Emma could stop them. She looked round quickly to see if anyone had heard. It seemed that no one was about. She let out a long sigh of relief. She'd made it back to the Regency, wearing the lace gown, but she'd left the dressing room key in her coat pocket, back in the museum. Ah well, it couldn't be helped. Another time, perhaps?

She was alone, thank goodness. But where was she this time?

It was some kind of sitting room. There was a fire in the grate and candles in the wall sconces. There were portraits on the walls, too, but nothing she recognised. So she assumed it must be someone else's house.

Whose? And why was she here?

Above the crackle of the logs, she thought she could hear music. Was that a flute? She went to the door and opened it a crack. Yes, music. Quite a large group by the sound of it. Several stringed instruments and woodwind as well.

If there's a small orchestra playing, then it's a ball or, at least, a pretty large musical soirée. And if I'm here, in my ballgown, it's because I was invited.

96

Is Will here, too?

It couldn't be the Rutherford ball, could it? Not unless she was doubling back on herself. She'd been in the Regency on the night of the Rutherford ball and she had stayed at home, trying to fathom out how the lace gown worked. It had been very late when she'd started to take the gown off and found herself back in the museum.

The gown couldn't have brought her back to an earlier time, could it?

Somewhere a clock began to chime. One, two. Followed by silence.

Two o'clock? In the morning? What time was it when I took the gown off?

Emma tried to remember. She'd been waiting for half past three, to go down to the entrance hall, but it had been much earlier when she'd taken the gown off. After midnight, certainly. But after two?

She didn't think so.

Even if she couldn't go back to a time she'd already "lived" in the Regency, it might be the Rutherford ball. Balls went on for hours after midnight. This seemed to be a case in point: it was two o'clock in the morning and the orchestra was still going strong.

I don't know whether it's the Rutherford ball and it doesn't really matter. Will is probably here. And I'm going to have to talk to him. So I might as well get it over with.

She pulled the door wide, raised her chin and sailed out into the corridor, following the sound of the music until she found the source.

It was a ball, all right. The ballroom was enormous, lit by what seemed to be thousands of candles and heaving with people. The heat was overpowering. Several of the gentlemen were perspiring visibly in their layers of evening clothes, especially the soldiers in tight dress uniforms with high gold-braided collars. Most of the ladies were fanning themselves pretty hard, too.

Emma opened her own fan and waved it gently as she stepped forward into the room. She looked, she hoped, like a late arrival who had not yet been affected by the heat.

Was she a late arrival? Or had she been here earlier, in her doppelgänger guise? No way of knowing. She'd just have to brazen it out.

I'm getting better and better at being brazen. She almost laughed at the thought. There were definitely advantages to being a haughty aristocrat. No one dared to question what she chose to do, even when it was outrageous.

"Good evening, Lady Emma."

Will. Yes, it had to be Will. And he was being remarkably circumspect. Was that because there were so many people about?

She responded in kind, dipping a tiny curtsey in response to his elegant bow. "Good evening, Sir William. How very pleasant to see you again. You are well, I trust?"

He dropped his voice half an octave. "As well as I was when I left you this morning."

Oh.

"You mean...?" She let the words trail off.

"Have you forgotten already, ma'am? You wound me. You do indeed. May I remind you that I had the honour of escorting you for a space in Green Park? We discussed, er, milkmaids. And cows."

He might have lowered his voice but he was definitely enjoying baiting her, even though he must know it would do her reputation no good at all if she were known to have met him in the park. Or anywhere else, for that matter. Will Allmay definitely had a nasty sense of humour.

"I fear you are mistaken, Sir William. If you discussed something as...as *agricultural* as cows, it must have been with some other lady. What do I know of cows, pray?"

He raised his eyebrows. Rather scornfully, Emma thought. "Forgive me, ma'am. I fancied you might have taken an interest in your late husband's prize herd of longhorns. I'm told they are quite a sight to behold."

She bit her lip. He was enjoying this, blast him. And he clearly knew more than Emma did. "My husband's herd was special, sir, and quite out of the common way," she said quickly. "The animals in the park, so I am told, at least, are merely simple milking cows. Why should you think I would interest myself in such beasts?"

"Why, indeed?" He cocked his head. The orchestra had begun to play a waltz. "But shall we forget the agricultural in favour of the cultural? Might I ask for the honour of this dance? It is a waltz, you know." There was a wicked glint in his eye as he added that last, and totally unnecessary, rider. He was telling her how much he wanted to hold her in his arms.

Emma wanted it too. But did the High Stickler dare to dance, publicly, with the greatest stud in London?

He held out his gloved hand. And waited.

"I—" She fiddled with the dance card hanging from her wrist. "I'm not certain I am free," she began.

He seized her card and opened it. "As I thought," he muttered in a low voice. "Every dance is free because you have only this moment arrived. But I am glad, for I had begun to think you had broken your promise and would not appear at this ball at all."

"Sir, I made you no promise," she protested. Then she, too, lowered her voice to a bare whisper. "I said we would talk the next time we met. But I made no promise to attend this ball." She drew herself up. "I do not break my promises."

"No," he replied simply, "you do not. And it is one of the things I admire about you, my sweet. One of the many things. So now – will you waltz with me?"

What choice did she have? She put her hand into his, walked with him onto the dance floor and was drawn into his arms.

Chapter Twelve

BEING IN WILL'S ARMS WAS HEAVEN. Second only to being in his bed, lying naked together.

Emma tried very hard to put that thought out of her mind, but with his left hand clasping her fingers, and his right against her back, it was impossible, even though he was not actually touching her: his skin was separated from hers by his gloves and her lace. Yet it felt as though her back were burning. She fancied that, when she looked at her skin in the mirror, there would be a fiery handprint where his palm had rested.

They barely spoke during their waltz. For a long time, Emma could think of nothing to say. And Will, it seemed, was content to be holding her. At last, as he whirled her round the floor, dancing with control and elegance, she managed to say, tritely, "How well you dance, sir."

He chuckled low in his throat. "For an uncouth sailor, you mean, ma'am? I should perhaps say that a good sense of balance is essential for dancing the waltz." With that, he threw her into a reverse turn which she managed to follow, just, though it was the last thing she had expected. "And a sense of balance is one thing that we uncouth sailors acquire pretty early on in our careers. Indeed, if we fail there, our careers tend to be, er, rather short. When one climbs a mast, in a rolling sea, a sense of balance is – shall we say – useful?" He chuckled again and then fell silent.

Emma couldn't bear to look into his eyes, so she fixed her gaze on his mouth. No, another mistake. She tried his cravat, and that strange gold pin, instead. Less arousing.

After several more turns, he said, very quietly, "It is usual to converse with one's partner while dancing, ma'am. Or, at least, to look at him occasionally."

Oh. "I—" She glanced up quickly into his face. It was a mad thought on her part, but he seemed to be *drinking* her in.

Don't look at me like that. She thought it, but she managed to stop herself from saying the words aloud. It would have been such a confession of failure on her part. He would know that, when she was in his arms, she was incapable of coherent thought or action. If he did not know it already.

They continued to waltz in silence. She thought his hand tightened a little against her back but it might have been wishful thinking. She loved being held close to him, but she was afraid of what the other dancers, and the onlookers, might see. It was a highly dangerous proceeding, waltzing with Will Allmay. If she had any sense, she would never do it again. But the temptation, she knew, would be very great.

The waltz ended. She dipped a curtsey, as convention required, and he bowed in response. It was not his normal elegant bow, but a rather quizzical move, little more than a nod. If the onlookers clocked the familiarity of that, the tittle-tattle would certainly begin.

"Where would you like me to lead you, ma'am?"

"I beg your pardon?" Emma said, puzzled.

"You will not wish to be seen in my company any longer, I dare say, but I cannot simply abandon you. Are there friends hereabouts with whom I may reunite you?"

Emma looked around. She could see some of the ladies from the musical soirée, but she had never learned their names. She might try a tactical retreat to the ladies' retiring room? She must not be seen to remain with Will. Much too dangerous for her reputation.

She was still hesitating when Will glanced over her shoulder, his attention caught by someone in the far corner of the ballroom.

His mouth twitched a fraction. It might have been a grimace but it was difficult to be sure. "Ah," he said. "My godmother is beckoning to us. She wants to meet you, I collect. May I bring you to her?"

Will's godmother? "I do not think I know...?" Emma began, with a clear question in her voice.

"Lady Augusta Sinclair-Smythe. You will not have met her. May I introduce you to her?"

Emma gulped. But then, why not? Lady Emma was an aristocrat, a respectable widow and as good as anyone in society. She supposed that Will's godmother must be a proper person for her to know. Will would not introduce them if that were not the case. "Certainly." They started to stroll across the floor. "Which is she?"

"The tall lady in maroon silk with blonde lace."

Emma studied the woman covertly. There was something formidable about the way she stood and stared out across the ballroom. She had the air of a general reviewing his troops. A single button out of place, and some hapless soldier would be hauled off for a flogging. Emma knew, in her head, that she was immaculately dressed in her gold lace and evening slippers, but her heart was thumping before they had come within three yards of the woman. Close up, Lady Augusta was the general to her fingertips. Her sharp black eyes narrowed as she surveyed Emma from head to toe, looking to find fault, no doubt. Lady Augusta pursed her thin lips before saying a word. Then she turned abruptly to Will and said, "Introduce your companion, William, if you please."

Not a general. A field marshal.

Will seemed to take it all in his stride. Emma's hand was still on his arm and she could feel no tension in his muscles. He bowed. "Good evening, Godmother. How very pleasant to meet you here. May I present Lady Emma Groatster, recently come up from the country?" Turning his head slightly towards Emma, he added, "Lady Emma, this is my godmother, Lady Augusta Sinclair-Smythe."

So that's my name. Groatster? Weird. I've never heard anything like it before. And—

Lady Augusta extended two fingers to Emma.

One of those. Not only domineering, but arrogant with it.

Puzzling over her strange surname would have to wait, Emma decided. She touched the outstretched fingers with two of her own and sank into a half-curtsey. "Delighted to meet you, ma'am, " she murmured, just loud enough for the older woman to hear.

"And you, child," Lady Augusta boomed. "William?" She turned to her godson. "I should like Patience to meet Lady Emma. Go and find her for me. She is—" she waved a hand in the general direction of the far side of the ballroom "—somewhere over there. Ah no. She must have seen you. She is coming to bid you good e'en."

Will's smile looked genuine enough. "How delightful," he said. "I have not seen Patience for an age."

A slim woman in deep cornflower blue was threading her way towards them. She was dressed, Emma noticed, in the height of fashion rather than in the modest white muslins usually worn by young single women. Her exquisite gown was exceedingly low cut; her guinea-gold hair was piled high on her head, with a single long curl hanging enticingly across her bare breast. Striking, rather than pretty, Emma decided. The Regency probably called her "handsome".

With a mother like that, she will be either a shrinking little mouse, or a general-in-waiting.

"Patience, my dear. Here is William." Lady Augusta paused. Then came the obvious afterthought. She turned to Emma. "Lady Emma, may I present my daughter, Miss Sinclair-Smythe?"

Miss Sinclair-Smythe sank into a very elegant curtsey, with just the correct depth due to an aristocrat whose station was high, but much lower than a duchess. "Delighted to meet you, ma'am."

Emma responded with a curtsey of her own, though not as deep as Miss Sinclair-Smythe's. It was unnecessary to extend her hand. She murmured, "Delighted," and smiled a company smile.

The young woman – she could not be termed a girl, for she must be somewhere in her mid-twenties, Emma reckoned – passed quickly from Emma to Will.

"William, it seems months since we have seen each other." She did not ask what he had been doing since their last meeting, Emma noticed, wondering if the young woman knew about Will's reputation. Salacious gossip was not usually shared with unmarried females, but with a mother like Lady Augusta, anything was possible.

Miss Sinclair-Smythe pushed between Emma and her mother in order to grasp Will's hand firmly in both her own and reach up to kiss him soundly on the cheek. "We have missed you," she said quietly, offering her own cheek for him to return her kiss. He did so, without the least show of reluctance, Emma noticed. There was a moment of slightly awkward silence and then Patience said, rather too gaily, "Oh, listen. They are playing another waltz. How lovely."

Poor Will, Emma thought. *He doesn't stand a chance with these two.*

At the same moment, Will was bowing and offering his hand to Patience. "Will you do me the honour, Patience?"

"Oh, go along," said Lady Augusta, flapping a hand. She looked, to Emma's mind, like a purple penguin trying to shoo away an amorous rival. "You young things need to become reacquainted. Meanwhile, Lady Emma and I shall join the chaperons and have a comfortable coze. Go along with you now, do."

That puts me in my place. Among the chaperons and the dowagers, indeed? Well, I am not that much older than her precious Patience and I don't think he lusts after those guinea curls half as much as he lusts after my red ones.

Emma had no more time for her own thoughts. Lady Augusta had been talking non-stop as they walked across to the chaperons' corner and it was risky not to pay attention. The woman was clearly quite determined to keep Emma away from Will Allmay and to swamp her with gossip and inanities. Her questioning, when she finally got round to it, was sharp. "Do you ride, Lady Emma?"

"Yes," Emma replied, without stopping to think. "To be sure, I do. Everyone rides, do they not?" she added, trying to sound offhand. Emma had ridden regularly before her marriage and had enjoyed it very much. Julian, who did not ride, had convinced her to give it up. They should enjoy their hobbies together, he said. And, blinded by her own misplaced love and what she thought was his love for her, she had done as he asked. It was only long afterwards that she realised it was all about control. If she was doing something that he could not, and doing it well, too, he would be failing to control every aspect of her life. That, for Julian, was totally unacceptable.

Lady Augusta was prattling on about riding in the park. Emma, lost in her own painful memories, had not been paying enough attention. "...enjoy riding out with Patience. You will make a remarkable couple, you so, er, *red*, and she so fair. What horse do you ride? A grey, I suppose, with your colouring?"

Emma suddenly had a mental picture of herself, in the flowing skirts of a Regency riding habit, mounted on a grey horse. Side-saddle. *Side-saddle?* But she didn't know how to ride side-saddle. "I...I have not brought my horses to London, ma'am."

Lady Augusta waved a dismissive hand. "No matter. You may borrow one from our stable."

I have to stop her before this ends in disaster. "Thank you, ma'am, but no. I do not ride in London." She thought rapidly. "You will understand that, while I was, er, in the country for so long, I did not ride. It would have been inappropriate to do so," she added, pompously. Let Lady Augusta make what she liked of that. The newly widowed and highly conventional Lady Emma would certainly not ride out for pleasure while she was in mourning. "As a result, I am somewhat out of the way of it. I would not wish to disgrace myself by making a first appearance on horseback in company with your daughter who is, I imagine, a fine horsewoman."

Lady August simpered. "She is said to have an excellent seat, it is true. And I am sure you have, also. Or you will have, once you have taken to it again."

"Perhaps your daughter would enjoy a carriage drive with me instead?" Emma suggested, in desperation. She had to do something to escape the prospect of riding side-saddle for the first time in her life. In the Regency. In public. What if she fell off? Lady Emma the High Stickler would be the laughing stock of London society.

Lady Augusta seemed to hesitate, for once.

Emma made the most of her chance. "When Miss Sinclair-Smythe returns from her waltz, I shall suggest it." She turned slightly so that she could see the couple on the dance floor. "They move most elegantly together, do they not?" she said, trying not to sound grudging. Patience did dance beautifully with Will, probably better than Emma did, for Emma had not had years and years of instruction.

"Yes, they do make an elegant pairing. I have long thought so."

Really? An aristocrat's spinster daughter and the greatest stud in London? What's going on here?

"Do you think, ma'am, that Miss Sinclair-Smythe might enjoy a drive with me?" Emma said again. "At a time to suit her, naturally. We might make an arrangement for a day when the weather is warmer?" And a day a long way in the future, Emma hoped.

"The weather seems set fair and warm enough," Lady August pronounced. "Tomorrow would be very suitable. Patience is free in the afternoon, I collect. You will call for her at four? You may drive round the park. Most of fashionable London will be there, as you know."

What could Emma do but agree? She had been railroaded by a master of the art.

Emma found herself smiling inwardly at her own choice of words. Lady Augusta, a Regency woman, knew nothing about the railroads to come.

~ ~ ~

Emma was claimed for many more dances, by gentlemen who greeted her as old acquaintances. She learned the name of only one of them, but she discovered nothing about how any of them might have met her.

She did catch the odd glimpse of Will on the dance floor, usually with older married ladies, and once, later, dancing a second time with Patience, but he did not approach Emma again. Was he angry with her for staying so quiet while they danced? He couldn't, surely, have expected them to discuss intimate matters in such a public place? Anyone might have overheard.

He had promised that he would agree to any conditions she chose. And he knew that one condition was the preservation of her reputation. Was that why he was keeping his distance?

By three in the morning, Emma had had enough of being a society lady and holding a fixed smile. Besides, her feet ached. Silken evening slippers, she had discovered, provided no support at all. So, since Will clearly had no intention of resuming their conversation, she would leave. The question was: how? Should she find a spot where she could be alone to take off the lace gown? Or should she summon her carriage and return to her London house? If she went back to her own time, she'd be able to research Lady Emma, now that she knew the surname to look for. It would be fascinating.

It would be cowardly. You're trying to find an excuse for leaving, because you're afraid of being alone with Will.

She was honest enough to admit, to herself, that it was true. And she didn't want to be a coward where Will was concerned. She wanted to be alone with him, preferably somewhere with neither onlookers nor clothes, and she ought to give him a chance to seek her out.

Honesty won out over the lure of research. She could pursue her researches at any time, after all. But there might not be many chances of being alone with Will.

Decision made, she put a hand to her mouth to conceal a pretended yawn and strolled casually down to the entrance hall. The main door was standing partly open so it was quite chilly, especially after the heat of the ballroom. Several liveried footmen were standing to attention under the eagle eye of a black-clad butler. She had only to raise an eyebrow and one of the footmen hurried across for her orders.

"Summon my carriage," she ordered crisply. She did not give her name. It was the butler's job to know who everyone was, wasn't it?

The footman bowed. "Your ladyship's carriage. At once." He bowed again and started for the door, presumably to issue the necessary summons.

Emma did not wait to see what would happen. It was too

cold, dressed as she was. And a lady would never loiter in a hallway, in any case. She swept off down the corridor in search of an antechamber where she might wait in comfort. Alone.

She soon found an empty saloon with a welcoming fire in the grate. Leaving the door ajar, she crossed to the fireplace and sank into a wing chair, holding out her gloved hands to the flames. It was wonderful to take the weight off her feet, too. She decided she would call for a warm foot bath as soon as she got back home.

Home? Since when was she thinking of Regency London as her home?

"Your ladyship's carriage is at the door." The footman had appeared without a sound, her velvet evening cloak draped over his arm. He shook it out and held it for her.

Snugly wrapped in her cloak, she made her way to the front door. The hallway was empty of guests. No one who mattered was there to see her leave.

Will had not come to find her.

Chapter Thirteen

AFTER HER SOOTHING WARM FOOTBATH, Emma slept very soundly in Lady Emma Groatster's bed. When she eventually woke up, she had to ring the bell to find out what the time was.

Bailey must have been waiting for a summons. She appeared in less than a minute with a cup of chocolate and some sweet biscuits.

"What time is it?" Emma asked, yawning.

"Just after noon, m'lady. At least this time, you have slept properly, as a lady should. You do need your sleep if you stay out dancing and, and suchlike, until so very late." Clearly, Bailey was in fusspot mode.

Emma grinned. "I'm not at all sure what kind of 'suchlike' you think I may be guilty of, Bailey. I did dance a great deal, as it happens. But I can assure you that no 'suchlike' took place." Well, nothing very much, apart from dancing a waltz where she was held very closely against the hard body of the greatest rake in London. "My poor feet are not used to so much dancing," she added, with a laugh.

"You should have known that before you started." The abigail certainly believed she had the right to tell Emma off if she did something that Bailey thought unbecoming. "One minute you are sitting in seclusion, as a proper widow should, and the next you're dancing the night away. With a selection of ne'er-do-well 'gentlemen', I have no doubt."

"You go too far, Bailey," Emma said, trying to sound stern. "It was a *ton* ball. Only the cream of society was admitted, as you very well know. My dancing partners were all gentlemen, I assure you."

Bailey grunted. "Even him? He *was* there, I suppose?"

Bailey was partly confidante and partly mind reader, Emma decided. And there was no point in trying to lie to her. She was too sharp, and too well used to Emma's ways. It would be impossible to pull the wool over her eyes for long. "Sir William was at the ball, yes. And before you ask, Bailey, I will tell you that I danced with him once only. He presented me to his godmother, Lady Augusta Sinclair-Smythe, and then he left us together. I did not speak to him again."

Bailey nodded knowingly.

Emma began to wonder why she was telling Bailey so much, or why she felt the need to make excuses for her conduct to a mere servant. She had done nothing wrong. Since she was acquainted with Captain Sir William Allmay, and everyone who mattered knew that to be the case, it would have been highly impolite for her to have refused to stand up with him.

One single dance. Why such a fuss?

Because the dance was a waltz. Accepted in the late Regency, yet viewed as more than a little daring, because the gentleman got to hold the lady in his arms. Against his body. Breast to breast. And worse.

Time to change the subject. "What is the weather like?"

Bailey answered by crossing to the windows and pulling open the long heavy curtains. Sunshine streamed in.

"Excellent," Emma said. "I have arranged to go driving in the park. At four o'clock, or a little earlier. Pray ensure that the carriage is ready in time, Bailey."

Bailey narrowed her eyes. "Certainly, m'lady. Will you be wanting the open carriage? Or perhaps the closed carriage is more to your taste? The one without the crest?"

Emma laughed out loud. Bailey's suspicions were totally unfounded, for once. "The open carriage, of course, Bailey, for such delightful spring weather. And I dare say you will make sure we have plenty of rugs, in case the wind should be chill."

"We?" The abigail's eyes narrowed even more. Was she speculating about what hands might get up to under cover of a fur rug?

"Yes, indeed. I have arranged to drive out with Lady Augusta's daughter." She watched with inner glee as Bailey's expression morphed in an instant from suspicious to inscrutable. Emma managed to give her abigail Lady Augusta's Mayfair address without laughing again, but it was a close-run thing. "I shall collect Miss Sinclair-Smythe at four o'clock precisely. Tell the coachman that I do not want to be even a minute behind my time. I shall be ready to leave from half past three."

"As you wish, m'lady."

"And in the meantime, Bailey, I shall take a bath, I believe. Followed by a light luncheon, here in my chamber."

Bailey nodded. "As you wish, m'lady. And which gown would your ladyship desire to wear for this outing to the park?"

Ah. She'd lost that round. And she'd been doing so well, she'd thought, playing the part of the haughty aristocrat. Emma, the costume specialist, might have a pretty good idea of what a high-born lady would wear for driving in the park, but she had absolutely no idea which day gowns Lady Emma Groatster possessed.

She sighed out a long breath. "Do you know, Bailey, that I am at a loss to decide? You will have suggestions, I am sure. Show me what you would recommend and I shall chose one. Your taste is always impeccable."

Bailey grunted again, but she was flattered all the same, Emma could see.

Round two to me, I think. On points.

Bailey produced three elegant outfits for Emma to choose from. Each had a matching hat.

Not one of the hats had a veil.

~ ~ ~

Emma's open barouche drew up outside the Sinclair-Smythe house at precisely one minute to four in the afternoon. The door opened immediately. A footman came out to greet her and to invite her to step inside to meet the ladies. Emma declined. She did not wish to keep her horses standing, she told him, loftily. She would wait in her carriage for Miss Sinclair-Smythe to appear.

It was, as she intended it to be, a rebuke. She was not at all sure why she had allowed herself to be manoeuvred into this tête-à-tête with Patience Sinclair-Smythe, but she would certainly not allow herself to be manoeuvred any more. A drive at four o'clock had been agreed. And if guinea-gold Patience kept her waiting for more than ten minutes, Emma would drive to the park on her own.

It was just after five past four when the door opened again and Patience Sinclair-Smythe came out. She was all smiles – until she clapped eyes on Emma's carriage. Her smile became a little forced then, for Emma's glossy black barouche was upholstered in golden velvet.

Not the best contrast for those guinea-gold curls, Emma thought triumphantly. Whereas Emma's dark red hair looked remarkably well against a gold background.

Miss Sinclair-Smythe quickly recovered her poise and allowed the footman to help her up into the carriage. Emma offered her hand. "Good afternoon, Miss Sinclair-Smythe. Do sit here beside me. There is plenty of space. May I say that that is a most fetching hat?"

Over her flounced white carriage dress, Patience was wearing a forest green pelisse that flattered her colouring. Her tall Leghorn hat was decorated with leaves, and perched jauntily on the side of her head so that most of her golden hair was on view for any gentleman who cared to admire it. She was well aware of her best features, Emma decided. Her sarcenet pelisse swayed beautifully to catch the light, showing off her slim, elegant figure. Emma placed a silent bet with herself that, once they reached the park, Patience would suggest they leave the barouche and walk for a while. Especially if there were eligible gentlemen around to see.

Why am I so suspicious of this woman? Emma wondered. *I don't know, but there's definitely something about her that doesn't ring true.* Emma had learned, over the terrible years with Julian, that her gut instincts were seldom wrong, even

112

when reason, or Julian, insisted on overriding them. So, with Patience Sinclair-Smythe, she would definitely be on her guard.

Emma nodded to her coachman and the carriage moved off in the direction of Hyde Park, where everyone who was anyone would be on show at this hour in the afternoon. Although the sun was shining, Emma took care to ensure that her guest was well wrapped up, for it was too early in the year to be truly warm. She kept up a flow of light conversation, about the weather and other harmless subjects, as they bowled along through surprisingly light traffic. But Patience responded only just enough to be polite.

As they approached the entrance to the park, Emma found she had very few acceptable topics left.

Your turn, Miss Guinea-Gold. I've made all the running so far. You, and your mama, were the ones who wanted this outing, after all. Time to tell me what the Sinclair-Smythes are really after.

"That is a most becoming gown you are wearing, Miss Sinclair-Smythe. As was your ballgown last evening. If I may venture to say so, your style is somewhat, er, different from your mama's. Do you and she patronise the same mantua-maker?" When the woman made no move to respond, Emma persevered. "Your mantua-maker, Miss Sinclair-Smythe?"

"Oh, please, won't you call me Patience? For we are going to be such good friends, are we not?"

Out of the blue, this woman was asking to be on Christian name terms with Emma. But why? And should Emma agree to such intimacy? Lady Emma was, after all, some years older than Patience, and a widow, besides. Not to mention that she was the daughter of an earl, at the least. No, a woman such as Lady Emma Groatster would not allow a mere Miss Sinclair-Smythe to presume to call her by her given name on such a slight acquaintance. Double-barrelled Patience was trying it on, Emma decided. For her own reasons. Emma did not trust the chit further than she could throw her.

Emma drew herself up a little, as befitted a high-ranking aristocrat. "I think, Miss Sinclair-Smythe, that we need to know one another somewhat better before we indulge in such informality." Patience looked disappointed, but only a little. So she had known perfectly well that she was pushing her luck.

"But you were going to tell me about your mantua-maker," Emma continued in a slightly friendlier tone. "Your style seems to me to be quite the latest thing. French, even. Does your mama permit you to choose all your own gowns?"

"There is a considerable difference in age between Mama and myself, you must understand," Patience said baldly. "So it is not to be wondered at if our tastes differ also. Mama has had her gowns from the same dressmaker *for ever*." She sniggered unpleasantly. "I have recently given my patronage to Madame Élise. She is, you may know, the most sought-after *modiste* in London."

This woman was making no attempt to conceal her disdain for her mother's fashion sense. And it was surely quite outrageous to share such disloyal opinions with someone she had only just met. Did she not consider the risk that her indiscreet comments might be repeated back to her mother? Patience was, after all, a single woman living at home with her parents and dependent on them for every penny.

"I had forgot. You do not know about my family, do you?" Patience continued, suddenly seeming very keen to confide. What had happened to the monosyllabic woman of a few moments earlier? She leaned across to Emma and lowered her voice. "The whole of London knows it, so it will do no harm to tell you, dear Lady Emma. And it will explain why Mama is so very much older than me and why our tastes, er, do not always agree. Mama says that she and Papa waited many years for a child. I imagine you will understand how she felt. You and Sir John were not blessed with children, were you? Such a pity."

Emma pursed her lips and looked away, saying nothing. It was not surprising news, but it was a little sad.

"As I said, Mama and Papa had all but given up hope when I was born. Mama says that when they were blessed with a baby girl, she could think of no other name but Patience, since that's what she and Papa had had to show for so long."

"How, er, how very interesting," Emma said quickly,

trying to hide her shock at such indiscretion. "I had wondered about your given name, I will admit. I had thought such names had fallen out of use centuries ago. I understand now. You were obviously a much-wanted child." And clearly a much overindulged one. Patience Sinclair-Smythe might well be an only child. Was she an heiress, too? Judging by her expensive wardrobe, there was no shortage of funds in the Sinclair-Smythe household. So why was double-barrelled Patience still unmarried in her mid-twenties?

Miss Sinclair-Smythe did not seem to have twigged that any of her confidences might be disconcerting. She burbled on, regardless. "You may be wondering, dear Lady Emma, about the fact that the only child of a wealthy family, such as mine, is unwed, at such an age. I am almost four-and-twenty, you know. Actually, it is all a great secret. But I am sure I can trust *you* with it. A marriage has been arranged." She paused, a dramatic pause, waiting for a reaction.

"Really?" Emma dutifully responded. "How splendid."

"Yes, indeed. It is a family arrangement, as such things so often are. Perhaps yours was also?"

When Emma remained silent, Patience shook her head and continued, "Well, even so. Mine has been arranged between the families. For years, as it happens. Because he... Well, he was not here. The wars, you understand."

"He was with Wellington's army? In Spain?"

Patience chortled and shook her head decisively. "No, no." There was still a laugh in her voice as she continued, "No, my intended was in His Majesty's Navy, where there were rich prizes to be won. He took many enemy ships, over the years, and returned with a very respectable fortune. Papa was most gratified."

"Oh."

"Indeed, you know him, I collect. You danced with him last evening. Sir William?"

"Oh." Emma's heart stuttered to a stop in her breast. And then it raced away, pounding painfully. She took a deep breath. She must not show how much this revelation had stunned her. After a moment, she managed to say, in something approaching her normal voice, "Really? How very interesting. I had not heard that Sir William was betrothed."

"It is not public knowledge. In fact, no one knows, apart from the closest family members."

So why are you telling me, a stranger? Emma thought. But she knew the answer to that, so she said, quietly, "This betrothal will be announced soon, I collect?"

"In due course. Mama says— Mama has made it clear that William must be allowed to sow his wild oats before any formal declaration is made."

"Wild oats?" Emma could barely get the words out.

"William was with the Navy for many years, you will understand, Lady Emma. Years and years at sea, with no female companionship whatsoever. He has been… Shall we say he has been deprived of what a normal man needs?"

Even modern-day Emma was shocked at that. This was straight talking with a vengeance. Patience Sinclair-Smythe might be a spinster, but she was far from naïve when it came to sex.

"Mama says William must be given space to sow his wild oats. And that he deserves it, after having been such a hero in the late wars."

"I see," Emma murmured. She was over the shock now, she told herself. Time to pay this woman back in kind for the hurt and embarrassment she had caused. "And these wild oats are…?"

"I do not trouble myself about what he does with women of a…a certain stamp. It is no concern of mine. Believe me, once we are married, there will be no more wild oats."

"Really? You will allow me to say, as an older and more experienced woman than yourself, my dear, that married men do very often indulge in a little dalliance, away from hearth and home. Their wives usually learn to turn a blind eye."

"There will be no such thing in our marriage," Patience declared stoutly. "William shall vow to be faithful to me. And only to me. I will not permit anything else."

"Very wise, my dear," Emma said. "Very wise."

And if you can achieve that, with a man like Will Allmay, you will be a very remarkable wife.

They drove on, in silence, for a good ten minutes. Patience

was looking around, rather smugly to Emma's mind, and clearly satisfied that she had delivered the message, and the hands-off warning, that she and her mother intended.

Emma was trying to process the astonishing news that Patience had delivered. Will Allmay might promise eternal love and devotion to Lady Emma Groatster, but he was promised, and had been for years, to his godmother's dreadful daughter. Well, if he were prepared to go through with a marriage like that, he would deserve every miserable moment it would bring him.

At least Emma knew, finally, what this special outing had been all about. Patience, and her scheming mama, must have seen the way Will danced with Emma and deduced that she might be a threat to their plans. They would know that Lady Emma Groatster was a widow with a spotless reputation. They would assume that such an upright lady would never stoop to becoming Will's mistress but that, especially now he had a large fortune of his own, she might try to entice him to the altar. And, as long as the betrothal to Patience was unannounced, any other marriage prospect for Will was a real danger. So Emma had to be warned off, in no uncertain terms.

Was she prepared to heed the warning?

Being honest with herself, Emma admitted that she did not know. She had lived with a serially unfaithful man in the twenty-first century. Was she prepared to become involved with another, in the nineteenth? Will was probably a deal less manipulative than Julian but what did that matter? Emma was not prepared to become the long-term mistress of Patience Sinclair-Smythe's husband.

And short term?

Short term, he was not Patience's husband. Not yet. Nor even her betrothed.

For the moment, he was free. And available.

I love him, Emma thought, *and I want him. I will not share him, but I do want him now. This designing woman does not have him yet. And she shan't, not ever, if I have any say in it.*

Chapter Fourteen

"IT IS SUCH A BEAUTIFUL DAY, Lady Emma. Might we stop the carriage and walk a little?"

Yup. Knew she'd do that. She's seen those splendid military types coming towards us and she wants them to admire her face and figure. She's a fast little piece, as the Regency gossips would say.

"Certainly, if you wish, Miss Sinclair-Smythe," Emma said courteously. "It will be easier for you to greet your friends and acquaintances when you are down on their level, will it not?"

Patience's eyes narrowed for a second but she quickly smiled again. If she had caught Emma's poorly concealed barb, there was nothing she could do about it and she probably knew it was unwise to try. Instead, she made a great show of allowing the footman to hand her down from the barouche and then fiddling with her straw-coloured parasol which – she said – would not open properly. "It is new and stiff. It needs a man's strong fingers. I fear mine are not up to the task. Stay, here is Captain Musgrove. I'm sure he will be able to help me."

Three military gentlemen were, by this time, close enough to have heard her words. One of them, very fine in scarlet regimentals, strode forward and saluted. "Miss Sinclair-Smythe. Good afternoon. I believe I may have heard you asking for my help?"

Patience made doe eyes at him. In a pathetic little voice –
the voice of a child rather than a woman of twenty-three,
Emma thought – she explained her problem. Predictably,
Captain Musgrove opened the parasol with no trouble at all.
As he restored it to her, he said, very politely, "I think I have
not had the honour of being introduced to your companion."

Emma bit the inside of her lip to stop herself from
laughing, for Patience had miscalculated there. She'd wanted
the officers' attention all to herself. But now she would have to
share. And after that nasty bombshell about the betrothal, it
was time for Patience to be put in her place. Emma fancied
that a few lessons in top-class flirting – where Georgette
Heyer had given her plenty of inspiration – might be in order.

So she took a step forward, looked Patience squarely in the
face and waited for the inevitable. It came, but several seconds
too late for good manners. "Oh. Oh, yes, of course. Lady
Emma, may I present Captain Musgrove of the— Oh dear. I
fear I have forgot the name of your regiment, Captain."

"No matter, ma'am. It is the 44th." He saluted very smartly,
keeping his eyes fixed on Emma and clearly appreciating the
view.

"Oh yes. I will try to remember," Patience said quickly.
She stepped between them and gestured towards Emma.
"Captain Musgrove, this is my very good friend Lady Emma
Groatster, lately returned to town."

*Very good friend, eh? Cheeky little madam. Well, she's
made one mistake too many. She deserves her comeuppance.
And she's about to get it.*

"Your servant, Lady Emma," Captain Musgrove said
politely.

Emma opened her eyes a little wider and beamed at
Musgrove, as if she, too, liked what she was seeing. Then she
tipped her head to one side and extended her gloved hand. "I
am delighted to meet a member of the gallant 44th, Captain
Musgrove. Were you at Waterloo? Your regiment performed
distinguished service there, I know, and the whole country was
grateful."

Captain Musgrove blushed and stammered a little that, yes,
he had been in the battle, but no, he had not done anything

particularly heroic. It had been all down to the other fellows.

"I am sure you did your duty right honourably, sir, whatever you may say."

Musgrove was now gazing at Emma with glowing eyes. He must be younger, and less experienced with women, than she had supposed. Time to let him off her hook. "Will you introduce your fellow officers, Captain? I should be very pleased to make the acquaintance of your friends."

"As would I," said Patience tartly, lifting her chin a little.

Unfortunately for Patience, Captain Musgrove was not paying her any attention at all. He beckoned his friends over and presented them to Emma. One was a younger colleague from the 44th, Lieutenant Taylforth. The second, in the green and black uniform of the Rifles, stepped forward in his turn and saluted.

Emma smiled warmly at him. "Ah, that is a uniform I recognise. The green of the intrepid 95th, I collect?"

Musgrove agreed that it was and proceeded to present his friend, Captain Grimond, who declared himself delighted to meet a lady who knew so much about military matters.

"Well, not as much as I should like," Emma said, extending an arm to include Patience in the conversation. "Miss Sinclair-Smythe, on the other hand, knows exactly how to dress to match the uniform of the Rifles. Allow me present you to her."

So, in the end, it was Emma who presented the pair to Patience, who had been beginning to look more than a little put out. She soon swallowed her ill temper, though, once she was able to chatter gaily with the officers.

Poor kid. She may be going on twenty-four, and she has the mother from hell, but she really doesn't have a clue.

"I say, you chaps," muttered Captain Musgrove suddenly, indicating the path behind him, "here is Will May All." Sure enough, Will was striding towards them. "Oh dear." Musgrove coughed nervously. His neck had gone very red. He seemed to be struggling to get his words out. Luckily, Patience did not seem to have heard his hasty comment and Emma was able to pretend that she had not, either.

"Perhaps the ladies would like to walk?" said Captain

Grimond quickly, turning his back on Will and offering his arm to Emma.

Clearly the officers were all familiar with Will and had suddenly remembered his unsavoury reputation. They were trying to prevent Emma and Patience from being forced to acknowledge a man they should not wish to know.

Emma took pity on them and stood her ground. "Thank you, Captain, but we must decline, for here is Sir William come to join us. Lady Augusta Sinclair-Smythe is his godmother, you know. So we ought, at the very least, to wish him good day."

Captain Musgrove's sigh of relief was a little too heartfelt.

Will raised his hat and sketched an elegant bow. "Good afternoon, Lady Emma. Patience."

This time, Patience merely dropped a curtsey, Emma was glad to see. Kissing Will would have been highly improper in such a public place. The girl did have some sense of decorum, after all.

"I must say that I am surprised to find you ladies in company with such reprobates as these three," Will added, grinning.

"Reprobates?" gasped Musgrove. "Why, coming from you, that's—"

"He's roasting you, Musgrove," Captain Grimond intervened calmly. "Best not to rise to the bait."

"What? Oh. Oh, yes." Musgrove frowned at Will who was still grinning wickedly. The captain swallowed hard but said nothing more.

Emma decided it was time to take charge. "Would you gentlemen care to walk with us for a space? May I suggest that Patience, in her green, would make a splendid picture between you two red-garbed gentlemen? Perhaps you would each offer her an arm? Meanwhile, I will happily make an ill-assorted trio with Captain Grimond and Sir William." She held out a hand to each of them. Being gentlemen, they did precisely as she asked. Patience was stymied.

Another point to me.

"Ill-assorted, indeed," Will exclaimed, loudly enough for the Rifleman to hear.

121

"Well, Captain Grimond is very fine in his Rifle green. I am sadly ill-matched in blue, while you, Sir William, are..."

"...wearing the tail coat and pantaloons of any gentleman taking a stroll in the park, ma'am. Sadly we civilians cannot compete with regimentals. You have the advantage of us there, Grimond."

Captain Grimond chuckled. "You could, if you wished, sir, appear in all your naval finery so that we lowly army captains would have to defer to you."

"Hmm, yes. There is that. Perhaps I should try it one day." He sounded perfectly nonchalant. But there was nothing nonchalant about what his fingers were doing. First his thumb stroked her gloved palm where it rested on his wrist. Then he pushed something small and sharp-edged inside her glove.

Emma stiffened automatically. What was he up to now?

"I shall take *note*," Will continued without a pause, "for the future."

Emma let out a breath. She hadn't missed the emphasis on the word "note". The sharp-edged intruder in her glove was a note from him. He was a clever and conniving man, she realised. He had come to the park prepared to pass a note to her, even though he'd had no way of knowing she would even be there.

Am I taking on more than I know, pitting my wits against Will Allmay?

She glanced up into his face and then quickly away. It didn't matter. Given the way his eyes rested on her, and how she felt about him, she had no choice.

~ ~ ~

Will's note seemed to be burning into her hand. She longed to discover what he had said but she was not fool enough to retrieve it while Patience Sinclair-Smythe was around. Patience's long elegant nose was quite capable of prying into anything. So Emma forced herself to be patient – like Patience's formidable mama, she reminded herself – and went through all the conventional elements of a stroll in the park with four eligible gentlemen and one lady.

In fact, Patience soon tired of the company of her red-coated rattles. They had fought in battle, to be sure, and were probably mature and capable officers in the field, but their society conduct needed work. They were lightweights, both of them. Perhaps after all the horrors they had seen, it was understandable? Yet Captain Grimond, of the Rifles, was no lightweight, even though he seemed to be no more than a year or two older than the men of the 44th. Captain Grimond was a sensible man who knew how to behave in company and could converse most entertainingly with a lady.

Emma focused much more on Grimond than on Will, on her left. She was trying very hard to put out of her mind that her hand was on Will's arm and that his message was tucked into her glove. So she fixed her gaze on Captain Grimond, trying to remember all that she knew about the Rifle Brigade. She had read historical accounts during her researches, but she was also a fan of the Sharpe novels. If the fictional Richard Sharpe epitomised the officers of the Rifles, with their independence of mind and innovative flair, it was perhaps not surprising that Captain Grimond was so much more personable than his infantry friends.

She found herself wondering whether it might be worth getting to know Captain Grimond a little better. Competition for Will? It would depend on whether Grimond was eligible, of course.

Almost any gentleman is more eligible than Will Allmay.

They had been chatting and laughing for some fifteen minutes when the sun went in and the wind became suddenly much colder. Emma stopped, shivering a little in her thin spencer. "I think, gentlemen," she said, loudly enough for all four to hear, "that Miss Sinclair-Smythe and I shall return to the barouche. It grows chill. But we do thank you, indeed, for your most entertaining company." She raised an eyebrow to Patience. "I am sure you will join me in thanking them, Miss Sinclair-Smythe?"

"Oh, certainly," Patience said, not very convincingly. She extracted her arms from her companions and came across to join Emma. "Perhaps you would escort me back to the carriage, William?" she said pointedly. "Since Lady Emma is having such a comfortable coze with Captain Grimond, she will not miss you, I dare say." She smirked as she tucked her arm into Will's and towed him away.

It was left to Emma to perform the courtesies with the other young men. "Gentlemen, it has been a pleasure to walk with you and I thank you for your company. On behalf of both of us. I do hope we shall meet again soon." She dropped a tiny curtsey in response to their salutes. It was the least she could do after Patience's lack of manners.

By the time Emma turned back to Captain Grimond, Patience and Will were a good twenty yards ahead of them on the path.

She really needs to prove she can take him from me. Emma clenched her fists involuntarily. Will's note, which she had finally managed to forget about, dug a corner into her palm. She almost laughed aloud.

Poor Patience. If only she knew.

Having helped Patience into the barouche, Will was standing by the carriage door, talking to her, but clearly waiting to offer his hand to Emma in turn. It was an unnecessary courtesy. Captain Grimond was perfectly capable of performing that service himself. Emma decided that she would ignore Will's hand and look for Grimond's. Anything to show Will that he could not order Emma's conduct as easily as he seemed to believe.

But it did not pan out that way. Will was not only older than Grimond, he was also much senior in rank. So when Will moved forward to offer his hand to Emma at the carriage steps, Grimond immediately stepped politely back. Yes, Captain Grimond was a very polished gentleman.

Will merely nodded to Grimond and stood waiting for Emma to put her hand in his. And when she did, she felt the distinct pressure of his fingers. No, whatever Patience *thought* she had going with Will Allmay, she was mistaken. Will was totally focused on Lady Emma.

At least for now.

~ ~ ~

It was hard, but Emma waited until she was alone in her own bedchamber before she stripped off her gloves and extracted Will's note. Was it a farewell, maybe? She doubted it. Not after that pointed encounter at the side of the barouche.

The note itself was very small and scribbled in pencil. It looked like a scrap of paper torn from a pocketbook. So had Will written it in the park when he spied her from a distance? That was certainly possible. And it made him seem less coldly calculating than she had first thought.

Emma's pulse was racing as she opened it and pounding fit to burst by the time she finished reading.

It contained very few words: *Come tonight. Cab waiting from 8 in Mews behind your house.* There was no signature, not even initials.

The room started to spin. She collapsed into her chair with a thump but it didn't help. She clutched the arm of her chair for support and closed her eyes. Eventually, the dizziness subsided and she could begin to think. What was she to make of it? Where did he plan to take her? Did he have some backstreet hideaway for his assignations? He must have somewhere discreet for meeting all those mistresses.

He will not take me where he takes them.

Emma was not sure why she thought that, or why she was so certain of it. But she was. And if she went, she would be putting herself in his power.

And what did he mean about a cab?

Presumably, he'd realised that she could not drive to a rendezvous in her own carriage with her own servants. But why was he sending a hackney for her? Why not a proper carriage?

Because a carriage or its horses might be noted or recognised. Will was certainly practised in the art of seduction. He would count on the fact that no one would remember one hackney cab among so many in London.

They might not remember the cab, but they might well remember the passenger. For Will's cab trick to work, Lady Emma had to get into it without being seen.

Hmm. And to do that, I would have to get out of the house alone and also without being spotted. Not exactly the easiest thing I've ever done.

Emma rang the bell to order a tray of tea. She needed to think of ways to leave the house alone and without summoning her own carriage. What's more, she needed to be wearing the lace ballgown. Just in case she needed to disappear. It was a knotty problem, the kind that Sherlock Holmes might have called a Three Pipe Problem.

It was only when she was drinking her second cup of tea that she realised what she was doing.

I have decided to go to him, haven't I? I must be out of my mind. He professes to love me, but he is going to marry that woman. What reason do I have to trust him now?

It made no difference. If she could find a way, she would go to him.

Chapter Fifteen

"THE GOLD LACE *AGAIN*, MY LADY?" Bailey sounded outraged, rather than surprised.

Of course, it would reflect on the abigail if Lady Emma were not seen to be at the forefront of fashion. Emma allowed herself to sound a little annoyed when she replied. "I have told you before, Bailey. I am working to win support for my charity from the wealthy ladies of the *ton*. I plan to wear this gown so often that none of them can avoid the issue."

Bailey harrumphed.

"So let us have no more discussion about often I choose to wear this gown. Will you put up my hair now? Perhaps something a little more daring for this evening?"

"As you wish, m'lady." Bailey reached for her comb.

She could certainly work wonders with Emma's curly red hair. In the space of less than fifteen minutes, it had been pinned up into a very flattering style with loose curls hanging down behind Emma's left ear.

Not quite as far down my breast as Patience's, Emma thought uncharitably, *but then my lace gown is not nearly as low-cut as her cornflower blue one. If she'd leaned forward, she'd have fallen out of it.*

"There," Bailey said, with a last twitch of the long curls. "Does that please you, m'lady?"

"Very well indeed, Bailey, thank you. You are a wonder with a comb and pins."

Bailey smiled, for the first time in the best part of an hour. "For what time shall I order your ladyship's carriage?"

Ah. If the carriage was ordered and Emma did not go down to meet it, she would be rumbled. "I have no need of my own carriage this evening," she said quickly, grabbing the first idea that came into her head. "Lady...Lady Mumford offered to call for me in her carriage so that we could go to the rout party together."

"Lady Mumford?"

"Indeed, and what is so strange about that, pray?"

"Um. Nothing, m'lady."

"Quite. Her ladyship offered and I accepted. I thought it was time that my coachman had an evening to himself."

"Oh." Bailey was visibly stunned at the idea that servants might get a night off.

Careful, Emma told herself. *Behaving in ways that are too unlike the real Lady Emma is risky. The servants will start watching me more closely, if only to see what strange things their mad mistress might do next.*

"And the horses need their rest too." That was better, judging by Bailey's expression. Horses had to be cosseted; servants did not.

"At what time should we expect Lady Mumford?" Bailey asked, reasonably.

"Ah, later. I can't quite remember the exact hour that was agreed. I made a note, somewhere. But I know it was later. In the meantime, help me to dress, please."

Bailey gave her a quizzical sideways look, but said nothing. She fetched the lace gown and helped Emma into it. It looked very fine. It was definitely earning its keep, these days. "What jewels will your ladyship wear this evening?"

Ah. More potential pitfalls. "Um. I don't know. What would you suggest, Bailey?" Emma was making a habit of this, but what choice did she have? There must be a jewel case somewhere, though Emma could not remember having seen it.

"The emeralds, perhaps?"

"Fetch them and I will decide." Bailey disappeared into the

128

dressing room, giving Emma a few blessed moments to herself. She had no clue yet how she was going to get out of the house unnoticed. And how was she going to account for the fact that Lady Mumford's carriage, so carefully "arranged", was not going to turn up at all? Emma's spur-of-the-moment, and lame, excuse for turning down her own carriage could lead to all sorts of problems.

She was tying herself in knots. Again. Running assignations in the Regency was turning out to be very difficult indeed. But other people, other ladies, managed it. Will had had many other women in his bed. So how had they escaped their servants? Or indeed their husbands?

She was no further forward when Bailey returned, carrying two flat jewel cases. "I brought the sapphires as well, m'lady. In case you should not have a fancy for the emeralds. Diamonds would be quite wrong with that gold lace."

"True." Lady Emma must be extremely rich. Not only emeralds and sapphires, but diamonds as well?

When Bailey opened the first box, Emma only just managed to swallow a gasp. These emeralds must be worth a fortune. "Hmm. I'm not sure that I want to wear anything quite so heavy this evening." The emeralds were stunning, and full of mysterious fire, but for Emma's taste there were rather too many of them in the heavy necklace. The long earrings, on the other hand, were beautiful, with single square-cut stones suspended from a column of diamonds set in gold.

Bailey opened the second box. Yes, that was much better. A pendant of a single teardrop sapphire surrounded by baguette diamonds that pointed outwards like jagged lightning flashes. The pendant hung from a delicate gold collar. There were matching eardrops, too, on a slightly smaller scale. And all the sapphires were an astonishing shade of ultramarine blue with subtle hints of purple. To Emma's eyes, it could have been a modern piece. And it was fabulous. "I think I prefer the sapphires, this evening, Bailey."

"The emeralds would better reflect the colour of your eyes, m'lady."

That would be true, but Emma doubted that Will needed emeralds to encourage him to look into her eyes. "Thank you for the compliment, Bailey, but I see no reason to wish for anyone to admire my fine eyes. I am not in the mood for flirting tonight." No, she was not. She was in the mood for some very serious lovemaking. And the glow, deep in her belly, was reminding her of that, more and more.

The clock chimed eight.

That's all I need, Emma thought. *A reminder that his hackney is already waiting for me and I still haven't a clue how to get out of the house to meet it.*

Bailey finished fastening the pendant around Emma's neck and hooking the eardrops into her ears. She fussed a little with the left-hand earring, to make sure it would not become tangled in Emma's hanging curls.

"That looks very well. Thank you, Bailey. You may go now."

"Were you not planning to come down to the saloon, m'lady?"

"Not for the present. I have a slight headache. I shall lie down and close my eyes for a moment or two. I dare say it will be gone soon."

"Let me help you off with your gown—"

'No!" That was too sharp. "No, there is no need. On second thoughts, I shall sit quietly by the fire. The headache will pass, I am sure. If it should become worse, I will ring for you, Bailey, and you may help me to undress. I would not have my lace become creased. It has much work to do, these coming weeks." She stroked the skirt fondly and managed a little chuckle.

Bailey sniffed her disapproval but said nothing.

"I wish to be alone for a space. If I need you, I will ring. You deserve a few hours to yourself."

To Emma's surprise, Bailey blushed.

"Bailey?"

"Well, m'lady, you see—" Bailey took a deep breath and began to speak very fast. "Tonight is Mr Bendridge's weekly prayer meeting. I am not often free to attend, but I should very much like to do so if your ladyship does not need me."

Prayer meeting? It was the first Emma had heard of it. Bendridge, she remembered, was the name of her butler.

"Who usually attends?" That was a safe enough question.

"Mr Bendridge insists that all the staff attend, particularly the maids and the footmen. He is a fine, stalwart Christian. And he takes his duties very seriously as the moral guardian of the household below stairs. He has doubts, you see, about the morals of some of the younger men—"

"Really? I hope I am not harbouring rogues in my household?"

"Not rogues, m'lady. Mr Bendridge says – only in the privacy of the housekeeper's room – that they are very young and unschooled in the ways of the world. They are always on the lookout for a chance to make mischief with the maids, he says. Feeling their oats, he called it."

More oats? Emma seemed to be surrounded by lusty men sowing wild oats. But what did that matter? This could be her chance. Her heart had begun to beat very fast. Taking a deep breath, she said, as solemnly as she could, "So Bendridge insists that the young men listen to his lectures on morality, does he?"

"Not exactly, m'lady. He reads them edifying extracts from the Good Book in order to show them a higher path."

Emma doubted her butler's plan would work. Testosterone-fuelled young men would always have an eye to the main chance.

And this might be hers. But she needed to be sure before taking the plunge.

"Did you say that Bendridge required *all* the footmen to attend?" she asked.

"Yes, m'lady. He is most insistent on that."

"Why, that is outrageous. My front door will be left unattended. Any of the thieves and vagabonds of London could enter and rob me."

"Not unattended, m'lady, no. On prayer meeting nights, Filch begins his duty earlier than normal so that the door will be safely guarded."

"Filch does not attend the prayers, then?"

"Um. I fancy," Bailey began carefully, "that Mr Bendridge believes a man of Filch's advanced years does not need quite so many warnings against vice as the younger men."

Emma had to work hard to stop herself from smiling. "I dare say Bendridge is right, Bailey. And I am pleased to learn that someone is guarding my door against intruders. Go now, then, and enjoy your prayer meeting. Will it have begun already?"

Bailey glanced at the clock. "No, m'lady. It wants another ten minutes until it starts."

"Very well. You will be early for once. And you may be sure that I shall not ring for you while you are engaged in God's work. As I said, I shall sit quietly by the fire until Lady Mumford arrives. Until then, I do not wish to be disturbed."

"As you wish, m'lady. If Lady Mumford should arrive while we are all downstairs with Mr Bendridge, Filch will let us know and I can come to find you."

That was no threat, for no Lady Mumford would arrive.

"Good," Emma said. "Oh, and before you go down, perhaps you would lay out my cloak and gloves?" Bailey nodded and bustled about for another few minutes. She laid Emma's velvet evening cloak across the chest at the end of the bed, along with long kid gloves, a fan, and a little gold reticule suspended from a braided golden cord.

"Will there be anything else, m'lady?" Bailey was obviously itching to join the God-fearing folk in the basement.

Julian would have called them "God botherers", Emma remembered suddenly. But such modern-day attitudes to religion were totally out of place in the Regency and Emma must not forget it. It was her duty, as a Regency lady, to ensure she ran a good Christian household.

"No, thank you, Bailey. Enjoy your prayer meeting."

Bailey dropped a curtsey and silently hurried out.

So I have a chance after all. God bless Bendridge and his Christian morality.

She looked at the clock and began to calculate. The prayer meeting would probably last the best part of an hour. Or perhaps longer? Bendridge was a pompous and self-satisfied man. If he believed in his own morality and saw it as his duty to impart it to the lower ranks of his staff, he probably would lecture them at length. What mattered, though, was Filch, down in the hallway. The old man would soon be sitting

132

comfortably in his porter's chair. At night, he was always asleep. But would he be asleep this early in the evening?

There had to be a chance of it. If Emma was lucky, Filch would have a Pavlovian reaction to sitting in the chair. Sit down, sigh, slump, sleep?

It was certainly the only opportunity she would get, so she would have to try. She might even say this chance was heaven-sent.

She would wait fifteen minutes, no longer. Then she would steal down the stairs and attempt to escape through the front door without being spotted.

She crossed to the bed for the velvet cloak. It was beautiful, but not exactly warm. And since she didn't know how far she was to travel in Will's hackney, she needed something sturdier. A few minutes of rummaging in her dressing room produced the very thing – a winter cloak of heavy wool. And with a hood, too.

Emma looked down at her feet in their delicate evening slippers. Not the thing for walking outdoors. She retrieved her walking boots instead – she had taken careful note of where Bailey stored them – and put them on under her lace gown. It looked ridiculous, but it was the only practical solution. She rolled her slippers into a rough ball and stuffed them into the silk reticule. She could swap her boots for her slippers and be properly dressed for any grand occasion she might be taken to.

Moment of truth. Time to go.

The prayer meeting must be well under way by now. She was as safe as she was ever going to be. Donning her cloak, she put an ear to the panel of her door. Silence beyond. She opened the door wide – there must be nothing surreptitious about her behaviour, just in case someone was around to see – and sailed across the landing as though it were the most normal thing in the world to be strolling out in a ballgown and boots.

She sniggered a little nervously to herself. If Filch were to catch her, she would send him off to the basement to fetch something, she decided. Or to take a message. If he were awake, she would have to get him out of the way, somehow, so that she could slip out of the front door. But, if the god of sleep was on her side, she wouldn't have to conjure up any more daft stories.

Drawing her cloak together so that no one would be able to see the ballgown beneath, she began to go quietly down the carpeted staircase. She heard nothing, and no one, until she reached the hall.

Her first step onto the marble floor made a horribly loud crunching noise. She froze. Walking boots and marble floors were not a good mixture.

She listened. There was no sound of movement. If Filch was here, in his porter's chair, he had failed to hear his mistress's arrival. She risked another step. Carefully.

And then she heard it. A delicious little snore.

Bless him. Filch was in his chair. Asleep.

Since he would not see her, Emma could take precautions to ensure she wasn't heard. Rising on tiptoe, she crept across the floor to the door.

Filch's snores were getting louder. Wonderful.

Emma turned the handle and pulled. The door opened silently. Bendridge, master of morality, clearly ran a well-oiled household. It was the work of moments to slip out and close the big black door behind her.

I've made it.

Emma pulled her hood even lower to shadow her face and scampered down the steps to the flagway. Flambeaux were blazing by the doors of two of the houses in the row opposite, but there was no other sign of activity. Holding her cloak close, she scurried along the pavement, round the corner and into the mews behind her own terrace. Sure enough, a hackney was there, waiting. Its driver was slouched in his seat, sucking on a clay pipe, but the moment he saw her, he jumped down, ready to help her in.

"Good evening, yer ladyship," he said. His voice was gruff and he had an accent that Emma couldn't place. "Please to come aboard?" He opened the door and offered a hand. Even through her glove, she could feel the calluses on his fingers.

Emma shivered. She couldn't help herself. "Where are you taking me?"

"Ah. The Cap'n said as I wasn't to blather to yer ladyship."

134

The Cap'n? Was this one of Will's former crew?

"I see." She wouldn't betray her fears by saying any more.

"But he said I were to assure yer ladyship that ye'd be safe wi' me." He nodded several times to emphasise his point. He was quite an old man, by the look of him, though if he'd been before the mast for years, he might not be as old as he looked. He could probably be a fierce man in a fight – all Navy men were battle-hardened, weren't they? – but at the moment he was smiling at her in a very fatherly way.

In for a penny?

Emma climbed up and in. And discovered, to her surprise, that it was not a normal hackney at all.

This one was sumptuously upholstered in black velvet rather than the normal cracked black leather of London cabs. There were fur rugs too, to put over her knees for warmth as she travelled. Emma almost laughed, though she knew her reaction was mainly nerves. Will Allmay was a Casanova of the first order, clearly. He had done a makeover on a standard London cab so that he could convey his paramours around the capital in comfort without risk of discovery. Very clever indeed.

The driver, up on his box, clicked his tongue and gave a swish of his whip. They were off.

She had no idea where she was going. And back in her household, no one even knew that she had left. She could disappear off the face of the earth and no one would have a clue where to start looking for her.

Emma had given herself into Will's keeping. It was now much too late for second thoughts, even though all her experience in modern life had taught her that trust was a mug's game. Will was a rake. And he was going to marry Patience. So what did that make Emma?

The hackney rocked soothingly as it bowled along. Somewhere in the back of Emma's mind, that rebellious inner voice suggested that Will must have had the springs replaced, as well as the upholstery. The blasted man was determined that nothing would be allowed to upset the amiable and obliging mood of his lovers as they were delivered to him.

Like a sultan ordering his concubines to be primped and

pampered before they were carried to his bed, Emma thought, with a jolt. *Is that what I am? Is that what HE is?*

There was no point in going there. She pulled the fur rug up to her waist, leaned back into her corner, and closed her eyes. It would not do to spend too much time and effort wondering about what might have happened during Will's other liaisons.

Or what might be about to happen with hers.

Chapter Sixteen

THE SLOWING OF THE CARRIAGE SHOCKED her awake.

How long had she been asleep? She had no idea. Nor how far she might have come. She peered out, but it was impossible to see where she was. Everything was so very dark.

Ah well. She was probably arriving at wherever it was that Will wanted her to be. No doubt she would see him soon. She took a deep breath. And then several more, trying to slow her unruly pulse. He must not be allowed to think that she was afraid.

But, in truth, she was. A little.

The cab wheels were crunching on gravel now. And it was slowing even more. After what seemed a long approach, but was probably less than a minute or so, the cab swung sharply to the right and stopped. She had finally arrived at her rendezvous with Will. She took a deep breath and swallowed hard.

She was not afraid. She was not.

After all, she was wearing the lace gown. Just a few seconds of isolation and she could disappear from anything, or anyone, that threatened her.

Emma fancied she could smell woodsmoke. But how could she smell smoke in a closed carriage? And yet it was a cheering, homely smell. It conjured up pictures of hearths, and blazing logs, and comfort. Nothing frightening at all. The smell of woodsmoke seemed to be even stronger when the carriage door was opened. Where could it be coming from? She strained to see, but there was almost no light. She fancied she heard a very low voice – Will's voice? – murmur, "You have brought her then?"

"Aye, Cap'n." The driver's voice was right next to the door. He was probably holding it open for her, but Emma could not make him out in the gloom.

Will's voice, less strained now, said, "Thank you, Sanding. I knew you could do it, if anyone could. I need you in the house. I am having trouble with the fire in the saloon, as you can probably smell." He chuckled. "And when you've seen to that, light a fire in the blue bedchamber, will you?"

"Aye, aye, Cap'n."

In the blue bedchamber? Among Emma's tumbling thoughts, two things registered: *bed* and *blue*. Not the Lamb House then? But a *bed*, all the same.

I will not sit in this hackney, trembling like a leaf. I am not in anyone's power. Not even Will Allmay's.

She rose from her seat, gathered up the skirts of her stout cloak and prepared to climb down. She expected Sanding to offer his callused hand to support her, but there, dimly outlined by the flickering carriage lamps, was Will. He simply reached up, put his hands to her waist and lifted her down. His hands lingered and stroked; he was holding her much closer to his body than any man should. But then, who was there to see or to object? Over her shoulder, he said, "Take the cab to the stables, and don't forget those fires. Supper can wait until you've done that. We don't want our guest to be cold."

Emma could hear the man climbing back onto the box behind her. And she could smell the smoke from Will's jacket. It had seemed comforting before. Now she was not so sure.

"My dearest Emma." Will dropped a kiss onto her hair. "Thank you for trusting me enough to come."

"But where am I? Your man would not tell me our destination." At that moment, the hackney started to move, presumably making for the stables. She could just make out the open front door to the house. Above the lintel, a stone lamb was eerily shadowed by the flame of an oil lamp in the hallway. "Oh," Emma breathed. "It *is* the Lamb House. I had not thought we had come so far."

Will smoothed his fingers down the side of her cheek. "I think you may have slept a little, my sweet. My hackney does that, I'm afraid. I did not design it to be so, but I know that it does happen."

And it has rocked many a lover to sleep in the past, has it not, O sultan of concubines? That image, bitter and resentful, rose unbidden in her mind.

But it didn't matter how many women he had had in the past, nor even that Patience was waiting in the wings. Emma was here, in Will's arms, and she realised that he was all she cared about.

It was not at all rational, she knew. Her emotions were seesawing about – anxiety, fear, panic, and then blind lust and longing. One moment she was afraid of being in his power, and the next, it was the only thing she wanted. Love was an arbitrary god. And that was the trouble. She loved Will. When she was not with him, she could see all the risks: she was well aware of the power imbalance between them, that men in the Regency ruled everything, while women had no status at all. But when she was with him, all her fears just melted away.

Besides, she told herself soothingly, *what has Will ever done to suggest that he might control or coerce me? Nothing at all. He has even promised, more than once, that I am to set the rules for our relationship.*

She leaned into him, allowing his warmth to enfold her. Her last coherent thought was: *I don't understand any of this. I love him. I trust him. I refuse to be afraid.*

With his arm round her waist, he led her up the steps and into the house, closing the door behind them and shutting out some of the cold. "I'm afraid it is not very warm and you can probably smell that I have made a pretty poor fist of lighting the fire in the saloon."

In the back of Emma's damped-down rational mind, a question poked up. "Surely the servants w—?"

"The servants are not here," he said, before she could finish her question. "There is only Sanding, my Navy steward, and the grooms in the stables. Everyone else has been given a holiday. I promised you discretion."

"And you keep your promises."

"Indeed. As do you, my darling Emma. I fear your supper tonight will be whatever Sanding can put together, though he can be a fair cook, as I discovered during our many years together on board ship. Supper may have to be delayed, however. I want your bedchamber to be warm first."

Emma felt herself blushing. "The *blue* bedchamber?" she said uncertainly.

"Ah, you have put your finger on the nub of things, my sweet. I am hoping, fervently hoping, I should say, that you will agree to share my bed; but a lady must have a bedchamber of her own, to dress in and to retreat to, if she wishes. So I have had another bedchamber prepared, just for you. It happens to be blue."

"Prepared just for me?" Given Will's reputation, surely any number of other females might have been installed in the blue bedchamber?

"I see that you doubt me, Emma. Shame on you, love. I have brought no other lover to this house. And the blue bedchamber was created especially for you. No other woman will use it, I can promise you that."

No one? Not even your wife? The question rose instantly to her lips but died before the words were spoken. The love in his face was so strong, and so all-embracing, that she could not resist its pull. The hateful words were vaporised, like morning mist in sunlight.

He led her into the saloon. Sure enough, his fire was a failure. It was giving out much more smoke than heat.

"Let me see to that," Emma said with a quick smile. Fires, she could do.

"No, you—"

But he was too late. She had thrown off her cloak, stripped off her gloves and was kneeling by the hearth, tending to the logs and then plying the bellows. In a very few minutes, the fire was drawing beautifully. What little smoke it produced was going up the chimney, as it should, and the flames were licking eagerly at the wood. Pleased with having achieved something useful, Emma rose, dusting off her hands.

Will was gazing down at her, with a glint of amusement in his eyes. "A lady of many talents," he said admiringly.

"A lady who needs to wash her hands," Emma said, holding out her dirty fingers for him to see. "And to change into her evening slippers, too," she added, poking a booted toe out from under her lace skirts.

He grinned at the absurd picture she made, in priceless lace and stout boots. "Come than. Let me take you upstairs. I'm afraid it will have to be the master bedchamber for the moment. Yours has no fire yet."

The *green* bedchamber. Where she'd first set eyes on Will. Oh well. What was it she'd told herself at the start of this evening's adventure? *In for a penny?*

~ ~ ~

The bedchamber was almost exactly as she remembered – the fire blazing behind its screen, the velvet-hung bed and windows, the silver candelabra. But this time, there was no bath and the candles were unlit.

And Will was wearing far too many clothes.

Emma's mouth went dry.

Will busied himself with lighting the candles on the mantelpiece and on the table by the bedside. He did not light the others, she noticed. It made the huge room seem less grand and intimidating. He crossed to the dresser and poured water into the china basin for her. "It is not hot, I am afraid, but at least there is soap, and a towel."

Emma nodded and joined him. She was incapable of speech. Automatically, she picked up the soap and washed her hands. Will was holding the towel for her. Like a servant. She took it, nodding her thanks. She still couldn't speak.

A moment later, he was kneeling at her feet, unlacing her boots and easing them off. His fingers lingered on the back of one heel, not stroking, just warming. But intimate, as if he were trying to learn every bone and sinew of her. "Your slippers, my lady?" he said softly.

"Oh. Oh, yes." She fumbled into her reticule and eventually managed to extract the sorry bundle of evening slippers.

He laughed, low in his throat, but said nothing about the pitiful state of them. He smoothed them out and caressed them, one by one, onto her feet. She thought her toes tingled under his fingers.

He rose to his feet. "Emma?" There was a question in his voice; and a slight tremor, too. "Are you quite well? You look a little pale, all of a sudden."

She struggled to clear her throat and managed to say, "I am quite well, thank you, Will. But this room—"

He smiled then. He knew. "It brings back memories?"

She closed her eyes and nodded.

He put a hand on her upper arm. The lightest of touches, neither possessive nor controlling. That gentle caress shivered down to the soles of her slippered feet. "I hope they are good memories," he whispered, in a voice that was as rich and dark as molten chocolate. And twice as tempting.

She didn't dare to open her eyes. She nodded again.

He drew her, unresisting, into his arms. "Oh, my love," he said softly, into her hair. He did not kiss her. He simply held her close against his body. And that was far more arousing than any number of passionate kisses would have been. Her head was resting against his breast, breathing in the scents of smoke, and soap, and warm living man. She could feel the beat of his heart, as loud as a military drum, it seemed, but steady, not tripping, nor racing away. It was so loud, so mind-blowing, that she was barely conscious of what her own heart was doing in response. It ought to have been pounding with desire. Or misgivings, for she did not know whether to trust in the love he professed so strongly. But somehow, held so close against his body, so safe, so enfolded, she was shielded from all her earlier doubts. She discovered that her own heart was beating in a calm, steady, contented rhythm. Because she was home. In his arms, where she belonged.

The last hint of tension flowed out of her.

After a long time, he moved to stroke her cheek with the back of his hand. The lightest of touches. Slow, soothing strokes. "Your skin is so soft. Beautiful. Too delicate to be real, especially against my rough sailor's hands."

She moaned softly in her throat.

He continued to stroke. The rhythm was intoxicating.

She managed to groan out his name. She wanted to ask him to kiss her, but the words would not come.

He rested his cheek on her hair. "Oh, my love, you cannot know how very much I need you. And want you." His words were barely audible. "The last time we made love in this room, I failed to satisfy you, I know. I will do better, if you will only give me a chance." She thought there was anguish in his voice.

Guilt lanced through her. She jerked her head back. She needed to see his face. "No, no. No, Will, you did not."

"But you ran from me. If I had given you what you needed— If I had satisfied you, you would have stayed, surely?"

She could see pain – and longing? – in his eyes. It hurt her, too. "No," she said firmly. "That was not the reason I left you."

"Why, then?"

Panic flooded her. He deserved an answer, but what could she possibly say? If she told him the truth, he would think her mad. Somehow words started to tumble out. "It was a mistake. I was— I was confused. But not because— When we made love, Will, it was wonderful. It was fulfilling. It was everything I've ever wanted. I left because— Because I was confused about what I was feeling. Not because I was dissatisfied. Believe me, I was not."

He looked unconvinced. "If you give me another chance, my love, I can show you how you can have the joy and the passion you deserve."

"I had it before, Will. With you." She smiled up into his eyes, willing him to believe. She fancied she might even be succeeding. Putting a hand to his cheek, she murmured softly, "But I would gladly have it again."

It was enough. He lifted her into his arms and carried her across to the great bed where he laid her down as though she had been made of the most delicate and precious porcelain. Then, for several seconds, he stood by the bed, gazing down at her. She thought there was wonder in his face. For her? She was not an object for awed admiration, like some rare sculpture on display. She was not marble. She was hot and alive. And she longed for this man.

She lifted a hand to beckon him down to her.

It broke the spell that had held him back. He dragged off his coat and let it drop. Then his waistcoat and cravat. His shoes thumped to the floor, too. But he seemed to hesitate.

She had the power here, it seemed. The greatest lover in London was waiting for a surer signal. From her.

It was the greatest gift he could have given her. And she knew now, for certain, that this love was right. For her, as well as for him. She reached out both arms to him. "Come, Will. Come to bed. I need you. Come to me now."

And then he was beside her and she was in his arms. First he removed her sapphires and laid them aside. "Beautiful," he murmured, "but hard. I want to uncover your softness, Emma."

Lace, and underthings, and finally stockings were peeled from her body, slowly and deliberately, with tiny kisses on her skin as each tie was undone. Emma had never imagined anything could be quite so sensuous. Her skin was glowing wherever his lips had touched. Even taking the pins from her hair was an arousing process, for he unwound each curl in turn, with the utmost relish, before laying them reverently on the pillow. He stroked the final curl across her bare breast with a deep sigh of satisfaction.

She groaned. She couldn't stop herself. She was floating in a sea of feeling, but she was floating alone. She needed more. She needed Will.

He was still wearing far too many clothes. She reached for his shirt.

He chuckled, low in his chest. She could sense the vibration under her hand. "Let me, love," he murmured. "It will be quicker that way, I promise." He tore off his shirt and tossed it on the floor. Breeches and stockings followed. In moments, he was as naked as she. And as beautiful as before.

Emma caught her breath at the sight of his hard, aroused body. There was a long white scar on the side of his chest that she had not noticed that first time. She touched a finger tip to it. When he did not recoil, she drew her finger slowly down its length. "You were wounded?"

"A long time ago. My first boarding. I was very young and not very skilled with a sword. I was lucky to survive."

She put her hand flat on the scar and closed her eyes. *Lucky to survive*. He might have died. And she would not have had this. "Kiss me, Will. Please."

He did. But it was not her mouth he kissed.

He started with the tender skin on the inside of her ankles. She shivered, but he persisted, kissing his way up the inside of one calf, and then the other. By the time he reached her inner thigh, her whole body was quivering with desire and her hands were fisted in the bedclothes. He must have felt her reaction, known what it meant, but he refused to be rushed. He kept on kissing his way up her body, inch by torturing inch, and muttering soft endearments in between. Emma thought she would die of longing if he did not take her soon. "Will," she pleaded. "Will, please."

"Soon," he whispered, kissing his way even closer to the core of her. Then, even more softly, "Now, Emma." He kissed her – there – and her world exploded.

She thought she cried out. A moment later he was with her, fully, sheathed in her quivering body and kissing her mouth with all the passion she could desire.

She came again as soon as he began to move within her. Her body seemed to be melting around him. As if she were being consumed by scorching flames. Her last coherent thought was to wonder why she was no longer afraid.

~ ~ ~

"This time, I shall not let you run from me, my love," he murmured, drawing her into a snug embrace and pulling the covers over them both.

She nestled even closer. Her whole body was glowing with a delicious languor. She didn't think she could run, even if she wanted to.

"You will not, will you?"

She took a long breath. Her breasts seemed to swell against his heated skin.

"Mmm." It was almost a groan. "That is delightful. And most inviting." He nibbled the lobe of her ear and she yelped. He laughed softly. "Not an invitation I intend to refuse.

Though I plan to take my time over certain parts of your body that I have yet to explore." He nibbled again. Her earlobe seemed to be linked to the very core of her. She felt the pull, deep in her belly, and the warmth began to grow all over again. She wanted this man. So very much.

He stroked a single finger down her cheek. "You have not answered my question, Emma." He pulled her even more tightly against his body with his free hand.

He was going to insist on an answer. But she could not promise to stay. She belonged in another world, another time. Though, at this moment, here in his bed and in his arms, there was nowhere else she wanted to be. She swallowed hard and leant her forehead against his chest. She did not dare to look into his face, even though she was not about to lie to him.

"You know I cannot stay with you, Will. Lady Emma Groatster has a fragile reputation to protect and you are—" She broke off, unable to find words that would not be insulting.

"And I am a rake, a philanderer, a destroyer of reputations, am I not?" he muttered bitterly. "It is no longer true, not since I found you, my love, but it seems that no one will believe it." He took a deep breath. "Not even you."

That sounded very like despair. And it was heart-rending.

There was only one thing to say. She lifted her head and fixed her eyes on his. "I love you, Will. There. Now I have said it. I was confused before, when I ran away from you. It is no longer so, I promise. But if we are discovered to be lovers, my reputation will be in tatters. You will always be accepted wherever you may wish to go, for you are a man, but I..."

He stroked her hair. "I know, love. And it is unfair of me to torment you with my unreasonable demands. I promise you, most faithfully, that I will do everything in my power to protect your reputation."

"Thank you. I know you will. And I promise I will not run from you. Not again. But you must allow me to leave when I feel I must. Please, Will. Can you not agree to that?"

He made an unintelligible noise in his throat. It might have been agreement, but if it was, it was unwillingly given.

Emma had to try to explain. Part of it, at least.

146

"Sometimes, being with you..." she began. "It overwhelms me." That was no more than the truth.

It seemed he was beginning to understand, for he said, gently, "As you do me, Emma. I will try my best to lessen your fears. And I promise I will not rail at you when you have to leave me." He drew her head down so that her mouth was only a breath away from his. "Provided," he added with a wicked grin, "that you do not try to do so tonight."

Chapter Seventeen

THE STRIKING OF A CLOCK WOKE her.

Three o'clock in the morning? Emma sat bolt upright in bed and discovered she was alone. What's more, someone had dressed her in a filmy nightgown that had wrapped itself around her legs as she slept.

She could tell she was no longer in Will's bed, but it was too dark to see anything clearly in this new room. The fire in the grate had burned low. There was just enough light to make out the dark shapes of the furniture. She slipped her feet from under the warm bedclothes and crept across the carpet. In spite of her caution, the floorboards shifted and creaked under her feet like live things. But it couldn't be helped. She needed light.

She touched a spill to the embers in the grate and lit two candles. That was better. She raised one to look around. Yes, it was a blue bedchamber, clearly the one that Will had promised as her private retreat. Her clothes had been laid neatly on the chest at the end of the bed. Her heavy cloak was draped across the back of a chair. Even her boots and slippers were there, waiting to be put on. But she couldn't possibly dress by herself. Not well enough to pass muster with Bailey.

She put her candle on the bedside table and slumped down onto the side of the bed. Her loose hair tickled the side of her chin and she brushed it aside impatiently.

148

That was another thing she could not do by herself.

But she must do *something*. Her household would be in uproar when the servants discovered she was missing. She had to get back, and soon, even if she arrived so dishevelled that the servants suspected she had been ravished.

She took her candle across to the dressing table and scrutinised herself in the mirror there. *Ravished* was exactly the right word. Willingly ravished. She looked like a woman who had been well and truly loved. She closed her eyes for a moment, remembering.

Their lovemaking had been too special for words – slow and languorous, then urgent and demanding, but always completely fulfilling. And when she had fallen asleep, deliciously exhausted, he must have dressed her in this frivolous wisp of silk and carried her here. Had he laid out all her clothes as well? Quite probably, for who else was there to do it, when all the servants had been sent away? She remembered how delicately Will had removed her boots. He was capable of many surprising things.

Except, she remembered with a chuckle, lighting fires. But she supposed there was not much call for that particular skill aboard ship.

The woman in the mirror was smiling a secretive smile. Emma shook her head at her own reflection. "It's all very well," she whispered, "but how do I get out of this?"

There was one obvious way. If she were to put on the lace gown and then take it off again, she would be transported back to the modern day. But Will would assume she had run away. And she had promised him that she would not. She sighed out a long breath. It had been stupid to make that promise, but promises had to be kept.

She thought she heard a knock at the door. Surely not at three in the morning? She paused, listening for movement beyond her door. The knocking came again. Crossing to the bedchamber door, she said softly, "Who is there?"

"Will."

Who else would it be?

She opened the door to find him standing on the threshold. Fully dressed. And looking more ridiculously handsome than ever. His eyes widened at the sight of her in nothing but her filmy nightgown, even though he must have chosen it himself. Embarrassed by his frank appraisal, she instinctively crossed her arms across her breasts, but his gaze then drifted down to the junction of her thighs. She resisted the urge to try to conceal any more of her body. He had seen it all, and kissed almost every inch of it, so why should she feel shy now?

"Forgive me," he said. He had coloured a very little. And his gaze was now firmly fixed on her face. "I had thought you would be dressed. I heard you moving about."

"I had not thought I was so heavy-footed."

"Ah." He smiled. "You are not, my love. But the floor of this room creaks. I have been waiting downstairs, listening for the creaks, to know when you got out of bed."

"Oh. A nightingale floor." Emma spoke without thinking.

"A what?"

"A nightingale floor. It's what the Japanese call deliberately squeaky floors. They use them in ancient palaces, as protection against intruders."

"Do they?" he sounded astonished. "How very inventive. And where did you come by that fascinating titbit of information?"

"Um. Do you know, I can't remember? Someone must have told it to me. It is of no matter." She paused, realising how clever he had been. He deserved her wrath. She drew herself up and narrowed her eyes. "It was calculating of you, sir, to provide me with such a bedchamber so that you could spy on me."

He had the grace to look a little sheepish. "Well, given how often you have run from me in the past, you will perhaps admit I had cause."

"I promised I would not run from you again, Will."

"Indeed you did. So, if you would prefer, I will have a different chamber prepared for your next visit. One without nightingales."

Emma shook her head. "I'm not sure there can be a next visit. My household will become very suspicious if I keep creeping out whenever they are at prayers."

"Is *that* what you did?"

"Yes. And I doubt I will manage to do it again."

"Then we must find a better solution for your escaping problem."

"At this moment, I'd rather find a solution to my unescaping problem."

"I beg your pardon?"

"I have to go home, Will. And in my present state—" she lifted some of her tangled hair and let it fall back onto her bare shoulder "—I'm not likely to manage that very successfully, am I?"

He grinned. "Just at the moment, you look like the most delicious invitation. That nightgown is even more enticing than I thought when I bought it."

Emma glanced sideways at her reflection in the mirror. That nightgown hid nothing. She could see the dark peaks of her breasts pushing against the sheer silk. She was becoming aroused, simply by being with him. And Will could see it, too.

She fought for control over her wayward body. Partly in desperation, she grabbed her heavy cloak from the chair and swung it round her shoulders. "I cannot think straight when you are looking at me like that, Will," she said.

"Well, you must admit that you made a lusciously tempting picture."

"I cannot afford to tempt you any more, Will. I must go home. It is already well after three in the morning. How shall I ever manage it?"

"I have been thinking about that, my love," he said, taking her in his arms and nestling her head against his shoulder. In spite of what he had just said, it was more of a comforting hug than a prelude to another adventure between the sheets. He stroked her hair back from her cheek. "I had a few ideas that might help, while I was waiting for you to wake up. I have a plain carriage here. You can return home in that. It can deliver you to your door and no one will recognise it as mine. I suggest you wear your evening slippers, though, rather than those boots."

"But I can't leave my boots here. Bailey will notice they are missing."

"True. I will put them up in a valise for you to take with

you. You may have it carried to your bedchamber once you arrive home."

That was a good idea. If she opened it when she was alone, she could sneak the boots back into their place. But there was a flaw in his plan. "How does it come about that I left with Lady Mumford and I returned in someone else's carriage, carrying a valise? There are bound to be questions."

"Well, I had the beginnings of an idea there, too. What if you met an old friend, a lady, needless to say, someone you had not seen for many years? She invited you to her house and you talked for hours and lost track of time. So now she is sending you home in her carriage."

"Hmm. Maybe." Emma's mind was whirring. "Yes, maybe."

"And perhaps you could visit this friend again, and stay a few days?" he added hopefully. "This friend might even send her plain carriage to fetch you?"

Will was indeed a conniving lover, but his calculations were falling a bit short here. "It won't do, Will. I am a woman of means. Why should I allow myself to be taken to and fro in someone else's carriage? And staying is impossible. My hostess would always expect me to bring my own abigail. I cannot take Bailey to a meeting with a lover."

"Perhaps your hostess has not enough room to accommodate an abigail?"

She shook her head again. "It won't work. If this hostess can afford to keep her own carriage, she can certainly afford to find a bed for a visiting lady's maid."

He sighed. "I am not doing very well, am I?"

"No, and nor am I. We are neither of us making a great fist of this tissue of lies we are trying to create. It would be better to keep it simple. Wait. I may have an idea," she added with a smile. "What if my long-lost friend were an invalid?"

"That's good."

"We were at school together," Emma went on, thinking aloud. "No, no, that won't do. Bailey would know all my friends from school. She has been with me for ever. No, this has to be a friend of a friend. And her name is— Hmm. She cannot be titled. Much too easy to discover where she lives.

She must be a reclusive Mrs Something-or-other. Another widow, I think. She is too ill to venture out and keeps a very small household. No, that won't do either. Why on earth would she keep a carriage if she never goes out? Oh this is impossible. I am tying myself in knots."

He stroked her hair again.

"I cannot think clearly when you do that, Will. In any case, I must dress."

"Let me help you," he said with a smile that began to melt her insides.

She pushed him away. "I don't think that would be a good idea. Your fingers excel at undressing a lady. I am not at all sure about the reverse."

He looked a little guilty, for once.

"Give me a few minutes alone, Will, so that I may at least put on my petticoats. I will need your help with some of my fastenings, however."

"And your hair? I cannot say that I have much experience as a hairdresser."

"I will pin it up as best I can." She looked round at the chest and then at the dressing table. "Do you know what happened to my hairpins?"

"Ah. I had forgot." He plunged his fingers into his coat pocket and pulled out a handful of pins. And her sapphires. "I have them here." He laid his haul down on the bare dressing table.

"Thank you." The jewels she could deal with. But her hair was a real problem. "Is there a hairbrush? Or a comb?"

"I will fetch them for you," he said, making for the door, "while you make yourself rather, er, more presentable to the world."

The door closed behind him. Just as Emma was starting to take off her cloak, the door opened again, a little way. Enough to allow Will to poke his head round and ogle her. "I should add that, looking as you do now, you are much *more* than presentable, my lady," he said, with a grin.

Emma cast about for something to throw at him. But by the time she turned back, empty-handed, the door had closed and he was gone. Just as well, for his wicked leer had made her laugh as he must have known it would. And laughter was by far the best way of getting a woman into bed. How many other women had he used it on?

She would lock the door. Not because she was afraid of him – she was not, not any more – but because she wanted to be in control of her own state of undress before she saw him again. She crossed to the door and found there was no key. And no bolt either. The blasted man had chosen a bedchamber with a nightingale floor so that he could keep tabs on her. And she couldn't even lock him out.

Well, she could do something about that. She picked up a hardbacked chair and wedged it under the door handle. That would show him.

On the other hand, what made her think he would enter without her permission? He had knocked and waited before.

No time for that. She must dress as best she could. She threw off her cloak and let the filmy silk nightgown drop from her shoulders. *I hope this is new,* she thought. *I would hate to think that one of Will's other lovers had worn it before me.* It seemed unlikely, though. He had gone to a great deal of trouble to prepare this bedchamber for her – for her alone, he maintained – so why would he not buy a new nightgown as well? He had said something of the sort, hadn't he?

She sneaked a quick look at her naked body in the glass. There were some tiny bruises on one breast. Love bites. She remembered those. They had been most arousing at the time. She fancied that Will had one or two on his own body, though she could not quite remember all the things that she had done to him. Or he to her. Her nipples were hardening at the memory of his caresses.

I must be practical. I have to get dressed and turn myself into something presentable so that I can go home.

With that, she dragged on her shift and then her stays and petticoats. Next came her stockings. Someone had smoothed them out carefully. Her garters had been placed neatly beside them. In the space of a few moments, she was dressed, all but her lace gown and her hair.

She stepped into the gown and put her arms through the puff sleeves. The simple act of putting it on made her smile. It was such a precious, magical thing. She reached round to tie a loose bow at the back of the neckline. That would do for the moment. When Will returned, he could help to tighten her stays and neaten the fastenings of her gown. With luck, he wouldn't bc too tempted in the process. And in the meantime, she would make a start on her hair, even without a brush and comb.

She lit more candles. That was better. Now she might see what she was doing. The floor by the dressing table creaked loudly as she went to sit down at the mirror. Goodness, what a racket. She would certainly demand a different retreat if she ever came again. The noise from these shifting floors would drive anyone mad.

Shifting floors? She took a moment to gaze round the room, telling herself to imagine it without any of the furniture. Would she recognise it if it were bare?

Yes, she would. She had been in it before, with Geraldine, the Lamb House manager. Her blue bedchamber was the one that was out of bounds to visitors because it would require a fortune to restore its shifting, and dangerous, floors.

A new idea poked its head up.

Emma put one of the lighted candles on the hearth and started to feel around under the rug. One of the floorboards was definitely promising. But her fingernails weren't strong enough. She needed—

Regency hairpins have their uses, she decided, as she bent one into a serviceable hook and knelt down again.

It worked. The end of the floorboard came up enough for her to peer underneath. There was a nice dry little space, plenty big enough for anything she might want to hide in it. Once the board was put back, no one would have the slightest idea that it had ever been moved.

She did a little victory dance. Luck was definitely on her side tonight.

Chapter Eighteen

EMMA MANAGED TO PIN UP HER tousled hair before Will came back with the promised brush and comb. There was definitely a lot to be said for natural curls, she decided. Even using only her fingers as a comb, the effect was not bad at all, although it was nothing like the elegant confection that Bailey had created earlier. For safety, Emma decided, she would keep her hood up until she reached her own room. Then she would drag her fingers through her hair, pulling out most of the pins and complaining that they were making her head ache. With a little more luck – Emma was already deeply in debt to Lady Luck tonight – Bailey would not have a chance to see the state of her mistress's hair before it tumbled down her back.

She clasped the sapphire pendant round her neck. That was the best she could do. She crossed her fingers and hoped she would pass in dim candlelight.

Footsteps outside. Will? Oh dear.

She raced across to the door to remove the chair. He mustn't find out she had done that. Though, since this room was to be her permanent retreat in this house, she was entitled to demand privacy. She would certainly ask him for a door key.

"Goodness, that is splendid," he said as he came in with a brush and comb in his hand. "How did you do that?"

"Female instincts." She grinned. "Desperation helped."

He laughed. "Do you need any help from me, my lady desperate?"

Emma turned her back. "Yes. Can you pull my stays tighter, please? And then do up my gown?" She heard him swallow hard. He made no move to comply. "Quickly, please, Will," she urged, hoping he would resist the urge to touch her skin. "I really must be on my way home or I'll never hear the last of Bailey's sermonising."

That made him laugh again. "She dares, does she?" he asked, starting to tighten her laces. He sounded fairly relaxed, she decided gratefully.

She needed to prolong this easier mood. "She dares, all right," Emma said lightly. "She admires my sanctimonious butler for the care he takes to discharge his Christian duty as the moral guardian of my household. She enjoys his sermons and prayer meetings." She forced a laugh. "So when she sees me meeting an unsuitable gentleman in the park, she makes her disapproval more than plain."

He had finished with her stays and was working on the fastenings of her gown. That was a lot safer. Emma's tension lessened a little. "A servant who has known one from one's cradle is bound to be outspoken, of course."

"Of course," he agreed. "And no matter what she says or does, you could not dismiss her, could you?"

Emma shook her head.

"What about your earrings?" he said, glancing across at the dressing table. "Surely Bailey will expect you to be wearing them?"

"I have them safely in my reticule." To emphasise the point, Emma picked it up and dropped it back onto the dressing table. It landed with a satisfying clunk. "I shall say I took them off because they were tangling in my hair. She won't be surprised. She was fussing with them earlier."

"Good. We seem to have covered everything." His gaze lingered on the neckline of her lace gown. It was not outrageously low cut; only a little of her bosom was on display. "Including you, sadly," he added with his infuriating grin.

"You go too far, sir," she said primly.

157

"I fear I do not go far enough." He reached for her cloak and wrapped it round her shoulders. "Sanding will drive the carriage back to town. Much as I should like to accompany you, I must think about your reputation."

And my sanity, Emma thought. *What would happen with just the two of us in a closed carriage for all those miles?*

His smile told her he was reading her mind. But he said only, "Let me escort you downstairs to your carriage, m'lady."

With that, he picked up the battered valise containing her walking boots, and opened the door that would lead her back to Lady Emma Groatster's respectable London life.

~ ~ ~

Emma did not sleep on the journey back to London in spite of the comforts of Will's carriage and the hot brick at her feet. She had more important things to do, working out the story of the invalid friend. She had decided that the lady would be a mere Mrs Smith, married young and widowed at an early age. Mrs Smith, sadly, suffered from a wasting disease which meant that she had difficulty sleeping, so she had been very eager to welcome Emma, even in the early hours of the morning. The poor lady could rarely leave her house because of her infirmities. But, on her very good days, Mrs Smith enjoyed a drive in the sunshine. As a result, she could never bring herself to dispense with her carriage. She had insisted on using it to send Emma home after the pleasant hours they had spent catching up on old times and old friends. And she was equally insistent, for the sake of exercising her horses as much as anything else, that Emma should use the Smith carriage to visit her in the future. Emma had not had the heart to refuse an old friend. And she had promised to go again soon.

Would the story convince Bailey?

First things first. Emma had to get into the house and fool Bailey about where she had been and what she had been doing.

She must not take a bath until the love bites had gone, she realised. For if the abigail saw those, she would know at once what her Lady Emma had been up to. She might guess anyway, for she was very sharp. But she was loyal to a fault. She would never betray Emma's secrets.

158

In private, however, her moralising might well become unbearable.

It was still dark when the carriage reached London. It was too early for heavy traffic, but Emma soon recognised the difference in the air. The fresh country smells of trees and damp rich soil had been replaced by less pleasant odours: dung, and decaying rubbish, punctuated by the occasional acrid note of burning flambeaux. She would soon be home. And she was ready.

The carriage slowed to round a corner. A few moments later, it came to a stop. Emma gathered herself together, pulling up her hood to shadow her face. The carriage door opened a little way. Sanding's voice said, "Shall I ring the doorbell for ye, m'lady?"

"No, no," Emma replied in an urgent whisper. Then, in a more normal voice, "I do not wish to wake the household at this hour."

Sanding pulled the door wide and offered his hand.

Emma needed a free hand for her skirts. She set the valise on the floor by the door and allowed Sanding to help her down. Turning to retrieve the bag of boots, she noticed that there was a second man on the box, holding the reins. "Oh," she gasped, surprised. "I had not expected a groom as well. But I suppose someone has to mind your horses while you help me down."

"This late, Cap'n said as 'twas safer with two, m'lady."

"Oh, but—" Surely Will had not wanted any of his grooms to know who his visitor was? This groom now had precise details of where she lived.

"Not to worry, m'lady," Sanding said in a fatherly way. "Yon lad won't talk none. He be dumb."

She glanced up at the groom again. He was slouched comfortably in his place, minding his horses and paying no attention at all to the passenger. Possibly a simpleton as well as dumb? He looked a big lumbering fellow under his old-fashioned tricorne hat. It warmed her to think that Will had given employment to such an unfortunate. It would have been an act of pure kindness.

"Your valise, m'lady."

159

"Thank you, Sanding. You may leave me now." She straightened her shoulders and mounted the steps. She didn't look back, though there was no noise of the carriage driving off. Sanding was probably under orders from Will to see her safely inside the house first. She turned the door handle and pushed gently. It opened as noiselessly as before. Emma prayed the sudden inrush of cold spring air would not wake Filch from his slumbers.

She slid inside. Yes, she could hear snoring. Luck seemed to be on her side. She turned to close the door, concentrating hard to avoid making any noise. The carriage had not left. Sanding had climbed back onto the box but had not yet taken the reins from the big groom, who did not appear to have moved at all. Sanding was looking over his shoulder, watching the door. He seemed to be speaking quietly to his companion all the while. Probably reassuring the simpleton that they would soon be home, Emma decided. She smiled up at the old steward – though, in the dark, he probably did not see – and pressed the door closed.

Filch's contented snoring continued without pause. Emma looked round quickly. She needed a light. There were two small oil lamps burning, one by the door, the other on the table at the foot of the stairs, along with a pair of unlit bedroom candles. She would take the lamp, rather than lighting a candle, for, in addition to the reticule dangling from her wrist, she would have to manage the valise and her skirts up two flights of stairs. It was much too difficult to shield a flickering candle as well. She crept across the marble hall, less concerned about noise this time since she was wearing evening slippers rather than boots, picked up the lamp and scurried up the stairs.

She made it safely up the second flight and into her bedchamber, closing the door behind her. She leant against it and let out the breath she seemed to have been holding since the moment she arrived in the front hall. She had been so anxious not to be detected. But she had made it. So far.

First things first. She put the lamp on the table by the door and glanced around. Phew. No sign of Bailey. Emma stuffed the valise under the bed and pushed it well out of sight. Her

160

abigail had the ears of a cat. She might appear at any moment, even though it must be nearly five in the morning.

Next, her hair. Emma tiptoed across to the wing chair by the fireplace and sank into it without stopping to take off her cloak. Now for the next part of her performance, even though she had no audience. She tossed back her hood and began to push her fingers through her hair, right down to her scalp, groaning theatrically as she did so. Hairpins flew in all directions. A couple pinged on the hearthstone. Most dropped silently onto the carpet, or the chair. She closed her eyes and leant back. She had done it. She groaned again, for good measure.

"You have the headache, m'lady?"

Emma jerked upright. Bailey was standing in the open doorway to the dressing room. She looked, as ever, neat as a pin. Did the woman never go to bed?

"Oh, Bailey. You should not have waited up."

"It is my duty, m'lady," Bailey said firmly. "And I was comfortable enough. There is a chair in the dressing room."

"But no fire," Emma said, concerned. "You must have been cold. It is quite cold, even here." She gestured towards the hearth and the dying embers.

"Let me ring for a maid to make up the fire."

"No," Emma said sharply. "There is no need. You may help me to undress and I shall go straight to bed." She yawned. For effect. "I am tired."

"And you have the headache."

"It will pass. Something about that hairstyle – so many pins – it was uncomfortable. I could not wait to pull them all out."

Bailey sniffed. "I am sorry that my work caused you pain."
Oh dear.

"It was probably because we talked so late, Mrs Smith and I."

"Mrs Smith?"

"A chance encounter with an old friend. I will tell you all about her in the morning, Bailey." She yawned again. "For the present, I am much in need of my bed."

Bailey harrumphed and began to undo the cloak strings at

Emma's throat, revealing the sapphire pendant. She stopped suddenly, her eyes widening. "Oh, goodness. Your eardrops, m'lady. Do not say you have lost them?"

"What? Oh, no. They were forever becoming tangled in my hair. I took them off and put them in my reticule." She allowed Bailey to remove the sapphire pendant from around her neck. While the abigail was setting the gold collar aside, Emma started to rummage in her bulging reticule. "That's odd," she said. "I remember putting them in here. I know I did." With a grunt of exasperation, she pulled the drawstring wide and upended her reticule into her lap. Handkerchieves, vinaigrette, a packet of pins, a tiny pocket book and other feminine necessaries tumbled out. And among them, a reassuring gleam of blue. "Ah, there we are. I knew I had remembered aright."

"But, m'lady, there is only one."

Chapter Nineteen

SAFELY TRANSPORTED BACK TO THE MUSEUM research room, Emma smiled to herself and patted the shredded lace gratefully as the sounds of St Mary's bells died away.

She should put the gown back into the costume store, but first she would go up to the staff room to make a celebratory cup of coffee, she decided. She deserved a reward. It hadn't been too difficult to persuade Bailey that the widowed Mrs Smith, friend of a friend, but with *so* many interests in common with Lady Emma Groatster, was real. The matter of the missing earring had taken longer, but Bailey had finally been reassured that her mistress could only have dropped it at Mrs Smith's house. That tale had the advantage of being true, too. Mostly. Lady Emma had refused to allow any fuss to be made. She would not permit her servants to disturb poor invalid Mrs Smith, and on a Sunday, too, with enquiries about a lost bauble. She would certainly be able to retrieve her earring on her next visit to her new friend.

Which – she had added very firmly – would be very soon.

Emma grinned at the memory. Poor Bailey had been thoroughly hoodwinked. The abigail hadn't even discovered the little valise until it was safely empty. It provoked a few questions, but Emma's cover story was well prepared and had the advantage of being simple. Mrs Smith, an avid reader, had asked Emma to lend her some books that she might enjoy. The valise was the invalid's, sent for that very purpose, so that Emma's people did not have to fuss around with brown paper and string.

Don't get too cocky, modern Emma told herself sternly. *There's plenty that can go wrong, especially with someone as sharp as Bailey.*

But, deep inside, she didn't think it would. She and Will – or rather, Regency Lady Emma and Will – were meant to be together.

She was still feeling euphoric an hour later as she drove home. She put her buoyant mood down to the combination of good sex and good luck. What more could she possibly want?

More of Will Allmay. She knew now why the Regency ladies touted him as the best lay in London. They were dead right.

She grinned at herself in the rear-view mirror, turned on the car radio and sang at the top of her voice all the rest of the way to her front door.

~ ~ ~

Emma spent most of the evening on the internet: first on the mundane, but potentially vital, task of finding a riding school where she could learn to ride side-saddle; second on the trickier task of trying to track down a Regency lady called Emma Groatster.

She succeeded on the first, but failed miserably on the second. There was no one at all with the surname Groatster. She tried various spelling permutations, but none of them worked, either. And she already knew that there was no Will Allmay in the records.

Yet they had both been at the Lamb House. So why couldn't she find them?

She could think of only two possible explanations, and both of them were seriously scary. What if she had dreamed it all? What if her "translations" to the Regency had never actually happened? Except in her ridiculous imagination?

If that was so, she was certainly losing her marbles. She should see a doctor.

But it couldn't have been all in my imagination. I brought back Will's dressing-room key. It's in my pocket. And it is definitely real.

That left the most far-fetched explanation of all, worthy of the best science fiction. What if Lady Emma and Will existed right enough, but in some kind of parallel universe rather than in the past of Emma's twenty-first century reality? It was difficult to get her head round that weird idea, but it did have the advantage of explaining why Lady Emma and Will appeared to have no history in Emma's modern world.

Parallel universe? She *was* going out of her mind.

If such a place existed, and if Emma was somehow getting there via the gold lace gown, she would never know what was going on. She had blithely referred to Waterloo when she was flirting with the officers in the park. So obviously there *had* been a Battle of Waterloo. But what about all the other historical details she thought she knew? Maybe there was no Princess Charlotte of Wales in Will Allmay's reality? Maybe George III was not mad and was still ruling the country? Or maybe the Stuart monarchs were still on the throne?

In one of her rasher moments, she had fancied she might risk telling Will about coming back from the future. If he really loved her, he would listen. She planned to back up her claims by telling him about things still to come, like Princess Charlotte's death in childbirth and George IV's accession in 1820. Or railroads. Will would undoubtedly pooh-pooh her fantasies at the time, but later, once they happened, he would have to admit that she had been right.

Provided she *was* right. In an alternative universe, she might not be.

She couldn't cope with such a mind-boggling idea. Her head was beginning to pound. And no wonder. The whole thing was utter madness.

She couldn't afford to worry herself into another migraine. It would ruin all her plans. She would park the idea of a parallel universe and put it out of her mind. Tomorrow, she was definitely going to the Lamb House. With Will's key. And a few other things, as well. As soon as she could manage to slip away, she was going to try Will's key in the dressing-room door. It would fit, she was sure. Then, once she'd proved to her own satisfaction that her time travel was real, she was going to make a visit to the nightingale bedchamber.

She had a feeling that those shifting floorboards were going to provide some of the answers she needed.

Newly determined, she shut down her computer and went into the kitchen to make herself some supper. She would sit with a tray in front of the television and watch the funniest, silliest programme she could find. She would have a couple of glasses of wine, too, since alcohol always made her sleepy. The last thing she wanted was to lie awake for hours, worrying about why she couldn't find Emma and Will.

~ ~ ~

Next morning, she prepared carefully for her drive out to the Lamb House. She felt she knew so much more about the place now, even though she'd seen only a few of the rooms while she was there with Will. He'd promised her supper, but she'd never seen the inside of his dining room or tasted Sanding's military cooking. Somehow, she and Will had got distracted.

What else did you expect from the greatest stud in London?

Her nagging inner voice was back.

She ignored it and turned up the car radio even louder. The sun was shining, it was a beautiful spring day, and she was going to solve at least one of the mysteries around Will Allmay. Old naggy could go and jump in the nearest lake.

She put her hand into her coat pocket and shivered when her fingers touched her rape alarm. That wasn't what she wanted to find at all. She had to dig deeper to reach Will's key. But it *was* there. Touching it made her heart feel lighter. For it was a real, tangible, provable link to the Regency man she loved.

Since the Lamb House had been reopened to the public earlier in the week, Emma needed to arrive well before any paying visitors were admitted. So she'd set off really early. Once the tourists began filing through the house, and gawping at Will's restored master bedchamber, she would have no chance of having his dressing room to herself.

There was only one other car in the staff car park when Emma drove in. It was probably Geraldine, the house manager, who was in charge of security and the house keys.

Geraldine had become a little leery of Emma on that last visit, but even Geraldine couldn't be in two places at once. Provided the other woman was busy with something downstairs, Emma would have time to nip up to the dressing room and try her key. Piece of cake, no?

Geraldine was in the basement staff room, making coffee.

Emma wished her a cheery good morning. "Is that real coffee? Wonderful. I'm no good in the mornings without an injection of caffeine."

Geraldine agreed that the same applied to her. She needed the real thing, she said, hence the filter coffee maker. It would be done in another few minutes and then they could both enjoy a quiet cup before the rest of the staff arrived and they all had to start on the mundane business of opening up for visitors. Given the fine weather, there would probably be loads of them.

"But that will be good for the house, won't it?" Emma said brightly. "Money towards upkeep and renovations?" Before Geraldine could reply, Emma said, "Oh, that reminds me. Something I have to check in the costume collection before we start opening the house. I'll just nip upstairs and see to it. I'll be back before you've finished pouring the coffee." She bustled to the door. "Milk, no sugar," she called back over her shoulder as she closed it behind her.

Now for it. She took the back stairs two at a time and was panting a bit by the time she reached the bedroom floor. She had not taken off her car coat. The vital key was in her pocket.

She raced through the master bedroom, still looking totally wrong with those garish red velvet hangings, to the dressing room on the far side. She checked the back of the lock. No key. Well, that was predictable. There was a key, and she had it. She took Will's key out of her pocket and tried it in the lock.

It wouldn't go in at all. For a second or two she stood staring at the door, thunderstruck. Her key must fit. Surely it must?

But it didn't. It was completely the wrong shape for the hole. She could see at a glance that the shank was much too thick.

How stupid of me. It was the key to the outside door that I stole. I remember now.

Shaking her head at her own mistake, she went across to the far door. Again, no key in the lock. This keyhole was bigger than the one in the connecting door. And the whole lock mechanism looked quite a bit older.

Emma pushed her key into the lock. It went in. Easily.

Yes, it IS the right key.

But when she tried to turn it, it refused to budge.

The mechanism was probably rusty inside. Maybe if she put some oil on the key, it would work?

She didn't have time to try that now, so she took the key out, spat on it, and tried it again. It moved a tiny fraction this time, but that was all. Emma muttered a curse.

"What on earth are you doing, Emma?"

Geraldine was standing in the doorway to the bedchamber, frowning angrily. This was her domain and Emma was clearly interfering where she had no right to be.

"Oh, sorry, Geraldine. I...I found this key back in the museum without its label. There was a scrap of label in the same box referring to the Lamb House and it looked as if someone had scribbled something about this dressing room on the back of it. I couldn't really make it out. So I was just trying the key, to see if—"

"To see if it would break the lock." Geraldine marched across the room and pulled Emma's key out of the door. "You, of all people, should know how easy it is to damage the fabric of an old house." She examined Emma's key for a moment. "And I can tell you this is nothing like the key to this door." She dived into her pocket and produced a huge bunch of keys, of all shapes and sizes. Choosing one, she inserted it carefully into the lock and turned it. There was no resistance at all. The mechanism was in perfect condition, clearly. No rust at all.

With a grim smile, Geraldine unlocked the door again and took out her key, holding it up against Emma's so they could compare them. The shanks were similar but the pattern of the teeth was totally different.

Emma knew she must be red to the roots of her hair. "I'm sorry. It was a stupid thing to do. I see that now."

"I'm glad you do." Geraldine sounded more like a headmistress than a colleague. "And if you come across any more artefacts that you *think* might belong at the Lamb House, I must ask you, please, to bring them to me." She made to pocket Emma's key.

No. That's Will's. And mine. You can't have it.

Emma raised her chin. "Since that key clearly doesn't belong here, I ought to take it back to the museum." She held out her hand, waiting.

After a moment's hesitation, Geraldine dropped the key onto Emma's palm and turned to go. "If you have no *costume* business here, perhaps we might go back downstairs? Come on," she added, sounding suddenly much less frosty than before. "Our coffee will be getting cold." She flashed a grin and led the way to the stairs. It seemed that Emma's faux pas had been forgiven.

Emma automatically followed her to the back stairs. Her thoughts were in turmoil. Her link between Will and the Lamb House was no link at all. The key didn't fit the lock. It should have, but it didn't.

Parallel universes? Was she in a Lamb House that looked the same, but wasn't?

She shuddered and had to grab the bannister for support. Nothing was working out as she had hoped and planned. Maybe she *was* going mad. It was easier to believe that than the ludicrous idea of a parallel universe.

~ ~ ~

Having worked on the costume collection for several hours, and shown it to a couple of visitors who had paid the extra charge to see it – they were both would-be Regency romance authors so their questions had been very detailed, and thought-provoking – Emma decided to risk the second part of her plan. That confrontation with Geraldine had been humiliating. Worse, it had been all for nothing, because Will's key didn't fit.

The blue bedchamber could be different, though. And Emma would never be able to stop brooding about it until she knew the truth. Since it was now late afternoon, Geraldine would be downstairs in the shop, selling guide books and postcards. The house stewards would be at their stations in the rooms open to the public, answering questions and keeping an eye out to prevent pilfering.

The blue bedchamber was out of bounds to the public. It had no prowling guardian.

Emma retrieved her treasures from her big shoulder bag, stuffed them into her pockets and made for the corridor. Once she was sure none of the staff was watching, she would slip into the blue bedchamber. The chamber of nightingales.

It was surprisingly easy. There weren't enough volunteers to have someone permanently on the landing. One person had to cover both the landing and one of the small saloons attached to the bedchambers. Emma loitered, pretending to be studying an oil painting on the wall. The moment the landing volunteer went back into her saloon, Emma slipped into the blue bedchamber.

Careful. Remember how much noise this floor makes. If there's anyone in the room below, they're bound to hear me.

In the modern room, there was no furniture at all. So Emma didn't cross the floor straight to the fireplace. She crept round the edge of the room instead, hugging the walls. As she'd suspected, the floorboards hardly shifted at all and there was no noise that she could hear.

She grinned to herself. Had her luck changed?

When she got to the hearth, she didn't kneel on the floorboards. Too risky. She knelt on the hearthstone instead. Not kind to the knees, but much less likely to creak.

She dug into her pocket for her makeshift hook tool and her pen with the little torch on the end. The edge of the board came up with a bit of a struggle – it probably hadn't been moved for decades, in this reality – and she bent her head down to floor level to follow the tiny torch beam into the dark. Her heart was thumping nineteen to the dozen as she focused it through the gap.

A glimmer of blue smiled up at her. Followed by the sparkle of a diamond.

Emma wanted to whoop with delight. Her sapphire earring was there, translated through two hundred years. She wasn't having hallucinations after all. Her Regency world was real.

She had the proof of it. Real proof.

She heard footsteps outside in the corridor outside. The volunteer was on patrol again. No time to waste on the earring. She had never intended to remove it, anyway. She was in the addition business here, not subtraction.

She pulled her treasures out of her other pocket. A small mango, sold to her as perfectly ripe but, in reality, a bit hard and green, and a cheap digital watch. She pushed the mango in beneath the floorboard. It was a bit of a squeeze and the fruit might get bruised, but what did it matter? Next she dropped the watch into the space at the stalk end of the mango. Then it was the work of seconds to push the floorboard back into its place and spread the dust across it with her handkerchief.

She stole back round the walls to the door, trying to scatter the dust as she went. The result wasn't great, but at least she was not leaving a clear track of footprints to show where an intruder had been. Emma stopped to listen at the door for a good minute. She heard the volunteer's footsteps pass and die away. The woman had returned to her post in the saloon. So it was as safe as it was ever going to be.

Emma opened the door.

There were two people in the corridor outside, inspecting some antique chairs. Emma's breath caught. Then she saw that they were only visitors. She marched out of the nightingale room and shut the door officiously behind her. She nodded to the couple as she passed them. "We'll be closing quite soon," she said. "Don't miss the restored master bedchamber before you go. It's absolutely splendid." She pointed. "It's down there." She made for the stairs without waiting for the pair to respond.

A great gush of joy was welling up inside her, desperately trying to burst out. She ought to suppress it, but she did allow herself to dance down one single flight of stairs. After that, she made herself go slowly, with the measured tread of a senior curator returning to her collection. If anyone saw her, they wouldn't be fooled, though. She was probably grinning like a loon.

She made it back to the safety of the costume collection without meeting anyone but visitors. Phew. Since the room was empty, she gave a couple of whoops of joy. Very discreet whoops. She would celebrate, for real, once she got home.

She was singing as she tidied away the costumes she'd been showing to the visitors and finished her paperwork. Before going down to the staff room to collect her outdoor things, she glanced in the mirror. There was a gleam of triumph in her eye, but if she kept her face straight enough, the others were unlikely to notice.

Some of the volunteers were already downstairs, chatting about their day and packing away their lunch boxes. Emma had noticed that very few of them used the Lamb House café. It had to be quite expensive, because the profits contributed to the upkeep of the house.

As the volunteers were about to leave for the car park, Geraldine appeared with a clipboard, part way through her routine for closing up the house for the night. "Oh, by the way, Emma. About that key."

Emma stiffened. Was she in for another dressing-down? In public, too?

Geraldine smiled. "I thought I should tell you. I had a look in the records this afternoon. They're nothing like complete, but I did find a reference to problems with some of the locks on the bedroom floor. It's possible that both the locks in the dressing room were changed, in the late Victorian period. So your key could be genuine. But if it is, the lock it fitted is long gone."

"Oh." Emma couldn't think of a thing to say. She knew she was staring, wide-eyed. At last, she managed, "Thank you for telling me, Geraldine. That's very, er, interesting. I'll put the key back in store with a new label saying 'Query Regency-era key to dressing room in the Lamb House, lock missing, replaced in late nineteenth century'. Then no one else will go off on a wild goose chase the way I did."

Geraldine nodded. "Good idea." She went back to her security checklist.

Emma drove home a bit distracted, turning the new information over in her mind. It was a very peculiar puzzle. According to available records, neither Lady Emma Groatster nor Will Almay had ever existed. And yet Emma herself had the possible proof provided by the dressing-room key, plus the definite proof of a hugely expensive sapphire earring. So the lovers must have existed. Somewhere.

What she needed was more proof. It was purely a question of finding it.

A glimmer of an idea tickled the back of her brain. And she was sure she had seen a book on the shelf in the research room that would provide the information she needed to make a start. To turn her latest off-the-wall notion into a full-blown plan, though, she would need a lot of background information and a great deal of guile, as well. A bit of luck could help, too.

Her new idea might prove the lovers existed. But, if it worked, it could also provide a huge boost to Emma's career. She ought to be focusing on that because, soon, she would have nothing else. Once Will married Patience, Emma would never make the transition again. Seeing him would be unbearable. So Emma would be alone, stranded in the modern world with not so much as a cat to love her.

Chapter Twenty

EMMA WOKE UP EARLY WITH A smile on her face. She couldn't wait to get back to Will. And it was Friday. A working day. So she could make the transition to where she was beginning to think she belonged. If she didn't make the most of this chance, she would have to wait three whole days before she could try again. Three days. It would be unbearable.

She snuggled down under the duvet for a few extra minutes. It reminded her of being in Will's arms – safe, and warm, and wanted. She heard herself making contented murmurs in her throat. Mmm. But she must get up soon. She needed to be the first to arrive at the museum so that she could do a few more of those blasted record cards. She doubted that anyone would have noticed, while she was at the Lamb House, that the data entry had not advanced at all in spite of the curator's late night working the day before. But the longer she left it, the more chance there was that someone would notice.

She allowed herself to lurk a little longer, remembering her triumph of the day before. That sapphire earring under the floorboard changed everything. It was there. In the twenty-first century. And it was there because she, Lady Emma Groatster, had put it there in 1817. So keys were not the only things that could migrate over centuries. Till now, the time travel had been in one direction only. The crucial question was whether migration worked backwards in time, as well. And tonight, she hoped to find the answer.

~ ~ ~

At the museum, Emma mentioned, during the morning coffee break, that she was planning to work late again. "You're overdoing it, Emma," Richard said in a worried voice. "It's no wonder you're getting migraines when you work so hard. And it's Friday, too. Everyone else will be off on the dot of closing time. They've got lives to live beyond work."

And so have I, but not in this century.

She threw a glance at Richard, silently thanking him for his concern. "Most of my life revolves around work at the moment," she said with a rueful smile. "And I'm really enjoying it, even the data entry part of it. So it's honestly no hardship to stay late and do a bit more. My weekend will be a rather boring affair – shopping and chores like house cleaning are not exactly attractive prospects." That was not the whole truth. On Saturday morning, she was going to have her first riding lesson in years – side-saddle. There would be nothing boring about that.

"You haven't forgotten you're babysitting for us tomorrow?"

In the excitement of finding the sapphire, she had. "No, no," she said quickly. "It will be the highlight of my weekend," she added, with a laugh.

"Well, I hope Chloë behaves herself, or it will be a highlight you'll want to avoid in the future."

Emma shook her head. "No, I won't do that. Chloë and I are becoming firm friends." That was true. Emma loved children and Chloë was an absolute sweetheart. "I wouldn't pass up another chance to spend time with her. No matter what she does tomorrow."

"That's very generous of you, Emma."

"Besides, I want to hear all about *Madam Butterfly*."

"Now that," Richard said with a grin, "is stretching the truth a bit too far. Didn't you say you detested that particular bit of Puccini? I didn't tell Melanie so, of course. In any case, she's such a fan she would be bound to rave about it, even if she knew you hated it."

The rest of Friday passed very slowly. Every time Emma glanced across at St Mary's clock, the hands seemed to be stuck. But at long last, closing time arrived and, as Richard had predicted, all the rest of the staff left promptly. They had wives and husbands and lovers to go home to. Whereas Emma's flat was a lonely place, with no one. But in her other life...

She smiled to herself. She had more than another hour to wait, so she could dig out that book from the research room. She spotted it immediately, bang in the middle of the shelf, exactly where she remembered seeing it before. It was a mine of useful information. As long as the people in Will's Regency reality matched the ones who were recorded in the history books – and after her success with the sapphire, Emma was much more hopeful on that score – she should be able to turn her vague idea into action. But she needed Mr Richard Cosway to be alive, and still working, in Will's version of 1817 London.

Pity she couldn't take the book with her. Written notes might transfer if she was holding them in her hand when she put the lace gown on, but she couldn't be sure. So Emma set herself to memorising the key facts about Cosway instead. She now knew a huge amount about him, including where he lived, how quickly he could execute his commissions, and the highest fees he had ever charged. Fantastic.

Provided a version of the historical Richard Cosway actually existed in Will's parallel London.

~ ~ ~

Emma wasn't surprised when the lace ballgown took her back to her own Mayfair house and her own bedchamber. Her silver clock showed a little after one.

One in the morning? It must be, since she was dressed in her ballgown.

But what day was it? And how long since she'd last been here?

She pulled the bell to summon Bailey.

The abigail took several minutes to appear. For once, she must have been downstairs rather than hovering in the dressing room.

"Help me to undress, please, Bailey. I'm more than ready for my bed."

"You're frowning, m'lady. Have you the headache again? Shall I order a tisane?"

Emma shook her head. "No. I'm simply tired." Once Bailey had removed the gold gown and her stays, and wrapped her in a bedgown, Emma sank into her favourite chair by the fire. "Oh, that reminds me. There's something I want you to do."

"Of course, m'lady. Now?"

Emma laughed. "No, certainly not. It's the middle of the night. First thing in the morning will do very well."

Bailey stood in front of Emma's chair with her hands loosely clasped against her skirt, the picture of an obedient servant waiting for orders.

"I want you to send one of the footmen to Mr Richard Cosway, at number two Stratford Place. He is to ask Mr Cosway to wait on me here, tomorrow, at his earliest convenience. And Mr Cosway is not to disclose my request to anyone. Not even to his wife."

"Might it not be simpler to send Mr Cosway a note, m'lady?"

Emma shook her head again, more decisively. "I have very particular reasons for wishing there to be no written record of my dealings with Mr Cosway, Bailey. You will make sure the footman is word-perfect in my message, if you please." She made Bailey repeat it, word for word, until she was satisfied. "Good. Thank you. First thing in the morning, please. And the footman is not to wait for a reply."

Bailey nodded and set herself to brushing out Emma's curls and plaiting her hair for bed. The long strokes of the brush were very relaxing. As was the warmth of the fire. Emma could feel herself beginning to doze.

Emma was on the point of getting between the sheets when Bailey suddenly said, "Oh, goodness, m'lady. I had quite forgot. What with the instructions for the footman, and Mr Cosway, and— It totally slipped my mind. I am so sorry."

"What on earth are you talking about, Bailey? What have you forgotten?"

Bailey dug into the pocket of her black gown. "This,

m'lady. A rather grubby note. It came for you while you were out." She sniffed. "I must tell you that I almost refused it when I saw the subscription, but the boy insisted it must be delivered to you. So in the end I let the footman take it."

She handed over a rather dog-eared piece of paper, roughly folded. On it was written, in black ink, "Lady E G". There was no address.

Emma reached for it. Could it be from Will? It did not look like a lady's hand.

For Bailey's benefit, Emma shook her head sadly and said, "I suppose the boy who brought it could not read and so there was no point in adding my address."

"But your name, at least, m'lady?"

"He probably had it by heart. Along with the address. Such boys have a degree of native cunning, you know. One should not underestimate them just because they cannot read."

"No, m'lady." Bailey was hovering, waiting for Emma to open the note and say who it was from. From the look on the abigail's face, she was suspicious.

Emma knew better than to dismiss the woman. It would only serve to increase her doubts. So Emma leant towards the head of her bed and broke the seal in the light of her bedside candle. With the paper at that angle, Bailey couldn't possibly see anything written on it.

"Ah. It is from Mrs Smith," Emma lied glibly. The note was from Will. And, bless him, it was dated. "She has my missing earring, you will be relieved to hear, Bailey." That was another lie, for Will knew nothing about what Emma had done with the earring, but mentioning it might help to divert Bailey's suspicions.

The abigail grunted.

Emma made a show of scanning the rest of the note. "Mrs Smith has invited me to visit her tomorrow evening. And to stay for a few days, as she is presently confined to her bed. She would much welcome the company, she says. I shall go. I shall need that valise of books."

Bailey nodded. "I will prepare your travelling cases, m'lady. Are you likely to need evening dress, do you think?"

Emma glanced back at the note. "I imagine I shall be

dressing for dinner, but I doubt that Mrs Smith will be hosting anything more elaborate."

Bailey nodded again. "You won't be wanting the gold lace ballgown, then," she said firmly. It was not a question.

Emma was stymied. Without the gold lace, she wouldn't be able to escape from Will. Not unless he allowed her to leave. She took a deep breath and considered her options. Did she trust him enough?

Yes. She did. Will was not Julian. Will was not controlling. She had promised not to run from him again. So she didn't need the gold lace as a sort of Regency get-out-of-jail-free card.

"At what time shall we be leaving for Mrs Smith's, m'lady? I presume you would wish me to order the carriage?"

"No. Mrs Smith is sending her own carriage for me at eight tomorrow evening. Or rather, this evening, since it is already Tuesday. She feels, er, she thinks she is imposing upon me quite enough by having me keep company with an invalid. And as I told you before, she likes to keep her horses exercised."

"Very well, m'lady. I shall be ready."

Uh-oh. Moment of truth. Get it over with. "I shan't be taking you with me, Bailey." When the abigail's eyebrows shot up, Emma added, placatingly, "Don't worry. Mrs Smith's woman can help me to dress and I shan't need one of your splendid hairstyles for reading to an invalid. It is a very small, quiet household. You would be quite at a loss for anything to do." Bailey still looked mulish, so Emma said, "It will give you time to change the trimming on my straw bonnets." She yawned and waved a vague hand in the direction of the dressing room. "I must say I am becoming thoroughly bored with them. What do you say to cherries, perhaps, instead of ribbons?"

Bailey grimaced. "Cherries would be quite inadmissible with your red hair, m'lady." She paused, her attention caught by Emma's professional challenge. "But carefully chosen flowers could look very becoming. Or feathers, perhaps?"

Emma smiled. It seemed she'd won that round. "I shall leave my bonnets in your capable hands, Bailey. And I shall expect to be pleasantly surprised at what your clever fingers have created, when I return from Mrs Smith's."

~ ~ ~

Richard Cosway arrived next morning before Emma had finished dressing. Bailey was frowning as she closed the door on the maid who had brought the message upstairs. "The man, Cosway. He is downstairs, m'lady."

"Goodness. Make haste with finishing my hair, Bailey."

The abigail continued her work at the same steady pace as before. "He is a tradesman," she said flatly. "He can surely wait."

"If he is a tradesman, Bailey, he is a tradesman with very influential friends. I believe his salon was frequented by the highest in the land when he lived in Pall Mall. The Prince Regent himself used to attend though His Royal Highness was not Regent then. He is much more conscious of his dignities now."

Bailey said nothing. She pinned a curl in place and picked up her comb again.

"Besides," Emma added, "Cosway is an old man now. We should venerate his years. Where have they put him?"

"In your bookroom, m'lady."

"Very well. I shall go down to him as soon as you have finished my hair."

Emma wondered what she would see. According to the reference books, contemporaries had described Cosway as a small man with a face like a monkey. In his younger days, he had certainly been mocked for his looks and for his extravagant and ostentatious modes of dress. He even had a nickname: "The Macaroni Miniature Painter". But he was undoubtedly an expert in his profession. Emma knew, even if much of the Regency did not, that Cosway had painted the famous miniatures exchanged between the Prince of Wales and Mrs Fitzherbert. She knew, too, that when the Prince – who would be crowned as King George IV – eventually died, he would be buried with that same Cosway painting of Mrs Fitzherbert next to his heart.

"There. That is done, I think, m'lady."

Emma glanced at her reflection. "That looks very well,

Bailey. Thank you." She rose to leave.

"Your earrings, m'lady?" Bailey was holding out a pair of neat pearl eardrops.

"Yes, very well," Emma said, curbing her impatience. She sat down again for a few moments while the abigail put the pearls in her ears. "I will see Cosway now. And in the meantime, Bailey, I need you to fetch me some ready money."

Bailey's eyebrows rose.

"Thirty guineas should be enough."

Bailey's eyes widened even more.

"Bring it to me in the bookroom."

"I can ask Mr Bendridge, of course, m'lady, but he may not have such a large sum to hand. Perhaps, your strongbox…?"

A strongbox. I am bound to have a strongbox in the house. But where do I keep it? And where is the key?

"That might present, er, difficulties," she said slowly, playing for time.

"I understand, m'lady. You would not wish to let a tradesman like Cosway see where your money is kept."

Yes! It's in the bookroom.

"No. And to be perfectly honest – I would not share this with anyone else but you, Bailey – I cannot quite remember where I left the key."

"Is it not in the drawer of your desk in the bookroom, m'lady? I do not recall seeing it up here in your chamber."

"I can't remember. I will check when I go down. In the meantime, try if you can obtain the money from Mr Bendridge. As you say, it would not do for Cosway to discover where I keep my money box."

Although it would be very useful for me to discover it. And the whereabouts of the key as well.

Emma allowed Bailey to drape a shawl becomingly around her shoulders and then sallied forth to meet the foremost miniaturist of the day.

Richard Cosway, RA, was a little old man with a rather scrunched-up face, but it was unfair of his fellow macaronies to have labelled him a "monkey", Emma decided. He had taken the liberty of sitting down in the bookroom while he waited. That was allowable, given his advanced years. He must be past seventy. He rose, with the help of a silver-topped ebony cane, and bowed low.

"Mr Richard Cosway?" Emma nodded to acknowledge his bow. "You are very prompt."

"Your summons was explicit, Lady Emma, and so I am here."

"Excellent." Emma crossed to the desk and sat down. "Pray be seated again, Mr Cosway. Our business need not detain us long. You have told no one of this meeting, I trust? Not even your wife?"

Cosway answered with a bow of his head. "No one. And my wife is at present in Italy."

"I am grateful to you for your discretion. I have a proposal to make to you. I wish you to paint my portrait. You continue to accept commissions, I trust?"

"Indeed, ma'am."

"Excellent. Then here is my proposal. I wish to have a miniature, an oval, on ivory, no more than three inches high; the exact size I leave to you. However, I wish there to be no written record whatsoever of the contract between us. Nor will you disclose to anyone that you have painted me."

The old man's eyes widened, but he said nothing.

"Furthermore, you will inscribe the back of the finished miniature with the name of the sitter, the date of completion, and the full details of yourself, as the artist. I take it that would present no problem?"

"It can be done, certainly."

"I will also require a letter, in your own hand, stating the conditions of our contract, namely that I required you to execute the commission in total secrecy, that you delivered the finished portrait into my hands, here at my house, and that, upon delivery, you were paid—" she paused for effect "—three times your normal fee."

The monkey jaw dropped a little.

"Your highest fee for such a miniature is thirty guineas, I believe?"

Cosway swallowed hard. His prominent Adam's apple stood out in his scrawny neck. He managed to nod in reply.

There was a scratch on the door. Bailey came in without a

word, handed a roll of banknotes to Emma and curtseyed herself out again.

Emma had hoped for guineas. Her plan would have to be adjusted. But only slightly.

"It is not the usual practice, I am aware. But this is not the usual commission. If you are prepared to agree to all my terms, Mr Cosway, I will pay you—" She began to count the notes onto the desk in front of her. Yes, there was enough. She breathed more easily. "I will pay you thirty pounds now and the balance on the day you deliver the portrait and the letter into my hands. Is that agreeable to you?"

Cosway had to swallow again and clear his throat before he spoke. His gaze was fixed on the pile of banknotes. "It is a very generous offer, Lady Emma, and, er, I should be delighted to have the opportunity to paint such a beautiful lady. Indeed, I would gladly do it for my normal fee."

"Oh?" Emma smiled a little.

"But I readily accept your ladyship's additional conditions. And therefore also your proposals as regards the amount and timing of my fee."

Yes, I thought you would.

"That is splendid, Mr Cosway."

She pushed the notes part way across the desk towards him, but kept her hand on them, waiting. She had more conditions to impose.

"How soon would your ladyship wish to sit?"

Ah. Difficult. How many days was she about to spend at the Lamb House with Will? She hadn't the foggiest idea. Will's note, which Emma had burned as soon as Bailey left the room, had been very specific about when and how Emma was to arrive for her stay with the phantom Mrs Smith, but had said nothing about delivering her back home again. Her naggy interior voice had noticed the omission, and pronounced it typical. *Your precious Will has a cock for a compass*, it had said.

That picture was too vivid, and too crude, for comfort. She pushed it away.

"I shall be from home for a few days," she managed to say, airily. "When I return, I will send you word. I cannot come to

Stratford Place to sit for you, you understand. You must come to me here."

The old man did not seem to be at all fazed by that, or by her requirements for secrecy, either. The Prince and Mrs Fitzherbert had probably been much more finicky and demanding. Their secret marriage was potentially treasonous, after all. Cosway calmly asked a number of practical questions about the best room to use as a temporary painting studio, and about how formal Emma wanted the finished portrait to be. It could all be done in about a week, he said, provided Emma was prepared to make herself available when he needed her. Their bargain was struck.

Emma rose, rang the bell and handed over her butler's thirty pounds. Cosway tucked the roll into an inside pocket of his beautifully cut coat. The macaroni style was long gone, but the painter was clearly spending a great deal with his tailor, in spite of his advanced years. Once a dandy, always a dandy?

"Thank you, Mr Cosway," Emma said when the footman appeared to show her visitor out. "Remember that I am trusting to your discretion in this matter."

Cosway bowed over his cane. "You may depend on me, Lady Emma."

The moment the door closed behind him, Emma scurried back to the desk and began to hunt for the vital key. To her surprise, she found it in the first drawer she opened. An unlocked drawer, too. Lady Emma Groatster's security was either very lax or she had very trustworthy servants.

The strongbox was in the unlocked corner cupboard. Surely it would be sensible to keep her money much more securely than this? On the other hand, the servants might start to gossip if Lady Emma suddenly changed her slipshod ways. And she couldn't very well keep her strongbox key on a ribbon round her neck, could she? Not when she and Will—

Emma's eyes widened at the amount of money she found in the strongbox: fat rolls of banknotes and rouleaux of guineas. She took out fifty pounds in notes, thirty to return to the butler and twenty for herself. She did not want to be beholden to Will while she was at the Lamb House.

You're lying to yourself, Emma Stanley. You're still afraid of being in any man's power, aren't you?

No. She wasn't afraid of Will. She wasn't. She trusted him. And she'd promised not to run from him.

It was just that, with money of her own, she could make her own choices. Wasn't it?

Chapter Twenty-One

"MRS SMITH'S CARRIAGE IS AT THE door, m'lady." The footman was holding the bookroom door for her. It was exactly eight o'clock.

Emma rose from the desk and picked up her reticule. The strongbox key was at the bottom of it, strung onto a piece of ribbon and wrapped in a handkerchief. She hadn't been able to bring herself to leave such a precious key loose in the drawer. Not when she knew that she could be out of the house for days on end.

"My valises?" she demanded loftily.

"Miss Bailey directed me to put them in the carriage, m'lady," the man said.

With a tiny nod of thanks, Emma made her way out. When the footman opened the door, Emma saw that Sanding was waiting by the carriage, ready to hand her in. Another glance showed the simpleton groom on the box, holding the reins. The poor fellow was in exactly the same slouching posture as before. Maybe his back was deformed as well as his tongue? Emma resolved to ask Will about the man's history.

I will, once I'm cool, calm and collected enough to make rational conversation.

Her mouth went dry at the thought of what she and Will might be about to do. Very little of it was likely to be rational. And none of it would be cool or calm, either.

"Good evening, Lady Emma." Sanding touched his forelock, navy style, and offered his hand.

"Thank you." The words came out as a strangled croak. Emma allowed him to help her in, glad she'd been alert enough to avoid using his name. It was the kind of unusual name that her servants might remember, and gossip about. Someone, in some other household, might well know that Will May All had a body servant called Sanding. And two and two could quickly make a very dangerous four.

Someone – probably Bailey, in spite of her irritation at being left behind – had provided a hot brick for Emma's feet. But as far as Bailey knew, this was to be a very short journey. A hot brick was over the top, surely?

Maybe Bailey's antennae had been twitching more than Emma realised.

She shrugged and settled back into her seat as the carriage moved smoothly off. Too late now. There was absolutely nothing Emma could do about Bailey and her clever insights until this visit to "the invalid Mrs Smith" was over.

By the time the crunch of wheels on gravel warned Emma that she was arriving at the Lamb House, she knew she was in danger of dissolving into a puddle of lust as soon as she tried to move. Just seeing Will waiting by the carriage steps would do it. She was going to spend days alone with Will Allmay – most of it in his bed, probably – and she couldn't think beyond that. She vaguely recalled that there were certain important tasks she needed to do while she was at the Lamb House. She told herself she would deal with them. Later. Once she was able focus coherently. Beyond the memory of being lifted into Will's arms.

The carriage door opened. Cold air rushed in. And disappointment. For Will wasn't waiting to lift her down and crush her in his arms. Sanding stood alone by the step. Very properly offering only a hand.

She took a deep breath, straightened her shoulders and stepped down. "Thank you, Sanding." She glanced round as nonchalantly as she could. There was no sign of Will. "I had thought your master might be here to welcome me." She was miffed and she didn't care if it showed. The blasted man was taking her for granted. She wasn't going to allow that.

A moment ago, I was all set to dissolve into his arms. Now I'm cross and longing to slap him. What is it with me and my moods?

Sanding shrugged. "If your ladyship will excuse me, I'll drive the carriage to the stables and see to your luggage." Without waiting for a reply, he climbed back up onto the box and drove off, abandoning Emma in the middle of the gravel sweep. How dare he be so rude? She might be the master's latest squeeze, but she was a lady and a guest at this house all the same.

She realised with a start that she wasn't alone. The simpleton must have climbed down while she was dealing with Sanding. The big groom was standing at the foot of the steps to the porch. Even though his disreputable tricorne was pulled low on his forehead, Emma sensed that he was gazing at her. Avidly.

She was Lady Emma Groatster. She didn't have to put up with such indignities. She might excuse the groom – he was dumb and simple and probably knew no better – but she would not excuse Will's rudeness. Will Allmay was about to get a piece of her mind.

Emma stuck her nose in the air, and marched up the steps to the open front door. She ignored the groom completely.

"Hoity-toity," said a voice behind her.

She swung round so quickly she caught her heel in her heavy cloak and staggered. Strong arms caught her and set her safely on her feet. "Careful, leddyship. Ye wouldn't want to be fallin' into the arms o' the loikes o' me, now would ye?" Will's yokel accent was a travesty. It wouldn't fool anyone. Least of all Emma.

He caught her wrist as she made to slap him. With his free hand, he removed his sweaty tricorne so that she could see his laughing face.

"You, you—"

He carried her hand to his lips and kissed it, letting his lips linger suggestively on her skin, while he looked up at her through his lashes. His eyes were sparkling with mischief. Will Allmay was enjoying himself hugely, the ratbag.

"That was you, on the box, all the time," Emma raged. "And you had the cheek to have Sanding tell me you were dumb." She pulled her hand out of his and punched him as hard as she could. The blow made no impression at all, which annoyed her even more. "He was so convincing, he had me feeling sorry for you, you great lummox."

"Thank you for that, my sweet," Will said in his normal voice. He replaced his hat and patted it into place. "If I managed to fool you, there's a fair chance that I fooled everyone else as well. Which was my intention."

"Oh."

"Did you really think I would allow you to be driven back to London, in the dark, with only Sanding to protect you? Shame on you, love. You should know me better than that."

Yes, she should. But at this precise moment, she was too overcome to say a word.

Will offered his arm. "May I escort your ladyship into the house?"

His formality helped her to regain a little of her normal composure. She took a deep breath, stepped back and looked him up and down. His coat was a disgrace, torn and smelly. And as for that hat—

She knocked it off his head with a backhand worthy of a Wimbledon finalist. "I will accept your escort, my dear sir," she announced primly, "when you are dressed as befits the gentleman you *used* to aspire to be." She sniffed theatrically and wrinkled her nose in disgust. "Perhaps Sanding did not like to mention that you *smell*?"

He threw back his head and laughed heartily. When he could speak again, he said, still grinning, "Like a sewer, I dare say. But that is easily remedied." He pulled off his enormous coat and dropped it on the step. He was wearing simple clothes underneath, but they were not torn. And a quick sniff told her they weren't smelly, either. Dressed like that, he could be a respectable yeoman farmer.

The way he was looking at her was not respectable at all.

He put his arm around her waist without a by your leave. "Enough of this funning, Emma." His voice seemed to have dropped at least an octave. "Come, my love. Come inside. I

189

need you." He dropped a tiny kiss on her lips.

The man was temptation incarnate. Her body swayed towards him, eager for one more touch.

He smiled down into her eyes. His voice became merely a thready whisper. "And if I am not mistaken, my sweet, the need is mutual."

~ ~ ~

Emma had no idea how long she had slept for. She lay on her back, staring up at the blue bed canopy. Her body was so heavy and sated that she couldn't summon enough energy to move a muscle. She had supped with Will, laughed with Will, frolicked with Will – on the rug before the fire, on the sofa, and finally in his green-hung bed – and then he had brought her here to be alone for a space. To sleep. He needed her to be well rested, he said. For he planned to return for her very soon. Then he'd faked a rakish leer that made her laugh. And had her insides turning somersaults.

Surely men weren't supposed to have that much stamina? The blue pill was a twentieth-century invention. But whatever the Regency equivalent might be, Will Allmay had it. Plus the ability to delight a woman in a thousand different ways. Oh yes – when it came to lovemaking, Will Allmay had it all.

He said it was because of me.

He said I was the only woman who had ever affected him in that way.

He said it was because he loved me.

Will had said a great many things while he was exploring her body with his fingers and his lips and his tongue. Emma had been too far gone to remember most of them. But she hadn't missed that fervent declaration of love. She had believed it at the time. Did she still?

How could she? If Will Allmay loved Emma, then why was he going to marry Patience Sinclair-Smythe?

Emma had no answer to that. Only Will could supply the answer. And Emma couldn't possibly ask him for it.

She sighed. Her bubbling happiness had evaporated at thoughts of Patience and the loveless marriage she had mapped out for Will.

But she hasn't got him yet. I have him. For now, at least.

She punched the pillow, wishing it was Patience's face. Childish, but satisfying.

What time was it? There was no clock in this bedroom so she had no real idea. It was either very late or very early. She found herself yawning. She ought to go back to sleep. That was why Will had carried her in here after all; so that she could sleep, alone, and in peace.

To be ready for their next bout of horizontal athletics.

Emma found herself giggling like an idiot at the modern vulgarity of her thoughts. It was something of a miracle that, whenever she spoke as Lady Emma, the words formed themselves into perfect, and perfectly polite, Regency sentences. Somehow the cruder twenty-first century speech patterns never made it out of her mouth. She doubted that Will, or anyone else in the Regency, would be able to cope with some of the expressions modern women used. She had a sudden vivid memory of the famous Ascot scene from the film of *My Fair Lady* when Eliza Doolittle shocked the cream of Edwardian society by shouting something very unladylike as she urged her horse on. Eliza's gaffe was pretty tame, though. Just: "Move your bloomin' arse!"

That, though shocking in the early twentieth century, would raise no eyebrows in the twenty-first, where effing and blinding was commonplace. But, in the Regency, no such words could ever pass a lady's lips. And no gentleman would ever utter them in front of a lady.

She closed her eyes, hoping to drift off again. Her bed was soft and voluptuous. Like a sultan's couch? No, that wasn't a good image. Will wasn't a sultan and Emma wasn't one of his concubines. She breathed deeply, trying to think of more appropriate images. Lovers lying on an Indian Ocean beach, maybe?

Why were all her thoughts exotic, and sultry?

Perfume.

She hadn't consciously noticed it before, but there was a definite perfume in the blue bedchamber. More of Will's doing, no doubt.

She inhaled deeply, trying to place it. It was rich and sensuous, the sort of scent that conjured up images of oriental

191

gardens with tinkling fountains and tables piled high with sherbets and fruit.

Mango!

For once, Will wasn't to blame. Emma was.

All her lethargy gone, she leapt out of bed and scrambled across to the fireplace. In her haste, she made a pig's ear of trying to bend one of her hairpins into a hook, and had to make a second one. Eventually, and with much swearing under her breath, she managed to prise up the end of the floorboard.

The mango might have been underripe when she tucked it into the hole, but it must be absolutely perfect now, judging by the scent that billowed out into the room. She eased the fruit out of its place. And then the sapphire earring from underneath. She put that with the strongbox key, wrapped carefully in the handkerchief at the bottom of her reticule.

There wasn't room for the mango as well, so she tucked it into one of the drawers of the dressing table.

But what about the digital watch?

Emma slammed the drawer shut and flung herself back down by the hearth. She didn't have a torch, obviously, and a candle wouldn't be much help for seeing under floorboards. She made do with putting her hand into the hole and feeling around for the missing watch. She made sure she explored every square inch of the hole.

It wasn't there.

Emma sat back on her heels and thought hard. The sapphire earring had migrated to the twenty-first century. And back again. The mango had made a one-way trip into the past. The watch hadn't.

The difference was obvious when she thought about it. And wasn't that why she'd picked that horrible cheap watch in the first place? It was essentially a computer encased in plastic, both things that hadn't existed in Regency England. If they hadn't been invented in 1817, how could the watch go back there? Whereas mangoes had existed for thousands of years. Time travelling was fine. For mangoes.

The watch would probably still be under the floorboard in the modern-day Lamb House. Emma made a mental note to retrieve it as soon as she had a chance. If it stayed there under that floorboard, it could ruin her grand plan.

She removed her makeshift hook and pushed the floorboard back into place with her foot. She even unbent her hairpin. No point it letting Will see that. He had a sharp eye for detail, honed in all those years of inspecting his ships. If he asked her what a bent hairpin was for, what could she possibly say?

~ ~ ~

The room seemed much lighter when Emma woke up again. It was morning. She must have been asleep for quite a while.

She sat up and sniffed the air. The mango scent seemed to have dispersed during the night. She could smell it, but only barely. And only because she knew it was there. Good. It was a complication she could do without.

Someone knocked softly on her door. Sanding? Or was it Will, anxious for a spell of morning frolics?

Emma's own silk wrapper was lying across the end of her bed. She dragged it on and tied the belt tightly. Once she was sure she was well covered and presentable, she went to open the door.

Will, fully dressed, was halfway down the corridor, but turned back at the sound of her door. "Emma. You *are* awake. I didn't want to disturb you if you were sleeping." He grinned. "I thought perhaps you needed more rest after your, er, exertions." Even in the gloomy corridor, she could see that his eyes were sparkling with mischief.

Emma frowned and tried to look stern. "You, sir, are a threat to any virtuous woman's peace of mind. Exertions, indeed. I'll have you know that—" She didn't get a chance to finish her sentence. In a couple of strides, Will had taken her in his arms and was kissing her. Passionately.

He took his time about it, exploring her lips as if they were totally new to him. When, finally, he was satisfied, and Emma was beginning to melt, he said, "Good morning, my love. You taste of nectar and sunshine."

Emma could think of absolutely nothing to say in reply.

"May I come in?" Will asked politely. "There are no servants about, I admit, but I'm not sure it's good for your peace of mind, dear virtuous woman, to be kissing a rake in a public corridor."

"Grr," Emma replied, trying not to rise to the bait. Will Allmay was too cocky by half. But after that toe-tingling kiss, she couldn't refuse him. From the look in his eye, he knew it, too. She tried to remind herself that he was a practised lover who knew how to manipulate women, and that she was not in the same league. It didn't help.

She let him usher her into the blue bedchamber and close the door behind them. He led her over to the bed and sat her down on it. She shivered a little, wondering if this was a preliminary to another new sexual adventure. Last night, they had done things together that she had not thought possible. It had been wonderful, though.

He stood back, gazing assessingly down at her. "Can you swim, Emma?"

Her jaw dropped. "Swim?" she croaked, eventually.

"Yes, love. Do you know how to swim?"

Emma managed to nod. Now what on earth was he up to?

"Splendid. So few ladies can, nowadays. Their parents seem to think it's more important to keep their bodies unseen than to teach them a skill that might one day save their lives." He made the comment with such feeling that Emma guessed there was something more behind it.

"Did you lose someone? To drowning?" she asked in a small voice.

He grimaced and ran a hand through his hair. "Oh, Lord. I hadn't realised I was quite so transparent. But since you ask, Emma – yes. My brother's wife. A bridge collapsed and she was swept away. John dived in to save her." He swallowed and turned to stare at the fireplace. "He was lost too."

"I am so sorry." There was nothing more Emma could say. Especially as it sounded as if the brothers had been close. This must be just the bare bones of the tragedy, but recounting it, Will had become distant. She wanted to put her arms round him, to offer comfort, but she was pretty sure he would push her away.

"Are you planning to take me swimming, Will?" she asked brightly, in an attempt to chase away his mourning shadows.

He turned back to her. He was smiling again and looking his normal, relaxed self. "I thought we might explore the bath house. Together," he added, wickedly.

"Bath house? But surely the Lamb House has no—" She caught herself before she said too much. "Um, I thought a bath house required a spring to feed it," she finished lamely. "You don't have one here, do you?"

"We found a hot spring when we were digging a well, actually. It was too good an opportunity to miss, so I had a bath house built over it. I like to swim."

Emma was gobsmacked. If Will had built a bath house, and found a hot spring as well, where had they gone? There was no sign of either at the modern-day Lamb House. She was sure of it. Was it a parallel universe after all?

"I have brought nothing suitable for swimming in," she said primly.

He let out a guffaw. "*Nothing* will be perfectly suitable," he chuckled, taking a quick step back to avoid the punch she aimed at his middle. She missed. "Tut, Emma. You will need to learn better science than that. Shall I invite Gentleman Jackson to give you lessons?"

She made a face. But it was useless to spar with him in this rollicking mood. Besides, it had made him forget his grief. She wanted to keep it that way, so she gave up the fight, and laughed with him. "So we are to swim, naked, in your pool, are we? How far is it from the house? You don't expect me to walk there naked as well, do you?"

He put his head on one side and inhaled deeply. "That *would* be a feast for the eyes. But I prefer to keep the sight of your body as a pleasure for myself alone." When she frowned, puzzled, he added, "We have to go past the stables, you see."

Emma felt herself reddening. She focused on retying the knot of her belt, trying to think of something to say. She came up with nothing.

"That's a very sultry perfume you're wearing, Emma. What is it?"

"I'm not wearing perfume. I—" Oh hell. He must have picked up the smell of the mango. Now he had it, he would follow it like a proverbial hound on the scent. So she'd better take the initiative. She crossed to the dressing table and produced the mango from the drawer. "I imagine you're smelling this."

"Why, that's a mango, isn't it? We used to eat those in the West Indies. Utterly delicious." He put it to his nose to inhale its intoxicating perfume and smiled in delighted anticipation. "But how did you come by a mango, here in England, Emma? Pineapples, yes, but a mango couldn't have been grown here, surely?"

For once, she'd prepared a Plan B. "I haven't the slightest idea where it was grown. It came as a gift. From an anonymous source, so I could not return it."

"You have an anonymous admirer, you mean?" He scowled for a moment. Then his face cleared and he said, "More fool him to have sent a choice delicacy without any means of claiming his reward. Your admirer may be as rich as Croesus but he sounds to have more hair than wit." He sniffed the mango again and sighed out a long breath. "To tell you the truth, I don't give a fig for his intentions, whoever he is. This mango is begging to be eaten. And I know exactly how it should be done." He looked round the room. "Where is your cloak?"

Emma nodded towards the cupboard.

Will laid the mango carefully on the dressing table, fetched Emma's cloak and wrapped it round her, over the top of her wrapper. "Put on some outdoor shoes, my love." He hefted the mango in one hand and held out the other to Emma. "Sweet delectation first, I think. Then a refreshing swim."

Chapter Twenty-Two

WILL HAD SHRUGGED OFF HIS COAT and flung it onto the daybed. He was now attacking the buttons of his waistcoat in a very businesslike fashion. The mango, and his clasp knife, were waiting on the little table by the side of the bathing pool.

It was all too prosaic for words. And, worse, it was the middle of the morning. Soon Emma would be confronted by a totally naked, and aroused, lover, probably with a ripe mango in one hand and an open knife in the other. At this precise moment, she could imagine nothing less alluring. Being escorted across the Lamb House park in the sharp spring breeze, and past the stables with their watching eyes, had made her much too conscious that the servants knew what she and Will had been doing, and might be about to do again.

She pulled her cloak tighter, ignoring the fact that Will's bath house was very warm inside. Steamy, in more ways that one.

"The best way to eat a ripe mango is naked. In a bath. Or followed by a bath, if you prefer, love."

She gulped. "And how, pray, did you come by that information, my dear sir?" she asked archly, playing for time. She might love him – she *did* love him – but she wasn't sure she was ready for something as brazen as this.

"You don't expect me to betray all my guilty secrets, do you, Emma?" He was now naked to the waist and kicking off

197

his shoes. "Would you believe me if I said I had it from a friend?"

The look on Emma's face must have been eloquent.

"No, I thought not," he said with a quick grin, tossing aside his second stocking, "but that is my excuse, nonetheless."

When he put his hands to the waistband of his breeches, Emma found herself turning away. She couldn't help it. Seconds later he was beside her, taking her face in his hands and lifting her chin so that he could look into her eyes. She couldn't quite read his expression. It seemed to be a mixture of concern and laughter, but that shouldn't be possible, should it? Either the man was sorry for embarrassing her, or he wasn't. If he was laughing at her, he couldn't possibly be sorry as well.

"I apologise, my love. I see that I go much too fast, and take too much for granted." His rueful and lopsided smile was clearly directed at himself, not her, Emma realised. And he hadn't undone his breeches after all. "If you will sit for a while," he said, gesturing towards the daybed, "I will take action to, er, subdue my ardour."

More confident now, Emma raised an enquiring eyebrow.

He grinned like a schoolboy caught out in a prank. "I had water piped to the bath house from the river, to mix with the spring water. It's too hot, otherwise. If I stand under the cold douche for a while, it will do the trick. Probably." He gave her a brotherly peck on the cheek and started for the corner of the building. Just before he disappeared, he called back over his shoulder, "If I were you, love, I'd take off that heavy cloak. You'll soon be as red as a lobster if you don't."

Lobster, indeed. Think yourself lucky, Will Allmay, that there's nothing here for me to throw at you.

She could have thrown the mango, but that, she told herself, would have been a waste. And she couldn't abide waste. It was nothing at all to do with the sexy picture Will had been trying to paint – the two of them, half submerged in steaming water, with mango juice dripping down their naked bodies.

Help, he's getting to me again, even though it is the middle of the morning and the stable lads are probably listening avidly for the sound of the master's cavortings.

198

She had two choices, she decided, sighing. She could go back to the house and wait for him to reappear. Perhaps somewhat chastened. Or she could sit and wait here, knowing that he would use all his wiles to seduce her as soon as he came back. The cold water might quell his ardour for a bit, but she knew that it wouldn't stay quelled for long. She'd had ample evidence of that in the previous few hours.

She was chewing her lip, trying to make up her mind, when she heard some extremely ungentlemanly language from the far corner of the bath house. *Serves him right*, she thought, unkindly. And then she remembered his rueful apology and began to feel sorry for him. A little. He was suffering for her, after all. An ice-cold shower would definitely smart on a man's aroused body.

Her own body seemed to be getting hotter and hotter. Admitting defeat at last, she threw off her heavy cloak. Underneath she was wearing only her silk wrapper and that flimsy, filmy silk nightdress that Will had provided on her last visit. Not much of a barrier to a man's questing fingers. She should put her protecting cloak back on.

She did nothing of the sort. She straightened her back, clasped her hands sedately in her lap and lifted her chin. To wait for whatever would come next.

Will was shivering when he reappeared, but at least he wasn't totally naked. He had removed his breeches but not his drawers. Unfortunately for Emma's composure, the water had plastered the linen to Will's body, so that the drawers didn't conceal much at all. The cold had done its work. For now.

Emma tried not to look.

He picked up a towel from the end of the daybed and started to dry his torso, humming to himself as he rubbed. "Mmm. Exhilarating. Makes the whole body tingle. You should try it, you know."

Her body was already tingling in all sorts of hidden places. She didn't need a cold shower to help it along. She shook her head but kept her eyes firmly focused on her clasped fingers. She sensed when he approached her, though. She could almost feel the heat of his body radiating towards her. Her mouth was too dry to swallow.

"For a woman who has been married, and who has, er, spent some hours alone in my company, you are remarkably shy, Emma." His voice had sunk, again, to the seductive bass-baritone that reminded her of lustrous dark velvet. "Would you be offended if I said I rather like it? It's part of what you are – a virtuous and very special woman."

Emma wasn't at all sure she could be termed "virtuous" when she was having a passionate affair with the greatest stud in London. On the other hand, she had never been promiscuous. Before Will, there had been only her husband, Julian. Emma felt sure that it had been the same for Lady Emma Groatster and Sir John. "I–I don't know what to say. But thank you, Will, for understanding. That I am not—er, not—"

"That you are not the kind of lady who would ever break her marriage vows. I do not doubt, my dear, that you were faithful to Sir John while he lived. And that you are now equally faithful to me." He lifted one of her hands to his lips. Drops of cold water fell from his hair onto her skin. She was sure they sizzled as they hit. "You do not ask, I note, if I am equally faithful to you?" he added, in an even lower voice.

She felt herself blushing. In spite of the scorching heat between them, the question had flashed through her mind as he spoke, even though he had vowed his fidelity many times. She ought to believe him, to trust him, but that tiny smidgen of doubt kept reappearing, to mock her. She had trusted and loved once before. And she had been so, so wrong. Had Julian killed her ability to love and trust without reserve?

"It is as I said last night, dearest Emma. I love you. No other woman has ever made me feel as you do. No other woman ever could."

It was all getting much too deep, Emma decided, in the tiny part of her brain that could still think. She was a twenty-first century woman. How could she possibly commit herself to a Regency man? How could there be love and trust when he did not understand, and never could understand, who and what she was? Emma was beginning to feel she was drowning.

In desperation, she resorted to flippancy. "If you are as devoted as you claim, sir, why is it that you have failed to give me any breakfast? Almost anything would be acceptable for this starving woman. Even mango."

She saw the flash of hurt in his eyes, but it was quickly replaced by humour. And mischief. He knew – at least, Emma fervently hoped he knew – that her failure to respond to his declaration of love was not a rejection. He knew she loved him.

"My lady shall have mango," he said, with a sweeping bow that belonged to an earlier age. He crossed to the table, opened his knife and deftly cut down each side of the central stone. He offered the vivid orange halves to Emma on his open palms. "Which would you like? Or perhaps you are so hungry you must have both?"

Emma could cope with light-hearted teasing. "I would not deprive you of such a delicacy. We will share. If you could cut the fruit out of its skin for me?"

"Certainly. But before I begin, might it not be wise for you to remove your silken wrapper?" He grinned when she reddened. "I do not say so to make you blush, Emma, though your blushes are delightful, but because that is your own wrapper. Your abigail will expect you to have it when you return to her. And if it is stained with mango juice, she will ask questions that you might find difficult to answer."

He was right, blast him. But at least she wouldn't have to strip naked. Since her nightgown belonged here at the Lamb House, it wouldn't matter if it was stained. Emma undid her knotted belt and shrugged off her wrapper.

Will folded it carefully and laid it aside. "Out of reach of any spatters," he said.

What he actually meant, Emma knew, was that it was out of *her* reach if she had another attack of modesty. Very clever. She had to admit that, in the seduction department, Will May All was very plausible indeed.

He cut a chunk of mango flesh and brought it to her lips. It smelled so divine that Emma closed her eyes, imagining how it was going to taste. She had always adored ripe mango and she was going to relish this one, above any other, because she was sharing it with her lover. He touched the juicy flesh to her lips. Once. And again. If the fruit had been a fraction warmer, it would have felt exactly like a kiss. Even so, its touch was incredibly sensuous. "Open your mouth, sweeting," he said softly.

She didn't. She was enjoying the sensation too much to respond.

Cold juice dripped on to her breast. "Ooh," she gasped.

Will popped the fruit into her open mouth with a chuckle. "That'll teach you, m'lady, to do as you're told. At least where dripping fruit is concerned."

Emma tried to brush the spill away but only succeeded in spreading it all over the top half of the nightgown. Not only was the silk now stained, it was also clinging to her skin.

Will touched the back of a finger to one nipple with a murmur of appreciation. Sensation shuddered through her. "Last night you were deep rosy red. Today you are tinged with orange, like a sunburst. If I were to taste you, there, would you be as sweet as I imagine?" He paused for her reply, but she couldn't say a word. "May I taste, sweet Emma?" he asked softly.

She managed a tiny nod.

Even through the silk, she was lost in the magic of his touch the moment he put his mouth to her breast. She gave herself up to pure passion.

~ ~ ~

Afterwards, he sliced the remaining fruit into pieces and brought them to the side of the pool so that they could feed them to each other with their fingers while they floated and caressed and explored. "So you see, love, that my friend was right. Naked in the bath is the only way to eat ripe mango."

Emma smiled a cream-pot smile and said nothing.

Will was floating on his back and pulled her on top of him, so that her buttocks were supported by his hips and her head was resting on his shoulder. From this angle, she had an exceptionally good view of the erotic paintings on the upper walls and around the skylight in the ceiling of Will's bath house. *No worse than Victoria and Albert had in their private bathroom*, Emma told herself. *Victoria adored sex. So why shouldn't I?* Emma was so relaxed that she thought she might drift off to sleep in the enfolding warmth.

"Can you imagine, Will," she mused, dreamily, "that one day in the future, all the exotic fruits you've encountered on your travels, mangoes, and pawpaws, and bananas, and pineapples, will be available in every high street greengrocer's, for anyone and everyone to buy?"

He chuckled. The vibration through his body and into hers was intensely pleasurable. "No, I cannot. For how would they get here before they rotted? Fly?"

"Why not? In the future, there will be flying machines to carry people and cargo all around the globe."

"I wouldn't rely on a flying machine to carry anything anywhere," Will said, scornfully. He blew softly into her ear. "Balloons go wherever the wind takes them. Useless for anything practical."

"But the aeroplanes of the future won't be balloons." She turned in the water so that she could see his face. "They'll have wings and they'll be powered by engines."

He chuckled again, shaking his head in disbelief. "Like Trevithick's steam carriage, you mean? My brother John saw it demonstrated in London, years ago. He said it was enormous and weighed several tons. How would an engine like that stay up in the air? And where would it carry all the coal for the furnace? Come, Emma, admit you've been reading too many fairy tales. Elves and fairies may fly in stories. In the real world, people keep their feet on the ground."

She gave up. She didn't know enough about engineering to be able to describe the internal combustion engine, and certainly not the principles of a jet engine. There was such a enormous gap of understanding between the primitive steam engines of the Regency – Stephenson's Rocket was more than a decade away – and the hugely sophisticated machines of the twenty-first century. And she hadn't said a word yet about men going to the moon. If she was going to convince Will that she came from the future, she would have to tell him about things, and people, that he could relate to. Perhaps she should try a mention of Queen Victoria? But not today. Emma had done quite enough kite-flying for one day.

~ ~ ~

It took so long for Emma's sodden hair to dry that she had to agree to stay another night with Will. It would be, she admitted to herself – but not to him – no hardship at all. She was learning to enjoy the delights of a man's body as she never had before. And she was becoming less and less shy about her own as the hours passed and Will took her to new heights of pleasure.

"Tomorrow morning, I must go home, Will," she said when they were sitting companionably over a glass of wine after Sanding's more than passable supper.

"Will you come for another swim in the morning before you leave?"

She shook her head. "I would love to, but I cannot. For two reasons." She fixed him with a stern gaze. "First, I would have exactly the same problem as today. My hair would be soaked. It takes hours to dry and, by the time it was presentable again, it would be too late to leave. I suspect, sir," she added, wagging an accusing finger, "that you were aware of that when you made the suggestion?" Will had the grace to look a little shamefaced. "Quite. And second..." She paused dramatically until all his attention was on her face. "Second, we have eaten all the mango."

He burst out laughing. "Emma, you are magnificent. And an absolute darling." He raised his glass to her and drank deeply. "It goes much against the grain, but I agree that you should go home tomorrow." Then he added, a little anxiously, "But you will come again? Soon?"

Did she dare? She'd got away with one secret tryst, provided there were no awkward questions when she got home, but could she do it a second time? She longed to be with Will, but it was a dangerous game. What if Will's servants returned early? What if one of his friends came to pay a call and caught sight of Emma?

"You can tell your abigail that you have agreed, at Mrs Smith's urging, to visit her regularly. And since the invalid has such difficulty in sleeping, you have volunteered to keep her company in the long watches of the night, with reading and conversation. In other words, you will normally stay at least one night each time you visit."

"You have a very glib tongue, sir." What else did she

expect from a lover as practised as Will Allmay? "But I suppose it is plausible," she added thoughtfully. Besides, it offered the chance to do exactly what she longed to do. She couldn't pluck up the courage to say so to Will, however. She was less shy than before, but that would be going too far. Instead, she said lightly, "By the way, if you send me a note again, can you make it look more like a lady's hand? My abigail is suspicious."

"She'll be even more suspicious if you receive another note from 'Mrs Smith' in a totally different hand."

Emma made a face. He was right. Again. What else did she expect from a practised adulterer?

"Tell Bailey that your invalid friend's handwriting has deteriorated due to her infirmities. That should do it."

"Yes, it should. Very clever. Just what a practised adulterer would suggest, of course." She had not intended to say anything so insulting, but she had certainly been thinking it and, somehow, the words had slipped out. She should apologise.

The corners of Will's mouth tightened. "I am not an adulterer," he said proudly. "You are not married. And neither am I."

Not yet. But Patience is waiting to get her claws into you.

Chapter Twenty-Three

LESS THAN TWENTY-FOUR HOURS LATER, as Emma's foot touched the flagway, her own front door opened and a fashionably dressed lady tripped down the steps, followed by her maid. Patience Sinclair-Smythe.

Of all the women in the world, why did it have to be *her*?

Patience came across to Emma, but before either of them could offer a hand, Patience stopped dead, staring wide-eyed at Sanding.

Oh dear. Out of the corner of her eye, Emma saw that the "simpleton" on the box was slouching even lower and had pulled his hat down almost to the end of his nose.

Patience pointed an accusing finger at the old man. "But you are Sanding, are you not? Sir William's man?" she demanded, in a voice that was rising to a shriek. "Yet this is not his carriage. Why should—?"

Emma took Patience firmly by the elbow and propelled her back up the steps into the front hall. She nodded to the footman to close the door after the maid and led Patience into the little saloon where they could speak in private. "You will allow me to say, my dear Miss Sinclair-Smythe," she began sternly, "that it is not seemly for a lady of your station to bandy words with a mere servant on the public highway."

Patience coloured a little, but recovered quickly. "But...

Oh, I see. I suppose William must have dismissed him. For cause, I do not doubt. Sanding is an old Navy man and much too uncouth to be personal servant to a gentleman." She dropped her voice to a confidential whisper. "I have already made up my mind that, once William and I are married, Sanding will be given his discharge from our service. I could not bear to have such a man about me."

Patience had a great deal to learn about handling men as strong-minded as Will Allmay. She needed helpful advice, but she would get none at all from Emma.

"Will you not be seated, Miss Sinclair-Smythe?" Emma said politely, taking a chair by the fire for herself. Patience must not be allowed to leave until Will's carriage was well out of sight.

Patience sank elegantly onto the sofa. "Thank you. Now that we are private, may I ask, ma'am, about that plain carriage you arrived in?" She leaned eagerly towards Emma. "Is it yours?"

"No, it is not." Patience had to be stopped in her tracks before her suspicions fixed on Emma and Will. Together. "And if you were planning to enquire about how the lady who owns the carriage might have come to employ that particular servant, I suggest you do not, for it would be an unpardonable breach of confidence if I were to provide you with any information on that head. You will excuse my plain speaking, my dear, but you are very young and inexperienced in the ways of the world." Yes, that was good. And since Emma was older and of much higher status than Patience, there was nothing the girl could do but grit her teeth and take the medicine that Emma was doling out. "You will allow me to give you a hint. It does not do for a young unmarried gel to be making impertinent enquiries about her elders. I am sure that, if your mama were present, she would say much the same."

Patience had been growing redder and redder as Emma spoke.

"If you wish to know what Sir William has done in relation to his servant, you should address yourself to him. Preferably not in public," Emma finished severely.

Well before Patience could seek Will out, Emma must

warn him of the need to cook up a credible story. Perhaps Sanding had been loaned to an indigent acquaintance? Yes, that might do. Emma would suggest it.

Will was probably on the case already, she realised, since he must have heard Patience's accusation and recognised the danger. They must get in contact quickly, though. They needed to get their stories in sync. If the dreadful Lady Augusta were to ask Emma about the incident with Sanding, Emma couldn't refuse to answer. And Lady Augusta's long nose would poke into every potential flaw in Emma's tale.

Time to paper over the cracks in Emma's relationship with Patience.

"Enough of such distasteful matters." Emma smiled broadly at Patience as if the girl were a welcome guest. "I am sorry I was from home when you called, Miss Sinclair-Smythe. But now that I am returned, may I offer you some tea?"

They conversed about mundane topics until the tea tray was brought in. The interlude seemed to have restored much of Patience's composure. As she took her cup from Emma, she said confidingly, "You must know that I was not solely making a courtesy call when we met outside, Lady Emma." She paused dramatically, waiting for a response.

Good manners required Emma to say something encouraging. "Indeed? Was there something particular you wanted to tell me, my dear?"

"I—that is, Mama said that, since you are so well acquainted with William, you should be told. In the strictest confidence, naturally."

Emma did not like the sound of this. Not one bit. Especially not the sly accusation that she was "so well acquainted with William". Denying it would achieve nothing, though, so Emma kept silent, waiting to see what would come next.

"Mama has decided that we have waited long enough. She has agreed that the betrothal may be announced next month."

Emma concentrated on stirring her tea, round and round and round. When she had regained enough control to speak, she looked up and said brightly, "Sir William is a fortunate

208

man. May I ask when the wedding is to be?"

"That is not yet decided. Mama says— Mama favours a summer wedding. Not this year, you understand." Patience tittered. "There would not be enough time to order my bride clothes. Once the season is over, Madame Élise will have fewer commissions from her other clients. I dare say she will be delighted to be designing my bride clothes in the autumn. It is immodest to say so, I know, but Mama says that it will be the wedding of the year."

I bet she does, Emma thought bitterly. *And I bet the old witch encouraged you to tell me so, too.*

"Your excitement is understandable, I am sure," Emma said. "I shall offer my congratulations to Sir William, when next I see him."

Patience raised a warning hand. "Would it be very *impertinent* of me, ma'am, to ask you not to do so until the betrothal has been announced? What if your conversation were overheard? Mama has *such* an aversion to tittle-tattle. She would be prostrated if there were to be rumours in the newspapers before the formal announcement."

Emma managed to nod and say, "I shall wait then." She drew on the last of her inner strength. "May I offer you more tea, Miss Sinclair-Smythe?"

But Patience had discharged her malign errand and clearly had no desire to remain one moment longer with a woman she saw as a rival for her future husband's affections. She rose, murmuring polite protestations of regret at being unable to stay longer. A brief handshake, and she was gone.

Along with Emma's peace of mind. And all her ridiculous hopes.

~ ~ ~

Emma sat by her bedroom fireplace and stared unseeingly into the flames. She had been so full of naive hopes and dreams. Then her nemesis, Patience Sinclair-Smythe, had appeared to dash her down. And to smile triumphantly while she did so.

Emma told herself, sternly, that she had been stupid to harbour hopes at all. She was a twenty-first century woman and Will was a Regency man. There could be no future for them, apart from the odd coupling on the sly. However enjoyable it might be, it could not continue for long. It was probably right that he should marry a woman of his own time and his own class, though Emma could have wished for a softer, kinder mate for him than Patience.

The real question was: what was Emma herself to do now?

She sighed deeply. By rights, she should be sobbing in despair at her lost love, or tearing her hair out, but all her emotions seemed to be in the deep freeze. She was not lovelorn Lady Emma Groatster, mistress of this fine house, but Emma Stanley, coldly rational museum curator, marooned in an alien time. And since Emma Stanley was going to have to return to the modern day, and stay there, she would make the most of her advantages here in the Regency, while she had the chance.

Her grand plan could still be made to work. It would mean remaining in the Regency for a little longer, but it would be worth it. It would help her to find out everything she wanted to know about Lady Emma Groatster – if there was anything to discover – and it would certainly be a huge boost to Emma's museum career. Since she would have nothing else, she was going to concentrate on that, from now on.

What's not to like, as they say in the twenty-first century?

The downside, she had to admit to herself, was Will Allmay. And the dreadful Patience. Emma would have to take steps to avoid them both.

If Patience calls, or her harridan of a mother, the servants will be instructed to say I am not at home.

Will would not call, but he might send another note. He might even ask Emma to visit their fictitious invalid again.

If Will sends a note, I will burn it, unread.

Decisions taken, Emma rose to pull the bell. When Bailey appeared, Emma gave orders that Richard Cosway was to be invited to start work at his earliest convenience. And that the painting room was to be prepared immediately.

"Yes, m'lady. Have you decided what you will wear to sit for Mr Cosway?"

On that point, Emma did not have to stop to think. It was all part of her grand plan. "I shall wear my gold lace gown, Bailey. It is my favourite, as you know, and becomes me very well, I think. I shall wear my sapphire earrings and pendant, also."

"And in your hair, m'lady? The diamond tiara?"

"No, that would be too much. And yet I should perhaps have something. Could you fix the sapphire pendant in my hair, do you think, rather than on its collar?"

"Hmm. That would look very well, I must say. In the style of an aigrette, perhaps? I will see what I can do." Bailey bustled away to start issuing instructions to the household.

Emma had nothing to do now but wait.

~ ~ ~

A note from "Mrs Smith" arrived late that afternoon, addressed as before. And in the same unladylike hand.

Bailey delivered it to Emma in the bookroom. "The boy did not wait for a reply," she announced with a frown of disapproval.

"Mrs Smith will not be expecting one," Emma said calmly, laying the note aside. "It will be to confirm the dates we have already discussed," she added airily. She could not throw Will's unopened note on the fire while Bailey was in the room. "Poor lady. She insists on writing her letters herself, but her hands are so twisted she can barely hold the pen." Emma picked up the note and waved it under Bailey's nose. "One would hardly credit that as a lady's hand. But it is so."

"As you say, m'lady. Will there be anything else?" Bailey did not sound totally convinced, but it was the best Emma could do.

"No. Except—yes. Have you made any progress with turning my pendant into an aigrette? Mr Cosway sent word that he will be arriving first thing in the morning, so you have very little time left, I'm afraid."

Bailey beamed at Emma. "Don't you worry your pretty head, m'lady. I'm almost done. You shall have your wish and you will look splendid, I promise." She sniffed. "I only hope that this Mr Cosway is skilled enough to do you justice."

"Mr Cosway has painted the Prince Regent, Bailey, and many other notables," Emma said. "I think that should be recommendation enough."

Bailey's compressed lips suggested she was swallowing an

indiscreet retort about the Regent and his cronies. In the end, she simply curtseyed herself out without a word.

The moment the door closed behind the abigail, Emma crossed to the fire with Will's note and reached for the poker to stir up the flames.

But what if the note was about Sanding?

Oh dear. It might well be. And it was always wise to prepare for the unexpected. So Emma would do better to open the note, read what Will was proposing as a story to cover Sanding's apparent dismissal, and *then* burn it. If there were endearments in the note, or an invitation to return to the Lamb House, she would not read them.

Will's note was full of the Sanding cover story. An elderly Portuguese lady, an old acquaintance from Will's Navy days, had arrived in London unexpectedly and was travelling to see friends in Shropshire, Hereford and south Wales. Since the Portuguese lady's English was not nearly as fluent as her French, Sanding was to accompany her as driver, general factotum and, when necessary, interpreter. On loan. Sanding's Portuguese was rudimentary but his French was adequate, Will added. At the end of the lady's visit to Wales, she would depart by ship from Falmouth without returning to London. She was "desolated" that she would be unable to renew her acquaintance with Lady Emma, but she had greatly enjoyed the time they had spent together. She was also immensely grateful to Sir William for the temporary loan of Sanding, who would be returning to London on the mail coach, at her expense.

It was a much more convincing tale, Emma had to admit, than the one she had dreamt up. By the time Will's cover story was shared with anyone, the "Portuguese lady" would be long gone from London, never to return. And it would appear that the only member of the *ton* she had met during her brief stay in London, apart from her old friend Will Allmay, was Lady Emma Groatster, to whom she had lent her carriage. Driven by Sanding, her temporary factotum. All very neat indeed. Yes, Will Allmay was a very clever and devious man. No doubt that was one of the reasons he had been such a successful commander during the French wars.

212

Emma's hand began to shake as she reached the end of the note. She had expected endearments from Will. There were none. Not one single word of love. The tears that had been buried deep in permafrost a few hours earlier were suddenly blurring her vision. She could hardly see to keep reading. At the very bottom of the page, squeezed in under the last line about the Portuguese lady, she could just make out a cryptic message in tiny writing. An afterthought, clearly. "Saturday. Hackney. As before."

And that was all.

She flung the note into the flames.

I won't go. I can't meet him again. Not after Patience. It would hurt too much.

She buried her face in her hands and let the tears flow.

It was a long time before she regained enough control even to begin to decide what to do. She was losing the man she loved. It hurt. Deeply. She wanted to lash out, to take revenge, to hurt Will as he had hurt her.

Why had he sent not one single word of love? Was that Patience's doing too?

Emma would not go to the Lamb House on Saturday. He would worry, a little, when she did not come to him, but he would assume she had been unable to get away without being caught. He would not expect a message, since he knew she had no safe means of contacting him.

She clung to her decision to refuse to see him. It was her only lifeline to rationality. No doubt "Mrs Smith" would send other notes, suggesting other meetings. Emma would not go to any of them.

If Emma really wanted to avoid Will, and anything to do with him, the obvious solution was to transition back to the modern day, and stay there, but she couldn't do that. She had to be ready to sit for Richard Cosway. She needed that miniature. It could be the key to her glittering future career.

She wiped the last of her tears and forced herself to think coherently.

The next day was Friday. Cosway could have the whole day to paint Emma. She was prepared to sit for hours, if necessary. And he could have all of Saturday, too, if he wished. By early evening, he should have left for his own studio to finish the background detail of the work. So Emma would be free to transition back to the museum as soon as he left on Saturday, which would be hours before Will's luxurious hackney arrived to lurk in the mews behind the terrace.

Once she was back in the museum, on her own twenty-first century turf, she'd be much more objective about her dilemma, she was sure. She would work out exactly what to do. She would have to return to the Regency one last time – there was no way round that, since she needed to get hold of the finished miniature – but she ought to be able to find a way of carrying out her plan without involving Will Allmay.

Preferably, she thought fiercely, *without setting eyes on him at all.*

Chapter Twenty-Four

"AND THE DEATH OF BUTTERFLY WAS so moving that I cried,"
Melanie said, shaking her head. "Richard didn't," she added
with a grin, "but that's par for the course. I can tell you that the
only time I've ever seen him shed a tear was when Chloë was
born. He tried to hide it, even then. Men, eh?"

Emma murmured sympathetically and nodded. Melanie
had been going on about *Madam Butterfly* all through the
meal. Since Richard and Melanie had been kind enough to
invite her to Sunday supper, Emma had had to pretend to be
more interested in the Puccini than she really was.

"Chloë really enjoyed her time with you last night,
Emma," Richard said, avoiding his wife's eye. "She said you
tell wonderful stories. Much better than mine."

Emma smiled and scraped up the last spoonful of her
lemon mousse.

"But she did complain about one thing. Apparently you
wouldn't get down on the floor to play horses with her. Must
admit I was surprised. I thought it was the game the two of
you always played?"

"Ah. Yes, well—" Emma began. "The truth is that I was
too stiff to do it last night."

Richard's eyebrows went up. "Must have been very
energetic housework you were doing yesterday."

Emma laughed. "Actually, I went riding yesterday."

"Horseriding?" Melanie said. "You've never mentioned that before."

"I rode all through my teens and at uni as well. I stopped after I got married. I, er, I couldn't fit it in." She swallowed and pushed the black memory away. "Anyway, I decided that my weekends were too boring these days – housework and shopping are not exactly riveting, are they? – and that I would start riding again. And I had this crazy idea that I ought to do something completely new. So I decided to learn to ride side-saddle."

"Side-saddle? I didn't think anyone did that nowadays," Melanie said, surprised.

"The Queen used to do it at the Trooping of the Colour. My instructor showed me a video of her. She looked very elegant. Before our time, of course," Emma added.

"I remember seeing her on TV," Richard said, leaning forward. "She used to ride a big black horse called 'Burmese'. It was a gift from the Mounties, wasn't it?"

Emma nodded. "The Queen did it as if it was the easiest thing in the world. I can tell you, from yesterday's experience, that it isn't. Having both legs on the same side of the horse feels weird."

"Doesn't it feel a bit unsafe?" Melanie asked. "Didn't you worry you'd slide off?"

Emma knew that Melanie had never ridden. "I was surprised at how safe it actually felt. There's a special horn on the saddle that you hook your leg around so it's a lot safer than it looks. The most difficult part of it was keeping my body straight in the saddle. The instructor said that upper body posture was the key to making it work. I think I got the hang of it, more or less, by the end of the lesson." In fact, her instructor had said she was a natural.

"So will you do more?" Melanie asked doubtfully.

"Yes, I think so. I really enjoyed it." Surprisingly, she had. And so, even though she wouldn't ever be riding in the Regency – she planned only one more, very short, visit to the past – she had decided to have more side-saddle lessons. She would do some normal riding, as well. "If I ride regularly, I

216

won't be as stiff and sore as I was yesterday. Tell Chloë I'm sorry. Next time I come to babysit, I'll do better, I promise."

"So you've been nursing your aches today, have you? Hot baths and embrocation?" Richard added, with a laugh.

"Well..." Emma made a face. Why not tell them about her discovery? She couldn't tell them the whole truth, though. "Actually, I spent most of the day at the Lamb House. Well, not in the house, but in the grounds. It was such a beautiful spring day and, after the fun of riding yesterday, I wanted to be out in the fresh air. No, Richard," she added, guessing the sarky comment that was on the tip of his tongue, "I didn't do my housework before I left home. I decided that housework could wait till next weekend." She chuckled. "I went there to enjoy the park and garden, but I think I may found something."

"Really? What?" he said, eagerly.

"I'm not sure exactly what it is," she began, untruthfully – she had gone there determined to look for Will's bath house and she was pretty sure she had found it – "but I think I've found the remains of a building under a stand of trees, near the old stables. It must have been demolished ages ago. Geraldine wasn't at the house yesterday so I couldn't ask her about it, but I'll do so the next time I'm there. If there really is something under those trees, maybe we can do a geophys survey to determine the extent of it."

"Fascinating," Richard said. "Any idea what it might have been for?"

Emma knew better than to push her luck. "No. Probably just for storage. Or something equally boring. I'll see what Geraldine says. If it was at all important, there'll be something in the archives, I imagine."

Richard nodded enthusiastically.

Melanie was looking bored. She obviously didn't share Richard and Emma's professional fascination for computer surveys of the ground to determine where buildings might have stood, centuries before. "Richard mentioned something about a damaged ballgown. Gold lace, you said, didn't you, love? It sounds fabulous."

"It's very badly damaged, unfortunately, but it would have

217

been quite dazzling when it was new," Emma replied. "It's not a court dress – ladies were still wearing dresses with hoops at court then – but it would have been worn to the highest of high society balls, I'm sure."

"Do we know who it belonged to?" Melanie was clearly much more interested in costume than in lost buildings.

"No, the records are very poor." Melanie looked so disappointed that Emma decided, on the spur of the moment, to tell her a bit more about the lace gown. "But I think – I'm speculating here, because I've got very little to go on – that it may have belonged to a rich Regency widow who was connected to the Lamb House in some way. I'm trying to research her, but it's difficult because I haven't been able to discover what her surname was. I'm pretty sure she was Lady Emma Something, though."

Melanie laughed. "No wonder you want to know about her. I'd want to follow up a mysterious Lady Melanie, if I came across one. Don't suppose I would, though?"

Emma shook her head. "It's a lovely name, but I don't think it was common in the early nineteenth century. They went for Mary, and Jane, and Catherine."

"And Emma," Melanie put in, with a grin. "Is the gold lace gown on display? I'd really love to see it. It sounds amazing."

"I can arrange a special showing, just for you, Melanie. I'll get it out, next time you and Chloë come to the museum. Chloë will have to learn how to look without touching, though."

Melanie winced. "That won't be easy, but I'll do my best." She started to gather up the dessert plates. "Would you like coffee?"

"Yes, please. Thank you for a lovely meal, Melanie. Much, much tastier than the microwave supper for one I'd been planning." Emma made a face. "It was very kind of you both to invite me."

"Least we could do when you filled last night's babysitting breach at such short notice," Richard replied, getting up to help with the clearing. "No, stay there, Emma. Our kitchen is barely big enough for two, far less three." After Melanie had left the room, he added, in a low voice, "And you were

218

remarkably restrained about *Madam Butterfly* as well. Melanie was a bit OTT, I thought. Thank you for putting up with her riding her hobby horse."

"I'd put up with anything for Melanie's lemon mousse," Emma said, with a grin, as he followed his wife into the kitchen. It was true that Melanie was a terrific cook. And sitting round the table in their cosy living room, chatting about opera and life in general, Emma felt very much at ease. In Will's Regency, had she ever felt this relaxed? The problem was that, when she was Lady Emma Groatster, she was constantly on edge, watching out for pitfalls. If she really got things wrong, she might even be ostracised. And then where would she be?

In the back of her mind, her conscience told her she was making a mountain out of a molehill, mostly in order to rationalise her cowardly decision to desert Will Allmay. Lady Emma Groatster, daughter of a peer of the realm, could get away with pretty much anything. Society would smile on her faux pas and call them merely "eccentric".

Emma sighed, remembering. Yes, there were rules in the Regency. No lady there could be as free as a woman in the twenty-first century, though a Regency widow could do very much as she liked, especially if she was as rich as Lady Emma Groatster. But a Regency wife was a different story. A wife was the property of her husband and bound by his decisions. A husband could be a tyrant.

Will Allmay would never be a tyrant to Emma.

But he wasn't going to marry Emma. He was going to marry Patience Sinclair-Smythe.

And married to that woman, Emma thought viciously, *he'll have every reason to end up being a tyrant.*

It could never be a happy marriage. Will, who loved to laugh and tease, would be shackled for the rest of his life to a humourless, detestable harridan who would probably end up as bad as her mother. Or worse. Marriage to Patience would be bound to make him miserable. Surely a woman who really loved him would try to save him from that?

Emma gulped. Did she love him enough to try? She honestly didn't know.

~ ~ ~

On Monday morning, Emma arrived at the museum bright and early, to do some more data input before anyone else arrived. She would have liked to go straight to the Lamb House, to quiz Geraldine about the demolished bath house, but unfortunately the museum was expecting an important visitor, an assessor from a charitable foundation. If he were really impressed with what Emma showed him, he might recommend a donation. And, after deep cuts in their Local Authority funding, the museum needed all the cash it could get its hands on.

Emma found she was actually enjoying the data entry work. It was satisfying to see the pile of index cards going down. Emotionally, too, she was on a more even keel after the excitement of the weekend. She had decided to take things one step at a time. She wouldn't decide anything about what she should do in the Regency until she'd sorted out all the loose ends about the modern-day Lamb House. She planned to spend the whole of Tuesday there. And to insist that Geraldine take her discovery seriously. If there was material in the archives about Will's bath house, Emma would need Geraldine's expertise to dig it out.

"Emma?" It was Richard, delivering the day's post. "This came for you. Looks like a book." He handed her a standard cardboard carton, big enough to contain a single paperback.

"I didn't order anything online," Emma said, puzzled.

"Perhaps it's a gift to the museum?" Richard said, dropping the package onto her desk. "Lovely to see you last night. Melanie sends her love. Sorry I can't stop to chat. I must get on with dishing all these out. We're very popular today, for some reason." He left the office with a cheery wave.

Emma ripped open the package. A small black book fell out, and a slip of paper which proved to be a gift card from an online bookseller. There was no sender's name.

Emma had learned to be very chary about anonymous gifts. Or anonymous phone calls. Or anonymous anything. The person behind them always seemed to be Julian. And his motives were always vindictive.

She checked the carton. It looked as if it had been sent

directly from the retailer, but it was always possible that Julian could have intercepted it en route. She should have been warier about opening it. Emma stopped and took a deep breath. She needed to stay calm here. And she should certainly be wary of touching anything Julian might have sent. She used a pen to lever the cover open. Her anonymous "gift" turned out to be a rather classy address book.

Why would Julian send Emma an address book, of all things?

She'd had quite enough of Julian's playacting and gamesmanship. She refused to let him get to her any more. If he were here now, she decided, she'd lob his damned address book at his head. Followed by every weighty tome in the place until he was buried under a mountain of them.

Something odd about the front page caught her eye. The book had gilded thumb-index tabs for all the letters of the alphabet.

There was no S. It had been cut out. And S was for Stanley. Emma Stanley.

Another one of Julian's mind games, was it? Well, this time she'd show him. She pulled the book open where the missing S should have been. The page was still there. It had been scissored into the shape of a large E. For Emma. And coloured blood red.

Fury flooded through her. She swore viciously. She tore out the bloody page and stuffed it into the shredder. Then she tore out all the rest of the pages, handful by handful, and shredded them too. When only the black board covers were left, she tossed them into the bin. Followed by the cardboard carton.

She hesitated for all of a second over the gift card. Should she use it to make enquiries about the sender? No, that was what Julian would expect her to do. He enjoyed putting Emma through the wringer. And it would be useless in any case, because there would be nothing to find. Julian was too good at covering his tracks.

She put the gift card through the shredder. And then she did a war dance round it, as if she'd put her bastard ex in there too. Because, at long last, in her mind, she had.

~ ~ ~

Next morning, in the shade of the stand of trees behind the Lamb House's old stable block, Emma and Geraldine began probing the ground. After half an hour's careful work, Emma sat back on her heels and laid her tiny trowel aside. "There is something here, isn't there? Don't you think we should follow it up?"

Geraldine was frowning. She must be thinking through the possible ramifications of the discovery. "A dig would be expensive, even if we used students and volunteers," she said. "Geophys would be expensive, too, especially with all these tress. And if it turned out to be the foundations of a common barn, we'd have wasted our money. We need it to be something that would attract more paying visitors to the house. Something with pizzazz, like an underground room for a Lamb House Hellfire Club." She smiled wryly. "As far as I know, the Lamb House was always rather tame."

Emma suppressed a smile. She wouldn't have called Will's erotic pictures "tame" at all. Still, she had an opening now; she'd better make the most of it. "If it turned out to be something interesting, we might be able to get a grant for the excavation. The assessor who was at the museum yesterday might be interested, you know. His foundation seems to have a lot of money to throw around."

"Really?"

"Look, Geraldine, why don't we have a trawl through the archives and see if we can find any mention of a building on this site? I know it's your domain, but I'd be more than happy to help with the donkey work." A bit of ego-stroking never did any harm at times like this. And it was access to Geraldine's precious archives that Emma really wanted, since excavation would find nothing. "You tell me what to do, and I'll do it."

Geraldine smiled. "Well… Yes, all right. I could spare some time this afternoon, so we could make a start straight after lunch, if you like?"

Emma wouldn't be having any lunch today. Her lunch break was going to be used to sneak into the blue bedchamber and retrieve the digital watch from under the floor.

~ ~ ~

When she turned up in Geraldine's archive room at two o'clock, Emma was beaming. The watch was safely stowed in the bottom of her pocket and she'd managed to cover her tracks pretty well too, she thought. She was ready for her next challenge.

Geraldine's expression wasn't encouraging. She'd obviously been in the archive room for a while because there were architects' drawings strewn across the big table. "I've looked through all the house plans, and there's no record of that building."

Emma wasn't daunted. In her gut, she'd known there was something odd about Will's bath house and its demolition. "But your records can't be complete, can they? There are clearly foundations there."

Geraldine agreed, reluctantly. "If the demolition took place centuries ago, medieval or earlier, it wouldn't be on any of the plans. But we really need it to be more recent than that." She brightened suddenly. "I know. I'll go through the prints and drawings of the house. They go back to the eighteenth century. Your building might be shown in one of them." She made for the drawers where the prints were stored. "Oh," she said, turning back to Emma, "there's also a big box of nineteenth century documents that haven't been catalogued yet. Can't say I'd fancy the job of going through them, myself. In some of them, the handwriting is almost impossible to decipher."

"I've done quite a lot of work with old written records," Emma said eagerly. "I could look through them, if you like, while you get on with the drawings."

"You're a sucker for punishment, aren't you?" Geraldine said, obviously relieved to be spared hours of tedious work. "Come on, I'll dig out the papers for you. The box is in the storeroom back here."

After hours of poring through documents that were mostly about business matters like rents, Emma found a little bunch of letters tucked between two leases in the bottom of the box. From the handwriting, they looked like a lady's letters, so there must be a good chance they would not be about the price of the latest stock bull.

She spread out the first letter and began to read. It didn't date from the Regency. It was from decades later, near the end of Victoria's reign when envelopes were commonly used. Unfortunately, none of these letters had its envelope so Emma had neither full names nor addresses. The first letter began simply, "My dearest Fanny," and was signed only, "Your affectionate friend, Sarah". The gossipy contents were fascinating. If Emma hadn't been on the hunt for information about the bath house, she would have spent happy hours devouring this stash. Instead, she skimmed them quickly, one by one.

In the second to last, she struck gold. Sarah was complaining that she would never now see the inside of the forbidden bath house, because Fanny's uncle proposed to demolish it. "I do not believe it could be so *very* bad," Sarah had written. "I understand, of course, that as a bath house it became useless after the hot spring ceased to flow, but the building could be used for some other purpose, could it not? Perhaps you might persuade your uncle to turn it into a summer house, so that visitors might view the art? If your uncle has truly decided on such a drastic step as demolition, he may be destroying works of real value."

Emma almost tore the paper of the last letter in her haste to open it. It was full of apologies. Sarah was almost begging Fanny not to end their friendship, though she was trying to justify her own position as well. "Needless to say, I respect your uncle's decision, dearest Fanny. He is a man of the highest Christian principles and, since he has decreed that the paintings are obscene, I would not, for a moment, suggest otherwise. It was just that it seemed to me somewhat drastic to demolish the whole building, and remove all records of its existence besides, for the sake of a few obscene paintings which could have been covered with whitewash. However, it is done now and I promise I will never mention it again. I would not have such a petty disagreement sour our friendship."

Emma gave a whoop of triumph. The friendship had probably foundered over the demolition of the bath house, for there were no more letters. But that didn't matter. What Emma had here was enough to prove that the bath house had existed and that some late Victorian do-gooder, inspired by puritan religious zeal, had had it demolished. He'd had all mention of it removed from the records, too, which would explain why Geraldine couldn't find it on any of the plans.

Emma rushed out to share her discovery with Geraldine.

The house manager was more than delighted. "Not quite as racy as the Hellfire Club, but worth pursuing, certainly. I wonder if there were any paintings below ground level? If the plunge bath itself had paintings on the sides, they might still be there to be excavated. Do you think your assessor friend might be interested?"

Emma knew perfectly well that there were no erotic paintings in the bath itself, but she promised to ask the assessor to visit the Lamb House. "I'm sure he'll be interested in what we've found out about the bath house. And even if he doesn't feel able to recommend a grant for a dig, perhaps we could interest him in the restoration of the bedchamber with the dangerous floors? If previous owners of the Lamb House had dodgy paintings in their bath house, they might have had some on the bedroom walls too, don't you think?"

Geraldine grinned. "Erotic paintings in the house itself would be a real draw. I'm not going to argue with your intuition, Emma. Not after this. You've certainly made a find about this bath house. You'll be written up in all the journals, I expect." She patted Emma on the back. "Better prepare yourself for being famous."

Emma ignored that. For the moment, all that mattered was that she had retrieved the watch and proved the existence of the bath house.

So Will's Regency Lamb House was definitely the place where she and Will had been together. What she had experienced was the past life of a real house. Were the people, Will Allmay and Lady Emma Groatster, real too? Without documentary proof, that was much more difficult to answer but, if her final trip back to the Regency panned out as she hoped, she would soon have the evidence she needed on that score, too.

Her modern-day career could wait until her return. There would be plenty of time for the triumph that would bring

Emma the professional recognition she was now determined to achieve. Perhaps, once she had that, she would be able to stop looking over her shoulder?

Chapter Twenty-Five

ON WEDNESDAY NIGHT, AFTER A PRODUCTIVE day at the museum, during which she had arranged for the charity assessor to visit the Lamb House towards the end of the week, Emma waited impatiently in the research room for St Mary's to begin to strike. The ballgown was laid across the table as usual. Everything else was the same, except that, this time, when she put her arm through the golden sleeve, she was going to have Will's dressing-room key in her hand. It needed to go back to where it belonged and this was Emma's last chance to return it.

Because this was definitely, absolutely definitely, the last time Emma was going to make the transition.

~ ~ ~

Fate was on Emma's side for once, she decided, for she arrived back in her own bedchamber in her own Regency house. And she was clutching Will's key, too. Excellent. She tucked it into her reticule before Bailey could appear and ask about it.

Emma sat down in the chair by the fire and held out her hands to the flames. How many days had passed since she was last here? If Bailey asked about her evening, Emma should be able to fob her off with platitudes about boring conversations and meeting the same people as she always did. Time was more difficult. And, in some ways, more important. She needed to find out what day it was. She hoped she would find a way of asking subtly, but she would be winging it. Would inspiration come?

She let the flickering fire calm her nerves for a good ten minutes before she rang the bell for the abigail.

Bailey appeared carrying a steaming cup. "I thought you might welcome a tisane to help you sleep, m'lady." She put the cup on the dressing table and began to remove Emma's jewellery. "You will deny it, I know, but I have noticed that Lady Mumford's parties often give you the headache."

Yes. Thank you, Bailey. But that's not the question I really need an answer to.

"I will admit to being fatigued, some of the conversation was tedious in the extreme, but I do not have the headache tonight. I will drink your tisane, though. It will be soothing. I am sure it will help me to sleep." She yawned theatrically. "Do I have any engagements tomorrow? I cannot quite remember." Emma hoped that tomorrow was not Sunday. If it were, her question would sound peculiar, given that Sunday was not generally a day for engagements other than divine service.

"Nothing of importance, m'lady. Nothing to stop you from sleeping late if you wish. Although I suppose—" Bailey pursed her lips. "I suppose I should mention that a message came while you were out. Mr Richard Cosway begged leave to wait on you first thing tomorrow morning to deliver your portrait. Shall I send to tell him to call in the afternoon, instead?"

"No, certainly not." So several days must have passed. But how many? "Since Cosway has finished my portrait so quickly, it would be courteous to make the effort to be available when he delivers it. Wake me in good time in the morning, please."

Bailey harrumphed. She clearly did not approve of suiting the convenience of someone she considered a mere tradesman. "I had always understood that paintings took weeks, or even months. It's been barely a week. This Cosway knows what he's about, does he, m'lady?"

"Indeed he does, Bailey. He did say it would take about a week. This is not a grand oil painting, after all. He works in watercolours. And the ivory is very small."

So it was about a week since she had sat for Cosway. To be absolutely sure of the date, she asked for the newspaper to be sent up. She pretended that one of the guests at Lady Mumford's party had mentioned something of interest that she wished to read for herself. Problem solved.

Emma congratulated herself. She would have both the day and the date. She would be able to sleep sound in Lady Emma Groatster's huge bed.

After an early breakfast, Emma took herself down to the bookroom to prepare for Cosway's arrival. He was commendably prompt. And he looked pleased with himself, too, as he handed over the work for her approval.

The miniature was stunningly beautiful, against a clear blue background. It was a pretty fair likeness, though Cosway had taken some liberties to make the image flattering to his sitter. He had painted Emma's eyes larger and more lustrous than they really were, and her neck much too long and elegant. The soft masses of red hair looked fuller than the real thing, too. But Emma wasn't going to complain. There was a lot to be said for having a portrait that was not an exact likeness of Emma Stanley, modern museum curator. It could raise far too many questions.

She turned the portrait over to check that he had carried out her instructions to the letter. There was a vast amount of writing on the back. And it was so small and crabbed that it was impossible to make out more than a letter here and there. She should have thought of that. Richard Cosway was a very old man. His hand might be deliberately steady and careful with a paintbrush, but with pen and ink he was obviously much more slapdash. He hadn't used normal black ink, either, but a watery sepia. Was black ink too dark to use on translucent ivory? Might it have shown through and spoiled the portrait on the front?

No matter how much she screwed up her eyes, she couldn't decipher his text. She would need a magnifying glass. She gave up, for now. But she had to be sure it was all there, so she said, in a reproachful voice, "I cannot *quite* make this out, Mr Cosway. Would you be kind enough to read it to me?"

He took the ivory from her and dutifully read from the back: "Portrait of Lady Emma Groatster, privately commissioned by her from the artist, and completed in May, 1817 by Richard Cosway, RA, RSA, et cetera."

Et cetera? There was a great deal more of that inscription than he had read out. Cosway's long *et cetera* must be the reason his writing was illegible. It had had to be microscopic in order to fit everything in.

She leaned across and pointed to the last few lines of the inscription. "What does it say, please?"

"It is my normal painting signature, ma'am." He read out a long screed of Latin.

Of course. Emma recalled the gist of Cosway's vainglorious Latin boast from her reference book: *Painted by Richard Cosway, RA, RSA, by Royal Appointment, Miniaturist to His Royal Highness, the Prince of Wales*. Or something of the sort. Cosway used it often on his work and it would certainly prove that Emma's miniature was genuine. So in the end, the microscopic writing didn't matter. It was giving her the provenance she needed.

Cosway put the miniature carefully into its little leather case and handed it back to Emma.

"You have my letter also, Mr Cosway?"

"Indeed, ma'am, I do." He produced a thick folded paper from an inside pocket.

It crackled as Emma opened it. Its style was very formal. "Madam," it began, "I have the honour, in accordance with your ladyship's instructions, to set out the terms of your ladyship's commission to me." Emma quickly scanned the detailed paragraphs that followed. Everything was precisely as she had specified.

Except for one thing.

Emma looked up from the paper. "Mr Cosway, the letter contains the details that we had agreed. Thank you. But there is one significant omission. There is no salutation."

"Indeed, ma'am?" He stretched out a hand. "May I see? I was sure I had written 'Madam' at the top of the sheet."

She handed him the letter. "Indeed, you did, Mr Cosway. But if you consider the letter with an objective eye, you will note that it does not specify the name of the lady to whom you are addressing yourself. I should like the name and style of your client to be clear on the face of the letter." She gestured towards her desk. "I have pen and ink here. Would you be so good as to add it?"

"You wish me to add 'To Lady Emma Groatster' at the top of the letter?"

"I do."

"As you wish, my lady." At Emma's insistence, he sat in a chair by her desk and – rather laboriously, Emma thought – squeezed the extra words into the narrow gap at the top of the letter.

Yes! Now she would have it.

Cosway sanded it and waved it about in the air to dry it before he handed it back to Emma. "I hope that is now satisfactory for your purposes, Lady Emma?"

"I am sure it will be," Emma replied, setting the paper aside with a broad smile. It was time to pay her debts. "Stay there, for the moment, Mr Cosway." She had one more thing for him to write. She opened the drawer at the side of her desk, extracted the little packet of money she had prepared and laid it in front of him. "The balance of your fee. Sixty-four pounds and ten shillings. Making a total of ninety guineas, as agreed. Perhaps you would like to count it?"

Cosway shook his head vehemently. "No, indeed, ma'am. I am sure it is exactly right."

"Then if you would be so kind as to write, at the foot of your letter, that you received payment in full?"

Cosway nodded and did so, adding the date and sanding the paper again.

Their business was at an end. Emma rose and offered him her hand. That was an honour he clearly had not expected, for he coloured a little. "Thank you, Mr Cosway. I know that I may trust to your discretion in the matter of this commission. It is never to be mentioned, to anyone."

He looked at her through narrowed, assessing eyes.

He would love to know why, Emma concluded, *but he never will.*

"Madam," Cosway said, with a little bow, "it was my

sincere pleasure to paint your ladyship. Sadly, I am now so old that I have forgotten all about it." The corner of his mouth quirked into a mischievous little smile. He might never know the reasons behind her strange conditions, but he had enjoyed the game.

The moment the door closed on Richard Cosway, RA, RSA, Emma grabbed his letter and peered at the scribble at the top of the paper.

And there it was. Even with Cosway's crabbed handwriting, Emma could make out the letters. It was not Groatster. It looked like G-J-R-O-R-S-I-T-E-S-T-E-R. Good grief. What a mouthful. Or rather, what a penful. Her name, her late husband's name, was another one of those English aristocratic handles that was pronounced in one way and written in quite another, like Cholmondeley/Chumly. Only Gjrorsitester/Groatster was much, much worse. None of the spelling variants Emma had tried came close to the real-life monstrosity.

It explained so much. She could jettison her fantasy of parallel universes. And she wasn't losing her marbles, either. Lady Emma Gjrorsitester would be in the records somewhere. As a sort of spelling mistake.

When she got back to the modern world, she would be able to look Lady Emma up. Lady Emma was probably as real as the bath house. Emma felt a new lightness. Was it relief at being reassured she was not going loopy?

First things first. The miniature and the precious letter of provenance had to be found in the twenty-first century. The best place for that would be the blue bedchamber in the Lamb House. Emma should be able to engineer that. If she was holding the miniature and the letter when she removed the lace gown, she would almost certainly arrive back in the museum with both vital items in her hand. But then she would have to conceal them at the Lamb House. What if someone caught her in the act of hiding them under that floorboard? What if there were forensic signs to prove that the items had been planted there in the modern day? And by her, Emma Stanley? Her career would be ruined if she were suspected of being involved in such a fraud. No, the only safe way would be to make her major find historically legitimate.

She gulped. Her heart began to race. She had counted on being able to avoid this. But she couldn't. She would have to hide the items in the blue bedchamber in Will's reality and then make certain that someone else in the twenty-first century was responsible for prying up the floorboard and discovering the hidden treasure beneath. It was the only sure way to protect Emma's modern-day reputation as an honest museum curator. And if she was going to achieve the successful career she craved, reputation was vital.

To hide the portrait, she would have to risk seeing Will again.

But what if he tried to make love to her again? Would she be able to resist him, knowing what she did about Patience and their imminent betrothal?

Emma wasn't sure. But she did need the miniature. It was the key to her future.

Her annoying conscience was reminding her that she ought to be trying to *save* Will from Patience, rather than trying to avoid seeing him at all. If she really loved him, that's what she would do, wasn't it? She would confront Will, face to face, and warn him about Patience.

She wasn't sure she was up to doing that. But she needed to get to the Lamb House. Did she really have any choice?

She swallowed hard and made up her mind to face down her fears.

When the next invitation arrived from "Mrs Smith", Emma would accept it.

~ ~ ~

The invitation came that very afternoon. And this time, it was couched as a note from "Mrs Smith" to her good friend Lady Emma. No scope for endearments at all. This note was written in terms that could be read by anyone. And the handwriting could well have been that of an arthritic invalid. Will Allmay was a very devious man.

"My dear Lady Emma," the note began. "I am most concerned that I have not heard from you this past week. I pray that you are not unwell. In the hope that you will be able to visit me this evening, as we arranged, my carriage will call

233

for you at 8 p.m. If you are unable to keep our engagement, it will suffice for your servant to tell my coachman so." It ended, "Yours most affectionately, J. S."

Had there been other notes from Will, these past few days? That final sentence in the note suggested that Will's carriage, or more probably his hackney, had waited in vain for Emma to appear. Was Will fretting because Emma had stood him up?

She rather hoped he was.

The question was: would Emma go to the Lamb House tonight? Or would she put him off until she was better prepared?

You're kidding yourself, Emma Stanley. You'll never be prepared for Will Allmay. He takes your breath away every time he touches you.

It was true. She could never be prepared for Will. So there was no point in putting off the moment of confrontation. But, to be on the safe side, Emma would wear her gold lace gown. If being with Will became truly unbearable, as she feared it might, she would leave him. For the last time. By disappearing completely from his world.

Bailey would say a ballgown was quite unsuitable for a quiet evening reading to an invalid. Which would be fair comment.

But Emma had thought of an answer to that. She would tell Bailey that "Mrs Smith" had heard about the gown and about Emma's efforts to raise money for wounded soldiers from the ladies of the *ton*. The invalid had asked to see the gown that was being used to achieve such charitable miracles. And so, for the sake of her bedridden friend, Emma had agreed to wear her gold lace this evening. Even Bailey couldn't cavil at that, could she?

Chapter Twenty-Six

"I'VE PUT YOUR VALISE IN THE carriage, m'lady," Emma's footman said, opening the front door for her. "Shall I help you in? 'Tain't the usual coachman tonight."

A quick glance showed Emma that Sanding was absent. There was no second man on the box. The "simpleton", muffled up in his huge smelly coat and with his tricorne pulled low, was in sole charge of the carriage tonight. Emma remembered that Sanding was supposed to be off somewhere in the wilds of Shropshire, or Wales, driving the Portuguese lady. It would clearly be unwise for him to be seen in Mayfair where news of his presence might come to the keen ears of Patience or her even sharper mama.

"The coachman cannot leave his horses, James," she said. "Pray help me in."

The young footman handed Emma into the carriage, closing the door securely behind her. She heard his officious call of "Drive on, coachman," and laughed to herself. If only he knew.

Will drove much faster than Sanding had, as if he were driving a racing curricle rather than a sedate lady's carriage. Emma couldn't decide whether he was anxious to reach their destination, and pull her into his arms, or angry at being kept waiting for a week. Well, she would find out when they reached the Lamb House. In the meantime, since she had no qualms about his ability to control his horses, she sat back in her corner and closed her eyes. She fully intended that, when they arrived at their destination, she would emerge totally relaxed, and even laughing at the experience.

It didn't work out quite as she had planned. When the carriage stopped in the sweep by the Lamb House's grand entrance, Will made no attempt to climb down from the box. Instead, it was Sanding who appeared to help her down. Again. The "simpleton" twirled his whip by way of greeting and drove off to the stables without a word.

Emma consoled herself with the thought that she had been looking for a way of avoiding a face-to-face confrontation. Will had just given it to her. She smiled at Will's man and said, calmly, "Thank you, Sanding. Would you be so kind as to bring my valise up to the blue bedchamber? And then a cup of tea? I have the headache, a little, and I should like to rest for a while." That would show uppity Will Allmay that he couldn't have everything his own way.

It would also give Emma a window of opportunity to plant the miniature and the letter. And, if she was truly determined to avoid Will, to remove the lace gown and leave the Regency for the very last time.

By the time Sanding arrived with the tea tray, Emma had hidden the miniature and returned the floorboard to its place. There was only one more detail she needed to settle before she was free to leave.

"Put the tray on the table by the fire, please, Sanding. I shall warm myself while I drink it and then I shall lie down for a while."

"Yes, m'lady. Will there be anything else?"

"No. Oh, wait, yes, there is one thing." She picked up the missing key from the dressing table and offered it to him. "I found this key in my valise after my last visit. I'm not sure what door it fits, but I do know that it does not belong in my house. So I am assuming it belongs here."

Sanding studied it for a moment. "I could be the missing key to the Captain's dressing room, I suppose. Though how it could have got into your ladyship's valise I can't imagine." He pocketed it. "I'll see it's returned to its proper home."

"Good. Thank you."

Sanding bowed.

"And thank you also for your kindness to me during my visits. I did appreciate it." Sanding's quick frown suggested he was reading far too much into her words. Cursing herself for making such a stupid slip, Emma continued quickly, "And I know I can count on your kindness and discretion in the future also."

Sanding smiled and left. Had she fooled him? Or had he left, believing that Lady Emma had decided never to come to the Lamb House again?

Crucially – if he had read her intentions, would he tell his precious Captain?

Emma slumped into the chair by the fire. She might not have long. And she had to decide what she was going to do. Was she going to take the lace gown off and abandon Will? Or was she going to stay long enough to warn him off the dreadful Patience? There was safety in returning to the modern day. But cowardice too. And a betrayal of her love for this man. If she stayed, though, she risked deep hurt. He professed to love Emma, but if she challenged him about his betrothal to Patience, would he finally admit that Emma was just one more in his long line of conquests? The truth was that Emma feared he would. And that it would hurt so much that she would never recover.

If she took the coward's way out, she would never have to hear the truth about what Will Allmay really felt about her. She would be able to kid herself that he had truly loved her. And that his marriage to Patience was purely a matter of duty.

Maybe it *was* just that?

It wouldn't make losing him any easier to bear.

She sat for a long time. Too long. The fire was warm and the chair was so comfortable that she dozed off, in spite of turning the same impossible questions round and round in her mind.

A soft knock on the door interrupted her dreams. Dreams of Will Allmay. What else? Emma was plagued by the man and by her feelings for him.

She sat motionless in her chair. If she made no noise, he

might assume that she was asleep on the bed and leave her in peace. She held her breath, listening hard for the sound of retreating footsteps.

They did not come. There was another knock, instead. A little louder. And then a whispered, "Emma?" He sounded concerned.

He would be. Will Allmay might be a rake but he was also a kind and generous man. He would not like to think that Emma was suffering in any way. And she would certainly suffer if she left without seeing him, just once more. It would break her heart.

She took a deep breath and rose from her chair. If she'd been going to leave, she should have done it as soon as she'd handed Sanding the key. She'd been conning herself ever since. Cowardice might be the safest tactic, but it wasn't what her heart was telling her to do.

She went to open the door to the man she was about to lose.

He looked magnificent, even in the half-light of the corridor. He was wearing full evening dress. The austere black tailoring emphasised his height and the breadth of his shoulders. The only spot of colour was that curious gold pin in his snowy white neckcloth. It seemed to represent some kind of animal, but not one that Emma had ever encountered. Perhaps it was mythical? A griffin or a sphinx?

Emma tried to focus on the puzzle of the gold pin rather than on the man who stood before her. Unfortunately, it didn't work too well. Especially when he bowed over her hand, as formally as if he were meeting her at some society ball.

"Emma, you look beautiful," he said softly, taking in the gold lace and the sapphires in one appreciative glance. "But Sanding said you had the headache?"

He was being ultracorrect, making no move to cross her threshold.

Emma took a step back to invite him in. "Tea works wonders for the headache," she said, truthfully. She did not want to sully their last time together by lying to him. "I did not expect to see you in evening dress, Will," she began, playing for time. "Do you have an engagement?"

"Only with you."

Oh dear.

"And you seem to have been reading my mind, Emma, since you too are in evening dress. I shall treasure the image of you in gold lace and sapphires."

That sounded like the preliminary to a farewell. Emma felt her eyes tearing up and dug her nails into the palms of her hands in an effort to control herself. She refused to blub like a lovesick schoolgirl.

Will closed the door quietly and crossed to the fireplace where he stood with his back to the flames, gazing at Emma, and waiting for her to join him. When she did not, he held out his hand to her.

She forced her leaden feet to move. But she did not take his hand. She could not.

It was difficult to read his features in the flickering light of her single candle. He looked... He looked uncertain. But she must be mistaken, surely? Will Allmay was never uncertain about anything. He was a man of action. And decision.

"Emma, my love, this last week has been torture," he said. "It has taught me, as nothing else could, that I am only half a man without you. You are the woman to make me complete." He sank to one knee. And took her unresisting hand in his. "Emma, my dearest love, will you do me the honour of agreeing to be my wife?"

Emma Stanley, who had never fainted in her life, had to grab the back of the chair to stop herself from falling. And then she said the first idiotic thing that came into her head. "But you are promised to Patience!"

"Am I?" Will rose to his feet and took her other hand as well, holding them both in a strong, reassuring clasp. "What on earth put that idea into your head?"

"Patience told me so." That sounded idiotic too, but Emma's brains seemed to have turned to mush. Will couldn't possibly have proposed marriage to her. Somehow, she must have misunderstood.

"Well, well, well." He made a face. "Shows just how wrong a man can be."

"I don't understand." She didn't understand anything. Least

239

of all the way her body was responding. She wanted to throw herself into his arms. But she must not. She must give him a chance to explain. Was he really saying that the formidable Lady Augusta had been building castles in the air over that betrothal? It seemed so very unlikely. And yet Will's distaste for the match was evident. Emma held her breath, telling herself to ignore her pounding heart, to wait for what might come next.

Will was looking distant, as if he were lost in long-buried memories. "I always thought Patience had a *tendre* for my brother," he said pensively.

"But I thought your brother died," Emma said, surprised into more unwary speech.

"I have— I had two brothers. John was the eldest. He died. As I told you." Will swallowed hard and continued brightly, "Daniel is a lot younger than me. Only a little older than Patience, in fact. But she hasn't met him for years so I suppose her tastes may have changed. He's in the army, you see. Refused the Navy." Will chuckled. He was uncertain no longer. "Can't really blame him. Poor chap couldn't stomach the idea of possibly having to serve with me as his Captain. He hasn't been home since Boney was sent to Elba, though. He likes the loose living on the Continent, I do believe."

"Oh." *Two* rakes in the same family?

"And Patience told you she was betrothed to me?"

This time, Emma thought before she replied. "Well, not exactly. She said there was an understanding between the families, but no formal betrothal. She hinted an announcement would come soon, though." It had been much more than a hint, but Emma couldn't very well tell him that.

"I suppose the title may have made a difference," he muttered darkly.

Emma wondered about that. Patience would become Lady Allmay if she married Will. She would probably revel in that new, elevated status. "I suspect it rankles that she is only *Miss* Sinclair-Smythe at present. She would like to be your *Lady*."

"Well, she is not going to be anything of the sort. There is only one woman I want to be my *Lady*. And, as it happens, she already has that title, from birth. Will you be *my* Lady as well as your own, Emma?"

Emma's heart stopped all over again. And then it galloped away, trailing impossible dreams. "I don't understand," she said again, in a strangled voice.

"Do you not? Do you really not understand when a man is proposing marriage to you, Lady Emma?" He shook his head sadly. "I know that it would be a huge step for any lady with such a spotless past to marry a man with a reputation as black as mine, but rakes have been known to reform before, you know. And I promise you that this one will. For you." He pulled her tight against his chest and wrapped his arms around her. "There have been no more mistresses since I have been with you, darling Emma. And I swear there will be no more after we are wed, either."

Emma swallowed and managed to turn a nervous titter into a cough. She couldn't help her reaction. In the back of her mind, she could hear Patience Sinclair-Smythe's whining words, about wild oats and worse. Emma had not believed, then, that it was possible for Will to turn into a faithful husband. Did she believe it now?

She looked into his eyes, and discovered that she did.

~ ~ ~

Will didn't attempt to take her to bed, which surprised her. He behaved as if they were in company, rather than alone, scandalously unchaperoned, at the Lamb House. He offered his hand and led her downstairs where he invited her to dine. Emma was not at all sure what to make of this new, reformed rake.

But having the table between them was a godsend. It gave her space to think.

She could not possibly marry Will Allmay. What would he do when she deserted him for her modern-day life? If he truly loved her – and Emma was beginning to believe that he did, poor misguided man – he would be heartbroken when he lost her. She must not do that to him.

Besides, a marriage had to be based on trust. There could be no trust between them unless Emma told him the truth about herself. But how could she? He would never believe a word of it. He had laughed when she described the air transport of the future. If she told him she had actually travelled back from that future, he would probably have her committed to an asylum.

She took a deep breath and tried to relax her shoulders. "I am deeply honoured by your proposal," she began formally, "but I—" She found she couldn't bring herself to say the words. "I cannot decide now, Will. You must give me time."

"Certainly. It is what I expected you to say." He smiled across at her but he made no attempt to touch her. "My proposal is unconditional. But if you wish to set conditions on our marriage – if you do me the honour of accepting me, of course – I will try to meet them."

That was a very great concession for a Regency man to make.

She broke off a morsel of bread and put it in her mouth, chewing slowly. Eventually she swallowed and said, "I would want a greater degree of independence than you might be willing to allow."

"You are a rich widow so that is understandable. I would ensure that you had quite as much financial freedom as you have now. I would replace your jointure with a similar provision."

Emma had no idea how much her late husband had settled on her, but it must have been generous, given the extravagant way Lady Emma lived. Normally, a remarried widow would have only pin money from her new husband, since he would assume responsibility for all her living costs. Will was offering her vastly more than pin money.

But independence was not only about money. If she made her conditions too onerous for him to accept, she would be able to refuse his offer without telling him the real truth. He would be disappointed. He might even be hurt. But, with the passage of time, he would come to understand that Emma would have made him an impossible wife.

"As my husband, would you expect to know where I went and whom I met? Would you expect to dictate where I lived and how I behaved?"

He stroked his chin thoughtfully. "Are you saying that you would require the freedom to do exactly as you liked without

242

any restrictions at all from me?"

Put like that, it sounded extraordinary. And, for a Regency marriage, unacceptable. Emma ploughed on. What choice did she have? "I *am* saying that, yes. I value my independence a very great deal. I cannot give it up. And...and I can see that it makes a marriage impossible between us. I am sorry, Will."

He smiled wryly. "I have not said that I reject your conditions, Emma. Perhaps we both need a little more time to think?" He leaned across the table to touch her hand briefly. "Shall we sleep on it?"

Oh. She felt herself reddening.

"I do not mean what you are thinking, sweetheart. I shall escort you back to the blue bedchamber and leave you there to sleep alone. This decision is too important for us to allow it to be clouded by, er, emotional entanglements." He grinned suddenly. "I fear I am become incredibly pompous this evening. Forgive me. May I ring for Sanding to serve our supper? It is very late and you have had only a crumb of bread."

Emma nodded gratefully. If they could talk of mundane things while they ate, she might be able to get her swirling thoughts into some kind of order. Will Allmay wanted to marry her. It seemed he loved her as much as she loved him. But it was an impossible dream. If she married Will, she would have to stay in the Regency for good. And she couldn't do that, could she? She had seen too much, and knew far too much about what was to come. How could she possibly keep up the pretence?

Sanding served them a light and tasty supper. The man seemed to materialise exactly when he was needed and then vanish again. For an "uncouth" fighting sailor, he was an exceptional servant.

Will kept up an easy flow of conversation, never once mentioning the matter of his proposal. Emma asked him about his time in the Navy but the stories he told her were pretty innocuous. He probably thought that a description of his battles would have been too much for her feminine sensibilities.

He needed to learn that females were not nearly as weak

243

and pathetic as Regency men seemed to think.

"I should like," Emma began musingly as they rose from the table, "to see something more of the world. I might travel to Africa, perhaps. Lions and giraffes and elephants. It would be exciting to see them in their proper habitat."

"You would be terrified, surely? Think of a great bull elephant leading his herd through the bush. You could be trampled in the stampede."

"Actually, elephant society is matriarchal," Emma said quietly. "The oldest, wisest females lead."

He stopped dead. "Females as leaders? Emma, you are a remarkable woman and capable of many things, but leadership is a man's role. Always has been. Always will be. Could you imagine a woman leading an army? Or leading a country like England?"

He looked so cocksure, so armoured in his belief in natural male superiority, that modern Emma broke through Regency Emma's shell. "There will be a woman leader, I promise you, Will. Less than two centuries from now. What's more, she'll take your beloved England to war. And win!"

Will began to chuckle, shaking his head at what he clearly thought was fantasy.

"You may laugh, sir. But you will laugh on the other side of your face when I tell you that she is– was– will be a *grocer's daughter*."

For a second he looked utterly astonished. Then he burst into a peal of laughter that went on and on. Eventually he was laughing so much that he collapsed back into his chair, holding his aching sides.

"Now that, my sweet," he spluttered when he had recovered some command of his voice, "is your best yet." He went off into another peal of laughter. "I swear you are quite wonderful. The things you say. And with the utmost seriousness, too. Almost as though you believed you were telling the truth."

"I *am* telling the truth," she replied, frowning crossly down at him.

"Of course. I'm sure your visions of the future are quite as real to you as...as this supper table. But a *grocer's daughter.*

Why, I—" Laughter overcame him once again.

Emma could see the case was hopeless. She was challenging his innate world view, not only about gender but about class as well. He would never believe a word of it. And, to be fair, it was ridiculous to expect him to. If she had been confronted by a person from the twenty-third century, telling her the future, she wouldn't have believed it either. Nonetheless, Will could have been a little more polite about listening to what she said.

She continued to frown down at him. He was still convulsed in mirth. Impossible man. With a snort of anger, she turned on her heel and marched out of the room, slamming the door behind her.

It was only when she reached her bedroom that she remembered the lace gown. If she removed it herself, she would not be here in the morning when Will came for the answer to his proposal. If she wanted to stay, she would have to ask for help. From Will? Or from Sanding?

She shook her head crossly.

From neither of them. After that little lecture about female fantasy, she had no intention of staying another minute.

Chapter Twenty-Seven

EMMA HAD AN ATTACK OF CONSCIENCE the moment she arrived back in the museum research room. Will would come for her answer in the morning and find her gone. Neither Sanding nor any of the stable hands would be able to throw any light on how she had left the house. Would Will start scouring the fields around, in case she was lying injured somewhere? Or dead? What would he do when he found no trace of her?

She should at least have insisted that he drive her back to her London house.

But it was too late to do anything now. The time window for travel to the Regency had closed for another day. She was stuck in the twenty-first century.

Perhaps, if she made the transition again the very next night, she would be able to retrieve the situation somehow?

She shook her head at her own indecision. *Fickle?* That was putting it mildly. So much for her resolution never to make the transition again.

But things had changed between her and Will. He had proposed marriage. She owed him an answer, even though it would have to be a refusal. Marriage, for them, was impossible. She was convinced of that. But she knew her refusal would hurt him. She couldn't disappear into the æther as well.

Other arguments were bubbling up, arguments about love and trust and the possibility of happiness. Troubling arguments. She pushed them back below the surface. She was too distraught, and much too tired, to deal with them. She needed to go home. To sleep.

~ ~ ~

She did sleep, but not well.

She kept half waking because something was nagging away in the back of her brain, but she could never quite catch hold of it and so she would fall back into the same restless sleep. At about six, she woke up properly and had it at once.

What a fool she'd been. Last night, she had been in the museum, with access to all its resources, and she had completely forgotten to search the records for Lady Emma Gjrorsitester, with the new, unpronounceable spelling. She wouldn't be able to do it today, either, because Owen Evans, the charity assessor, was to meet her at the Lamb House, first thing. Emma had carefully arranged the visit for a day when Geraldine would be off site, so that Emma herself would be able to show him around. Emma would be the only paid member of staff on site, which made her the obvious choice. She thought she'd done rather well there. She'd decided Owen was by far the best person to stumble across the loose floorboard by the fireplace in the blue bedchamber. No one would dream of suggesting there was anything fraudulent about a discovery made by someone as respected as Owen Evans.

She made herself a soothing cup of tea – she really needed that – and fired up her computer. Maybe Wikipedia had something about Lady Emma, with the new monstrous spelling? She found she was hesitating. Did she really want to know about Lady Emma? Who was also herself?

Yes, she really did. She carefully typed in the incredible name and hit the Return key.

Nothing.

Well, perhaps Lady Emma was not important enough to warrant a page on Wikipedia? Emma tried again, with a Google search. That produced nothing, either.

She sat back in her chair and stared accusingly at her

screen. It stayed resolutely blank. So what had she learned? She pieced together what she knew. It seemed that the house was real, and the bath house was real, but the past that she and Will were living was not real, because neither Lady Emma nor Will Allmay had existed. She sighed deeply. What a disappointment.

No, it was much more than disappointment. Emma was bereft, as if someone had cut out a part of her and wantonly destroyed it. Everything with Will had seemed so real, so alive. And yet it couldn't be. He didn't exist. And Lady Emma didn't exist either. So it could only have been some kind of parallel universe that she'd been visiting.

She took a large swig of her tea. That, at least, was no mirage.

What was she going to do?

Last night, she had decided, sort of, that she would go back to the Regency one last time, to say a final goodbye to Will and reassure him that she had not died in a ditch somewhere. He needed to know she was safe and well, in spite of her unexplained disappearance. She would politely refuse his proposal, on grounds that would not hurt his pride too much, she hoped. And then she would be driven back to her Mayfair house. From there, she would be able to return to her own modern time without hurting anyone.

And if her doppelgänger really existed in that weird parallel universe, it could take over the role with Emma's good will.

Back here in the twenty-first century, Emma Stanley would have the newly discovered bath house, plus a priceless Richard Cosway miniature with unassailable provenance, and she might even have secured funding for the restoration at the Lamb House. After that huge boost to her career, museums round the country would be competing to get her to work for them. She might even become a professor.

Her inconvenient internal voice insisted she would be sacrificing the only man she had truly loved for a sterile future in a harsh and unfeeling modern world.

Emma refused to listen.

She was cleaning her teeth after breakfast when a new

thought struck. If Lady Emma Gjrorsitester lived in a parallel universe, how could her portrait transfer to this universe? Would there be anything for Owen Evans to find under the floorboard?

She spat viciously into the basin. It was all too convoluted for words. There was only one place to find out the truth. And that was where she was going. Right now.

~ ~ ~

When Emma had so carefully placed the little miniature case under the floorboards of the blue bedchamber in Will's Lamb House, the leather had been new and supple and pristine. The case in Owen Evans' gloved hand was darkened with age and cracking in places. But when he opened it, the ivory miniature looked exactly as it had on the day it was completed. The colours were fresh and the brushwork was stunning.

"Well, well, well," Owen said in his lilting Welsh accent. "Isn't that beautiful? And wonderfully preserved, too. Miniatures so often fade when they're exposed to light. People should keep them in their cases rather than hanging them on the wall." He peered closer. "This one looks— Actually, I'd say it looks like a Cosway. That background is his signature Antwerp blue, isn't it?"

"I'm n–not sure," Emma stammered. "I haven't studied miniatures much."

Owen was beaming. "I've seen quite a lot over the years and I'd say that blue is unmistakable. We'd need an expert to confirm it, though. May I remove it from its case?"

"No reason why not."

Owen took his time over extracting the portrait. "I wonder," he said, almost to himself. "There's no signature on the front. Cosway never did that. But on the back?" He turned the ivory over. "Bingo! Yes. This is it, Emma. The real deal."

"I'm sorry?"

"When Cosway was in his pomp, he used to sign his works with a flourishing Latin signature. And that's what we've got here. I'll need a magnifying glass to decipher it all, though. The writing is minuscule."

"And what about the paper? What do you reckon that is?"

Owen picked it up. "I think perhaps you ought to deal with

this. It looks fragile to me. That kind of stiff paper can easily crack when it's been drying out for centuries. And if it relates to the miniature, it wouldn't be any later than about 1820, I'd say. Cosway died around then, I seem to remember."

Emma put on gloves and very carefully unfolded the letter. She read it aloud, deliberately stumbling over the difficult surname of Lady Emma.

"It does sound as if it relates to this miniature, doesn't it?" Owen said with a grin. "But we need to decipher the inscription on the back to be sure."

"I'll fetch a magnifying glass. I won't be a moment." She handed the letter to Owen and left him to it.

When she returned, he was frowning over the writing on the back of the painting. "I think I may have found something odd," he said. "Ah, thank you. Just what I need." He stretched out a hand for Emma's magnifying glass and went back to studying the inscription. "Yes, I thought I was right. Look here, Emma. The name on the letter and the name on the miniature don't match."

"What? But they must match. Cosway painted the miniature and Cosway wrote the letter."

"Well, they don't match. Look at the letter through the magnifier. You'll see that the ink for the body of the letter and the ink of the salutation are different."

"But the handwriting's the same?"

"It *looks* the same. Could be a forgery, I suppose," he added, with a grimace.

"The handwriting on the back of the miniature must be genuine, though?"

"Oh yes. I've seen it before. There's no mistaking it. But look closely at the description of the sitter. Look at the spelling of her name."

"Oh. Oh, goodness." The spelling on the back of the miniature was not the same as on the letter. On the back of the miniature, the name began G-Y-H-R- rather than G-J-R-. When Emma had forced Cosway to add the name to his letter, he had spelled it wrong, leaving out the H. Not surprising, given how complicated it was? And then Emma had compounded the mistake by misreading Cosway's Y as a J.

That could certainly account for why Emma had been unable to find Lady Emma Gjrorsitester in the records. She should have been searching on Gyhrorsitester.

Owen was staring at Emma, waiting for her to say something. "Oh, sorry. I was miles away. That name. It's so *very* odd."

"I'm not sure, but I think I may have seen it somewhere before," Owen said. "If it's the name I think it is, it's a sort of Flemish bastardisation of the French 'Grosseteste'. It means 'Large Head', as I'm sure you know."

"Yes. There was a Bishop Grosseteste at one stage, wasn't there?" When Owen nodded, Emma said, "So this woman, this—" she made a point of checking the paper "—this Lady Emma However-she's-pronounced was Flemish, you think?"

"I doubt that. It's not the name of any aristocratic English family I've ever heard of. It's much more likely to be her married name."

"Yes, I suppose so," Emma said uncertainly. Inside, she was cheering with glee.

"May I photograph these items, Emma? I won't use flash." With Emma's ready agreement, he did so. "This will be a wonderful find for the Lamb House. My Board will be sympathetic to making a donation to help with the restoration after this, I think." He beamed at Emma. "Cosway was the finest miniaturist of the time, you know. If the Lamb House trustees wanted to sell this, it would raise a good price. Especially with this provenance."

"But you said the letter was a forgery?"

"I said it could be, because of the difference in ink. I do think that the name at the top was added some time after the original letter was written. But, on balance, I'd say it all looks like Cosway's hand. It may well be genuine."

"Maybe the lady asked for it to be added?" Emma suggested. "The miniature includes her name, but the letter doesn't." She shook her head in assumed puzzlement. "It must have been a very strange commission, don't you think? She certainly wanted it kept a secret. And why did she hide it there? If she did hide it, that is."

"Perhaps she meant it as a gift? For a lover?" Owen said,

entering into the spirit of Emma's game of conjecture. "Perhaps the commission was secret because she was afraid that her husband might find out? Perhaps the lover abandoned her and so she hid the painting away? She couldn't bring herself to destroy it because it was so beautiful."

Emma chuckled. "That's a very plausible tale, I agree. You're good at conspiracy theories, Owen. If we can find out more about the lady in question, we might find the real answers, too. I'll start on the research as soon as I'm back at the museum."

~ ~ ~

Once Owen had gone, Emma rushed through the rest of her work at the Lamb House. She needed to get back to the museum early. Not because she wanted to make her last transition to say goodbye to Will – although she did – but because she was sure that she would now be able to use the museum's resources to find out about Lady Emma. There had been so many false leads about her surname. But this time, with the spelling from the inscription, Emma must have it right. Her instincts were telling her that, this time, she would find Lady Emma. The woman had not existed in a parallel universe; she was part of the history of this one. There might even be a link to Will. If so, Emma wanted to know about it before she saw him for the last time.

On her way back to the museum, the traffic was a nightmare. There had been a serious accident on the dual carriageway and the police had closed the whole road. Emma found the best detour she could, but lots of other drivers seemed to have had the same idea. The going was very slow. By the time she got within half a mile of the museum, it was already almost six o'clock. She would have very little time for her researches. And the nightmare drive had given her a thumping headache.

She didn't care about that. There was paracetamol at the museum. She could take a couple, if she had time, but it was much more important to follow up this last lead about Lady Emma. There would just about be time before she had to get the gold lace gown out of store. Once she was back in the Regency, her modern-day headache would disappear anyway, so what did it matter?

The museum car park was empty when she drove in. Everyone had gone home. The museum itself was dark. Good. There would be no one to ask her why she had come back when she was supposed to be at the Lamb House for the whole day.

She was smiling as she got out of her car and pinged the lock. She made for the staff entrance with a spring in her step. This time she was going to discover the truth about Lady Emma. She was sure of it.

"Slut!"

Emma whirled round. "Julian!" she gasped. She plunged her hand into her coat for her rape alarm. She couldn't find it. It should be there. It wasn't. She backed off a step, still scrabbling around at the bottom of her pocket.

"You've got that slut walk. That hip-swaying I'm-being-fucked-out-of-my-mind slut walk. I know. I've been watching you, bitch."

"You have no right," she spat. "We're divorced, remember?"

Julian was a big man, and strong. He was blocking the route to her car. And there was no one around to see what was happening.

Emma knew she had to divert his attention so she could use the self-defence moves she'd been taught. They might give her precious seconds to run back to her car.

Her scrabbling fingers found the museum keys. She pulled them out and pointed them, like a weapon.

Julian glanced down at her hand and laughed. Nastily.

"You don't own me, you bastard," she yelled, gripping her keys even tighter.

Julian's lips curled into a familiar snarl, the snarl that was always followed by a clenched fist. Usually to her gut.

Sweat prickled down Emma's spine. Automatically, she took another step back, to avoid the blow she knew would come.

No use. He was too close. And much too big.

He knocked her hand aside. His punch took all the breath out of her and doubled her up. She began to fall, arms flailing for support. But there was none. It felt like being in a slow motion movie: she registered the tiny quirk of triumph forming at the corner of his mouth, the quick double nod – masculine pride, at a job well done – as he turned to leave.

Emma's head hit the edge of the pavement. The last thing she saw was Julian's back as he strode away. Then everything went black.

~ ~ ~

The light had almost gone when Emma came to. How long had she been out for? Quite a while, possibly. She lifted her head, very painfully, and looked around. There was no one at all in the car park. Julian had disappeared, as he always did after attacking her. When the ambulance came, he was never there. And he always swore he never had been. Emma was on her own with her hurts, as usual.

She pushed herself to her knees and then, very gingerly, to her feet. She felt herself swaying and stumbled across the pavement to clutch at the museum wall for support. How her head ached. Her vision was a bit blurry, too. She put a hand to the back of her head where the wound was. Blood. Not bleeding a lot now. Just oozing. But her hair was thickly matted with it. So there must have been a lot of bleeding when she fell.

And then that vicious bastard smirked at how well he'd asserted his proper manly authority and stalked off without so much as a glance to see what damage he'd done. If only I could—

St Mary's struck the half hour.

No time to lose. Julian, and reporting the assault to Flo, would have to wait till Emma returned from the Regency. Time wouldn't have moved on in the twenty-first century so no evidence would be lost. But the window for the transition to Will was so very narrow. She mustn't miss it.

Where were her keys? She'd had them in her hand, hadn't she?

She found them on the ground near where she'd fallen. Bending down to retrieve them was touch-and-go. She almost passed out all over again.

Clinging to the wall for support, Emma felt her way along

to the staff entrance. It seemed to take an age to fumble for the right keys and then insert them in the complicated locks. But at last she was inside and the door was safely relocked behind her. She had managed to get to where she desperately wanted to be. And at least Julian couldn't touch her again while she was here inside.

She had to screw up her eyes to focus enough to check her watch. She found she had less that twenty-five minutes to open the key safe, retrieve the lace gown and get herself ready in the research room. And she so much wanted to go to the shower room and bathe her aching head. Would she still be bloody and faint after she reached the Regency? She couldn't be sure. And what would Will say, or do, if he saw her in such a state?

She had no time for agonising over that. She decided she could spare five minutes to bathe her wound with cool water, though. If she didn't, there was a fair chance she might pass out, right there in the research room, and lose the magic window to the past for another day.

That was a risk she wasn't prepared to take. Another day, another encounter with Julian? Anything could happen. Next time, he might kill her. He'd threatened it enough times.

She kept one hand on the wall for support, all the way to the shower room. There, she dragged the single chair across to one of the washbasins and collapsed onto it with a groan.

No time to waste. Got to bathe my head and then get out of these clothes before I go down to get the gown. Mustn't get any blood on the lace. Should I bandage the wound to make sure? No. No time for that.

In any case, the bandages were in the first aid box, upstairs in the staff room. Emma was going to have enough problems with the stairs down to the basement storeroom and back. She wasn't at all sure she could manage the flight to the staff room as well.

The paper towels by the basin made a fairly serviceable wound pad, even when wet. And the cold compress was bliss on the back of her head. But it didn't stay cold for long. After barely half a minute, she had to throw the bloody towels into the bin and make another pad. More cooling bliss. She allowed herself to repeat the process a couple of times more. And she was surprised at how much better she felt, even though her hair was still pretty matted and the wound was bleeding quite a lot faster than before, now that the clotted blood had been sponged away.

"I don't care. I can do this," she said aloud. "I can."

With one hand on the back of the chair, she pushed herself to her feet, toed off her shoes and began to unfasten her shirt. It took longer than usual to get down to her underwear, because she was wary of using both hands at once, in case she keeled over. But at last it was done.

Her watch showed twelve minutes to seven. Time enough. Just about.

It took precious minutes to open the key safe and grab the storeroom keys. She started for the stairs to the basement, telling herself that, barefoot, she was less likely to stumble and fall. She could do this. She would.

She was gasping for breath by the time it was done, but she did make it back up to the research room with the lace gown over her arm.

It was four minutes to seven by the church clock.

Emma spread the gown across the table and sank into her usual chair. She allowed herself a smile of triumph, though her cheek muscles did protest a bit. She was probably black and blue there, as well, but she didn't care. What mattered was that she had a chance to make the transition to Will. She desperately needed to make things right with him. She owed him. All she had to do was stand up, wait for the clock to chime and start to put her arm into the sleeve.

Two minutes to go.

One.

She pushed herself up and reached for the lace gown.

"I love you, Will," she whispered, as St Mary's began to strike.

Chapter Twenty-Eight

EMMA COULDN'T BELIEVE THE EVIDENCE OF her senses. Her head was whole again – no blood in her hair, no swelling on her face. Her body didn't ache either. She felt perfectly normal. Most astonishing of all, the blue bedchamber looked exactly as it had when she left it. It was surely impossible? She'd been in the twenty-first century for a whole day.

She checked round the room, more carefully this time. Yes, the single candle was sitting on the hearth where she had put it, for safety. The servants would never have left it there. And it didn't seem to have burned down very far at all. Nor had the fire.

Everything else in the room seemed to be the same too, even – she realised with a start – the bent hairpin she had used to lever up the floorboard. She had forgotten to unbend it. But that was something else that no servant would have left lying on the dressing table. So, almost certainly, no one had been in the room while she was gone. There hadn't been time. Twenty-four hours might have passed in the modern world, but she doubted if even twenty-four minutes had passed in this one.

One thing might have changed, though. Something she needed to know.

She grabbed the bent hairpin and knelt by the hearth to lever up the floorboard again. Was the miniature where she had hidden it?

The little space was empty. Her questing fingers found only dust. The miniature had been retrieved, in that other world, by kindly, lilting Owen Evans.

It was a good omen. Emma had a second chance. With Will. Who loved her, here in this world. Loved her enough to give up so many of a Regency husband's rights. Will's was a very special kind of love.

And in the modern world? Who loved her there? She had no family. She had colleagues and friends, like Richard and Melanie, but no one who was really close. She had her career, and rapidly increasing approval from her profession. She'd told herself it was enough but it wasn't. It never could be. It could never make up for being alone. And unloved. After Julian, she was always looking over her shoulder, never able to trust any man enough to start a relationship. With Will, it was different. As if their relationship had always been.

She had a free choice here. She could refuse Will, return to Lady Emma's Mayfair house and then to her modern-day career. It was the easy route. The cowardly one, too. Would she end up regretting the love she had rejected? Almost certainly.

The alternative was scary. Marriage to Will. She would have to give up all thoughts of ever returning to the modern world. She would have to trust Will with the rest of her life. If it turned out to be a mistake, she could never be free of him until one of them died. She might have a long time, under his control, to regret her decision. Hadn't she promised herself, after Julian, that she would never allow another man to control her?

Will was not Julian. Will was nothing like Julian. He had a Regency mindset about gender and class, as she had discovered over supper, but he wasn't planning to control Emma. He had offered her financial independence. And love. He was not prepared to give her total independence, though.

Did any marriage, in any world, offer that? A loving marriage needed compromise. It was a partnership that husband and wife worked out together. As Richard and Melanie had done.

What she wanted from Will wasn't total independence, she

realised. It was partnership. An equal partnership. If he agreed to that, she would marry him. And stay.

She needed to tell him. Now. She didn't care how late it was.

She plucked up her candle from the hearth and made her way back downstairs. Where was he? There was a sliver of light under the dining-room door. Everywhere else was dark. Cautiously, she pushed the door open.

The only light was from the remains of the fire. Will had drawn his chair back to the dining table which was bare except for a half-full decanter and a brandy glass in Will's hand. He was slowly swirling the liquid round and round.

How much had he drunk? And why? Because of her?

"Will?" she said softly.

He wheeled round in his chair and jumped to his feet. "Emma." He put the glass carefully back on the table. She thought he looked guilty. "You find me drowning my sorrows."

"Sorrows?" she repeated.

"More like self-inflicted wounds. I insulted you. And I laughed at you. It was unforgivable and no apology could atone for that. Though I *am* sorry." He sighed deeply. "Have you come for your revenge? I presume you are going to refuse me?"

"I have come to ask you a question."

He took the candle from her fingers and set it down. It flickered wildly, casting odd shadows across his face. He offered her his hand, but she shook her head. It would depend on his answer. If he said the words she hoped to hear, she would take his hand and keep holding it until the day she died.

He let his arm drop to his side. He looked— He looked beaten. Beaten? Will Allmay?

"When we spoke before, about conditions for a marriage between us, I asked for total freedom, independence to do exactly as I wished. I was wrong to ask for that, Will. It is not what I want. Marriage should be a partnership, where husband and wife love and trust and honour each other. I want a partnership. A partnership of equals."

He frowned a little but then his expression cleared. "I think

I had better know what you mean by that, Emma. We have had enough misunderstanding for one night."

She smiled up at him. "As your wife, I would want to be involved in everything to do with our life together, business as well as pleasure, and I would ask you to take no decisions about me without consulting me first."

"I can certainly promise to consult you about anything that concerns you personally, Emma. I would do nothing you did not want. But business decisions? Do you mean investments and the like?"

"I do. You would find that I know more than you expect about investing. I might be able to give you some shrewd advice. If you are prepared to consult me, that is."

"While I was at sea, my investments were left to my man of business." He shrugged. "I am only just beginning to get to grips with what I have and what I might do with it."

"Then perhaps we could learn together?" she suggested shyly.

"That sounds like a splendid plan." He smiled a little shakily. "Are you saying 'yes', Emma? Will you marry me after all?"

Emma lifted her chin and looked him straight in the eye. This mattered. She had to do it right. "I shall be happy to become Lady Emma Allmay," she said. She had made her decision. She would stay with the man she loved. The modern world offered nothing to lure her back.

Will ruined her romantic moment by snorting loudly. He sounded like an outraged plough horse, rather than a man receiving a 'yes' to a proposal of marriage. "I sincerely hope that no one would be so impudent as to use that name to you, my love. They call me that, I know, and worse, but to apply that name to my wife would be an insult beyond bearing. I would call out any man who did so."

"But you *are* Sir William Allmay, surely?"

She had rendered him speechless. He gaped at her. Then he shook his head as if trying to clear it. "How could you possibly think that?" he managed at last.

Emma began to stammer. "W–well, everyone c–called you simply 'Sir William' or 'Will Allmay'." That could not be the

260

whole truth, Emma now realised. Somewhere in their past, they must have been formally introduced. The problem was that Emma herself had no memory of it.

"We *were* introduced, you know, my dear Lady Emma," Will said pointedly. "But, then," he went on, more kindly, "you were introduced to so many people at that ball, and there was so much noise, that it is possible you misheard? Or perhaps you deliberately took no notice?"

Emma couldn't decide whether his second question was prompted by mischief, or hurt pride. "I can't imagine any lady of the *ton* failing to take notice of you, Will May All," she responded, too sharply. True, but the wrong thing to say. She put a hand on his arm and smiled up at him apologetically. "However it came about, I must ask your forgiveness, Will, for I had completely forgotten your proper name when we met again." Judging from his softening expression, it seemed he had accepted her far-fetched excuse. And forgiven the underlying insult, too. That was a kindness she did not deserve, but it confirmed much that she believed about the man she was about to marry. No – *believed* was the wrong word. She *knew*. Her Will was a very fine man. And would be a good and faithful husband, too.

"How did it come about that you were given the nickname Will Allmay? Or, indeed, Will May All?" Help. Why had she said that? "Actually, I think I can guess about the second of those," she muttered sheepishly. "No need to explain."

He gave a choke of laughter. Then he took both her hands in his and turned her to face him. "The first is simple, love. My full name, which you would never have heard, is William Alford Mayfield. The nickname arose in the Navy. After that first boarding, when I was so very stupid as to get myself wounded, I was a great deal more careful and more thoughtful about my planning. Partly as a result, some of my subsequent actions were very successful. Some of that was pure luck, I must say. But the young officers were so delighted at their share of our ship's prize money, they started to call me Lieutenant Allmay instead of Lieutenant Mayfield. And once the men became aware of it, they turned it into a rhyme that spread through the Fleet. There was no stopping it. So I became Will Allmay. Including, on occasion, to my face."

"May I know what the rhyme was? Only if you think it is fit for my ears, of course."

Will blushed and hesitated. "I had best tell you. I would not have you hear it from one of my fellow officers. Or, worse, from Sanding. *Prizes for All May be hoarding, When lucky Will Allmay leads boarding.* That was what the men used to say. Not true, I should stress," he added quickly. "We didn't take prizes with every boarding I led."

"I see." He was too modest to trumpet his successes, but there must have been a lot of them. That frescoed bath house, for example, could not have been cheap, yet he had thought nothing of commissioning it. Will Alford Mayfield had left the Navy a very rich man. But that was not why Emma was going to marry him. "I think I must retract my acceptance of your proposal of marriage," she said, with mock formality. She ignored his sharp intake of breath. "I shall be delighted and honoured to become Lady Emma Mayfield instead. It has a happy ring to it."

His shoulders relaxed and he beamed at her. Then he lifted her hands to his lips and kissed them, one after the other. It was a kind of vow. Emma knew it and she was sure he did, too.

"I am afraid that you will not be Lady Emma Mayfield for long, my love. I heard from my lawyers a few days ago. The court has finally declared John legally dead."

"Uh? I'm afraid I don't understand," Emma said.

"No, you would not know, I dare say. It was a very long time ago. The fact is that, although they found Isabella's drowned body, they never found John's. Everyone assumed it was swept out to sea, and lost. But there was no proof." He took a deep breath. "Now that more than seven years have passed, John's title will become mine. So you will not remain Lady Emma Mayfield for long. Soon you will become the Countess Lambester." He took her into his arms.

Lambester. The Lamb House. That curious gold pin in Will's neckcloth. A replica of the worn stone lamb over the lintel, of course. It all came together. Emma had been looking in totally the wrong places. But it didn't matter a bit. Her decision had been made, for the right reasons, long before she'd learned any of this.

Will sighed and pulled her even closer. "I never wanted the title. It was John's by right," he said seriously, stroking her hair. "But after he died, I had no choice. I hope you don't object, my love, to becoming my countess?" He laughed softly. It seemed he could never stay melancholy for very long. "At least it's not half as difficult to spell as your previous name. I never could remember all those silent extra letters and the order they went in. That's why my notes were always addressed to Lady E. G."

Emma had to laugh, too. "Lots of people had trouble with it. I did, myself." Will would never know quite how many problems that name had caused her. If Emma had known how her surname was really spelt – and if Cosway hadn't made that mistake on the letter – she might have found out all about herself ages ago. And about her second husband as well.

Fate had been on her side with all those false clues and dead ends. It was much better not to know, she decided. Peerage books included dates of death as well as dates of birth. Emma did *not* want to know now, at the outset of their marriage, how long she and Will would have together. They were going to be married, they were going to be together and, from this day forward, she was going to make the most of every second of her allotted time with the man she loved.

~ ~ ~

Much later, they sat together by the fire in the master bedchamber, with Emma in Will's lap. He nuzzled her ear. It was heaven. She wanted him to take her to bed, now, but he was making no move to do so. He hadn't wanted to make love earlier, either.

"Are you not tired, love?" she asked hopefully. "Perhaps we should go to bed?"

He shook his head. "I don't want you to leave me yet."

"I don't plan to. Your bed is big enough for both of us."

"Ah," he said. "I promised myself that I would not make love to you again unless and until you were my wife."

She pulled back from him. "That, sir, was a rash promise. And one about which you did not consult me. Am I to have no

263

say? What if I don't want to wait until I have your ring on my finger?"

"You won't have to wait long if you prefer not to, love. I, er, I took the liberty of procuring a special licence a few days ago. But if you would rather wait to arrange a grand society wedding, I promise I will not object."

"And you will be celibate in the meantime, too?" she asked, laughing.

He made a very glum face. "If you wish it," he said. "It would not be easy."

"No, *you* may be easy, my love. I do not wish to wait either. May we be married tomorrow?"

He beamed and pulled her close for a long, tender kiss. "We may. Sanding has taken the carriage to town. Your abigail should be here shortly to act as the second witness."

"Second wi—? I can see that this partnership of ours is going to require very careful managing. My partner-to-be seems to view me as an enemy ship to be outmanoeuvred so that it can be boarded and taken as a prize."

"You could never be an enemy, sweet Emma," he said, dropping kisses down her jawline, "but I think that the boarding and the prize will be worth the winning. For both of us."

~ ~ ~

Emma woke to find Bailey bustling around the blue bedchamber, unpacking and stowing clothes away. "I have brought a selection of your gowns, m'lady, so that you may choose which of them you wish to be married in. I brought your jewel case, also."

Oh dear. How was Emma to explain? If she got it wrong, it would sound sordid. Particularly to someone with Bailey's strong views on Christian morality.

'Bailey, I should tell you that Sir William and I— Um."

Bailey turned round from the clothes press and grinned broadly. "You mean your ladyship and Mrs Smith?" There was a distinct twinkle in the abigail's eye.

"You knew?" Emma asked, horrified.

"Of course I knew, missy. That man of yours ain't the only one who's fly to the time of day. I only wish you'd have trusted

264

me enough to confide. I could have helped you. Sneaking out to a hackney in the mews is not what a lady of your station should have been doing, you know." She tried to look prim, but failed.

Emma burst out laughing. Trust was going to be important for her life in the Regency. And it seemed that she had people around her who merited both trust and love. She was truly blessed.

Bailey managed a little chuckle, too. She came across to the bed and gazed fondly down at Emma. "It is so wonderful to see you restored to full health, m'lady. When we first came up to London after your accident, I feared you might never be well again. Some days you were almost your old self, but so often—" She sighed deeply, remembering. Then she smiled brightly again. "There's no chance that you will forget who you are now. Not when you're so happy in yourself, marrying Sir William. Bless him, he's lifted that black shadow and brought you fully back to us again."

A black shadow? There had been a dark shadow in Emma's mind, she realised, shrouding and distorting her thoughts so that she trusted no one, not even people who loved her. But now she was whole again and free of it. Will had held her hand while she pushed the shadow away.

"You'd best make a start now, m'lady. The vicar will be arriving in an hour, Sanding says. Which gown shall I lay out for you?"

"I think you already know, Bailey. There can be only one. The gold lace."

~ ~ ~

Will put his hands behind his head and relaxed into the pillows of the great green bed. He looked like a very happy, and very satisfied, man. "So, my love, you are married to a rake after all. Are you content?"

"No," Emma said emphatically. She was rewarded by a sharp intake of breath and the muscles of his torso tensing under her fingers. She smiled knowingly. She had power over this man, her husband, as he did over her. "I am *not* married to a rake, sir, I will have you know. I am married to a loving husband who has sworn to be faithful to me and only to me. I

265

do not think, therefore, that he qualifies as a rake, do you?"

Will laughed and pulled her very close. "I can see that I am going to have considerable trouble getting the better of the logic-chopping lady who is now my wife. But I fancy I shall enjoy the challenge she is going to present."

"Mmm." Emma dropped a kiss on his bare chest. "I think your wife might enjoy the challenge also."

"I can't resist you, darling Emma. Your quick wit disarms me."

She looked up into his eyes. "And you, my love, can always make me laugh. There is no better way than laughter to charm a woman into your bed. May I say that I sincerely hope you will not be making other women laugh, in the future?"

He pushed her away a little so that he could lay his hand on his heart. "I swear I shall not laugh any woman into my bed. Except you, my darling wife."

"I do love your teasing," she said. But there was something about it that she needed to know, and had not yet found a moment to ask. "May I say that I am surprised by it, too? My image of a fighting sea captain is of a stern disciplinarian, self-contained and aloof. Rather humourless, in fact. I had not imagined a fighting captain could be a man who teases, or laughs, as much as you do."

"No, and perhaps I did not laugh as much then. But, if you had spent as many years fighting as I did, and seen as many deaths of good men, you would want to make light of the world also, I dare say."

Oh. She had not thought of it in that way. "Was it so very dark, Will?"

"No, not always. I had a good ship's company in most of my commands, with efficient officers who knew their work and could be depended upon. Much of the time, our duty was routine patrol, manning blockades off French and Spanish ports. Blockade can become tedious after weeks and months out of sight of land, especially if the resupply ships do not arrive and rations have to be cut. The men get restless when they have no fresh food and little water. That is when there can be trouble below decks and your stern disciplinarian comes to the fore. I can tell you that a captain takes no

266

pleasure when he has to discipline his men. But order must be preserved aboard the King's ships. The captain's word is law, and must be understood as such by every member of the ship's company."

Shipboard discipline was brutal then, Emma knew, from reading Hornblower as well as history books. The thought of the cat-o'-nine-tails would make any modern woman shudder. And the sentence for mutiny was death. She would not, could not, ask if Will had ordered such punishments. He hadn't needed to tell her that he took no pleasure in it. She could well believe that he had hated it.

"And yet there were times when we worked so hard, and chased so hard, that we did not sleep for excitement." Will seemed to be shaking off his dark memories. "When the men thought there was a chance of a prize, they were more than eager for the fight." He chuckled. "I had some bonny fighters in my crew."

"Was Sanding one of those?"

He flashed a grin. "Sanding can certainly handle himself in a scrap. I have seen him fight with a pistol in one hand and a cutlass in the other. And take down two of the enemy. I would as lief have Sanding at my back as any of my officers."

"He seems very loyal to you."

"I would trust him with my life. What's more important – I have trusted him with yours."

There was nothing Emma could say to that. Poor Patience had been so wrong about so much. And she had certainly been wrong about Sanding. The man was as true as steel. It seemed that the bonds formed when a crew of men fought together at sea were stronger than anything that a civilian landlubber, like Emma, could ever understand.

She laid her hand over his, on his heart. "I dare say your years at sea were a great deal bloodier, and more dangerous, than you will ever admit to me."

"Yes, well. A lot of it was tedious, as I said. Though the solution to muttering among the men was a few hours of gunnery practice. By the end of that, most of them were so deafened by the noise that muttering was totally impossible. Everyone had to shout in order to be understood at all."

"And no one in their right mind shouts mutinous thoughts. Am I right?" Emma said with a wry smile.

"You are, my dear. You may not have spent time aboard ship but your sharp intelligence sees much that lesser men do not. I am learning, more and more, that the female of the species is not to be underestimated."

"True. And the female, they say, is deadlier than the male. Although I *think* that was a reference to venomous spiders, rather than human females. Female spiders have a habit of eating their mates once they have, um, performed their husbandly duty."

"I had not heard that before. You are a mine of fascinating information, Emma." There was a new gleam in his eye. He stroked a finger down her cheek to her jaw and said in a softer, deeper voice, "So if I were to… ah… perform my husbandly duty now, madam, would you sink your fangs into me?"

"I might. But, alas, my fangs are not venomous. My bite would do you no harm. Indeed, you might find the sensation enjoyable."

He laughed and swept her into his arms. And then there were no more teasing words.

There were no words at all.

~ ~ ~

Emma made sure that Will was sound asleep before she crept out of their marriage bed. Their clothes were strewn all over the floor, starting at the door where Will had carried her over the threshold, and ending by the bed where Emma's stockings and garters had been very slowly removed. In between kisses, she remembered, with a shiver of pleasure.

She quickly donned her silk wrapper, retrieved her gold lace gown from the floor by the door and crept out, taking the lamp with her. It was only a few steps to the blue bedchamber. The room was empty, as she had known it would be. But Bailey's scissors were lying where Emma had left them, by the chest at the end of the bed.

Emma opened the chest. It smelled of the lavender that was used to keep the moth away. She inhaled deeply. She had known it would be lavender. She had smelled it that first day, when the museum store room showed her the man she loved.

268

Closing the chest again, she laid out the gold lace gown and picked up the scissors.

~ ~ ~

It was nearly dark when Richard finally made it home on the day of the inquest. Little Chloë had been in bed for ages. Melanie was in the kitchen, quietly singing to herself as she made a pot of tea. Without a word to her, Richard sank into an empty chair by the table and dropped his head into his hands.

Melanie said nothing. She simply poured him a mug of tea and set it down by his hand. He didn't move to take it. He didn't even raise his head.

She took a deep breath and sat down opposite him. "Is it over?" she asked quietly. "The inquest?"

His head jerked up, as if he were coming back from a long way away. "What? Oh. Oh, yes. It finished this afternoon. But late, so I missed the fast train back." It seemed the tea registered with him, at last. He picked up his mug and took a large swig. "Natural causes."

"But…but she'd been attacked, hadn't she? What about that blow to the head? And the way you found her…?"

"There was no attack, according to the pathologist. She'd had a fall, he said, and hit her head on the edge of the pavement by the staff entrance. Forensics found her blood there. They think it was almost certainly an accident. Followed by a brain haemorrhage an hour or so later, inside the museum. All caused by a malignant brain tumour."

"A brain tumour? Good grief. And she didn't know?"

"Apparently not. There's no record of her having been to her GP or the hospital. You'd imagine she'd have had terrible headaches, wouldn't you? And now I think back, she did call in sick with migraine once or twice. But that wasn't the strangest thing." He shook his head, took another drink of his tea, and sat silent for a long moment, gazing vacantly out towards the garden.

Melanie reached out to put her hand over his and bring him back to earth. "Did the inquest explain why you found her in her underwear? And with that ruined ballgown?"

"What?' He gave a crack of mirthless laughter. "Oh no. I… Actually, no one *asked* me what she was wearing when I

269

found her. The police knew, of course, and so did the coroner, but no one asked about it, so I didn't volunteer anything. It was all so…so surreal, somehow, finding her half-naked in the research room, with the lace ballgown and all that blood. It looked as if she was about to try on the gown, in spite of the state it was in. But why would she do that? I can't imagine that she would ever do anything so unprofessional. In any case, she shouldn't have stayed at the museum. She should have gone to the hospital to have her head looked at. Or called an ambulance. Her brain must have been playing tricks on her. The tumour, I suppose. She got fixated on that blasted ballgown. And then she had the brain haemorrhage and…and died."

"But you did say she'd become obsessed with this Regency Lady Emma, didn't you? She was over the moon when she found the Cosway portrait."

"Yes, that's true enough." He made a face, clearly bewildered. "Yet she was a dedicated professional in every other aspect of her work. Maybe her obsession was caused by the brain tumour, too?"

Melanie nodded in sympathy.

"I'm glad I wasn't asked about the underwear, anyway. The papers will make enough of it, as it is, without giving them that sordid picture to perv over. Imagine what the headline could have been – *Death during Sex Romp in Museum*. Or worse. Eugh. She was a good colleague and a good friend to us. I didn't want some muckraking journo to trash her reputation. They probably will, though."

"How can they? If you didn't mention the underwear, I mean?"

"Because she told the police that her ex-husband was stalking her. She'd reported several incidents, they said. Phone calls, loitering outside the museum. That sort of thing. Threats, too, apparently. The police thought, at first, that the blow on the head might have been down to him. They were actually looking to arrest him. And that's the really strange part."

"Didn't they find him?"

"Oh they found him all right. In Australia."

"Australia?" Melanie gasped.

"Yes. And he'd been there all the time."

"But—"

"When the police looked again at all Emma's reports of stalking, they discovered there was no evidence to corroborate any of it. No phone records, no CCTV, nothing. At the time, they'd put it down to bad luck – camera malfunctions, that sort of thing – but the evidence from Australia was solid. He'd never left. She couldn't have seen him, because he was never here."

"So she was making it all up? *Emma?* But why on earth would she do that?"

"No." He shook his head sadly. "That's the really awful part. They don't think she lied. She reported what she *thought* was happening to her, they said. She would have believed it. Totally. She was probably having delusions of some kind. Related to bad things from her past life. It was the brain tumour, they said."

"Oh, poor, poor Emma. And what a terrible way to die, believing you were being pursued by someone who hated you. She'd have been so frightened…" Melanie shivered. "And so alone, too, poor woman. There was no one who loved her."

"Uh-huh." He sighed deeply. "It's incredibly sad. Still, she's at peace now. That's our only consolation. And hers." Straightening his shoulders, he raised his mug, and said, "If there's a heaven for you, Emma Stanley, I hope you found your precious Lady Emma there to welcome you. Wherever you are now, your agonies are over. Rest in peace."

~ ~ ~

Emma made the last cut with especial venom and stood back to admire her handiwork. She'd decided there would be no going back. No second thoughts. And now she'd taken her fate into her own hands. The shredded dress might have worked its magic in the twenty-first century, but in the Regency it had to be whole to work, she was sure.

Wasn't she?

Well, there's one way to find out for certain. I'm alone. I can test it right now.

She put down Bailey's scissors and caressed the mutilated lace. The gown was a wreck now. Such a shame. But it had been necessary. As long as she had an escape route back to the future, she could never be fully committed to her life here with Will. There would always be that little frisson of *what if I just...?* Love needed trust and commitment. Full on, one-hundred-percent commitment. That was what she had promised at the altar. And that was precisely what she was going to give him.

She pinned her hair up, out of the way, and turned back to the magic lace. In fact, the gown was easier to put on than she'd expected, given the state of it, though she didn't bother trying to do up the ties. She was going to take it off again immediately, after all, so there was no point.

She turned to look at herself in the pier glass. Even to her own critical gaze, she looked like a real Regency lady. The hairstyle and the absence of make-up helped, but there was more to it than that. Was it the way she held herself these days? That aristocratic hauteur?

She looked the part; there was no doubt of that. Except that it wasn't going to be a part any longer. This was going to be her life. For good.

Stop havering, Emma, and just DO IT. The moment of truth is now.

With her eyes fixed on her own reflection, she took a deep breath and held it. Then she raised her fingers to the top of her sleeve and began to ease it down her arm.

A second later, she tensed and closed her eyes, suddenly afraid of what she was doing. What if she'd got it wrong? What if she heard St Mary's clock again?

A single chime echoed in the silence.

Cursing, Emma squeezed her eyes even tighter shut. She wanted to scream, to block it all out. She didn't want to see the museum, ever again. She didn't want to hear that blasted church clock either. She'd screwed up, big time. How could she have got it so wrong? What if she couldn't get back to Will? What if—?

Another chime.

And this time, she really heard it.

Not a church clock at all. No, it was the musical chime of a sweet little carriage clock, a present from Will, sitting on her own dressing table. Balm to her shredded nerves.

She opened her eyes. And saw. She was still standing in front of the mirror, though the lace now lay in a golden pool at her ankles. She was still in the Regency. She was still safe with her beloved Will.

And she'd put paid to the magic of the golden gown. For good. Or perhaps not? Perhaps it was like a Sleeping Beauty? Perhaps one day, a couple of centuries in the future, another Emma would find the shredded lace and try it on, so that the circle could begin all over again?

She laughed softly to herself. It didn't matter. Not now she had Will.

She laid the lace in its lavender-scented new home and started back towards the green bedchamber. *Their* bedchamber. Where she belonged.

For this Emma, at least, the fairytale had run its course. She had found her prince. And her happy ever after.

THE END

Dear Reader : From Joanna Maitland

The ruined Regency ballgown that inspired this story is no phantom. The original is in the costume collection of the Hereford Museum, although I have to admit that I changed the material from silver lace to gold (in response to a reader poll). The damage is certainly real, though. Was it caused by a time travelling lover? Maybe. Who knows? Whatever the truth about the lace ballgown, I hope you enjoyed reading about how Emma and Will finally reached their happy ending, in spite of the two centuries that divided them.

This was my first venture into timeslip, so if you did enjoy it, I'd be really grateful if you could leave a review at your usual online store or on your favourite reader website. Your review can help other readers to find and enjoy my books, too.

Thank you!

For Competitions, Giveaways and Other Stuff

For news, free stories, competitions and giveaways, and lots of fun stuff, please visit the new multi-author website at Libertà Books https://libertabooks.com where you can have your say on the weekly blog, or maybe write a love letter to a favourite novel. Intrigued? Have a look and see whether you would like to join in. You'd be most welcome. We often host writers you will know and we talk about all sorts of books which probably include many of your favourites.

My old joannamaitland.com website is still available, but it's no longer updated. Information about me and my books is now all on my Libertà page at libertabooks.com/joanna. Or you can follow me on Twitter @JoannaMaitland to get all my latest news.

The Libertà hive tweets @LibertaBooks and you can find us on FaceBook/libertabooks, too.

Do come and join the fun in the Libertà hive where readers and authors chat and laugh about books, films, history, costume, the craft of writing and much, much more.

About the Author

Joanna Maitland has published 13 Regency historicals with Harlequin Mills & Boon since 2000 and has sold nearly one and a half million copies around the world, with readers in countries as diverse as Japan and Brazil. She is now an independently published author. She is continuing to write Regencies, but also hopping over the hedge into lush new pastures. Her first timeslip, *Lady in Lace*, was published in 2018 and there may be more. There will probably be medieval romances in the future, too. If there's history involved, Joanna is up for it!

Joanna is one of the founding partners of Libertà Books, a multi-author website https://libertabooks.com/ where readers and authors share their love of books, reading, and fun. She is also a proud and long-standing member of the Romantic Novelists' Association which recently honoured her by making her a Vice President of the Association.

His Silken Seduction

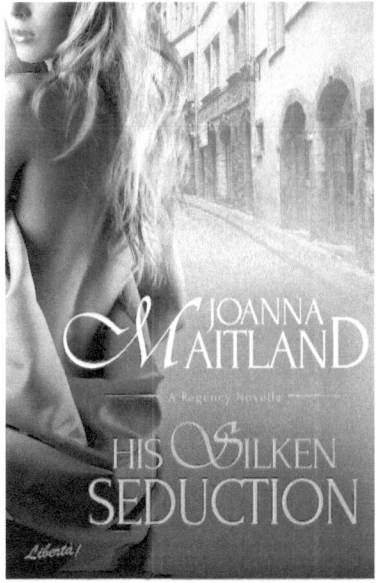

Wounded. Abandoned. In the enemy's bed

He's Wellington's spy, trying to survive in war-torn France.
He has a choice   duty, or desire.

She's his beautiful silk weaver. Day after day, her hands caress
his battered flesh. Her touch is driving him wild.
But she's the enemy. She must not discover who he is. Surely
she will betray him?

Will he dare to trust her
with his life, his mission, and his heart?

Read on for an extract

HIS SILKEN SEDUCTION
Chapter One

France, March 1815

THEY WERE COMING FOR HIM.

They had come out of nowhere. Five of them. And they had knives.

Ben started to run. What choice did he have? He was alone. No…no, Jack was about somewhere. Where? Ben couldn't see him, but he must be—

No time to think about that. It didn't matter anyway. Two against five was very poor odds, especially when the two were unarmed and the five were not. It was every man for himself.

Run, you idiot. The voice in his head was insistent. *Faster! If they catch you, you're dead meat.*

Ben put on a spurt. He could do this. He could.

He must.

He was almost out of the old port area. Just another few yards to the end of the quay. There must be safety up ahead. Somewhere. Somewhere less dangerous. With civilised people. If only he could—

Pain ripped through him.

Then – only then – he heard the report. A shot. One of those blackguards had shot him. And he was falling. Falling…

His last thought was to wonder why the ball had hit him before he had even heard the shot.

And then he was floating. Surrounded by shifting dark mists that rolled and twisted into fantastical patterns and shapes. Bringing with them strange, sun-drenched scents.

Am I dead? He dragged in a desperately needed breath. And discovered how much it hurt. *If it hurts, I can't be dead, can I?*

He sucked in another breath. And a blinding light burst through the pain. He remembered. If he was injured, how could they continue with their mission? Their mission for Wellington was vital. Nothing else mattered. Nothing. He groaned out the precious words. "Mission. Wellington." As if, by speaking them aloud, he could make all right again. "Mission."

Those perfumes were swirling around him once more. This time, they swept him off to a hot sunny hillside, where he found himself lying on springy grass, gazing up at the sky through yellow puffs of mimosa flowers, drinking in scents of lavender and rosemary. But with his next breath, the dark shrouds closed in again, suffocating him and swallowing the sky.

He wanted to cry out, to fight against the blanketing mists, but he did not have the strength. Their long grey fingers stroked him into darkness, deep as a pit.

Even in the darkness, there was pain. Piercing, unbearable pain, like daggers in his flesh. Ben tried to move, to throw them off, somehow, anyhow, but the enveloping web was looped round and under him, tying him in a tangled thicket from which it seemed he would never break free. And always the daggers. The daggers. He groaned and thrashed his body from side to side. If he was not dead, he must fight. He must.

"Sleep now," said a soft voice. It was barely a murmur but it soothed. It must have been sent from heaven. An angel? Cool clean linen was laid on his forehead, as refreshing as joyful rain on dry earth. Ben felt the knots unravel as his bonds receded into the grey mist, defeated by the angel's hand.

If I can sleep, I cannot be dead. If I can sleep... If I can only sleep...

It was not sleep that came. It was torture. Suddenly, he was being tossed back and forth between giants. And they were rejoicing at his groans of pain. This was not heaven. This was hell, full of red-hot needles and tongues of fire. From this, there could be no escape. His angel had forsaken him.

He cried out.

And his angel returned. His fair-haired angel. Calling his name, through the whirling flames. He wanted to reach for her, but he was pinioned. He could not escape.

"French," the angel said sternly. "You must speak only French. No English. Only French."

He was in a French heaven. Or was it hell? But his angel spoke French and so he must do so, too. "No English," he croaked.

Which language had he spoken? He could not tell. He could not hear his own voice. The circling shrouds were sucking it away, swallowing his words, swallowing everything. Were they trying to suck out his soul?

He gave a great cry of anguish. But it could not save him. The pit was opening at his feet and he was falling. Down, down, down. Into blackness.

He must climb out of the pit. He must. If he could free his arms, he could climb. He could claw his way out of this blackness. He began to struggle against the invisible bonds that held him...

"Herr Benn."

It was his angel's voice. No, not hers. Another's. Another angel?

He struggled even harder to break free of the darkness. To reach her.

"Herr Benn, no! You will injure yourself. Wake up. Oh, pray, wake up."

A hand on his shoulder. Shaking him.

He was out of the pit. He could open his eyes. There was light. Bright, blinding light.

And his angel was still there, still there behind the light, still speaking to him in that sweet, urgent voice.

"Herr Benn. Oh, Herr Benn, you are yourself again. Thank heaven. You were having such a nightmare and I could not wake you. Are you...are you well now?"

She was speaking French to him. And the room was spinning. Had he really been dreaming? The pit was not real? Nor the giants with their red-hot needles?

A hand stroked a cooling cloth across his brow. Then it brought a cup to his lips and helped him to drink. The prickle of sharp lemon on his tongue was no dream. He was alive. This was real.

He turned his head a fraction to search for his angel's face, hoping desperately that she, too, was real.

Everything was blurred. The light was too bright. In desperation, he screwed up his eyes against it, struggling to focus. There was... Yes, he could just make out a halo of fair curls filled with sunlight. And then, at last, a face.

He sighed out a long, thankful breath. His angel was still at his side. She was real.

And she was beautiful.

He did not know who she was, but all at once he understood the meaning of his dream. It was all true, even though it was a weird jumble of memories, interlaced with pain. He and Jack were on a spying mission for Wellington. They had been set upon by a gang of villains as they left Marseilles. And one of the assailants had had a gun.

"Did they shoot me?" he croaked, in French, gazing pleadingly at his angel. He was hot and aching. Covered in sweat. And the pain was certainly real. It seemed to be worst on his right side. He began to reach with his left hand, to find out how badly he was wounded.

Soft fingers caught his hand and held it. "Do not distress yourself, Herr Benn," the angel said, frowning down at him. "Yes, you were shot, but the bullet is gone and the wound is clean. Pray do not claw at your bandages. Your shoulder will heal better if you rest." She pushed him gently back on to feather pillows and laid his hand firmly on the coverlet.

"I... Where am I?" He had not seen this girl before, had he? She looked familiar and yet she was not. He would not have forgotten such fragile beauty.

She smiled at him. The frown melted away, leaving her skin smooth as a peach. "You are in Lyons. You were brought here by your friend, Monsieur Jacques, and my sister, Marguerite Grolier. You are safe here, in our weaving house."

That was why she seemed familiar! The silk weaver was her sister. And he had seen the silk weaver in his dreams, had he not? Had she not admonished him to speak only French?

He was having difficulty working out what was real and what was fantasy. "Jacques is here? I need to speak to him." Jack would be able to explain everything. Jack would set Ben's topsy-turvy memories to rights. Unless... "Jacques? Did they shoot him, too?"

"Be easy, sir. Your friend came off with a whole skin. As did my sister. You were the only casualty."

Ben sighed. What a relief. He said as much.

"For a German, you speak very good French, Herr Benn," she said, smiling broadly at him now. "You have very little accent."

Another piece of the puzzle slotted into place at her words. Of course. Since, unlike Jack, Ben could not speak French like a native, they had agreed that Ben would pretend to be a German. He had become Herr Christian Benn, while Jack had become Monsieur Louis Jacques, a *bourgeois* from Paris. Ben must remember to play his part. Was there anything else that he needed to remember? And beware of?

He must speak French. Only French. No English.

And he must find out the name of this fair-haired angel.

She offered him the cup again and he drank greedily. "Thank you," he said. "Thank you, Miss...er... Your pardon, ma'am. I'm afraid I do not know your name."

"It is Grolier, of course. Suzanne Grolier."

"Suzanne." He repeated it several times, relishing the taste of the syllables on his tongue. "It is a beautiful name. It suits you."

She was blushing. "You must not say such things," she said, flustered. She grabbed the cup and made a great show of gathering up the linen she had been using to bathe his face. Then she retreated towards the door.

"Please don't go," Ben said.

"I must. You need to rest."

"But I cannot rest if I do not have your promise to return. Will you promise?"

Her blush was even deeper now, but after a moment she bit her lip and gave a tiny nod. "I will come back later to tend your wound. Provided you promise, in your turn, Herr Benn, to do everything I tell you to."

He frowned, puzzled. He was missing something important here.

She took a few steps forward so that she was standing at the end of the bed, looking gravely down at him. "You are an invalid. I am your nurse. A patient must obey his nurse or he will never get well." Suddenly, she smiled at him, a mischievous smile that lit up her delicate features. "You do want to get well, don't you, Herr Benn?"

If getting well would lose him that wonderful smile, he was not at all sure that he did.

HIS SILKEN SEDUCTION
is available as an ebook from your local Amazon
Also available in paperback

www.ingramcontent.com/pod-product-compliance
Lightning Source LLC
Chambersburg PA
CBHW020958120726
47905CB00009B/2744